# By Light of
# Hidden Candles

Daniella Levy

Kasva Press

Alfei Menashe / St. Paul, Minnesota

Book design and layout: Yael Shahar

Cover design by Yael Shahar with photographs by Cathleen Tarawhiti, Iswanto Arif, and Warburg, used by kind permission.

First edition, 16 October 2017
Kasva Press LLC
Alfei Menashe, Israel / St. Paul, Minnesota
www.kasvapress.com
info@kasvapress.com

By Light of Hidden Candles

ISBN
Trade Paperback: 978-0-9910584-7-1
Ebook: 978-0-9910584-8-8

T 9 8 7 6 5 4 3 2

# DEDICATION

---

For Abi,
who, if this book were Catholic,
would be its patron saint;


and in fond memory of Dr. Gloria Mound (1930–2017),
researcher, historian, and activist,
who dedicated her life to helping descendants of crypto-Jews
find their way home.

–Daniella Levy

# THE KINGDOMS
## OF IBERIA
## (1461 – 1492)

## HIJA MIA

*Hija mia, mi kerida,*
*aman aman!*
*ne te eches a la mar,*
*ke la mar esta en fortuna,*
*mira ke te va a llevar.*

*¡Ke me lleve y que me traiga,*
*aman aman!*
*siete puntas de hondor,*
*ke me engluta el pexe preto*
*para salvar del amor.*

*¡Hija mia, mi kerida,*
*aman aman!*
*no te vayas a lavar*
*a la fuente de agua fria*
*onde el cavallero esta*
*dando agua al su cavallo,*
*mira que te va a llevar.*

*Ke me lleve y que me traiga,*
*aman aman*
*d'entre del romero en flor*
*ke la mi casa es muy chika*
*y no entra nunca el sol;*
*de entre estas paredes frias*
*pedri, madre, la color.*

*Si me lleva es porque kero,*
*aman aman;*
*en la mar me vo a kedar,*
*de mi cuerpo hare una barca*
*con mandil le vela va,*
*remos de los brasos haga,*
*ke en lo preto la luz hay.*

## MY DAUGHTER

My daughter, my darling,
alas, alas!
Don't throw yourself in the sea,
For the sea is capricious—
See, it will carry you away.

Let it take me, let it bring me
(alas, alas!)
Seven leagues deep.
Let a black fish swallow me
To save me from love.

My daughter, my darling,
alas, alas!
Don't go to wash
By the spring of cold water.
There's a knight there
Watering his horse—
See, he will carry you away.

Let him take me, let him bring me
(alas, alas!)
Amidst the blooming rosemary—
For my house is very small,
And the sun never enters;
Inside these cold walls,
Mother, I've grown pale.

If he takes me, that's my desire
(alas, alas!)
I'll remain in that sea.
I'll make my body a boat,
My clothing its sail,
My arms its oars—
For in that darkness is the light.

– Judeo-Spanish Folksong

# By Light of Hidden Candles

# One Last Story

"There's something I never told you."

Mazal started and lifted her head from the book of Psalms. She had been praying at her grandmother's side all night, by the light of the Sabbath lamps her mother had lit before sundown. For the past day or so, her grandmother Míriam had been lying motionless, only her chest moving up and down with each shallow breath. But now her eyes were wide open, gazing at her young granddaughter from beneath the scarf that was wrapped around her hair.

"About what?" Mazal closed the book and set it down by the clay lamps. She took her grandmother's hand.

"The ring," her grandmother rasped. "You have to try to return the ring."

Mazal's eyes scanned the room. One of the lamps was empty, its wick dark, but the other still burned low, casting flickering shadows on the mud walls and the curtain that separated them from the mats on which the rest of the family slept. A hint of light crept in from the window above their heads, already bringing with it the suffocating desert heat. She could barely make out the sparse contents of the room, but she already knew there was no jewelry to speak of, except the few silver bands that were always on her mother's wrists.

A *muezzin* sounded in the distance, calling the Muslims to prayer.

"What ring?" Mazal whispered.

Míriam took a shuddering breath, closing her eyes again, and then slowly reached for her collar. She drew a leather cord from beneath her robe. Dangling from it was a wide golden ring. Mazal's eyes widened. She had never seen anything of such value in her grandmother's possession.

"Where did you get that?" she breathed.

"There is something I never told you," Míriam repeated, "about our escape from Spain. Something I have never told anyone. Not even your grandfather." Her breath caught in her chest and she coughed weakly.

Mazal's heart began to pound. "Should I get Mama?" she whispered, shifting her weight as if to stand up.

"No." Míriam grasped her hand tightly. "This is only for you." She beckoned Mazal closer.

"Before I tell you," she whispered, her voice barely audible, "You must promise that you won't tell anyone else."

Mazal swallowed. "I promise."

"And that you will do everything in your power to accomplish what I failed to do in my lifetime…and return this ring to its owner. Or his heir."

Mazal stared at the ring in her grandmother's hand, glinting in the flickering lamplight.

"I…I will try…"

"And if you are not successful…you will pass it to your daughter…or your granddaughter, *inshallah*. And my *ketuba*, and your mother's. And you'll tell her the story. Maybe one day…" Míriam's voice trailed off, and she closed her eyes again, her grip on Mazal's hand going slack.

"Abuela?" Mazal whispered urgently.

Míriam opened her eyes again.

"Tell me the story." Mazal raised her grandmother's hand to her lips and kissed it. "I promise to do everything I can."

Míriam looked deep into her granddaughter's eyes, her own welling with tears. Then she took another rattling breath, and began to speak.

# Alma

"Oh hell no. There is no way I'm going in there."

Mimi was staring into the storage room of our late grandfather's Judaica store, her lips curled in a look of disgust. I had just flipped on the light, a naked bulb dangling from the ceiling, and it revealed two cramped aisles of shelves buried in cardboard boxes, packing paper, and bubble wrap. And the dust—it was everywhere. Clinging to the walls, the boxes, the peeling laminated wood flooring; floating through the air, filtering the already-faint light from the bulb and making it look even yellower.

I tried to say something snarky, but all that came out was a coughing fit.

"I can't afford to get that gunk on my clothes," she went on, smoothing out the skirt of her business suit. She cast a wistful glance at the narrow staircase behind us that led down to the back of the store. "I'm supposed to be heading straight for the job interview of my dreams after this."

"Well, that's fine," I wheezed, slipping my inhaler out of my pocket and taking two hearty puffs. "I'll just sit here and suffocate in the dark."

Mimi turned to me with an arched perfectly-plucked eyebrow. "Alma, you forfeited the right to use asthma as an excuse for anything the minute you decided to move to Manhattan."

"I didn't decide to move to Manhattan," I protested, covering my mouth with my sleeve and taking a step into the room. A cloud of dust rose under my shoe in response. "I decided to transfer to NYU. It's not my fault it happens to be in Manhattan."

"I came here to help you move in to Grandma's apartment. Taking a dust bath in my interview suit was definitely not part of the plan."

"Oh, stop being such a JAP."

The acronym for Jewish American Princess earned me a playful smack on the back of the head, knocking my glasses askew. But it also hit its mark: she took a tentative step in behind me, teetering on her high heels.

"She really needs to hire someone to organize this," she said.

"Shhh. Don't give her ideas, she'll get me to do it."

"Gotta earn your keep somehow, li'l sis." Mimi started scanning the shelves in the aisle on the right, and I stepped into the one on the left. "I can't believe the supplier didn't have a website," she went on. "How does anyone keep track of information when the only record of it is on a piece of paper?"

"You expect Grandma to be entering this stuff into a computer?" I snorted. "See anything that looks like it might have the record books in it?"

"If I were willing to touch anything, I might be able to move some boxes around and look."

I rolled my eyes.

I paid for my moment of passive-aggressive scorn: my foot caught on the corner of one of the boxes on the floor, and it knocked me off balance. I grabbed at one of the shelves to my left to steady myself. That turned out to be a bad idea. The shelf rested precariously on a pair of metal supports, and it gave when I grabbed it. Not only did I fall on my face, I ended up with a big box landing squarely on my back. It knocked the wind out of me and I couldn't even yelp in pain. The box then tilted over and spilled its contents—heavy books, from the sound of it—onto the floor.

"Whoa, Alma, are you okay?" came Mimi's voice, muffled by layers of cardboard.

I extricated myself from the mess, straightening my glasses and cursing under my breath. Mimi was standing behind me, but she seemed to be focused on something other than my plight.

"Hey, Alma, look." She pointed at the wall where the shelf had been. Disgruntled at her lack of sympathy, I followed her gesture. I promptly forgot my irritation; the box had been concealing a small metal door built into the wall. It looked like the door to a safe.

"Huh," I said. I inspected the round knob in the center of the door. There was a little keyhole underneath it.

My heart started pounding.

The one advantage of digging through the storage room was that sometimes real treasures turned up—tarnished silver menorahs, crystal candlesticks studded with rhinestones, or rare, out-of-print editions of Jewish scholarly volumes. And if those things were lying around in boxes…

"What would they have hidden in a safe?" Mimi voiced the rest of my thought.

I groped in the pocket of my denim skirt for the keys to the store, and then started going through them one by one, searching for a key that looked like it might match. After a few tries, I found one that slid neatly into the hole, and with a little jiggling, I managed to turn it in the lock and swing the safe door open.

Inside was a plain, rather flat wooden box. I scrunched my mouth to one side in disappointment. "Well, that's anticlimactic," I said.

"*Nu?*" Mimi urged. "Take it out and see what's inside."

I slid the box out of the safe and pulled off the lid.

The inside was lined with maroon velvet, and resting in it was a pile of what looked like old parchments. I squinted at the one on top through my glasses, and Mimi leaned over my shoulder to peer at it. It was a formal Jewish document of some kind, inscribed in beautiful Hebrew calligraphy. Mustering all my twelve years of Hebrew school, I scanned it, trying to figure out what it was. It didn't take me long to spot my grandfather's name: *"Hachatan hana'im... Gershon ben Moshe l'mishpachat Dahan, amar la laKalah, Alma bat David..."*

"Grandma's *ketuba*," Mimi said. "This is weird. Why would she be storing it here?"

I peeked underneath it and saw a very similar document. Underneath it was another. They all looked like *ketubot*, Jewish marriage contracts; and when I examined the dates on top, they seemed to be going back a generation each time. My eyes widened as I noticed that the pile was pretty thick. "How far back do these go?" I wondered aloud. I carefully lifted the pile from the box and let the parchment on the bottom fall gently onto the velvet. I squinted at it in the dim light.

*On the third of the seventh month, five thousand, two hundred, fifty and two years to the creation of the world...*

5252. What Jewish year was that? Math was not my forte, but I did know that we were somewhere in the 5770's.

I took a sharp breath.

"Mimi," I rasped, "this *ketuba* is five hundred years old."

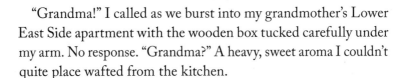

"Grandma!" I called as we burst into my grandmother's Lower East Side apartment with the wooden box tucked carefully under my arm. No response. "Grandma?" A heavy, sweet aroma I couldn't quite place wafted from the kitchen.

I led Mimi across the small living room, past the old leather couches tucked around the walls, and walked through the open doorway that led to the kitchen. When I saw my grandmother, I stopped short and Mimi almost crashed into me. Grandma was sitting on one of the wicker chairs by the tiny breakfast table, her head rolled to one side, her headscarf askew and her wispy white hairs peeking out underneath. Her walker was parked by the wall next to the doorway. She was snoring loudly.

Mimi put her finger to her lips, her eyes wide beneath voluminous eyelashes. Her makeup was immaculate for her interview today, and her black hair was ironed perfectly straight. Between that and the suit showing off her figure and long legs, she looked particularly stunning. She had always been the pretty one.

Well... and the smart one.

Well... she and Shoshana were both pretty and both smart.

Is there a third category in this sister-classification system?

Mimi made a "hands off" gesture, and I nodded in agreement. If you valued your life, you never, ever woke Grandma.

Mimi looked at her watch. "I need to go," she whispered. "You interrogate her for me as soon as she wakes up, and report back."

"I will." I gently rested the box on the table next to Grandma. "Hey, Mimi," I said, turning to her. "Thanks for bringing me and my stuff down here."

She grinned. "You're welcome." She leaned in and kissed my cheek.

"Good luck with the interview."

"Good luck with Grandma. And school. And... everything."

She pulled back and took my hands, studying me for a moment.

"Are you sure you know what you're doing?" she asked.

I groaned in frustration. "Why do you all keep asking me that?"

"You would have made a great nurse."

"No, I wouldn't have. Because I never would have passed the boards. I barely scraped by in most of those courses."

"You'd have pushed through. I just..."

"You think this degree is pointless. I know. I've heard it all before. Abba and Ima have lectured my ears off about it. Stop trying. It's done already. I'm here. Deal with it."

She crossed her arms, still giving me a piercing look. "This better not be all about David."

"Even David isn't all about David," I countered. "The whole thing just...reminded me how important this is."

She did not look convinced. But she sighed in defeat and turned toward the door.

"I'll see you back in Albany for Rosh Hashana, yeah?" she tossed over her shoulder.

"Unfortunately," I answered.

There was a pause.

"Ima will have a fit if you're not there," came her stern voice.

"I'll be there, I'll be there."

I heard the front door shut behind her.

I glanced back at Grandma, who hadn't moved at all. Then I turned my attention to the pot on the stove. There was some diced fruit, maybe apples or pears, boiling gently. The liquid was a kind of deep orange and seemed pretty thoroughly boiled down. I looked at my grandmother and then back at the pot. With my free hand, I slid open the silverware drawer next to the stove, took out a fork and was about to poke one of the chunks of fruit.

*"No no!"*

I jumped, almost dropping the fork, and whirled to see my grandmother, perfectly alert, shaking her finger at me with one hand and fixing her headscarf with the other.

"Top silverware drawer is for meat! That pot is dairy! Don't you go *treifing* my kitchen!"

My shoulders slumped sheepishly. "Sorry, I didn't notice the blue tape."

Her weathered, olive-skinned face relaxed and she let out a laugh, swinging her upper body forward to heave out of the chair. "How are those quinces doing? Mmmm, they smell good."

She stirred the pot, and then suddenly froze and looked at me.

"Where is Mimi?"

"She left just a minute ago." But her question reminded me of the box on the table.

"Oh, Grandma!" I exclaimed, crossing the kitchen toward it. "Care to explain this?" I picked it up and turned to face her.

Grandma glanced at it and then did a double take. She reached out and took the box from me, her pale green eyes widening.

"This..." she breathed.

"Look familiar?"

She put the box on the breakfast table and pulled off the lid. She gasped. "The *ketubot!*"

"Are they what I think they are?"

I watched her gently finger the edges of the parchments, counting under her breath in Spanish. "*Veinticuatro,*" she said finally.

"Whose are they?" I insisted.

She looked up at me with wild eyes. "Get me my reading glasses."

I launched off in the general direction of the kitchen counter, and floundered around for a few moments before realizing I hadn't the faintest idea where her glasses were. "Um...where are they?"

My grandmother gave me a withering look. "I forgot that I own a priceless historical treasure, and you expect me to remember where my glasses are?"

"So they *are* what I think they are?"

"If you think they're the original marriage contracts of our maternal ancestors, going back twenty-four generations, then yes."

"Really?" I squealed.

"I'm pretty sure. My grandmother gave them to me before she died—except for the last one, which is my own." Her voice was soft and strained with emotion.

I looked back down at the box, and noticed her reading glasses folded neatly right next to it.

"Um, Grandma." I pointed.

Grandma followed my gesture, spotted the glasses, and sighed deeply, putting them on. "There was something else, though. It wasn't just the *ketubot*. There was an object... something very valuable." She pulled the papers back out, her eyes scanning the bottom of the box. I leaned closer, squinting at the maroon velvet, and noticed something glinting gold wedged into the padding at one of the corners. I reached for it, pulled it out, and held it up in my palm for both of us to examine. It was a ring, wide and heavy, with a flat bezel featuring an engraving of some sort of bird.

"This feels like solid gold," I murmured.

Grandma took the ring from me, turning it over in her hand. Her brow was wrinkled deeply.

"There's a story with this. Something my grandmother told me. I just know it. And I remember that it was very important." She gave a frustrated sigh. "But I just don't remember what it was."

"I can't believe you forgot that you had these!" I sank into a chair. "I asked you about seventeen times in the past three months if you had any documentation, and you said you didn't think so!"

"Well, then our timing is rather fortunate, wouldn't you say?" She slipped the ring into her pocket and stacked the *ketubot* back into the box. "When are you starting that genealogy program?"

"I'm not sure. The semester in Madrid is supposed to start in the spring."

"Good! So you'll have these to jump-start your research." She closed the box and hobbled over to the stove.

"But you never even mentioned them to me!" I pressed. "My whole life! Mimi said she'd never heard of them either! Even back before you started having issues with your memory..."

She turned off the flame and began rummaging in the silverware drawer.

"Well... no," she said. "I think... well, if anyone else were to find out that I had them, I'd never hear the end of it. Someone would insist I donate them to a museum or a university or something." She began scooping pieces of fruit out of the pot with a slotted spoon.

"Maybe at least that way they wouldn't get lost."

"Don't you start," she warned, stabbing the spoon in my direction. She turned back to the fruit and began chopping the cores off the fruit pieces. I watched her hunched figure as she worked. Her multicolored scarf clashed horribly with the baby-pink housecoat that stopped short right above her bare ankles. She had a remarkable amount of energy for cooking projects at 78 years old, especially considering that virtually every other task inspired many groans and complaints.

"Seriously, Grandma," I insisted. "Can you imagine if I hadn't found them and no one knew about them? They'd be lost forever... what if you forget them again?"

"I'm not giving those to anybody until you figure out what that story is."

"What story?"

"The one about the ring."

"The one you can't remember? How am *I* supposed to figure it out?"

"Aren't you going to Spain this spring?"

"I...I plan to," I said, grabbing one of the pieces of fruit, "but I have to actually, you know, apply for the program, and—"

"Maybe something you find there will help jog my memory."

I shook my head, sighing, and popped the fruit into my mouth. "Hmm," I said, savoring its flavor. It was somewhere between an apple and a pear, with the texture of a potato. "What are these things?"

"Quinces. *Los membrillos*. You've never had *bimbriyo?*"

"I don't think I understood half the words in that sentence you said just now."

Grandma shot me a look of incredulous exasperation. "What

does your mother *do* in her kitchen?"

"Wait, so how is my tracing our family line back to Spain going to help you remember a story your grandmother told you?"

Grandma sighed deeply again, wiping her brow on her sleeve. "I don't know. I just hope so." She scooped the quince back into the pot and started mashing it with a fork. "Getting old is awful, Alma. I don't recommend it."

I blinked. "Well, um. I think it's...probably better than the alternative."

"*B'ezrat haShem,* when you get old, may they have pills that make you feel not a day older than fifty until the moment you die. Peacefully. In your sleep." She pretended to spit on the floor three times, since apparently such a statement required warding off the Evil Eye. Then she grabbed my chin and gave it a little shake, making a high-pitched affectionate noise. "*Kapara,*" she said, then released my chin and kissed her hand. She put down the fork and waddled back to the breakfast table. "Stir that," she instructed, scooping up the box. She tucked it under her arm and grasped the handles of her walker.

"Hey, wait, where are you taking that?" I protested. "I want to see..."

"You saw enough. I'm putting them away. Exposure to this damp air is bad for them." She wheeled out. "Just keep stirring," she tossed over her shoulder. After a beat, she added: "With a *dairy* spoon."

# Míriam

"Mmm. Are those quinces I smell?" Abraham de Carmona pulled back the curtain hanging over the doorway to his neighbors' kitchen. His daughter Míriam and their neighbor, Hanna, were huddled over a ceramic pot on the fire. Míriam turned and smiled at him, her eyes widening with joy. Wisps of her dark hair peeked out from under her headscarf, matted against her sweaty brow, and her apron was covered in flour. She brushed the hair away from her pale green eyes with her bent wrist, trying to avoid smearing more flour on her face with her fingers. She dusted her hands on the apron as she crossed the kitchen.

"You can smell them a league away, can't you, Papa." She embraced him. "I missed you."

Abraham kissed her and held her close. "I missed you as well. I'm so glad to make it home in time for Rosh Hashana."

"So are we," Hanna piped up from behind them. "When you were gone last year, Jacob Aventuriel was the *chazzan*. It was a musical experience I'd rather not repeat."

"Oh, he wasn't that bad." Míriam pulled back and untied her apron, smoothing out the folds of her plain brown linen dress. Abraham smiled, straightening the hat atop his graying hair. He peered around the room.

"Where are your little charges?"

"We sent them with Solomon to the butcher."

"I hope you asked him to pick up a lamb's head for us as well."

"Don't be ridiculous!" Hanna didn't bother to turn from the pot.

"You are having the meal with us. We're counting on your stories from Cartagena."

Abraham laughed. "You have never said no to me, Hanna. How could I say no to you?" He held Míriam at arm's length, his brown eyes twinkling. "You are looking well, my girl."

"Thank you, Papa. How did your business go?"

"Well. Very well, thank God."

"I hope that means you've found her a match," Hanna piped up again. Míriam turned to shoot her a sour look. Hanna did not turn around. "Sixteen years old, beautiful, from a pious family…the neighbors are starting to talk."

Abraham looked thoughtfully at his daughter. "Let them talk."

"No, let *us* talk," Míriam said. "I want to hear about Cartagena."

"Come, help me unload the spices from my cart and I'll tell you how it went."

Míriam followed him through the narrow entrance room and out of the house toward the street. The Jewish Quarter of Lorca was alive with holiday preparations. The sounds and smells of washing and cooking wafted from every household, and the wild laughter of excited children echoed off the thick stone walls of the fortress in which the *judería* was tucked. Míriam could not remember the last time she had set foot beyond the Fisheries' Gate where the *judería* ended and the outside world began; since she and her father had established themselves in Lorca, she had never given much thought to what lay outside the wall. The *judería* was her world: the whitewashed plaster walls of the houses, with brown tile roofs scattered haphazardly over the uneven terrain of the hill, the zigzagging paths and steps connecting them, and at the center, the pride of the Jewish Quarter: the synagogue, with its high arched ceilings and decorative tile flooring, its expensive glass lamps and elaborate plasterwork. Across the courtyard was the *beit hamidrash*, the house of learning, which was always buzzing with the sound of men discussing the words of the Torah and the Sages; and up the road to the northeast was the building that housed the *mikveh*, the ritual bath, where Míriam had accompanied several of her friends celebrating their ritual purification before their wedding night.

She could smell her father's cart before she saw it: a rich harmony of exotic scents from faraway lands. There was nothing more wonderful than helping him unload his goods, breathing in the aromas, imagining the dishes she could flavor with the small samplings of spices that he would let her keep. She surveyed the wooden cart piled high with fat sacks.

"Did Don Tomás have anything new this time?" she asked her father.

"No, not in particular. But you can always count on Tomás to get his hands on the best cloves and cinnamon on the market. Here, smell this." He hoisted a large sack from the top of the cart and offered it to Míriam, who paused and made the blessing over smelling something pleasant, then closed her eyes and inhaled deeply.

"Mmmm. We should use these for *besamim* for *havdala.*"

"He insisted that I stop by his estate to rest before starting up the hill toward home." Abraham looked up beyond the roofs of the Jewish quarter at the square tower that loomed over them, stroking his graying black beard. "I know the *judería* is up here because the fortress protects us, and I am grateful for that, especially these days. But do I wish it were not such a steep climb!"

"I bet Moreno feels the same way." Míriam grabbed one of the sacks and hoisted it onto her shoulder.

"Oh yes. He's the most exhausted donkey in all of Murcia."

"I'm sure he'll be...glad...for a few days' rest thanks to Rosh

Hashana," Miriam grunted, carrying the sack toward the door to the cellar. She lifted the door handle with her foot and kicked it open, then descended the stairs, blinking to adjust her eyes to the dim light. She threw the bag onto one of the empty shelves and turned around to get another one, but something caught her eye and made her turn around to look at the wine barrels. She narrowed her eyes at them. Something wasn't right. She stepped closer, counting them.

"Papa," she called up to her father, who was a few steps behind with a giant sack of his own.

"Yes, dear?"

"The wine."

Abraham continued to the shelf and threw down his sack. "What about the wine?"

"Two barrels are missing." She put her hands on her hips, narrowing her eyes at him accusingly. He didn't turn to face her.

"Are you sure?" he asked absently.

"Papa!" Miriam scolded. "Where are they?"

Abraham sighed deeply and finally turned to her. "I dropped them off at the secret passageway. Sánchez has probably collected them by now."

Miriam glared at him. "You know what will happen if you get caught!" she hissed.

He lowered his eyes. "I know."

"And besides what will happen to *you*...what will happen to *me*? Isn't it enough that I lost one parent?"

Abraham raised a hand. "Miriam, please."

"You know you are all I have in the world. And for what? For those *marranos*, those pig-eaters, to have a sip of kosher wine on the holiday?"

Abraham's eyes flashed. "Do not call them that. Don't you think for a moment that you are better than they are, Miriam. You have never stood in their place. It is only by the grace of God that we did not have to face what they faced. We were simply in the right place at the right time, and they were not."

Míriam exhaled and lowered her eyes. "I'm sorry. I just don't understand why it's so important that they have kosher wine when the rest of the time they are eating everything the Christians eat."

"That's exactly why I said you have never stood in their place. You don't understand." Abraham's eyes almost glowed in the dim light of the cellar. "You don't understand what it is like to face the choice between death and baptism. You don't understand what it is like to wear a mask every moment, to be a pretender, in order to keep your own life and protect your family. You don't understand what it is like to feel that you can do no right in the eyes of anyone—not the Christians, not the Jews, and certainly not God...you are a sinner no matter what you do. Holding on to that one spark of Torah is what is keeping those *conversos* alive, Míriam. They know that at least they can sanctify the holidays in silence by bringing pure wine to their lips—and you will never understand how much comfort it brings them."

Míriam felt angry tears welling in her eyes and quickly brushed them away. "But Papa...who will comfort *me* if you are caught by the Inquisition? Who will comfort me if I have to watch you burn at the stake? You may feel sorry for them, but they *are* sinners. Who are they that you should sacrifice yourself for them?"

"Who are you that you should judge them?!"

Míriam winced and shushed him, looking up at the cellar door. He followed her gaze, then turned back to her, taking a deep breath.

"I just..." he went on quietly, "I can't stand by idly and watch them disappear. Who knows...maybe if we help them hold onto a little of their Judaism...maybe one day the Christians will become more tolerant, and they will be able to cast off their masks and live free as Jews again."

"Will you stand by idly and leave your daughter an orphan?" Despite her efforts to hold her tears back, several escaped and streamed down her face. Abraham saw them and gathered her into his arms.

"Miriam...Miriam... I'm sorry. I'm sorry. You're right. I'm being selfish. I will tell Sánchez that this is the last time. All right? Just please...don't weep anymore. I can't stand it."

Miriam took a deep, shuddering breath.

"Thank you, Papa," she murmured into his shoulder. "Please. I worry about you enough without your sneaking around under the noses of the Tribunal. You know how closely they watch those *conversos.*"

Abraham sighed, pulling away and giving her a sad smile. "You worry too much. Maybe Hanna is right and it is time to find you a husband you can worry about instead of me."

Miriam half-sobbed, half-laughed. Abraham drew a handkerchief from his belt and handed it to her.

"Here. Sit here and calm down. I'll unload the rest of the spices, and when I'm done we will have some coffee and I'll tell you all about Cartagena. All right?"

# Manuel

Usually when I walked past a Judaica shop I averted my gaze.

Okay, maybe sometimes I would venture a peek out of the corners of my eyes, just to catch a glimpse of the strange and beautiful items on display. After all, where I came from, such things were more likely to be found in museums, not stores.

Something was different this time, though. I wish I could say I didn't know what it was. Or that it was something about the shop itself... only it was very much like the dozens of other Judaica shops I'd passed on the grimy, bustling streets of New York City: frayed black Hebrew print on the display window, polished silver and ceramic items arranged just so on the dusty blue velvet...

But no. I did know what it was.

It was the girl behind the counter.

In my defense, it wasn't that she was pretty. Well, I should say it wasn't *just* that she was pretty. She had shoulder-length black hair that curled gently at the ends and high cheekbones accented by the frames of her glasses. Her large, almond-shaped eyes were narrowed and her full lips were pursed in what looked like annoyance, probably at whoever was on the other end of the cellphone pressed against her ear.

Where was I?

Oh yes. It wasn't just that she was pretty. There was an odd familiarity to her that I couldn't place. She did look more or less Mediterranean... maybe even Spanish? I started racking my brain trying to figure out where I might have seen her before. And it was as I did this that I found my hand pressing against the glass of the door. And pushing it open. And setting off a faint sound of bells.

The girl glanced over at me and raised her eyebrows.

My heart leapt to my throat.

She waved a greeting, and then turned her attention back to the phone.

I didn't have to walk in. I could have just turned around and left. In fact, that's exactly what I wanted to do. But somehow, it just did not happen. My feet would not heed my command to turn back. They carried me down the steps into the store.

I ducked into the nearest aisle, facing away from her, trying to regroup and figure out what on earth I was going to do next.

"Listen, Ima," the girl was saying in a sharp tone, "I really can't have this conversation now, I'm at the store, I've got customers here…"

I glanced around to locate these other alleged customers. It seemed that she was referring to me in the plural.

"Yes, I told you, it's right here in the pamphlet in my hand at this very moment, it's legitimately a part of the degree."

Her side of the conversation faded from my awareness as I noticed the contents of the shelves in front of me. The top shelf contained what appeared to be sets… of what, I couldn't imagine. The only items I recognized were goblets and plates for the trinkets to rest on. On the shelf beneath these were stacks of brown and white leather-bound books. There was Hebrew print embossed in gold on the covers. I breathed in their scent—new paper, fresh ink, and leather—and extended a hand to touch them. But I stopped midway. This was not what I walked in here for.

*Wait. What* did *I walk in here for?*

"…Do you really think I'd be traipsing off to Spain without making sure of that?"

My ears automatically locked back onto her voice.

"Okay, okay, we'll talk about it some other time…"

I straightened my back and turned slowly to peek over the shelf behind me at the girl. She lowered the phone from her ear and pressed something on the screen. Then she tossed it carelessly on the counter in front of her and said, "Why are parents so annoying?"

Was she talking to me? I instinctively glanced around for someone else she might have been talking to. But when I turned back, she was looking right at me. "Sorry about that," she said. "Can I help with something?"

"Eh..." Panicking a little, I reached behind me, groped on the shelf and plucked an odd-looking silver item from it. "Mm... I was wondering what this is." I held it up.

She glanced at it. "Oh, that? It's a *besamim* holder."

I blinked. "Sorry?"

"A container for the *besamim*. The spices for *havdala*."

I cleared my throat. "I'm sorry. For...what?" I emerged from the aisle, my footstep muffled on the threadbare brown carpet. All right, so I sounded like a total idiot, but at least we were talking now.

Her face melted into a friendly smile. "*Havdala*," she repeated. "It's the ritual for ending the Sabbath."

"Ah." I had no idea what she was talking about, but never mind. I inspected the object. It was a curious little thing, a sort of silver cage on a stand crowned by a conical spire, with a tiny silver flag on top. "Eh...how do you use it?"

She studied me. I was close enough now to see that her eyes were a pale sea green, and her eyelashes were so long they brushed against the lenses of her glasses when she blinked. I was too fascinated with this to focus on what she said next. When I realized she had asked a question, I started. "Sorry?"

She paused, still surveying me over the glasses. "I asked if you have any idea what I'm talking about."

I gave a sheepish grin. "Now that you mention it, no."

She removed her glasses and put them on her desk, rubbing her nose where the glasses had left little indentations. "We have a little ritual to end the Sabbath, called *havdala*, which means 'differentiation'."

She stood up behind the desk, reached out and took the trinket from me. I found myself watching the way her hair spilled toward her collarbone as she leaned forward.

*Dios mío. Focus, Manuel.*

"You put spices in this. Cloves are easiest." She pulled off the spire, showing me the empty silver cage. "And then, during the ritual, you smell it." She closed it and demonstrated sniffing it.

She handed it back to me. I studied it, biting the inside of my lip. I mustered every gram of courage I had and looked up at her.

"I know this sounds crazy, but have we met before?"

"Alma!" A muffled voice came from somewhere near the back of the store.

"Yeah?" the girl called back.

*Alma. Her name is Alma.*

"When are you going to bring down the *Gemaras* for Mr. Steibel? He's supposed to be here any minute."

An old woman appeared on the narrow wrought-iron staircase at the back of the store, clutching the railing and scowling in our general direction. Her hair was covered in a colorful scarf, and her skin, like Alma's, looked darker than that of the Jews I'd seen in my neighborhood in Brooklyn. When she caught sight of me, her gray eyebrows rose.

"Ah!" she exclaimed. "I see you found me a strapping young man to do the job."

I blinked, glancing at Alma in alarm. She was rubbing her forehead in exasperation.

"Ignore her," she instructed me, sliding off her stool and making her way around the desk. "Coercing random people into hard labor is her idea of customer service. I'll get them, Grandma."

I hesitated, regarding her short but full-figured frame, trying not to notice the way her pale green shirt and denim skirt hugged her curves as she stepped toward the aisle.

Inevitably, I heard my mother's voice screeching in my head: *Manuel! Did I raise a gentleman or a philistine?!*

"No, wait," I stuttered, placing the whatsit-holder on the desk. Alma stopped, raising an eyebrow and looking at me over her glasses. "Please, sit down. I am happy to help."

I turned back and approached the staircase. The old woman smiled down at me triumphantly.

"Now, there's what those Ashkenazim call a *mensch*," she said. She had a vague accent that sounded familiar, but I couldn't quite place. "You see, Alma? People love to help. And I worry about you carrying all these heavy loads. You're supposed to be making me great-grandbabies someday."

I cast a glance back toward Alma, who had followed me to the back of the store. She rolled her eyes.

"Grandma, I am perfectly capable of carrying a box of books down the stairs!" she insisted.

"Sit," her grandmother ordered, and Alma obeyed, but not without some disgruntled muttering. I followed her grandmother up the narrow stairs and found myself facing an enormous cardboard box on the landing. I wrestled with it, finally managing to lift it and start tottering back down the stairs. Good thing I had spent all summer stocking shelves at Garcia's grocery!

When I reached the floor, I tried to minimize the exertion in my voice: "Where do you need this, ma'am?"

"Just put it on the front desk," she said.

"Here," Alma's voice came from behind the box, and I felt its weight lighten somewhat.

In a series of awkward maneuvers, we finally managed to get

it through the middle aisle without breaking anything. We set it down carefully on the desk and shook out our arms. The grandmother was slowly lowering herself down the stairs.

"Well, thank you, young man," she said, seizing a cane that was waiting for her on the landing.

"It's nothing," I said quickly.

She gave me an appraising look as she approached me. Then she opened her mouth, and a question in perfect Spanish came out:

"*¿Eres hispano, chico?*"

That was about the last thing I had expected to hear.

"*Sí, señora,*" I responded, a little taken aback. "*¿Y usted?*"

She laughed. "*I was born under the Spanish protectorate in Tétouan, Morocco,*" she continued in Spanish. "*Castilian is my first language.*"

It took me a few seconds to recover from the shock. I had a vague idea that there were Jews in Morocco, but I never would have guessed that they spoke Spanish. "*How is Castilian your first language?*" I finally asked.

"*My ancestors fled Castile in the fifteenth century,*" she said. "*And you can take the Jew out of Spain, but you can't take Spain out of the Jew.*" She winked at me. "*My grandparents and parents spoke a North African dialect of Judeo-Spanish called Haketía. We reverted back to Castilian when the Spaniards took over.*" She turned to Alma and switched back to English: "Did you call the cab, *mami?*"

"Yes, he should be here any second," Alma said, grabbing her grandmother's elbow to help her climb the two steps that led up to the street. "Please don't forget to tell the doctor about those spells of shortness of breath, okay?"

"I know, I know." The grandmother pulled open the door and they made their way out to the street.

I stood there, trying to absorb what I had just heard. On the one hand, I still had no idea what had gotten into my head walking in here in the first place. I could almost feel Padre Carlos's disapproving frown. *You ask too many questions about the Jews,* his voice echoed in my head. *This is not good for you.*

On the other hand, my curiosity about Alma had only grown. She and her grandmother were completely different from anything I had known about Jews up until that point. And having lived in Brooklyn for the past five years, you'd think I would know.

"I'm so sorry about that," came a voice from the door. "My grandmother is a little...eccentric."

I realized I had been standing there staring blankly at the candelabras on the shelf behind the register. As my eyes swept the surface of the desk, they caught something I hadn't noticed before: the emblem of NYU on the pamphlets Alma had been looking at earlier. My eyebrows went up and I reached for them.

"Do you study at NYU?" I asked, turning to her and nodding at the pamphlets. "I'm about to start my second year there. Iberian studies."

"No way!" she exclaimed. "I just transferred from SUNY Binghampton to that exact program. I have my heart set on getting into this special honors program." She tapped the pamphlet I was holding. It read, *The Spanish Heritage Project: Research Your Family's Past with NYU Madrid.* "In the fall semester, they teach you how to do research in the historical archives in Spain, and then you spend spring semester in Madrid doing just that."

I riffled through the pages, a strange feeling of urgency rising in my chest. "That actually sounds...really interesting," I murmured. I was thinking about my father, and the pages of records he had so painstakingly researched, now tucked away in a cabinet somewhere in my mother's room.

"My father..." I said. "He managed to trace our paternal line back to Granada of the 1500's."

"Oh, cool!" Alma exclaimed. "So you wouldn't even need this program."

"On the contrary," I said. "He never achieved his goal. He believed we are related to one of the old noble families in Castilla—our surname is Aguilar—and he wanted to prove it, but never made a definitive connection. The oldest ancestors he was able to find seem to have been commoners." I flipped the pamphlet over and examined the glossy picture of the National Historical Archive on the back.

"So," Alma said. "I take it you're not Jewish."

The comment caught me off-guard. For a moment I had forgotten that I was standing in a Judaica store, talking to a Jew, for no apparent reason.

"Ehhh, yes," I stuttered. "That is, no, I'm not. I'm Roman Catholic." I studied her, trying to gauge her reaction to this information.

"So..." Alma narrowed her eyes at me questioningly. "Were you here looking for a gift, or...?"

"I...no," I said, my eyes drifting back to the silver object I had grabbed when I first walked in the store. "I was...only curious." I picked it up and carried it to the shelf, replacing it carefully on the tray.

"Curious about the *besamim* holder, or about Judaism?"

I spun around, surprised by the directness of the question. She was watching me expectantly. I paused, unsure what to say.

"Both, I suppose," I answered slowly.

She raised an eyebrow, her smile almost teasing. "So just how Catholic are you?"

I laughed. "I was seriously considering attending seminary before we left Spain."

"That bad, huh." She laughed, too. "To be a priest?"

"Yes."

"What made you decide not to?"

"I did not really decide. I just put off the decision for now." I smiled. "And just how Jewish are you?"

She shrugged. "Oh, you know...traditional? I keep kosher and observe the Sabbath and all that. We Sephardim don't buy into the Ashkenazi obsession with labels and boxes, but if you insist, I might fall somewhere between Orthodox and Conservative. Conservadox, if you like."

She gestured a lot as she spoke. It was adorable.

"I...see."

She seemed to register that I didn't—at all—because she smiled apologetically. "Never mind. Jews. We're a complicated bunch." She regarded me for a few moments. "So, you're from Spain."

"Yes. Granada, in the south."

"Of Alhambra Decree fame. Of course."

I couldn't tell if her voice went somewhat cold or if it was my imagination, but I felt uncomfortably conscious of the implications of our common heritage. Had my own ancestors been responsible for her ancestors' expulsion from Spain?

I shifted awkwardly, not meeting her eyes. I had been brought up with an acute awareness of how badly my country had treated its Jews; but never until now had I met a descendent of the victims. Finally I had an opportunity to say what I had been feeling for years: "I am...sorry for what my ancestors did to yours."

Alma laughed. "It's been half a millennium. I think I'm over it."

I felt a little lighter in the chest, and gave her a cautious smile.

"How long have you been in the US?" she asked.

"Five years."

"Five years? No way! Your English is great!"

I felt my face get warm and waved away the compliment. "My accent is very strong."

"No, it's adorable!" she blurted, and then flushed a little herself and cleared her throat. "But...then why are you taking Iberian studies at NYU? Seems a little silly to come all the way from Spain to New York to study...Spain."

"Well, I simply thought it would be easier to study something familiar. With a lot of material in Spanish."

"Oh. I guess that makes sense." She nodded at the pamphlets in my hand. "So...you want to keep those?"

I glanced down at them again, then looked up and grinned. "Actually, I think I do. Is that okay with you?"

"By all means! At least that way I'll be able to tell my grandmother I didn't let a customer leave the store empty-handed." She winked.

"Thank you," I said. "Thank you very much." I took a step back toward the door. "It was lovely to meet you."

"You too," she returned, kind of absently, as something on her phone caught her attention and she leaned over to examine it. I shoved the door open, lingered for a moment, then turned and walked out, swallowing hard as the door swung closed behind me. I stood there, trying to reorient myself and figure out what on earth had just happened. Then the door behind me burst open, hitting me in the hip. I dropped the pamphlets and they fluttered to the ground.

"Ooh! Sorry!" she gushed, rushing to gather the pamphlets.

"That's all right, I'm fine..." I tried to bend over to help her, but she snatched up everything first. She stood up quickly and handed them back to me.

"I just, um..." she said, hastily brushing back her hair, "I realized I hadn't gotten your name."

"Ah." I smiled widely, warmth rushing to my cheeks. "Manuel. Manuel Aguilar."

"Manuel Aguilar," she repeated slowly, squinting her eyes. "Manuel." And she went back into the shop, lost in thought. Then she turned and opened the door again, as if remembering that she hadn't finished the conversation yet. "I'm Alma."

"I caught that. It is a Spanish name." I grinned.

"Actually it's Hebrew, too," she said. "Nice to meet you! See you at school, I guess!"

"Ehhh...yes."

And she closed the door again and went back to her perch behind the desk. I watched her, smiling, for a little longer before folding the pamphlets carefully, tucking them into my pocket, and continuing down the street.

# Alma

"Okay. This is ridiculous," I blurted aloud when finding myself, for the fourth time, facing the fountain at the center of Washington Square Park. I buried my face in my hands, trying to take a deep breath, and once again drew my crumpled campus map from the back pocket of my skirt. I brushed my bangs out of my eyes and squinted at the map. I looked up again. The trees obscured my view, the buildings seemed incredibly vast and sprawling, and no matter how hard I tried, I could not figure out which side of that stupid arch I was on.

*This is hopeless.*

Out of the corner of my eye I caught sight of a guy in sunglasses sitting on a bench under one of the trees. He seemed to be craning his neck to look at me. I walked toward him.

"Hi," I called. "Can you tell me how to get to the Academic Resource Center?" He stood up and took off his sunglasses. I stopped in my tracks. Recognition jolted through me, but I couldn't place him. He was tall and kind of lanky, with a rather dark complexion and a shock of loose black curls that fell lightly around his face. But the thing that was really burned into my memory was his honey-brown, soulful eyes—there was something in their depth that made my spine tingle. Where had I seen them before? I cocked my head at him. "Hey. Have we met before?"

"Yes. I believe we have." A wide smile brightened his face, and at the sound of his accent, I remembered.

"Oh! Yes! You're the Spaniard who carried that box down the stairs for my grandmother!" I was surprised at how much relief

I felt. I guess any vaguely familiar face is welcome when you're lost in Manhattan. "I remember everything about our conversation, but…" I winced, biting my lip apologetically. "I'm really terrible with names."

"Manuel."

"Yes! Manuel. Good to see you!"

He leaned back, sizing me up. "You seem lost."

"Yes. I am." I grinned sheepishly.

"So you are terrible with names, and have a terrible sense of direction."

"Exactly. You have me all figured out there."

"Well, I am pleased to assist a lady in distress. The Academic Resource Center," he turned and pointed, "is that building right there."

I looked where he was pointing and felt my cheeks burn. "You mean, the one that says 'Academic Resource Center' in extremely clear lettering that's easily visible from the spot we are standing on?"

He laughed. "Yes. That's the one. It just so happens," he said, stuffing the book he'd been holding into his bag, "that I should be on my way there myself."

"Oh, right! Are you coming to the Spanish Heritage Project introduction?"

He nodded.

"Oh, nice!"

He hoisted the bag onto his shoulder and gathered his coat in the crook of his arm. Then he gestured toward the building. "Shall we?"

I fell in step next to him, and we crossed the street together, leaving behind the smell of the freshly cut grass and the cool, moist shade of the trees as we approached the row of buildings.

"So. What are you hoping to find in the archives?" he asked.

"Well…" I sighed. "I know it's a long shot. I know they probably don't have records from the time period I need. But my grandmother is adamant that I have to go and look. I can't really explain it..." My voice trailed off as I looked at him. "Well, you're from that part of the world. You probably get it. There was always this really strong sense of family lore in my grandmother's family. It was...lost in the last generation in a way, so I think I'm kind of her last hope."

We had arrived at the glass door to the building. He swung it open and held it, then looked at me expectantly.

"Aww," I said.

His thick eyebrows knitted in confusion. "What?"

"Nothing." I walked in, biting back a smile, and he followed. I paused in the lobby and glanced at my watch. "Well...we still have ten minutes."

There was an awkward pause. I fiddled with the map in my hands.

"You, um...want to sit?" I gestured to the little coffee tables nearby.

Manuel hesitated.

"Unless you, um, I don't know, have something else to do," I said quickly. "Or want to go to the classroom first. Or—"

"No...let's sit. I want to hear more about your grandmother." He headed for the nearest vacant table, pulling out a chair for me and setting his bag on the opposite end of the table before sitting down. I smiled again at this old-fashioned chivalrous behavior. *Gotta love Europeans.*

"You were saying that you think you're your grandmother's last hope."

"Right."

"So...hope for what?"

"I'm not even sure." I sighed in frustration. "Her memory isn't what it used to be, and she says there is something she wants to figure out about how our ancestors left Spain. I don't know what she's hoping I'll find…but I'd like to find proof that they were from Spain in the first place."

He nodded slowly. "So…what you are telling me is that you transferred to New York University to spend a semester in Madrid, not because you want to travel or study there, but because your grandmother told you to."

I blinked. "Well, when you put it that way…"

He laughed.

"Actually, it wasn't just my grandmother," I went on. "I have this cousin I grew up really close with, and in the past few years he's been sort of distancing himself from the family and from Judaism in general. I mean, a lot of my cousins aren't religious, and some of them have very little connection to Judaism. But last year David started dating a—" About half a millisecond before it was too late, I realized who I was talking to. I blushed a little and stuttered, "That is, you know, he just started doing things that really crossed the line for my family, and he isn't on speaking terms with most of us anymore. It was kind of the straw that broke the camel's back for me, and I realized I had to do something to preserve our family's heritage. And maybe…" I shrugged. "Maybe find some information that can get the rest of them excited about it again."

He was nodding slowly. I wondered if he knew what I'd been about to say before I caught myself.

"Also," I added quickly, "I kind of hated nursing school."

"That's what you were studying before?"

"In a manner of speaking."

There was a pause. I cleared my throat.

"So! What about you? How did you end up at NYU? Or… New York, for that matter?"

He sighed. "My mother," he said simply.

"Why did she want you to come here?"

"I…don't know." It was remarkable how his whole manner

changed. He crossed his arms and his mouth pursed in irritation. "She's a little crazy, my mother."

"So it's crazy to live in America?" I smiled.

"No no, that's not—" he protested, eyes wide.

"I'm joking, I'm joking."

"Ah. Sorry."

"It's fine. Quit apologizing."

"Sorry? I mean…" He put his hand over his mouth, his cheeks reddening.

*Aww,* I thought. *He's so cute. Too bad he's not Jewish.*

I laughed. "You don't need to apologize for not understanding. You've been here—how many years, again?"

"Five."

"There are people who've known me for twenty years and still don't get my humor. You're ahead of the curve." I glanced at my watch. "Hey, we should go."

---

Professor Rodriguez had told me over the phone that attending the introduction didn't guarantee that I'd be accepted into the program, but I'd meet the other students considering it, and get a feel for what kind of work would be involved. I had tried my hardest to convince him that my Spanish grades from Binghampton were only so-so because the professor was evil and that I would work really hard to improve my language skills. He had not seemed particularly convinced.

As Manuel and I walked into the classroom, though, and heard the chatter of the students already sitting there, I started to wonder if maybe Rodriguez was right to be skeptical. There were six students sitting on the hard plastic chairs in front—four girls and two guys—all of them talking animatedly in rapid-fire Spanish.

I couldn't understand a word.

Well, of course they were Hispanic. They were all there to research their Spanish heritage, weren't they?

Manuel took a seat and burrowed back into his book.

One of the girls facing the door noticed me standing there and looked up, smiling. "*Hola*," she said, and then something else in Spanish I didn't quite catch.

I cleared my throat nervously. "Um. I actually don't speak Spanish that well." Five other faces turned toward me, bearing expressions with varying levels of perplexity. "I'm Alma."

The girl exchanged glances with the girl sitting next to her. "This class is an introduction to the Spanish Heritage Project," she said. "Is that what you were trying to find?"

"Um, yes. I actually do have Spanish heritage, but..."

"Where from?" the girl asked.

"Um... Morocco. That is... it's complicated. I'm a Sephardic Jew..." I registered six blank stares, and after a few moments of awkward silence, I found myself launching into a rambling speech about Sephardim and Morocco and the expulsion of the Jews from Spain. By the time I was wrapping it up, the two guys had returned to their conversation, the girl who had spoken to me was playing with her phone, and the remaining three were watching me and looking politely confused.

Finally one of them cleared her throat. "So what you're saying," she said slowly, "is that your family is originally from Morocco, but they probably came from Spain before that."

Well, when she put it that way, it sounded awfully simple.

"Um... right," I said. I sat down in the empty seat next to her. "So... what about you guys?"

We chatted for a few minutes about their own backgrounds—all of them Latin American—but the conversation soon seemed to melt back into Spanish and I got left behind. The twinge of doubt

I had felt when entering the room grew stronger. I gritted my teeth and forced myself to listen, trying to pick out words I recognized from the river of sounds.

"Good afternoon," came a voice from the door, and Professor Rodriguez walked in carrying a stack of papers. He dumped the stack onto the desk at the front of the classroom and surveyed us, counting under his breath. "Six...seven...eight. Good, you're all here."

He spent the next half hour explaining about the NYU Madrid program and how our project would integrate with it, and what the grade requirements would be. "I imagine you—well, most of you," he said, his eyes lingering on me, "will be taking the advanced classes taught in Spanish. You, on the other hand," he said directly to me, "will probably want to take the Spanish-language track." I nodded, shrinking a little in embarrassment at being singled out as the class idiot.

He went on to introduce us to Spanish paleography, showing us slides of various documents from different historical periods. The closer we got to the fifteenth century, the more my stomach twisted in nervous knots. How on earth was I ever going to be able to read those illegible scribbles? Projected alongside one document on the screen was a chart identifying the letters, and Professor Rodriguez asked us to take a few minutes to try and see if we could figure out what the top sentence said. I squinted at it, then flopped back against my seat in resignation.

"Are we really ever supposed to figure out how to read what that says?" Andrea spoke up from next to me.

"That's what we're going to be working on for a major portion of this semester," Professor Rodriguez said.

Manuel cleared his throat from two seats over. "Professor," he said quietly. "Does it say, *'Pater noster, qui es in caelis'*? The Lord's Prayer in Latin?"

We all turned to stare at him.

Professor Rodriguez's face lit up.

"Yes," he exclaimed, "yes it does! Very well done, Mr. . . . "

"Aguilar," Manuel reminded him.

"*Muy bien.* Can you read this one?" He clicked to the next slide. Manuel took a moment to look it over and to study the chart, and then, very slowly, began successfully identifying words from the sentence.

"Very impressive! Is this your first time reading fifteenth-century documents, Mr. Aguilar?"

"Yes, Professor." Manuel squirmed a little under all our astonished gazes.

Professor Rodriguez shook his head, grinning widely. "Some people just have a knack for it," he said. "You are very fortunate, Mr. Aguilar. This will make your work much easier."

The professor continued to explain a little more about the structure of the research, but I was having trouble concentrating. My chest was tight with anxiety. Of the eight of us, I was clearly at the greatest disadvantage. If I ever did manage to get to a point where researching the archives would be in the realm of possibility for me, I would be working at half the speed of the other students.

Then I caught half a sentence the professor was saying: ". . . So, I recommend trying to work in pairs or small groups and helping each other out with your respective projects. It may seem to take up more of your time, but it usually ends up making you more efficient because another pair of eyes can often make a big difference."

I glanced over at Manuel. He was fiddling absently with a pencil, his forehead wrinkled a little in concentration, a stray black curl fallen over his eye.

*If I could get* him *to help me . . .*

And the more I thought about it, the more it made sense. He was a Spanish speaker. His Spanish, in fact, was probably closer to medieval Castilian than anybody else's, because he was actually from Spain. And if he could read archaic scripts like that on his first try, he'd be reading them like his own handwriting by the beginning of next semester.

I glanced around the room, wondering how many of the other students were having the same thought. I felt another wave of anxiety. I had to make sure to get to him first. My entire twenty-six-generation family legacy depended on it.

*On the other hand...*

I bit my lip, feeling guilty about the fact that I even considered the fact that he was Catholic a reason to hesitate. I mean...it's not like I hadn't had non-Jewish friends in the past. But they were all female. And...well...an image of my cousin David's face floated into my mind.

*Oh, don't be ridiculous,* said a voice in my head. *He wants to be a priest. A Catholic priest. That's, like, only a notch less safe than a gay guy.*

*Not that I've ever actually had a gay friend. But theoretically...*

It was at that point in my inner monologue that I noticed that the professor had dismissed us and the other students were standing up to leave. I jumped up, looking for Manuel, and caught sight of his shoulder bag as it disappeared around the doorframe. I grabbed my backpack and sprinted after him.

"Manuel!" I called as I skidded out into the hall. Fortunately, being half a head taller than most of the other students, he was easy to spot. He stopped and turned around, his eyebrows raised in surprise. I jogged up to him.

"Um..." I started, feeling my cheeks get warm. "Hi."

"Hi," he answered with an uncertain smile.

"So listen," I blurted. "Remember the list of my faults you already have?"

He blinked.

"You know, that I'm really bad at directions..." I reminded him.

"And you are terrible with names?"

"Right! So I have another thing to add to that list. My Spanish. It sucks."

He squinted at me in confusion. "Okay..." he said slowly.

"My chances of staying in this program, never mind having any success whatsoever with the genealogical research, are fairly abysmal. So...um. I noticed how good you are at paleography and between that and your Spanish I was wondering if you'd be willing to pair up with me for the research," I said breathlessly.

Now it was his turn to blush a little. "Eh..." he said with an embarrassed smile. A group of students jostled past us.

"I...it's totally okay to say no," I said quickly. "Or to think about it. You don't need to tell me now. I just, um, wanted to put it out there..."

"I think I see what is going on here," he said. "You want to exploit me for my ability to read fifteenth-century manuscripts." He was still smiling.

"Well, yeah," I answered. "What else would I exploit you for?"

He laughed. "It's just that I'm still not sure I'm going," he said. "My mother is not going to be happy when she finds out I'm thinking about it."

"Why, you think she'd mind?" I asked.

He studied me for a moment. "I'm her only son," he said. "My father is dead and so are my grandparents, and if she even has living cousins, my grandmother was completely cut off from her family and my mother doesn't know them. So...yes, my mother would mind."

"O...kay," I said. "I'm hearing a lot of stories there. But I still don't understand what that has to do with you going to Spain. She's going to have to face the fact that you're an adult someday. How old are you?"

"Twenty-three. But you don't realize how much she sacrificed for me to finish college here."

"You will. You'll just do one semester in Madrid. What's the big deal?"

"Well, you are very persuasive," he said. "Maybe I'll simply give you her phone number, and you can resolve it between you." He pulled his phone from his back pocket.

"Sure, hand it over!" I extended my hand helpfully.

He froze, looking a little alarmed. "I...did not...I was joking."

"Why?" My heart sank a little.

"She's...trust me, you don't want me to put you in that position."

I narrowed my eyes at him. This was sounding more and more like an excuse to get out of telling me he didn't want to be my research partner.

"So, is that a no?" I ventured. "'Cause I'm totally serious. I will talk to her if that's the issue."

He shifted uncomfortably.

"It's okay," I said quickly. "You don't owe me an explanation. I understand—"

"It's not just my mother," he interrupted me. He was staring at the floor now, kicking at an empty gum wrapper with the toe of his sneaker. I waited, dread filling my chest. Was it the religious difference? Maybe he felt uncomfortable with my being Jewish? I hadn't really thought about it before then, and the idea made my fists clench.

He cleared his throat. "I'm not sure we can afford it," he said in a small voice.

Guilt immediately washed over me. I nearly kicked myself for making such an uncharitable assumption.

"I'm on financial aid," he went on, "and I'm quite sure it doesn't cover international programs. I have some savings, but..." his voice trailed off. "I certainly would not count on my mother paying for it."

I studied him.

"Listen," I said slowly, "no pressure or anything. But Professor Rodriguez was super impressed with you just now. I bet he would be willing to work on some kind of arrangement to make sure you can participate in the program. I bet there's financial aid for students who want to study abroad."

He fiddled with the zipper on his bag, still not meeting my eyes.

"I get it. You're shy," I said. "I'll come with you and do all the talking."

He peered up at me from beneath his black curls, smiling sheepishly.

"As you may have noticed," I went on, "talking is pretty much the one thing I'm good at."

He laughed. "All right," he said. "You win."

I cleared my throat. "So, then. . . is this a yes to my original question?"

He blinked. "What original question?"

"The one about us being research partners. If you do end up going."

He hesitated again, and my old suspicion resurfaced.

"I. . . sure," he said.

I narrowed my eyes slightly. "You sure? You okay working with a Jesus killer? 'Cause I don't want to ruin your priesthood prospects or something." I hoped my voice was more playful than stinging, but I wasn't sure it came out right.

He leaned away, looking a little surprised and maybe a little offended. Then he fired right back. "And what about you? You're okay working with a Christian boy? I don't want to invoke the wrath of a Jewish mother."

We regarded each other awkwardly for a few moments.

"That was a joke, Alma."

I felt my cheeks get warm, and let out an awkward laugh, turning away from him. "Yeah, I know. Come, let's go find the professor."

# Míriam

The day after Abraham's return, Míriam woke early to help Hanna
with the preparations for the two-day holiday. This mostly involved
entertaining the children so that Hanna could cook in peace, and
usually she would bring them over to Míriam's house to play. But
today Rabbi Meir was going to teach a special class for all the kids
aged three and up, so it was only two-year-old Rebeca who needed
minding. Míriam attempted to slice vegetables and knead dough with
Hanna while keeping an eye on the child; but the constant interrup-
tions to pull Rebeca away from the fireplace were very frustrating.

"Just leave it," Hanna said. Her eyes had dark circles underneath
them and she rubbed them wearily. She was the midwife of the
*judería,* and had been up most of the night attending a birth. "Take
her outside, let her play in the mud, I don't care. They're all getting a
bath later anyway. I need to lie down for a little while."

Míriam carried Rebeca toward her own house, but stopped
short when she saw a young man standing there shifting his weight
uncomfortably from one foot to the other, peering toward the window. He was tall, with curly black hair that fell gently around his
face and a wide-brimmed hat with a large plume. His surcoat was
elaborately embroidered. Míriam didn't need to note the absence of
the red circular badge that Jews were required to wear to know that
he was Christian. She hung back, not sure what to do. He noticed her
out of the corner of his eye and turned to face her. His eyes were
honey-brown and had an intense, soulful quality to them that made
Míriam lower her gaze.

"Pardon me, *señorita*," he said, sweeping off his hat and bowing. "Is this the residence of Abraham de Carmona?"

"Yes, *señor*." She eyed him apprehensively.

"My father sent me to show him some documents. We understand that you have a holiday this evening and sincerely apologize, but it is urgent."

"Ah. Is your father Don Tomás?" Míriam asked, starting to catch on.

"My apologies. Yes. My name is León. Are you Abraham's daughter?"

"Yes." Míriam felt her shoulders relax a little. Don Tomás had been her father's friend and business partner since shortly after they had arrived in Lorca, and she knew that her father trusted him. "He is at the *beit midrash* studying."

"I beg your pardon, at the what?"

"The house of learning. The building across the courtyard from the synagogue." She pointed up the street. "Up that way, turn right and then right again into the courtyard. The entrance is up the stairs to your right."

"I'm...not sure I will recognize the synagogue," he said uncertainly.

"You can't miss it."

"*Gracias, señorita.*" He bowed again and took off in the direction she had pointed. She watched him for a few moments, then swung open the door to her house and carried Rebeca in.

A few minutes later there was a knock on the door. Míriam got up from the bench built into the wall of the living room and went to answer it. It was León again, his cheeks reddened and his head bowed.

"I am so sorry to disturb you again. I have some difficulty following directions. Could you explain again..."

Míriam smiled, feeling her discomfort with him slowly melting away. "Why don't I take you there?"

He looked up, his shoulders relaxing in relief. "I would be greatly obliged."

"Come, Rebeca!" Miriam called to the little girl, who had been spreading a pile of cloth scarves all over the floor. Rebeca ignored her. Miriam sighed in frustration and went to pick her up. As they approached the door, Rebeca grabbed Miriam's headscarf and yanked hard. Miriam gasped as her hair spilled over her shoulders in a long black cascade, curling gently at the ends near her waist. She blushed profusely, putting Rebeca down and feverishly wrapping her hair up again. León stared politely at the ground. When Miriam had firmly tied the scarf back on, she picked Rebeca up again and swept past León.

She closed the door behind them. Rebeca, who apparently felt she had not filled her quota of mischief, reached out and snatched León's hat right off his head.

"No, no, Rebeca!" Miriam scolded, wrestling the hat from her. León's eyes softened and he smiled.

"That's all right," he said. "She can carry it if she wants."

Miriam cleared her throat. "This way." Rebeca stared at León from over Miriam's shoulder, the hat swinging from her hand.

"I am most grateful for your offer to escort me." León fell in step behind her. "Your neighbors seem very suspicious of me."

It was true. As they passed by Miriam's neighbors, many of them stopped what they were doing to stare in their direction.

"We are suspicious of anyone who isn't Jewish," Miriam said. "And I'm sure you can imagine why."

León shrugged. "These days, everyone is suspicious of everyone else."

They continued in silence down the street. Rebeca lost interest in the hat and dropped it on the ground. León stooped to retrieve it and dusted it off, jogging to keep up. Miriam led him past the neighboring houses into the synagogue's courtyard, and then up to the steps of the *beit midrash*. As they approached, the hum of voices became louder and louder. To Miriam it sounded like a normal, lively discussion of the rabbi's lecture, but León looked a little alarmed.

"Are they fighting?" he asked.

Míriam laughed. "No, they are studying."

León raised his thick eyebrows, looking at her skeptically. "By shouting at one another?"

"Well...it's more...shouting *with* one another."

"This explains quite a bit," León mumbled.

"What do you mean by that?" Míriam asked sharply, shifting Rebeca to her other hip.

"Never mind. Will he hear me if I call him?"

"No. You'll have to go in and get his attention."

He hesitated. "Am I allowed? I'm a Christian..."

"And I'm a woman, so between the two of us, you might as well go." Míriam turned and carried Rebeca back up the street.

"*Señorita?*" León called. She stopped and turned around. "I'm sorry, I don't remember your name."

"I didn't give it." She paused. "It's Míriam."

"Míriam. I thank you most sincerely for your gracious assistance."

Míriam hesitated, giving him a scrutinizing look. "You're welcome." And she turned back and left, leaving him to watch her a few moments before entering the *beit midrash*.

# Manuel

The aroma of frying eggs greeted me as I opened the door to our apartment and shoved past the coats hanging in the hallway. I tossed my shoulder bag aside and took the two steps toward the kitchen. Sure enough, my mother was bent over the stove, the sizzling and crackling of eggs issuing from a pan she was swirling. Her dark brown hair, streaked with just a few strands of gray, was pulled into a tight bun on the back of her head, and her tan sport jacket and pencil skirt put the finishing touches to her no-nonsense-high-school-Spanish-teacher look.

She glanced up.

"Did you know that blood spots in eggs mean that the chickens laying them were distressed?" she boomed in her strong Murcian Spanish. "Makes you wonder what they worry about, no?"

My father taught me a long time ago that when it came to Mama, you just needed to smile and nod a lot.

I smiled and nodded.

"Have a seat, *cariño.*"

I sat.

"You hungry?"

"No, Mama."

"So just one egg?"

Mostly, it's just no use to argue with the woman.

She dumped the egg onto a plate in front of me and stood there. I stared at it. She stared at me.

"When, exactly," she said suddenly, "were you planning to tell me about this?"

She flopped a pile of papers onto the table. I peered around my plate at them, and when I realized what they were, my stomach dropped.

"Why were you rummaging around in my room?" I demanded.

"I asked first. What is this?" She tapped the pile sharply with her finger.

I sighed. "They're... pamphlets. For a university program."

"In Madrid!"

"New York University in Madrid. It's a special honors program for Spanish genealogical research. It would be part of the degree I'm already doing at NYU."

"And you are thinking of attending this program?"

I poked at the egg with my fork. Finally I said, "I was thinking that I might want to continue Papa's work."

My mother threw up her hands. "If I had wanted you to attend university in Madrid, we would have moved to Madrid!"

"It's just one semester, Mama."

"Granada has a perfectly good university! I could have sent you there! Do you think I'm stupid?" She glowered at me.

"Mama," I said, finally looking up at her. "Why are you so worked up about this? It's still an American university. And I'll still have to spend another two years on the New York campus to complete the program. It's not like I'm moving back to Spain."

"Oh? If there's nothing for me to be worked up about, why were you hiding this in your desk?"

"Why were you *looking* in my desk?" I countered.

To no avail. "You think I put myself through that impossible foreign-educator program as a single mother while you were in high school to bring you to New York to get a decent education so you could go back to Madrid in the middle of your degree?!"

"If this is about me getting a decent education, it makes absolutely no sense for you to be opposed. What do you have against my going back to Spain? Why does it make any sense for you to stop me from finishing Papa's work and researching our family? You have always been curious about it too!"

"I am fine with researching your father's family. I just don't want you to go back there now. I know you will be tempted to stay because it is easier to remain in a place with a familiar culture. Especially since you haven't really been all that happy here."

I stared at her. I hadn't realized that she understood that.

"Why don't you want me to be happy, Mama?" I asked softly, my voice shaking slightly in anger.

"My job is not to make you happy, boy. My job is to make you a good person. And that is why I want you to stay in America."

"Then let's just put this plainly, Mama. You don't want me to go because you think Spain is inherently evil."

"Oh, don't be so dramatic," she snapped. "There are plenty of good things about Spain. But there are things ingrained in the culture that are very problematic. I don't want you absorbing more of that anti-semitic and racist garbage that Padre Carlos used to preach."

A surge of anger washed over me and I shoved the plate at her, standing up from the table. "I can't believe the way you talk about the man who was like a father to me after Papa died," I hissed at her. "Especially after he passed away himself last year."

She narrowed her eyes and drew her lips into a thin line in her most defiant expression. "Yes. Clearly, I am an insensitive, ungrateful heretic. But I am also your mother, so watch your tongue. And eat your egg." She shoved the plate back at me. I crossed my arms and glowered at her. She turned away, grabbed the sponge by the sink and wiped down the counter furiously, even though it was already immaculate.

Finally, she turned back to me with a sigh. "Listen," she said, her voice softening. "He really was a wonderful man. I owe him a lot. And I know how important he was to you, and how much you gained from what he taught you. But I never liked the way he talked to you about Jews. And I don't like the way you relate to them now that we live in a place with so many of them."

I clenched the back of the chair as my anger surged again. "Are you implying that *I* am anti-semitic?"

"Do you have a single Jewish friend?"

"Yes!" I blurted without thinking.

"Oh?" My mother's eyebrows shot up. "Who?"

"Just...someone...from school," I stammered, immediately realizing my mistake.

She gave me her narrow-eyed scrutinizing look, which then melted into a sly grin.

"So *that* is what this is all about," she said. "The sudden interest in this program you never mentioned before. It's a girl."

I rolled my eyes. "Why do you *always* think everything is about a girl?"

"Am I right?" She cackled a little. "An American girl who wants to go to Madrid and you want to go with her to be her little Spanish-speaking hero to help her with her studies. Tell me I'm right."

I took a deep breath, trying to restore my composure. "A *friend* mentioned that she was going to join this program to research her genealogy in the national archives. I thought it would be a good opportunity for me to do the same."

She turned back to the counter and pulled a mug and the sugar bowl from the shelf with that infuriating grin still plastered on her face. "Very nice, *cariño*," she said, scooping sugar into the mug. "Maybe my plan is working after all."

"What plan?"

"You would never be dating a Jewish girl under Padre Carlos's watch."

"I am not *dating* her. I couldn't date her even if I wanted to."

Mama glanced at me with a knitted brow. "Why not?"

"Because Jews don't date non-Jews."

"What are you talking about? I saw the Rosenberg boy with an Asian girl not two days ago. She was definitely not Jewish."

"Maybe secular Jews do. Not religious ones."

"She is religious?"

"Yes. But it doesn't—"

"Well, maybe you can change her mind."

"I don't *want...* Wait. Why are you so excited about the idea of my dating a Jewish girl?" I demanded.

She shrugged, turning to the coffee maker on the counter to pour herself a cup. Finally, she said simply, "I like Jews."

I kept a suspicious eye on her as I slowly sat down.

Of course, I knew this about her. Back in Spain she constantly complained about the anti-semitism, even though there were practically no Jews around to be offended by it. And in contrast to my own social isolation after our move, my mother had flourished in America. She never got along with our neighbors in Granada, and had only one good friend there. Here in Brooklyn, on the other hand, she was the belle of the building, always visiting and chatting with our Jewish neighbors. They were constantly knocking on our door on Saturdays, asking my mother to do weird things like flip light switches on their Sabbath. She loved every minute of it.

"Why Jews in particular?" I asked her.

"I don't know, *cariño.* There's something about them." She laughed softly, joining me at the table with her mug. "When I was a girl, kids at my school used to sing about Jews having tails. I always thought that was ridiculous, seeing as Jesus was a Jew, and the Bible never mentions *him* having a tail."

"And if he did, we should all want to have tails."

"Exactly. I just don't understand what people have against them.

The Jews have done so much good in the world." She sipped, staring out the window absently. Then her eyes drifted back to the pamphlets on the table, and without another word, she scooped them up and tossed them into the trash behind her.

"Mama!" I yelled. "I needed those!" I jumped up from the table and ran to the garbage can. I stared down in dismay, seeing that the papers had already soaked up stains from the remainders of breakfast.

"Ah, I'm sorry," my mother said, idly sipping her coffee and not sounding sorry at all.

"This is ridiculous, Mama." I leaned forward and snatched her coffee from her hand, spilling a little on the floor as I set it behind me.

"Hey!"

"Listen to me." I leaned in, looking her straight in the eye. She looked at me, one eyebrow raised, her lips a thin line. "You wanted me to come here so I could learn American ideals, right? Well, you can't choose *which* American ideals you want me to learn. Americans are all about independence, right? *Let freedom ring?*" I said in English, spreading my arms wide like a pop singer about to hit the climax of "The Star-Spangled Banner". "So here's your Americanized son. Are you ready for him?"

Her eyebrow arched further.

"I am an adult and therefore I make my own decisions. So it doesn't really matter what you think. Whether I go to Madrid is up to me, and there is nothing you can do about that."

She continued to watch me, unimpressed.

"Are you finished?"

"For now."

"There's just one little thing you're forgetting, *cariño.*" She reached across the table, scooped up her purse, pulled out her wallet, and waved it in front of me. "You're an adult now? That's cute. Pay for it yourself." She stood up and reached behind me, grabbing her coffee cup. She sat back down, ceremoniously stuffing her wallet back in her purse.

Well, at least this part I was prepared for. I still have no idea how Alma managed to make it happen, but after a ten-minute chat with Professor Rodriguez and a brief phone conversation between the two of them and the financial aid office, Alma informed me that all I'd need to pay for would be the ticket to Madrid. I relayed this information to my mother, trying to leave Alma out of the story as much as possible.

I should have known my mother would see right through me.

She narrowed her eyes. "*You* went to negotiate with the financial aid people?"

I said nothing.

The sly grin crept over my mother's face again. "I think you need to tell me more about this Jewish girl."

I rolled my eyes and stalked out of the kitchen without another word.

# Alma

*"HaShem yishmor!"* Grandma shrieked, invoking divine protection as I slammed the brakes, narrowly avoiding the bumper of the car that had just swerved into my lane. *"Ya mahabool!"* she shouted, rolling down her window to gesture angrily at the driver. *"Yikhrib beytak!"*

I took a deep breath to calm myself, and then rolled her window back up. "Grandma, I don't think cursing at him in Arabic is going to help much."

She continued muttering to herself in a mixture of Hebrew, Arabic, and Spanish, until she finally closed her eyes, let out a deep sigh, and said in English, "I hate these roads. Next year we're taking the train up to Simon's for the holiday."

"Sure, Grandma. We'll just leave three days earlier so we have time for you to go down the stairs."

"Not funny." Grandma gave me a playful smack on the thigh. She leaned back against the seat and was silent for a few moments. "Sometimes I think your mother is right. Maybe I should just move to Albany."

I raised both eyebrows.

"Don't you dare tell her I said that," she added quickly.

"My lips are sealed." I bit back a smile. "Anyway, I need you to stay in Manhattan for three more years. Then you can move to Albany."

"Well, you know, I don't actually have to *be* there for you to live there."

"Yeah, but I'd be so sad!" I glanced over at her. "This is the first time we've really been able to spend this kind of time together, you know? It almost makes me not want to go to Madrid in the spring." I sighed. "I wish you could come with me!"

"Oh, me too, honey." She patted my knee. "I'll be honest with you, I am not looking forward to the noise and bustle of Rosh Hashana this year. I've been enjoying our quiet *Shabbatot*, just the two of us."

"Me too. I wish they would get over the all-the-extended-family-has-to-be-together-for-the-holiday thing. Couldn't we do rotations or something?"

Grandma snorted. "We're Sephardim, Alma."

I sighed, and we were silent for a while. Grandma stared out the window, and began singing that song, the one in Judeo-Spanish she always started humming when we were quiet for long enough. *"Hija mia, mi kerida, aman, aman, aman..."*

She narrowed her eyes, staring ahead of us as we passed a huge billboard that said "JESUS SAVES."

"Alma," she whispered.

"What?"

"Christians. Christians saved them."

"What? Who?" I glanced at her, wondering if this was grounds for an urgent neurologist appointment.

"The family!" She stared at me, her eyes glowing. "That's what it is! It was a Christian family. Our ancestors were being pursued by the Inquisition, and the Christian family helped them escape..."

I pulled the car to the shoulder of the road with a screech. As we jerked to a stop, I looked at her wildly. "Tell me everything you remember," I said, pulling my phone out of my pocket. "But hold on a second, I want to record you. Just in case." I feverishly flipped through my apps, finally finding the voice recorder and turning it on. "There. What do you remember?"

"I just... I remember my grandmother, shortly before she died, giving me the ring and explaining how it had been handed down to her; then she told me that she needed to tell me a story." Her forehead wrinkled.

"And she told you that our ancestors were pursued by the Inquisition, but a Christian family helped them escape Spain?"

"Yes..." she said hesitantly.

"And?" I prompted.

She gave a frustrated sigh. "There was something else. That's not everything she told me."

"And you don't remember?" My heart sank.

She shook her head.

"Well..." I said, my mind racing. "Maybe if you think more about the details of the scene it will help you remember. Where were you? What did the room look like?"

"It was in our old apartment in Tétouan. Abuela had lived with us my whole life. She was lying in her bed... it was terribly hot, but she was under a colorful wool blanket. I remember her handing me the ring... and telling me something about it. She wanted me to do something with it."

"Give it to somebody?" I ventured.

Her eyes narrowed. "Yes, that's it!" she said finally. "Give it back to the descendants of the Christian family."

It took me a few seconds to register what she had said.

"Wait a minute," I said. "Seriously? She expected you to track down the descendants of some anonymous Christian Spanish family from five hundred years ago, so you could hand them a piece of jewelry?!"

Grandma leaned listlessly against the back of the seat. "I know. It's crazy."

"So... is that the thing you couldn't remember?"

"I don't know. I have this niggling feeling that there's another detail that I'm not remembering."

We sat, the recorder running. After a few minutes, Grandma just shook her head.

I sighed, turned off the recorder app, and slipped my phone back into my pocket. I turned the ignition key, frowning. "Well, I hope you aren't expecting *me* to track down those descendants," I said.

"Who knows, Alma?" Grandma asked as I turned back onto the road. "Maybe if you find some records from the Inquisition, they will tell you some details that could lead you to them."

"And then I'm supposed to trace that family down twenty-four generations? All in one semester?"

Grandma was silent for a few moments. "Okay, so it won't happen this spring. But maybe you, or somebody else, will be able to finish the work at some point later. This is *the* time to do this. While the new generation has access to the information, and the old generation is still around to remember..." She chuckled. "Well, just barely."

I shook my head, staring at the road ahead. "Twenty-four generations... half of Spain is probably descended from that family at this point. And a good chunk of Latin America."

"Then that increases your chances of finding one, no?"

I sighed. "This is going to be an extremely expensive, time-consuming wild goose chase."

"Well..." Grandma reached over and pinched my cheek. "You're a very smart goose."

~~~

By the time we managed to get all the adults and about a third of the kids sitting down to eat the festive Rosh Hashana dinner, I was so exhausted from trying to keep track of what was going on, who was saying what, and who was yelling at whom that it was all I could do to keep from burying my face in Grandma's shoulder and refusing to move. All thirty-six of us were crammed around Uncle Simon and Aunt Gila's table, extended to its fullest length, or at the two full-sized plastic foldable tables spilling out into the living room. The seating was basically divided by level of religious observance. Seated at the far end of the plastic tables were the rebellious teens constantly getting yelled at to put away their phones and have some respect—including my brother Zack. My grandmother was ceremoniously placed at the head of the main table, and sitting next to her were me, my cousin Eliezer in his black and white ultra-Orthodox garb, my sister Shoshana—who was constantly getting up to rescue the houseplants from her two-year-old—and her husband Josh. My aunts were bustling around, squeezing between the chairs to deliver and remove platters of salads, appetizers, and entrees. Shoshana's newborn was in a baby seat placed a little precariously on the couch, and I was really jealous of how the hum of constant chatter was actually keeping her fast asleep.

"So, Alma," Mimi shouted at me from across the table. "Are you going to Spain next semester in the end?"

I opened my mouth to respond but threw up my hands in despair as my Aunt Ziona let out a loud, percussive laugh that drowned out pretty much everything else. I pointed at the vacant seat next to mine where Shoshana had been sitting, and Mimi got up and walked around the table to sit next to me.

"Almost for sure yes," I shouted into her ear. "Whether I'm going to be able to do the research for Grandma is another question..."

"Didn't you tell me you found a research partner?" Grandma yelled from next to us. I turned, surprised she had managed to make out anything we had said over the din. Our end of the table quieted a little as my cousins and aunts picked up on what we were talking about.

"No," I said, and I found myself flushing a little. "I said I found someone who might be able to. He's not sure yet."

"He, huh?" Mimi elbowed me. I rolled my eyes.

"Yeah, I know you think this whole college business is all about meeting boys, don't you."

"You know I've been dying for you to find a boyfriend already."

"Well, this isn't it, okay?"

"Why not?"

I paused as a twinge of foreboding tugged at my chest. "He's Catholic."

The table suddenly got a lot quieter.

"Who's Catholic?" my mother asked from five seats down.

Manuel's voice echoed in my head: *I don't want to invoke the wrath of a Jewish mother.*

"Nobody, guys. Sheesh. Why are you all listening all of a sudden?"

Mimi narrowed her eyes at me. "You're seriously considering traveling to Spain with a Catholic guy to do research?"

"Oh my God!" I groaned in frustration. "First of all, I'm not traveling to Spain with a Catholic guy to do research. I am traveling to Spain to do research with a *group,* which is doing an academic project, and said Catholic guy may or may not be my research partner within that group. For credit. It's not like we're going to be frolicking on the beach drinking martinis. Come to think of it, Madrid isn't even anywhere near the coast..."

Mimi raised an eyebrow. "Yeah. Because frolicking on beaches is totally your idea of a perfect date. As opposed to getting cozy with some old books in a library somewhere."

I rolled my eyes. "It's the *books* I'd be getting cozy with, okay? I mean really. Medieval records of trials and torture. Sounds way romantic."

"Anything sounds romantic in Spanish," my fifteen-year-old cousin Elisheva piped up from the cellphone end of the table. I glared at her.

I heard some complaining sounds coming from the baby seat and glanced back toward baby Shira on the couch. She appeared to be stirring. As I turned back to look for Shoshana, I caught a glimpse of my grandmother. She was giving me a very odd look.

"What?" I demanded.

"You didn't tell me he wasn't Jewish," she said.

"Well, what did you expect?" I snapped. "It's a Spanish heritage program. Everyone but me is Hispanic. How many Hispanic Jews do you know?"

"I know one from Cuba," Uncle Shalom offered.

"Don't you think it would be wiser to work with a girl?" my grandmother asked.

"Oh come *on!*" I groaned. "This is ridiculous! I'm not David, okay?"

The words were out of my mouth before I could stop them. The table was very quiet now.

"Is there a problem with David?" My cousin Rachel's voice was very sharp.

"Of course there's a problem with David!" my grandmother shouted at her, knocking over her wineglass and spilling red wine all over the white tablecloth. Mimi and I rushed to soak up the spreading stain with our napkins but my grandmother ignored it. "You'll notice that he doesn't even have the courage to show his face around here on Rosh Hashana—"

"If you would let him bring Cathy—"

"I want nothing to do with his *goya* girlfriend!"

"*Stop it!*" Shoshana yelled, rushing into the room with two-year-old Jonah on her hip. "Stop it! We are *not* having this conversation again. Not on Rosh Hashana. Please. Please. Can't we just enjoy the meal?"

Both Rachel and Grandma shot her dirty looks, but they both picked up their forks and shoved more food in their mouths.

"We're not talking about David," my mother snapped, glaring around the table at her six younger siblings, their spouses, and their children. "We're talking about Alma." She fixed me with an appraising look. "It's different."

"That's what I'm saying," I quickly agreed. But my father's brow was knitted and his lips pressed together in an unmistakably disapproving look. "Come on, guys," I insisted, "don't you trust me?"

"This isn't about trust, child," Grandma cut in. I turned to look at her. She was eying me warily. "It's about wisdom."

"So you're saying I'm stupid."

"No. I'm saying don't *be* stupid."

"I'm *not*. I have no intention whatsoever of getting romantically involved with someone who's not Jewish. You know Jewish continuity is extremely important to me, and you know that I know what happens after a few generations of intermarriage."

"You know what they say about good intentions, right?" my father mumbled.

"So you're saying that traveling to Spain with some random guy I hardly know will inevitably end in my falling desperately in love with him, despite everything that's important to me? Geez, hasn't anyone here ever had a friend of the opposite sex? If only it were that easy, I'd totally be fishing around for a nice Jewish guy to drag there with me..."

"I'm..." Grandma sighed. "Just forget it. You said he's not sure. I'm saying, why don't you just try to find someone else?"

My father shook his head. "If anyone is asking me, the whole Iberian Studies thing is a waste of time anyway."

"Now that you mention it, no one *is* asking you," my grandmother shot at him. "We all know your opinion."

"I'm just saying, it's not a career," he continued. I sighed deeply and looked at Mimi, who rolled her eyes and mouthed *Here we go.* "Your sisters have solid career paths. In this economy—"

"Enough, Isaac." My mother elbowed him.

"In this economy?" my grandmother boomed. "Do you have any idea what kind of riches we're rolling in compared to what I grew up with?"

"That's not the point—"

"No, *you* listen to *me*, son," Grandma pressed, pushing her plate away, her pale green eyes flashing. "There are things far more valuable than money. Do you have any idea how many people are documenting the history of my community from Tétouan? Practically none! Any idea how much is left of our culture, or of Haketía, the language my ancestors spoke for hundreds of years? *Your* family was from Algiers, just one country over, and they had never met a Spanish-speaking Maghrebi Jew in their lives."

Aunt Sara giggled. "Remember the look on their faces when they tried to speak to us in French?"

My dad sighed deeply.

"Your daughter," Grandma went on, "is the only one in this family who has even bothered to take an interest in our heritage—"

"Can we please stop talking about me?" I pleaded. But they ignored me and continued to bicker about the merits of my choices, in the way of mothers- and sons-in-law. I buried my face in my hands. *This is why I was so glad to leave Albany,* I reminded myself. *At least they're distracted from the Manuel scandal.*

I flopped against the back of my seat and stared at my plate, rage surging in my chest again. *And what was up with that?* I thought. They knew nothing about him. Nothing at all. Heck, even *I* hardly knew anything about him. *So what if he's Catholic?*

At this point my grandmother was standing and waving her arms in the air and shouting something about her dead relatives as more of my aunts and uncles joined the argument.

I shook my head and stabbed my fork into my stuffed artichoke. Beneath all the noise, a random memory crept into my head: a game David and I played as kids at the synagogue while our parents attended services. He always wanted to be Judah Maccabee, and I always wanted to be Queen Esther, and we somehow managed to work out a story where those two Jewish heroes existed in the same time and place. When we were teenagers we read Aryeh Kaplan's books to each other in the synagogue's library and held lively debates about them. I would never have imagined he'd be absent from our Rosh Hashana table this year, choosing a non-Jewish woman over us.

I shot a glance toward Rachel, who was now engaged in conversation with our cousin Tova. It was true, I was upset with David like everybody else; in fact, it had been the fight between him and the rest of us that finally spurred me to go ahead and transfer to NYU and dive into researching our family history. But...I couldn't help but think that Rachel was right to be angry at the family. If what she said was true, it wasn't that her brother didn't want anything to do with *us*, it was that the family didn't want anything to do with *him*—or, more accurately, with his non-Jewish girlfriend. Were we really so insular, so unaccepting, that we couldn't set aside whatever disputes we might have about Jewish continuity and treat Cathy like a human being?

The more I thought about it, the more determined I became that Manuel *would* be my research partner.

*To hell with them*, I thought, shoving the last bite of the artichoke into my mouth.

# Manuel

I found it hard to concentrate at church that Sunday. It was a cloudy day and the combination of the dim light of the sanctuary and the soft singing made me feel very sleepy.

Moreover, my mother's words from that morning about Padre Carlos rang in my ears, and I couldn't get the image of his face out of my mind. I knew this was the point where I would have wanted to consult him about Madrid and my mother and Alma… but he was gone.

I felt tears form as I walked up the aisle to get in line for communion, the familiar ache clutching my chest. Throughout my adolescence I had gotten used to that ache, the longing for my father. Now I felt it for both of them.

I looked up and saw the priest smile at a little boy a few paces ahead of me. Father Greg had kind but piercing blue eyes and brown hair that was thinning and graying around the edges. His skin was pasty white under the dull light sifting through the tall, narrow windows on the opposite wall. I watched as he handed the boy his wafer. He was so much more relaxed, less solemn, than Padre Carlos was during Communion. And he had been so patient in that first year or so when I struggled to confess in English.

*Maybe I should talk to him.*

When Mass was over, I hung back, watching Father Greg say goodbye and chat with the congregants slowly shuffling out through the heavy wooden double doors. I sat on one of the pews nearby, idly grabbing a book of Psalms that had been sitting there and scanning the cover as I waited. Finally, I caught his eye and walked over to him. He extended his hand.

"Manuel, right?" he said. I nodded, offering my hand. He held it between both of his. "How are you?"

"Good, thank you, Father. I was wondering if you have some time to talk."

---

Father Greg's office was a small room on the second floor of the building. It contained two leather chairs at forty-five degree angles to each other, and a very cluttered antique desk with an office chair squeezed in behind it. He gestured to one of the chairs.

"So," he said, sitting down in the other chair. "How can I help you, Manuel?"

I sat down and studied him for a moment. "When I lived in Granada," I started slowly, "my priest was like a father figure to me, and I used to consult him about many things, not just about practicing our faith. When we moved here, I would call him sometimes. But he passed away last year."

"I am sorry to hear that. May God rest his soul."

"Amen. Is that kind of consultation customary in your church too?"

"Absolutely. You know our faith touches all areas of life. And all priests have training in counseling. But I should mention that if it seems to be something that would be better handled by a professional, I will refer you to someone who is better qualified."

"Oh, it's nothing that serious," I assured him. "I just...I have been..." I sighed. "I don't know where to start."

"Well, pick a spot, and we'll take it from there." He smiled.

"I suppose it starts..." I allowed my eyes to drift toward the window. The shades were drawn. "Ever since I was a little boy, I always found Judaism fascinating. I know it is strange because there are not many Jews where I came from. But in Spain it is like... there is this echo of them there. There are these streets still called by Jewish names, and buildings that have been churches for centuries that are still called *sinagoga*... I grew up in the Realejo district in the center of town. It was the old Jewish quarter before the Catholic Monarchs conquered Granada and expelled the Jews. I remember spending a lot of time looking up at the statue of Yehuda ibn Tibon that stands there, wondering about all these ghosts of Jewish culture that remain in that place." I finally turned back to look at Father Greg to gauge his reaction. He just nodded, still looking pleasantly curious. "I don't know how to explain it. Every time I came across something Jewish it was like I could not tear my eyes away..."

He waited, watching me patiently; and when I didn't continue, he said, "Well, you know Judaism is the root of our faith."

I was a little taken aback. "Well, yes, I know that. But Padre Carlos discouraged me from this interest... he said the Jews are misguided and getting too close to them might increase temptation and confusion."

Father Greg's brow furrowed slightly. "What did he mean by getting close to them?"

"Well... when I told him I had always wanted to go into a functioning synagogue and speak to the rabbi, he told me that was a very bad idea."

"Because he thought it would lead you astray?"

"Yes."

"So..." Father Greg shifted in his chair. "What brings you to me on this issue?"

"I... I met this girl in college... well actually I met her when I walked into her grandmother's Judaica shop in Manhattan. It was the first time I had ever gone into a place like that. It turned out that she is descended from Spanish Jews who fled to Morocco.

She is the first Jew I have really spoken to."

Father Greg's expression did not change. He kept watching me thoughtfully, resting his chin on his hand.

"She is planning to go to Madrid to research her family, and when she mentioned the program she was joining, I remembered the genealogical work that my own father had done before he died and how I had always wanted to dig deeper. So I met with the director of the program and attended the introduction. Afterwards the girl came up to me and asked if I'd be willing to be her research partner. She does not speak much Spanish and I know I could be of help to her. But the problem is…" I sighed. "I don't know if I want to do this for the right reasons."

Father Greg uncrossed his arms. "What would the right reasons be?"

"To finish my father's work. To have a chance to go back to Granada and visit his grave. It's an honors program, and I think it will be very interesting."

"And the wrong reasons?"

"To get away from my mother." I hesitated. "And to get closer to this girl…and maybe Judaism, too."

Father Greg nodded and drew a deep breath. "So let's make some order here. Getting away from your mother is not a sin, as long as you are not disrespecting her."

"Well, that's the trouble. She does not want me to go."

"Why not?"

"I don't know, Father. I'm not sure even she knows. She does not want me to go back to Spain now. I think she feels that the culture there is a bad influence or something."

"I see. Well, that makes it a little more complicated, but I don't think that, in and of itself, should be a reason not to go. As for the question of Judaism and this Jewish girl…" He smiled. "Well, that also depends. Are you attracted to her?"

I opened my mouth to answer but wasn't sure what to say.

"Let me ask another way. Do you think there is a reasonable possibility of some kind of romantic relationship between you?"

*Well, that's easier.* "No. Basically zero chance. Religious Jews don't date non-Jews. And I am still considering attending seminary after I finish my degree. So it's a mutual *no.*"

"Do you think either one of you might be tempted away from those commitments, though?"

I paused, feeling uncomfortable. "I don't know her well enough to say."

He smiled again. "I like you, Manuel. You are a very honest man. I think you have a lot of self-awareness, and that leads to refinement and self-discipline. In my opinion, you don't need to worry about this."

"About what?"

"About going to Madrid. Many of us are moved to make decisions for reasons we don't entirely understand, some of which are pure and some of which are impure. At the end of the day, it doesn't really matter, so long as we remain conscious of our conduct and always strive to do God's will. It sounds to me like something is calling you to join this young woman in Madrid and finish your father's work. And it definitely sounds like the Jewish roots of the Christian faith are calling you to explore them. I respectfully disagree with Padre Carlos. I think it can be very positive to connect with those roots. Jesus himself was a Jew, you know. I am good friends with a number of rabbis myself." He nodded toward my chest, which is when I noticed that I had been absentmindedly fiddling with the crucifix hanging there. It was a simple gold pendant that had belonged to my father. "Just be sure to keep in mind what those roots grew into. That part the Jews aren't so clear on." He smiled. "Who knows, maybe you will influence her to come closer to your faith."

My stomach turned a little in discomfort at that.

"As for your mother, you'll just have to see if she comes around. Try your best to stay respectful."

I gave a wry smile. "As you know, that one is sometimes hard for me."

He grinned. "Do your best, and if not, well, that's what confession is for." He winked, and I laughed, feeling much lighter in the chest. "Also," he added, "I would recommend praying whenever you are struggling with doubt. God has a way of giving us answers when we ask." He stood from the chair and crossed the room, reaching for a small notepad on his desk. "It is my custom," he said, picking up a pen, "to give those I counsel a verse or two from the Scriptures to take away from our conversation." He scribbled for a minute, then tore off the page and handed it to me. "I think these are yours."

I took the note and read: *If I have the gift of prophecy and understand all mysteries and all knowledge, and if I have a faith that can move mountains, but I do not have love, I am nothing. Love bears all things, believes all things, hopes all things, endures all things. (1 Corinthians 13:2/7)*

"Is there anything else, Manuel?"

"No," I said softly, staring at the note. I folded it and slipped it into my pocket as I rose from the chair. "No, thank you, Father. You have given me a lot to think about."

# Míriam

Rosh Hashana was always one of Míriam's favorite holidays. Her father served as the *chazzan,* the cantor, during services. She watched him through the wooden lattices of the women's section on the second floor of the synagogue, overlooking the main hall. The men sat around the benches along the walls, wrapped in their silk or woolen prayer shawls, swaying back and forth in concentration. Her father stood at the wooden podium in the center and led the congregation in the prayers in his low, rich voice.

She found her thoughts drifting to the Sánchez family, down in the main part of the city, and the other *converso* families who would be drinking her father's wine tonight. Their ancestors had been forced to convert during the wave of riots and massacres across Iberia a hundred years before. Once baptized, they could not change their minds and rejoin the Jewish community even if they wanted to—especially now that the Inquisition was in operation.

Míriam tried to turn her attention back to the prayers, feeling a wave of fear rising within her. *Well,* she thought, *at least Papa promised me he won't help them again.*

After the service, they met in the courtyard with their neighbor Solomon Guerson and walked with him back to his house. It was very dark out, with just a sliver of new moon hanging low in the sky, but the holiday lamps from all the houses in the *judería* glowed in the windows and cast soft shadows on the ground. A gentle breeze was weaving through the houses, bringing the salty smell of the sea from the coast, about seven leagues from the city.

Hanna was waiting for them, the table set with her decorative ceramics and her finest tablecloth. The younger two children were in bed already, but Azaria, the six-year-old, and Mose, the eight-year-old, were roaring through the house in vigorous play.

"Don Tomás made a stop in Almería and inquired about the siege," Abraham was telling Solomon as Hanna brought out the salads. "Granada will fall any day now—mark my words."

"We all knew it was a matter of time," Solomon sighed. "It's going to be a great upheaval. A lot of Jews in this area depend on cross-border commerce for a living. When the Alhambra falls, Castile won't need us here anymore."

"And not needing us, and not wanting us…that's a bad combination," Abraham agreed. "I've heard talk…"

"Yes, I've heard it too."

"Talk of what?" Miriam asked.

"That the monarchs are considering an Edict of Expulsion."

Miriam dropped her stuffed grape leaf and stared at Solomon. "Expulsion? Again?"

"Not just from a specific region. From the entire joint kingdom of Castile and Aragon."

Hanna shook her head and clucked her tongue. "Nonsense. It must be gossip. Why would they do such a thing? Jews are an irreplaceable part of the economy."

"That hasn't stopped them from supporting mass conversions and massacres in the past, has it?" Solomon said wryly, scooping some pomegranate seeds onto his plate.

"Well, the mass conversions are what they want," Hanna said. "And the queen hasn't supported the massacres. She has tried to protect us."

"Are you forgetting the La Guardia blood libel?" Solomon challenged.

"That was Torquemada's doing, not the queen's," Hanna replied.

"Acting under her orders," Solomon insisted.

"Things are changing, Hanna." Abraham looked up thoughtfully from his eggplant salad. "Queen Isabel has been giving more and more power to the Inquisition. King Fernando will surely do the same in Aragon once he is not distracted by the war with Granada. The Church is very concerned about our influence on Christians. They think we are a corrupting force, especially for the *conversos*."

Míriam exchanged a pointed glance with him.

"And when Granada falls, they will no longer have a need for our ties to our brethren in the Emirate," he continued. "They might as well expel us."

"God forbid! You shouldn't even mention such things on Rosh Hashana." Hanna spit three times onto the floor to ward off the Evil Eye.

Abraham chuckled. "I think God has other things to take into consideration while writing the decrees for the coming year. And besides, He *is* on our side."

"Is He really?" Míriam spoke up. Everyone looked at her. "I don't know, Papa. It is hard to feel like we are the Chosen People when we are constantly being oppressed, slaughtered, expelled, and exploited. He did not stop the big massacres a hundred years ago. He did not prevent the executions of the innocent Jews who were accused of killing the child of La Guardia."

"The *mythical* child of La Guardia," Solomon cut in. "They never even named him. There was no body. He never existed."

"We know, we know, Solomon," Hanna sighed. "It is amazing what people are willing to believe about Jews."

"Those are important questions," Abraham addressed Míriam. "We have no way of knowing what God's calculations are. All we know is that we have survived this long, despite every enemy that has risen to destroy us. In every generation. *For not just one has risen to destroy us…*" he began in Hebrew.

"*But in every generation they rise up to destroy us,*" Miriam continued the quote from the Passover Haggadah. "*And the Holy One, Blessed Be He, saves us from their hands.*"

"Exactly." Abraham's eyes shone in the lamplight. "It has been true for thousands of years. The Holy One, Blessed Be He, will never abandon us, even though it may feel like He has. We have suffered greatly, but we have survived...and we have thrived. Look at us." He gestured around the table. "Jews have lived here since before Christianity even existed. We've seen the rise and fall of many different kingdoms, and we've had to constantly adapt to the religious and political changes over the years. And yet, here we are, still celebrating the same holiday our God commanded us at Mount Sinai so long ago. Despite the Babylonians, the Assyrians, the Egyptians, the Greeks, the Romans...despite the Crusades... This is nothing new. He will see us through."

Miriam closed her eyes and breathed deeply. "Your words give me comfort, Papa. But it is hard to feel protected when there is still so much suffering. Where would we go if the Monarchs expelled us?"

"Let's just focus on where we are right now," Abraham said, reaching toward her and giving her chin a gentle stroke. "It's Rosh Hashana, and here's to a sweet new year." He raised his goblet. "*L'shana tova u'metuka.*"

# Manuel

I spotted her at the back of the lecture hall, scribbling furiously in a notebook. I took a deep breath and climbed the stairs to join her in the back row.

"Well, hello."

She started, jerking her head up from her notebook, and then recognized me and relaxed into a smile.

"Well, hello!" she echoed, lifting her bag from the seat next to her so I could sit. "I forgot that you're taking this class too."

"Where have you been? We missed you at the project meeting last Tuesday."

"Could have called me. Well, on second thought, that wouldn't have helped. It was Rosh Hashana. I was in Albany with my crazy family." She must have registered the confused look on my face, because she continued, "We don't use electronic devices on Biblical holidays or on the Sabbath. Rosh Hashana was Tuesday and Wednesday, so the whole week was a bit of a blur."

I slipped into the seat next to hers. "Rosh Hashana is the Jewish new year, right?"

"Right."

"So, happy new year."

"Thank you." She scanned her notebook again, then sighed and flipped it closed.

I reached for my laptop and set it on my desk. "How do you celebrate it?"

She smiled at me. "Oh, you know, the usual."

"Forgive my ignorance, but what would that be?"

"Okay. Crash course in Judaism: it's all about food. Okay, and in the case of Rosh Hashana, a lot of praying. And also blowing a ram's horn, called a *shofar*. But mostly food."

Silence fell over the hall as the professor entered and greeted us. I felt a pang of disappointment as Alma smiled apologetically and opened her notebook again. I opened my laptop and found my notes file for the class, but as the professor began talking, my mind was wandering. I wanted to ask more questions. In fact, my mind was suddenly flooded with questions. I tried to focus on the professor's voice and the slides he was showing, but I just couldn't. I glanced over at Alma and noticed that she had paused in her note-taking, staring ahead at the professor. I reached over tentatively and slid her notebook toward me. She cast me a bewildered look. I fished a pen out of my pocket, wrote on the margins of her notebook, and slid it back to her:

*Biblical holidays? What other kinds of holidays are there?*

She read my question and smiled mischievously.

*I wasn't under the impression that this class was supposed to cover that...* she wrote, passing her notebook back to me.

*I don't care. This is more interesting than eighteenth-century Spanish literature.*

*Will there be a test?*

*Are you deliberately not answering my question?*

*There are also rabbinical holidays, like Chanukah and Purim.*

*So Biblical holidays are ones mentioned in the Bible, and the rabbis established the rabbinical holidays?*

*Basically. Purim is mentioned in the Bible too. But not in the Torah.*

*Isn't the Bible the Torah?*

*Nope. Just the first five books.*

*Curious, I thought Chanukah was "the" Jewish holiday.*

*That's because it happens to be so close to Christmas. Rosh Hashana, Yom Kippur, Succot, Passover and Shavuot are all more important.*

*You Jews have many holidays.*

She drew a checkmark.

*You don't even know the half of it,* she wrote.

We scribbled back and forth through the entire class, discussing the intricacies of Jewish holidays and how they related to the Christian ones. By the time it was over, neither of us had more than an extremely vague idea of what the class we had theoretically been attending was about.

"Maybe you should join my minor," Alma said, winking at me as we stood up and stretched.

"Your minor?"

"Judaic studies. There are a good handful of non-Jews in my classes. Some of the classes count toward Iberian Studies too—like Hebrew language and Sephardic medieval poetry."

"I think I'm having too much trouble with my second language to start studying a third."

"Oh shut up—your English is better than my Spanish will ever be." We shuffled out from behind the desks and descended the stairs together. "So...anyway." Alma cleared her throat. "Any progress with your mom?"

I sighed. "I'm not sure."

"I told you, I'm totally willing to call her. I want this to be a done deal."

I turned to look at her in surprise. "You mean the trip? Or me being your research partner?"

"Both. Honestly I don't think I'll make any headway at all without your skills." She stopped and turned to me, and I noticed that we were standing in the hallway. "Where are you headed?"

"Mm...not sure. My next class is in an hour."

"Let's go to the library." She turned and started walking down the hall.

"Eh...Alma."

She spun back around. "What?"

"The library is that way." I jerked my head in the opposite direction.

She gave me a sheepish look. "See? What would I do without you?" She jogged back to me. "Seriously, can you imagine me in a foreign country? I'd be hopelessly lost in three minutes."

---

I had thought she wanted to sit in the library and talk, but she actually took me over to the Jewish bookshelves and plucked a worn Hebrew Bible from one of the shelves. She handed it to me, and a tingle ran down my spine as I opened it and saw the pages of Hebrew print.

"Such a beautiful alphabet." I breathed in the book's scent—old paper and ink and leather. I had always loved that smell.

"I told you you should take Hebrew." She winked.

She then proceeded to give me a somewhat rambling introduction to Jewish religious literature, from the Bible down through the Talmud and other important rabbinical writings. She tossed out bits of information about Jewish history that I had never heard before as she went through the shelves, pulling out various tomes and handing them to me. It was a little overwhelming.

"I have so much to learn," I sighed, replacing a book of modern Jewish philosophy on the shelf.

"Don't we all?"

I closed my eyes and breathed in the library scent again. Then I opened them and turned to smile at Alma. "Thank you for showing me."

"My pleasure, Manuel." She turned and started walking down the aisle. "Your name has too many syllables. Don't you have a nickname?"

"Mm...no."

"Your mother doesn't call you Mani or something?" She headed for the chairs next to the glass wall that overlooked Washington Square Park.

"No." I made a face. "It's only one more syllable than yours..."

"Well, now's your turn," she said, sitting down and unzipping her backpack. "I need help with my Spanish homework." She froze and looked up at me. "Unless you have some other work to do."

I did.

"No, that's fine, I'm happy to help you."

---

As it turned out, her dismal assessment of her Spanish proficiency had not been overly modest. I tried not to wince too much; but she could tell that I was finding this painful, and she kept burying her face in her hands and moaning that she'd never get it.

"Don't be so negative! You will learn," I tried to comfort her.

She sighed deeply. "I knew a few girls in high school who spoke Spanish fluently because they loved to watch those terrible Latin American telenovellas."

"Then maybe it's time to watch some terrible telenovellas?"

She shot me a look of horror. "I would rather scrub every toilet in Madrid."

"I don't blame you."

Alma looked over my shoulder, her eyes narrowing. "I think that lady is calling you."

I turned around and my heart sank as I watched my mother approaching us. She was dressed smartly in her gray suit, her hair in her usual tight bun at the back of her head, her footsteps so firm and sure that her stilettos clunked audibly even on the carpet.

I stood up, trying to move in front of Alma to block her from my mother's view.

"*There you are,*" Mama huffed at me in Spanish. "*I've been looking all over! I almost forgot that we've got that family-locator thing installed on our phones. Why didn't you answer your phone when I called you?*"

"*It's on silent. I was in class.*"

"*But you aren't now! Why didn't you check it?*"

"*I was busy. What do you want?*"

"*I need you to help me with these bank forms.*" She shoved a few papers into my hands. "*Se supone que debo devolver estos al banco hoy, y no sé...*" her voice trailed off as she noticed Alma behind me. "My apologies." She switched to her heavily accented English. "I am being rude. I am Raquel Elvira, Manuel's mother." She extended a hand. Alma's face lit up and she jumped up and pushed past me to shake my mother's hand.

"Manuel's mother!" she exclaimed. "So happy to meet you. I'm Alma Ben-Ami." Then her forehead scrunched in confusion. "Elvira? I thought your last name was... Ag... um... something else?"

"Manuel's is Aguilar. Mine is Elvira." She smiled. "In Spain, women don't change their family names when they get married."

"Oh... I wondered how that worked out, with all the confusion of inheriting both the paternal and the maternal family names. So you just keep the names you're born with."

"Exactly."

My mother glanced appraisingly between the two of us. I hid my face in the forms, scanning them to see if she had filled them out correctly.

"*Está bien, mamá.*" I tried to hand them back to her. She ignored me.

"So," she shot at Alma. "You are the girl who is trying to drag my son to Madrid, eh?"

Alma didn't flinch.

"Yes! Listen, I know you're concerned, but this is really, really important to both of us." She was gesturing excitedly. My mother watched her with her eyebrows raised. "I know your late husband—may he rest in peace—would be proud of Manuel for continuing his work in researching his family."

I caught a sparkle in my mother's eye. "Nice try," she said evenly, "but..."

"I promise you I won't let him get into trouble, and I'll take good care of him, and I'll make sure he stays around Americans as much as possible, and..."

I stared at Alma in dismay. She was talking like I was my mother's prize poodle. But my mother's face had taken on a thoughtful look, and I stopped myself from protesting.

"You are Jewish, yes?" she asked.

Alma blinked. "Umm...yes."

"So you will keep him away from the Opus Dei."

I buried my face in my hand.

"Uh, I don't even know what that is. But, um, sure."

"Mama..." I groaned.

"You will know it when you see it," my mother said to Alma, continuing to ignore me. "And you will make sure he comes back with you. After *one* semester."

"Yes. Of course."

Alma's hands were clasped at her chest and she was looking up at my mother expectantly. My mother stared right at me, and I could almost hear the cogs in her head turning.

"All right, Manuel Aguilar y Elvira. But remember, *you* are paying for the tickets." She snatched the forms from my hand and turned on her heel, stalking away in her stilettos. I turned back to Alma. She was doing a little victory dance, pumping her fists and bouncing up and down. She flushed when she saw me looking at her in amusement and toned down her enthusiasm ever so slightly.

"We're going to Madrid! Score!" She raised her hand for a high-five, and I gave it. "So funny..." she said, examining me. "You look nothing like her."

"You were right," I admitted. "I should have let you talk to her in the first place."

"Why didn't you?"

"It's just that... she..." I felt my face grow a little warm. "I think it's her passive-aggressive way to persuade me not to become a priest. Whenever I so much as mention a woman, she automatically assumes that I am interested in dating her."

Alma snorted, sitting back down. "Well, that one's easy. Just tell her that religious Jews don't date non-Jews."

"I did," I answered, a little too quickly. "She's not buying it. I told you, she's a little crazy."

Alma paused, as if deliberating whether to say something. "Well, if it helps, my family basically freaked out when I told them my potential research partner was a Catholic guy. It was really disconcerting. And kind of infuriating. Like, sheesh, don't they trust me?"

I wasn't at all sure how to feel about this information.

"Hey, um..." Alma was studying the clock on the wall behind me. "Aren't you late for class?"

I gasped and shot a look at my watch. "Yes! Thank you!" I grabbed my bag and took off, tossing a "So sorry, see you later!" over my shoulder.

# Alma

The leaves in Washington Square Park turned red, orange, and brown, fell off the trees and carpeted the grassy areas, and then disappeared as the snow began to fall. The Spanish Heritage Project group met every three weeks, and with each meeting, my sense of inferiority faded a bit—that is, when I wasn't sitting next to Manuel and watching him breeze through the transcriptions. Zoe and I seemed to make a pretty good team; believe it or not, I was better at identifying letters than she was, so when I was able to make out parts of the word, she was able to complete it if she recognized it from Spanish.

"Then why don't you switch and be partners with her?" Grandma asked when I told her this. She was dropping balls of dough into a pot of boiling oil on the stove. I scowled at her from my usual spot at the kitchen table.

"Because she and Nicole are cousins. They're working on the same family tree. It would be stupid for them not to work together."

"Well it doesn't have to be pairs, right? Ow!" She jumped back from the pot, flapping her hand around.

"Grandma! Careful!" I ran to her and herded her over to the sink, turning on the cold water, grabbing her hand and plunging it into the stream. "*Sfenj* is totally not worth another trip to the emergency room, okay?"

"Oh, calm down!" She shoved me away with her shoulder, but kept her hand under the water. "I'm all right. Always happens when I deep fry. It's one of the prices you have to pay for Chanukah."

"I wasn't aware that Chanukah was about paying prices," I grumbled, watching her warily.

"Being Jewish is about paying prices." She took her hand out of the water and frowned at the blister forming on her thumb.

"Sit down, Grandma. I'll get you some aloe and take over from here." She sighed, but shuffled over to the table without protesting. I rummaged through the cupboard for the first aid kit and brought it over to her. "You okay managing with that?"

"For goodness' sake, I'm not dying. Go mind the *sfenj*. They might be ready to flip by now."

I turned to the pot and peered in, trying to keep a safe distance myself as I grabbed the slotted spoon and gingerly poked at the doughnuts.

"I don't want to find a different research partner," I said. "I have no reason to. This is really my only hope for getting anything out of this whole adventure—and with his help, I've been able to maintain a high enough average to stay in the program. You should be thrilled."

"I *am* thrilled. I am. I'm really excited for you." Grandma was intently wrapping her finger in a bandage.

"You sound ecstatic," I said sarcastically. "Where's the 'but'?"

"Did I say 'but'?"

"I'm not an idiot. You're worried about me getting too friendly with Manuel."

"You said it, child, not me."

"Did I mention that he wants to become a priest?"

"How does that help matters exactly?"

"Catholic priests are celibate."

My grandmother finally looked up, her eyebrows so high they almost disappeared into her headscarf, and then just turned back to her finger without another word.

*"Ande le dan al tiñoźo, le corre sangre,"* she mumbled.

It was never a good sign when she talked to herself in Spanish. Or Haketía. Or whatever.

"What was that?" I demanded. "Something about blood?"

"'Wherever you hit the man with ringworm, he bleeds.'"

I scrunched my forehead. "What? Ringworm? Who has ringworm?"

"If you didn't think there was a grain of danger in this, you wouldn't be getting so upset about it."

"*No!*" I banged the spoon on the counter and whirled to glare at her. "I'm upset because this is going to be the most important thing I've ever done in my entire life and the fulfillment of your own family legacy and something that's been important to you and your family since *forever*—because *I'm* the only one who cares enough about our heritage to get off my lazy butt and fly it over to Spain, even though I really struggle with Spanish and I could totally have chosen to do something easier with my time in college... and *you* think that my friendship with a Christian is going to make me break with tradition."

My grandmother looked up at me, pursing her lips. "I think you better flip those."

I rolled my eyes and did as she told me, but I refused to change the subject. "It's insulting. Really. I can't believe you think I don't have the self-control to maintain proper boundaries. That you automatically assume there has to be romantic potential there just because he happens to be male."

My grandmother looked like she was struggling to decide whether to say something, and then shook her head.

"I don't know, Alma. Maybe you're right. Maybe I'm overreacting. I do trust you. You know I do. I just want to make sure you know that sometimes these things are out of our control. Love is funny that way."

"But you know that love and infatuation are not the same thing.

You're the one who always told me that. You don't 'fall in love' like you fall in a hole. Love isn't the butterflies and the fireworks, it's the commitment and the choosing every day to stay committed. Right? It's a choice."

"Yes. Absolutely." She paused. "But this infatuation business... can be very powerful too."

I shrugged and turned back to the *sfenj*. "Well, it's not relevant. So relax." I looked up at the kitchen window. In the fading light, I could hardly make out the bare branches of the maple tree in the alley between our building and the next. "Hey, it's almost time for candle-lighting."

# Manuel

I studied my reflection in the bathroom mirror, straightening my tie and rubbing the three-day stubble on my face. *I think I need a haircut,* I thought, casting a dismayed look at my wayward locks, which were really starting to get out of control. I ran my hand through them, trying to get them to fall a little more neatly. *More ruggedly handsome. Less scraggly caveman.* My attempts were all in vain.

My phone buzzed in my pocket. I sighed and drew it out, but my heart instantly lightened when I saw who the text was from.

*Hey, Merry Christmas, Catholic Boy.*

I smiled.

"You need a haircut." My mother's voice startled me and I whirled to see her standing at the bathroom door.

"Do you mind not standing there watching me? It's creepy."

"I ran into your priest yesterday," Mama said, talking past me as usual. "Father Greg. I like him. He's a nice man."

I studied her. "Is this your way of proposing coming with me to Mass tonight?"

"No, no." Mama stepped back, and I swept past her into the hallway. She followed me to the kitchen. "You know I don't go to church."

"You planning to go to synagogue instead?"

She arched an eyebrow, looking a little surprised and somewhat amused.

"Why not, Mama?" I asked. "It's Christmas. Papa used to go."

She shrugged. "I didn't go with him—even when the cancer got worse. I see no reason to start now."

"It's never too late to start."

"Oh stop it, you sound like a priest." She sighed and reached out to tug at my tie. Before she turned away, I saw her eyes glistening with tears. "And you look just like your father."

The air in the room suddenly became heavy and crushing. I felt like I was struggling to breathe. I drew the air in deep and slow, having grown accustomed to these moments. They were less frequent now, but they did come, especially around the holidays when my father's empty place at the table tore open the wound that could never quite heal.

My mother was leaning against the back of the chair, her back turned to me, her shoulders shaking. I put my hand on her back.

"Mama."

She turned and hugged me furiously, burying her face into my chest. "I just miss him so much, Manuel."

There it was, the familiar burning ache in my chest, the prickling in my eyes. Thirteen years had passed, but I was still that little boy, holding onto his sobbing mother in the hospital ward, not understanding how the world could possibly move forward from here.

My tears dripped onto her hair. "I miss him too, Mama," I choked.

"Do you remember how he used to sing…"

*"Pero mira cómo beben los peces en el río…"*

"Yes, and he used to make that ridiculous fish face to make you laugh…"

"I remember, Mama…"

"And his *belénes*…"

"He spent months setting up those nativity scenes. Took up half the living room."

"He would have been quite an artist if his parents had let him." She pulled back, reaching for the box of tissues on the countertop, not meeting my eyes.

"Remember how he taught me to draw that eagle?"

"The family emblem? Of course. I had it on the fridge until we moved. I think I still have it somewhere. He really drove that sense of lost heritage into you, no?" She dabbed at her face with a tissue and blew her nose. *"Por Dios.* Why does it always get so much worse around Christmas?"

I swallowed and looked out the little window at the street, where the lampposts and trees lining the sidewalk glittered with Christmas lights. "There's something about this time of year..." I murmured.

"I thought that maybe once we moved here it would be easier, in a place with no memories of him..."

"It probably didn't help that we never had any other family to make Christmas memories with," I pointed out.

"Yes, once your grandparents died, it was just the three of us." Mama sighed, closing her eyes and leaning against the doorframe. "If I had been able to contact any of my grandmother's relatives, we might have had cousins to invite."

"You never told me why she was cut off from her family."

Mama shook her head and clucked her tongue in irritation. "If I knew, I would tell you." She turned her face up to me. "Is my makeup running?"

"A little."

She muttered an expletive and shoved past me toward the bathroom. I drifted toward the doorway and began putting on my coat, scarf, and hat.

"You sure you don't want to come, Mama?" I called to her. "It's a really nice service."

"I'm sure, *cariño.* You go. Go pray for all of us."

# Miriam

It was a warm morning a week after Rosh Hashana, and Miriam hummed to herself as she shifted the weight of the heavy water jug from one hip to the other. She spotted her friend Basseva hanging laundry outside her family's house and tried to get her attention, but she seemed too engrossed in her work to notice.

Miriam approached the front door of her modest home, noting that the wooden shutters on the bedroom window were coming loose and she would have to try to fix them later. She almost walked inside before a figure in black caught her eye. She turned to look and gasped. The jug slipped from her grasp and shattered on the stone step at her feet, splashing water all over the bottom of her dress.

The man was leaning against the wall of the house, his arms crossed, looking straight at her with a cold smile on his face. His dark mustache and beard were neatly trimmed. He was wearing black robes, a wide-brimmed hat, and a huge silver crucifix; and while Miriam had rarely been outside the walls of the *judería* since her childhood and had never seen one before, she was absolutely certain that she was looking at an officer of the Inquisition.

She stood there staring at him, trembling, for what felt like an eternity.

Finally, he spoke. "Is this the de Carmona residence?" His voice was soft and even.

Miriam's voice shook as she answered that it was. She glanced around her, looking desperately to see if there was someone around who could help her. But she knew that no one could.

"I hear," said the churchman, in the same hair-raisingly soft voice, unfolding his arms and taking a step forward, "that Abraham de Carmona makes an excellent wine."

Míriam's heart leapt to her throat. Her chest constricted in fear and she felt like she could hardly breathe.

Her visitor nodded toward the cellar door in the ground to the right of the house. "Is this his cellar?"

Míriam glanced at the door and back again, not knowing what to do.

"Would you be so kind as to show me where this...legendary wine is kept?"

Míriam's mind raced. She understood that if she cooperated, it might lead to her father's arrest. But if she didn't cooperate, the consequences would probably be even worse. The Inquisition did not make arrests without evidence, and even so there was usually a grace period. There should be time to warn her father. On the other hand, he was a Jew, and the laws that regulated the Inquisition were supposed to apply only to Christians. Who knew what they would do to a Jew who had been helping *conversos* maintain their Jewish traditions?

Nevertheless...there was no way to know what the Inquisition knew, and whether the remaining wine in the cellar would be evidence enough to condemn her father.

Míriam took a deep breath. "With pleasure, *señor.*" She stepped gingerly over the shards of the broken jug, swept past the official, and bent down to open the cellar door. She felt almost sick with fear but tried to stay focused. The official followed her down the stone steps. Once her eyes had adjusted to the gloom, she pointed to the five small barrels to the right. He took a step toward them, removed one of his gloves and ran his hand over the wood. When it hovered over the cork, Míriam half-shouted, "No!"

He looked up, his eyebrows raised, more in amusement than anything else.

Miriam flushed furiously and looked at the ground. "It's just…if you open it…it won't be kosher anymore…"

He smiled a sinister sort of smile, letting out a little laugh. "Is that so?" He pulled the cork out. Miriam's shoulders sank. He closed his eyes and took a deep sniff. Then he dipped his finger into the hole and took a taste.

"Hmm." He straightened and squinted at Miriam. "Not bad for a Jew."

Miriam blinked back tears, staring at his boots.

"Well. Since you apparently have no more use for this barrel, I trust you won't mind if I take it with me?" He shoved the cork back in the hole and picked up the barrel without waiting for an answer. He started up the stairs. Miriam paused, then followed him. As she swung the door shut, he stopped and turned back to her.

"Yom Kippur is tomorrow night, is it not?" he asked.

She blinked in surprise.

"Good thing Jews don't eat or drink on Yom Kippur…isn't it? No one will need kosher wine on *this* holiday."

She did not respond.

"Well. Thank you for your generosity, *señorita*." He lifted the barrel with that same sinister smile, and swept off, his black robe billowing in the wind.

Miriam stood frozen in place, and waited until he rounded a corner and disappeared from sight before she bolted into the house, shutting the door behind her. She leaned against the inside of the door and sank to the ground, burying her face in her hands.

"Master of the Universe," she sobbed. "What should I do?!"

She had half a mind to go tell Hanna what had happened, but she didn't want anyone else to know about what her father had been doing, since it might endanger them as well. She had to get word to her father immediately—but how? Going down to Plaza de Santa María herself was risky in all kinds of ways; single Jewish women simply did not do that, and she was sure to arouse suspicion. Maybe she could find a boy to send with a message.

She stood up and went outside the house again. She wandered through the narrow streets of the *judería*, trying to keep up the appearance of composure, and looked for potential messengers—but all she could see were women and young children. Finally, she spotted Yehuda, a ten-year-old neighbor boy, who was playing quietly with sticks in the courtyard of the synagogue.

"Yehuda!" she called. "Can you do me a favor?"

Yehuda eyed her suspiciously. "For what?"

"I'll give you some candied quince. I need you to run as fast as your legs can carry you and deliver an important message to my father at Plaza de Santa María. Can you do that?"

Yehuda stood up. "What should I tell him?"

"Tell him…" Míriam paused. "Tell him that I told you to say that a man in black took some wine, and that he is in danger."

Yehuda screwed up his face in confusion. "What? A man in black?"

"Repeat it after me: a man in black took some wine."

"A man in black took some wine."

"And my father is in danger."

"Your father is in danger."

"Say it again."

"A man in black took some wine and your father is in danger."

"Good. Now go. And come back to me immediately and tell me what he says, and I will give you your candy."

Yehuda took off toward the Fisheries' Gate. Míriam watched him, then walked back to her house to clean up the broken jug…and to wait.

# Alma

I sat on the floor of my room in Grandma's apartment with a sigh, kicking up a cloud of dust from the carpet. I coughed furiously, clutching my chest.

"Everything okay in there?" I heard my grandmother call from the living room. I struggled to slow my breath, then reached for my inhaler and took two puffs.

"It would be," I wheezed, "if you'd get this carpet vacuumed once in a while."

"'Get' the carpet vacuumed, huh?" she called. "I think I should file a complaint with the lazy granddaughter who's supposed to be keeping my house..."

"Very funny."

"Are you done packing?"

I glanced over at the suitcase next to me. "I guess. For now."

"Then come over here."

I struggled to stand up, still coughing, and walked to the living room. Grandma was sitting in her armchair. On her lap was the wooden box I had found in her store six months earlier, the one with the *ketubot*. My heart pounded in excitement.

"Finally!" I exclaimed. I inched around the coffee table to sit on the leather couch next to her, and reached out for the box.

"Ah-ah!" She snatched it away. "Let me show you first."

She gently pulled off the cover.

"Oh my God, this is so exciting!" I squeaked.

Grandma grinned up at me. "I know!" She set the box on the coffee table. "Twenty-four generations," she said, tapping the pile on her lap. "Starting with my *ketuba*." She tenderly picked up the parchment at the top of the pile, scanning it with a gentle smile. "Now, obviously, I'm not letting you take the originals to the Land of the Pickpockets over there. I had them copied for you." She nodded at a large folder that had been resting on the coffee table.

"Photocopied?!" I exclaimed in horror.

"Oh no. I had them professionally scanned." I let out a breath of relief, and Grandma chuckled. "Take out a piece of paper now and start drawing the family tree. You probably won't need all the names; I just want you to visualize the connections."

"Hold on, let me get one of my notebooks." I stood up and ran back to my room, grabbing one of the new spiral notebooks I had packed for school and returning to my spot on the couch. "Oops. I'll need a pen too."

"Here." My grandmother handed me one. "Start by writing yourself."

I wrote my name on the top of the front page. *Alma Ben-Ami.* "Now your mother." *Hannah Dahan.* "Married to?" *Isaac Ben-Ami.*

"Now me." I smiled. *Alma Solomon, m. Gershon Dahan.* "Put the date as well. June 9th, 1956. 30th of Sivan, 5716." I scribbled down the dates. "Okay. Now this is my mother's." My grandmother slipped her marriage certificate under the rest of the pile and handed me the next one. We worked through the pile and I wrote down the names carefully. After twenty-three certificates, we finally reached the oldest one, which Grandma handed me very, very carefully. My heart pounded as I examined it for the second time.

"*Míriam bat Abraham v'Orosol A"H, l'veit mishpachat de Carmona,*" I read. "The third of Elul, 5252…which would be…"

"Summer of 1492."

"And the *A"H?*"

"Acronym for *aleha hashalom.*"

"'Peace be upon her'?"

"Right."

"So we know her mother was dead... Orosol? I've never heard that name before..."

"It's Spanish. It means—"

"'Gold sun'. My Spanish isn't *that* bad. But it doesn't sound like a Jewish name..."

"Sure it is. Like Yiddish names—Gittel, Frieda, Golda..."

"But Yiddish is a Jewish language."

"And what is Haketía? Buddhist?"

"Oh. Right. Well, you said Spanish, not Haketía."

"Spanish Jews spoke Castilian. Haketía is the dialect of it that developed in the Maghreb after the Expulsion. Anyway, the important thing is that she was married just under a month after the Expulsion."

"Do you think that means she arrived in Morocco before the Expulsion?"

"I would assume so, but we can't know for sure without more evidence. With a family name like 'de Carmona', I would think they were originally from Andalusia, but Jews moved around a lot during that period so it's basically impossible to know where they were before they got to Morocco."

"Do we know for sure that they escaped the Inquisition? Maybe they didn't even come from Spain..."

"Well, that's the whole point, *mi Alma.*" Grandma took off her reading glasses and rubbed her eyes. "Beyond these documents, we don't know anything for sure."

"So..." I said. "What about the ring?"

"The ring?" Grandma narrowed her eyes at me.

"The ring! The gold ring that was in here with the *ketubot.* Oh, God. Please don't tell me you forgot about it."

Grandma rubbed her chin, her eyes searching.

I dug around feverishly at the bottom of the box. The ring wasn't there.

I felt my throat tighten, and my breath caught in my chest.

"Grandma," I pleaded, "please remember. You have to remember. It was a gold ring. Your grandmother gave it to you. She said we have to return it to the Christian family who rescued our ancestors."

"Right…" I could see the memory returning to Grandma's eyes. "So where did you put it?"

She pursed her lips, concentrating hard.

"I wanted you to bring it with you," she murmured, more to herself than to me. "I wanted you to wear it…around your neck!" She looked up at me suddenly, and burst out laughing.

"What? What's so funny?"

Grandma reached for her collar and pulled a chain out from beneath her housecoat. At the end of it dangled the ring.

"Sometimes one must search far for what is near," Grandma grinned, and we both burst into hysterical, relieved laughter.

Grandma unclasped the chain from around her neck and clasped it around mine. Then she took my hand and held it in both of hers. "I can't tell you how much it means to me that you're doing this, Alma."

"You don't have to." I smiled back at her and saw her eyes welling with tears. "Oh, Grandma, don't cry!"

"Let me give you a blessing." I knelt by her chair, and she placed her hands on my head. *"May God make you like Sarah, Rebecca, Rachel, and Leah,"* she said in Hebrew. *"May God bless you and guard you; may God shine His countenance upon you and be gracious to you; may God lift His countenance to you and give you peace."* She took a deep breath. *"May you journey in peace, may you return in peace.* And may God assist you on your journey, opening your eyes to the path that you seek," she continued in English. "May He protect you from evil, and from confusion, and from fear. And may He grant you joy always." She leaned down and kissed the top of my head. By this point, tears were streaming down my own face, and Grandma saw them as I rose. *"Ay, hija mía.* Who was just telling me not to cry?" she scolded, grinning through her tears. I leaned over and wrapped her in a hug.

"I'm going to miss you so much," I sobbed.

"Me too, sweetie. But you'll be back before you know it, and then we'll have another two years to get completely sick of each other."

I laughed, standing up and wiping my eyes on my sleeves.

"Knock knock," came a voice from the door. I turned to see my mother pulling off her gloves and stuffing them into the pocket of her bulky red winter coat. "Freezing out there."

"Ahh, there's my Hannah." My grandmother's eyes lit up.

My mother squeezed around the coffee table to kiss her on the cheek. I snatched up the wooden box with the *ketubot* from the coffee table before my mother's coat could push it onto the floor. "How are you ladies doing?" she asked.

Grandma and I sighed simultaneously.

"You ready to go?" she addressed my grandmother. "Or should we wait until Alma's cab gets here?"

Grandma narrowed her eyes at my mother. "Go where?" she asked.

My mother sighed impatiently. "I drove down here to bring you to Albany. To live with us while Alma is away. We discussed this a million times over the past few months. Remember?"

"Oh..." Grandma glanced around the apartment. "And who's going to run the store?"

"Lara. Same person who's been running it while Alma's been at school."

Grandma looked up at me.

"Come on, Grandma." I offered a hand. She gave another resigned sigh and let me help her to her feet.

# Manuel

There is always something surreal about the atmosphere of an airport, especially at night—the vast space, the murmurs and echoes of voices and footsteps, the bright lights against the darkened floor-to-ceiling windows. My mother accompanied me to the security line, wringing her hands and plucking at my clothes whenever I let her near enough. "I really hope that old SIM card works in your phone. Did I give you that letter to send to Marta when you get there? I thought I put it in your backpack..."

"Yes, I have it. Mama, calm down. You can always mail something to me if I forgot."

"I know. I know. I just get so nervous about traveling."

I laughed. "I'm the one traveling, not you!"

She gave me a weary look. "It's much the same thing." She sighed and scanned the line. "This is ridiculous. It'll take you an hour to get through here. Maybe we can sit and wait until it gets a little better..."

"It won't get better. It's the TSA, Mama. Inefficiency is their *modus operandi*. If I wait any longer I might miss the flight."

"How is the Jewish girl getting here?"

"By taxi, I think."

"I like her, you know."

"Yes, I know. You should go, Mama."

She just stood there for a moment, looking small and uncertain and restrained. Then she straightened and reached up to put her hands on my shoulders. "You're right." She pulled me down and kissed me on each cheek. Then she cupped my face in her hands

and looked into my eyes. "You know he would be so proud of you."
She gave my face two sharp pats, then abruptly turned around and walked off.

*"Hasta luego, mamá."*

She paused and turned, giving me one last appraising look.

*"Hasta luego, cariño.* And for the love of God, get a haircut when you get there."

And with that, she disappeared into the crowd.

---

I waited for Alma at the gate, watching the other passengers to see if I could spot other NYU students heading for the spring semester in Madrid. There were eight of us in the Spanish Heritage Project, but a couple dozen others participating in the regular NYU Madrid program. The other Heritage Project students arrived in pairs; Zoe and her cousin Nicole, Andrea and Melissa, and then Lucas and Lorenzo. I let their flirtatious chatter wash over me, compulsively checking my watch. Boarding time was approaching and I was contemplating giving Alma a call when I saw her jogging toward us, breathless, her ponytail a mess and her glasses askew.

"Random security check," she was mumbling as she plopped down next to me. "God Almighty. Do I look like a terrorist to you?"

"It's supposed to be random, no?"

"They *claim* it's random. I tell you, the guy had it in for me the moment I explained that my luggage is so heavy because it contains pots and pans."

I blinked. "Why does your luggage contain pots and pans?"

"How else am I going to keep kosher in a non-kosher kitchen?"

"Even if the pots are clean?"

"If you haven't noticed yet, Judaism is the most

obsessive-compulsive religion on the planet. . ." She paused, registering the blank look on my face, then drew a deep breath and launched into one of her long-winded explanations: "Kashrut is like a spiritual allergy. According to the laws of kashrut, metal pots and pans and ovens absorb the flavors of the non-kosher food that was cooked there, so we're not allowed to use anything that's been used to cook non-kosher food."

"What if the kitchen is vegetarian?"

"There are still cheeses and other products that may contain non-kosher ingredients. . . and there are a bunch of other issues besides non-kosher meat and separation of milk and meat. . . it's really complicated. And even if I bought brand-new pots in Spain, I'd have to go through a whole elaborate procedure before I could use them."

"Ah. For a moment I thought it would maybe be okay for you to eat in my kitchen."

She shot me a suspicious look. "Does that mean you're a vegetarian?"

I nodded. "My mother always has been. We never had meat in the house."

She raised her eyebrows and nodded slowly.

"What? Is there a problem?"

"No, no problem," she said, her voice kind of high-pitched. "No problem. All I'm saying is. . . good thing I can't marry you."

I opened my mouth wordlessly for a moment, then collected myself and cleared my throat. "Was this. . . a possibility you had considered before this devastating revelation?" I grinned.

She blinked, looking a little flustered. "Well. . . *possibility* would imply that it was, you know. . . possible."

I bit my lip and nodded, smiling at the ground. I was enjoying this a little too much. "I think. . ." I turned back to her. "You did not answer my question."

"I think…" she said, "you really don't need an answer. I'm gonna go get a Coke. Do you want one? I'll get you one." She jumped up and took off for the nearest newsstand.

I sighed as I approached my row and double-checked my boarding pass. Yes. Middle seat.

I glanced around. Alma was sitting in the middle seat across the aisle, between Lucas and a girl I didn't recognize. Lucas seemed a little disappointed with the arrangements too, and when I followed his gaze I had a hunch I knew why. I studied him for a few moments, a smile tugging at the corner of my mouth, then glanced between him and Melissa, who was in the seat next to mine.

I approached him.

"Would you mind switching seats with me, *amigo?*" I asked him. He looked up in surprise.

"Where is your seat?" he asked skeptically.

"There," I said, nodding casually in Melissa's direction. I almost laughed when his eyes lit up.

"Sure, no problem," he said, scooping up his bag and standing up.

I shoved my bag in the overhead compartment and sat down next to Alma. She was engaged in conversation with the girl next to her, who noticed me and smiled in my direction.

"Hi," she said.

Alma turned around and blinked in surprise. "Manuel! Wasn't Lucas sitting here a second ago?"

"He was kindly willing to switch with me."

"You seem to be developing a habit of following me around."

"Much as I enjoy your company," I said, "I'm afraid my motivation was the aisle seat."

"Ahh." She nodded. "Tall-person problems." She turned back

to the girl next to her. "Olivia, this is my friend Manuel. He's in the Spanish Heritage Project too."

"Nice to meet you," said Olivia, grinning widely. She had a round sort of face, olive skin, and very straight black hair that spilled around her shoulders.

"Manuel, this is Olivia. We just figured out that we're roommates." I nodded politely.

"¿Hablas español?" Olivia addressed me.

"He's from Andalusia, so *castellano*," Alma answered.

"Ah. I'm from Arizona, but my parents are Mexican," Olivia said, still addressing me.

I gave another polite nod, feeling increasingly uncomfortable. I leaned forward to dig a book from my bag and began to read as Alma and Olivia continued chatting. Eventually their chatter died down. I continued reading in silence.

"So have you been back to Spain at all since you moved here?"

It took me several seconds to realize that Alma had spoken to me. I looked up from the book, blinking in surprise.

"Back to Spain?" I echoed, trying to register her question. "Ehhh...no."

"Geez, this must be exciting then!" she continued. "Are you planning to meet up with friends and family in Granada?"

"I don't really have any family. And I have not stayed in touch with my friends." I paused, studying her. "But I'm definitely planning to go visit my father when I can. His grave, I mean."

She nodded. "How far away is Granada from Madrid?"

"Not sure exactly. It's a different part of the country. Several hours by train, probably. Spain is much smaller than the USA." I smiled at her. "Maybe you should come with me—it's a beautiful city."

"I bet. Well, we'll have to see. Religious Jews do not make great travel companions, you know."

"You should have warned me before we got on this plane. Why not?"

"We're a pain in the butt. We can't eat anywhere. We can't do anything on Saturdays. And this makes us totally obsessed with finding other Jews with whom we can share our bad food and whine about it all. Not to mention visiting Jewish heritage sites, which are all extremely depressing in Europe."

"I would not mind showing you some Jewish heritage sites. My mother dragged me to all of the ones near us when I was growing up."

Alma cocked her head at me. "Your mom has a thing for Jews too, huh?"

"She definitely does. She seems much more at home in Brooklyn than she did in Granada, to be honest."

"She's a funny lady."

"That's one way to put it."

Alma reached forward and started rummaging through her bag under the seat in front of her. Finally she fished out a small digital video camera.

"What are you doing?" I asked suspiciously.

She turned the camera on and twisted the lens around to face her, then clicked *Record*. "Semester in Madrid, day one!" she said to the camera. "As you can see, we're all settled here on the plane, waiting for the engines to get started... and here is Manuel..." she turned the camera toward me. "Looking... exasperated."

"Are you going to be doing this the entire time?" I asked, rubbing my forehead.

"Well, someone's grumpy!" She turned the camera back to herself and smiled at it. "And this here is our new friend Olivia..." Olivia started at the sound of her name and looked up, smiled, and waved for the camera. "And we should be taking off very soon! See you in Madrid!" Then she turned it off, her smile abruptly disappearing, and turned to me. "Listen, buster, I'll catch hell from my family if this trip isn't extremely well documented. And I expect you to be fully compliant."

"Did I sign for this? I don't think it was in the contract..."

"Oh, quiet!"

"Ladies and gentlemen, we are pleased to welcome you on board flight F750 to Madrid..."

"Oh my God, I can't believe this is really happening," Alma clapped her hands in excitement. "You know I've never flown internationally before?"

"Then maybe you should pay attention while she explains the safety procedures."

"You're just trying to get me to shut up."

"Mm, yes. I'd like to listen."

"You're such a goody-two-shoes."

"Shh."

<hr />

The flight was uneventful, unless you count Alma's occasional outbursts of "I need to get out of here!"—clawing past me to pace up and down the aisle—as events. I didn't mind much that she did this, because I could not get comfortable enough to sleep for more than twenty minutes at a time anyway. It certainly didn't help when Alma poked me awake to inform me that I was snoring.

We were greeted in baggage claim by a guy holding a sign and introducing himself as Dave; but as more and more of us joined the group with our luggage, Alma was left standing by the carousel, increasingly agitated, watching suitcases disappear off the track until there were none left at all.

"It happens sometimes," Dave told her. "Don't worry, we haven't had a student yet whose bags were permanently lost. It might take another day or two."

"Great, well, I guess it'll be all packaged food for the next few days..." she grumbled as I accompanied her to the Lost Luggage desk.

"Oh right, your pots..." I said.

"I told you that security guy had it in for me. That's probably why the bag was delayed."

She filled out the forms at Lost Luggage and the guy behind the desk told her they'd be in touch. We rejoined the NYU group, where Dave was giving out keys and maps and helping students figure out how to get to their lodgings. Alma was in an independent rental a block down the road from my homestay, along with Olivia and one of the other female students.

"Is there a way to make the kitchen kosher?" I asked. "Maybe they'd be willing to keep it kosher for a few days..."

Alma gave me a sarcastic grin. "Yeah, sure, there's a way—but trust me, it ain't gonna happen."

"Why not?"

"Just trust me."

"No, I want to know. What would you have to do?"

She looked up at me over her glasses. "You really want to know?"

"Yes."

"Well...you asked." She shrugged. "So first, you'd have to scrub everything completely clean..." and she launched into a complicated explanation that involved scrubbing, boiling, pouring boiling water, leaving ovens on, and blow-torching. As she was getting into the finer details of which materials could and could not be made kosher, she skidded to a stop and stared at me. "Why are you even still *listening* to me?"

I blinked. "Why not? It's interesting!"

"No! It really isn't!" She looked me up and down. "Are you *sure* you're a Christian?"

"Manuel, right?" came a voice from behind me. I turned around.

It was a solidly-built guy with a long curly ponytail, and he extended a hand. "I'm Rob, we're gonna be roommates at Señora Ortega's."

"Pleased to meet you," I said, shaking his hand. "This is my friend Alma."

"Nice to meet you." They shook hands. "So..." he turned back to me. "I was gonna head over there now. I thought you might want to tag along."

I hesitated.

"Go ahead," Alma said. "I'll be fine."

I regarded her. Her ponytail was coming apart, strands of black hair frizzed wildly around her face, and her pale green eyes were bloodshot and puffy.

"You sure?" I asked.

"Yeah, yeah. Go on. I should go join my roommates." She pulled her phone from her pocket. "Just give me your new number."

⁓

As we boarded the airport shuttle, I noticed that it felt strange to be surrounded again by people speaking Spanish. For the first time, I realized how much mental strain I'd become accustomed to simply because I was surrounded by English speakers. In the USA, my ears automatically picked out Spanish conversations among the hubbub of English, as if my brain were somehow thirsty for its most comfortable language. Here, everything suddenly became so much easier to understand.

Fortunately for me, Rob was not very talkative, and I was able to stare out the windows and contemplate the view as we approached the city. I had visited Madrid a few times in my life, but it was so long ago that I didn't really recognize anything. What did feel comforting and familiar was the huge sky. Spending all my time in New York City, I was used to seeing only strips of gritty blue between the crowded buildings. Madrid's architecture was lower, more quaint. The pace was slower; people on the street were strolling, not rushing. The city definitely felt more like home than Brooklyn did, but it was not Granada. The sunlight was too gentle.

Rob and I navigated the streets with little trouble and found ourselves on the sidewalk in front of a yellow brick building about five stories high. We entered, climbed the stairs to the second floor, and knocked on the door. A short, round lady in her sixties greeted us and introduced herself as María Ortega. She seemed more disappointed than anything else to learn that I was a Spaniard, especially when she heard my Andalusian accent. Northerners tend to associate the "lazy, sound-swallowing" southern accent with the lower class. I wondered if I should take my mother's advice while I was here, and use the "refined" Castilian Spanish she had insisted I master when I was a teenager.

Señora Ortega's apartment was cramped but meticulously tidy. She showed us our rooms, and told us that when we were done unpacking she would show us around the kitchen.

Rob and I each had a small room with a wardrobe, a bed, and a desk. I set down my suitcase and sat on the bed, patting the mattress. I had forgotten how much narrower European beds were. Light streamed in from a small window above the desk. I walked toward it and peered out; a grassy little park lay below, with a swing set and a slide. A woman sat on a bench and read while a little boy ran around the equipment. Another apartment building rose behind the park, red brick with flourishes in white stucco around the windows.

I turned back to the room and unzipped my suitcase.

When about half the contents were put away in the wardrobe, my phone rang. I dug through my bag to find it. Alma's name was displayed on the screen.

"Hello?"

"Manuel?"

This didn't sound good. Her voice was shaking.

"Alma? What's wrong?"

"I just... I'm not... I'm tired and hungry and I can't think straight, and I don't know what to do about the food, I forgot to pack the list of packaged kosher products in my carry-on and our Internet here isn't set up yet and even if it was I don't know how to get to the nearest supermarket and I can't decide if I'm more tired or hungry and I might just fall asleep on the way there anyhow but I'm so hungry and—"

"Alma, I can't understand a word you are saying...what can I do to help you?"

"I don't know!" she sobbed.

"You said something about a list of kosher products. If I find it for you, will that help?"

"I don't know because I don't even remember if it had anything useful on it and honestly I just need an actual meal right now and I have no idea what to do..."

"Wow. You Jews really *are* awful travel companions."

"Don't mock me in my hour of distress!" I couldn't tell whether she was laughing or crying.

"Alma, give me the address of your apartment and I'll come over there and see if I can help you. Okay?"

⸺⸺

Two minutes later I found myself sitting on Señora Ortega's couch, staring at the yellow pages open in front of me. *This really shouldn't be so hard*, I thought. *Just do it.*

*Why can't she do it? Text her the number and be done with it.*

*But...her Spanish. And I heard what kind of a state she's in. She won't be able to thread two words together.*

*Oh, but he has to speak English. Come on. He must interact with Jewish tourists all day.*

*Why is this so hard for me? He's just a rabbi. A Jew like Alma. They don't bite.*

*But... a rabbi.*

*I'm not going to marry him, I'm just going to talk to him on the phone! Even Padre Carlos wouldn't have a problem with this...*

*But he* would *have a problem with the reason I'm calling.*

*I'm just helping a friend!*

"*¡Basta!*" I said aloud.

"Sorry?" Rob called from the other room.

"Nothing." I sighed, closed my eyes, and whispered, "*Dios... ayúdame.*" I reached into my pocket for my phone, still not sure whether I was going to use it to call the number or just text it to Alma. But as I drew out the phone, a note came out with it and fell onto the couch next to me. I picked it up, curious, and opened it; then drew in a sharp breath as I read Father Greg's handwriting:

*Love bears all things, believes all things, hopes all things, endures all things.*

I cast an incredulous look toward the ceiling, and offered up a silent "*Gracias.*" Then I dialed the number, pressed "call", and put the phone to my ear.

# Míriam

Míriam paced through the house, back and forth, back and forth. It had never been so agonizing waiting for someone to come back from the market. It must have been two or three hours already, and soon it would have been time for her father to return from his market stall anyway. She couldn't bring herself to do housework or even eat anything.

Finally, she heard footsteps approaching the door. She flung it open and saw little Yehuda standing there, red-faced and out of breath.

"Well?" she prompted him.

"I'm sorry, Míriam. I looked everywhere for him. I couldn't find him."

Míriam's stomach dropped.

"His stand was there and his spices were on display. People were just helping themselves. I asked them where he was and no one knew."

Míriam felt dizzy and leaned against the doorframe for support.

"Yehuda..." she said. "Here...come here... I'll give you the quince..." She pointed to the shallow ceramic jar on the table in the middle of the room. "Take what you like...just listen..." She grabbed his shoulder and turned him to face her. "Don't tell anyone about this. Understand? Not a word to anyone. At least not for the next few days. You promise me?"

Yehuda gave her a quizzical look, but he promised.

"Okay. Go take the quince and go home to your mother."

He did as he was told, and when he had left, Míriam bolted the door shut and stumbled to the bedroom, collapsing on her bed by the front window. She hugged her knees to her chest and cried, rocking back and forth, trying to gain some control of her thoughts. *Maybe he was warned by someone else. Maybe he has already fled. Or maybe he was already arrested. There is no way to know. All I can do is wait. All I can do is wait.*

The sun was setting behind the mountains. She sat on the bed by the window and watched it sink below the roofs of the houses across the street. She couldn't eat, couldn't sleep. She just sat in the gathering darkness, waiting.

Eventually she must have drifted off, because she was awakened by a rustling sound outside her window. She bolted upright, listening carefully. There was a very light knock on the door.

Her head spun. *What if it's the Inquisition?* She didn't move.

The knock came again, this time a little bit louder.

*The Inquisition would not knock gently.*

She tiptoed to the door, resting her ear against it. The knock came again, and this time a voice.

"Míriam de Carmona," the voice whispered. "Are you there?"

*That definitely doesn't sound like the Inquisition.*

"Who are you?" she called through the door.

"León."

Míriam jumped back from the door in astonishment. Don León? Don Tomás's son? What was he doing here at this hour?

"Míriam, please open the door and let me in." His voice was very quiet and so muffled through the door she could hardly hear him. "I know where your father is. It is dangerous for me to be out here. Please let me in."

Míriam opened the door. León swept inside, closing the door behind him and removing his dark hood. He fumbled for the lock.

"Don't lock the door," Míriam blurted.

León looked at her in confusion. "I'm just trying to keep—"

"I know. But it's improper." She did not feel like explaining. He raised his hands in defeat. He was dressed all in black, and in the darkness she could hardly make out his silhouette against the door. "Where is my father?"

"Hidden at our estate. There's an extra room in one of the towers, where the seamstress and her assistant used to sleep."

Míriam stared at León. "Your father is hiding him?"

He took a deep breath. "Yes."

Míriam was at a loss for words. Giving refuge to a fugitive from the Inquisition was treason of the highest order. After a few moments, she whispered, "Is your father out of his mind?"

There was a pause. "To tell you the truth, that's exactly what I asked him." He regarded her. "But he is my father and I do as he says. He sent me to come get you." He tossed a black piece of cloth at her. She caught it and examined it. "Put that on and we'll go. Your father told me where the secret passageway is."

Míriam eyed him skeptically. "Aren't you the one who has difficulty following directions?"

She saw a flash of white in the dark, and was able to see that his face had broken into a smile. Somehow, Míriam started to feel a little better. "Yes, but I manage to find my way when it really matters."

Míriam took a step back. "I'm just going to go get some of my things…"

"No, no. No time. We have everything you need. Just put on the cloak and come now."

Míriam hesitated for a moment, sizing him up. "How do I know I can trust you?"

León sighed. "Do you have a choice?"

She slipped on the cloak, and with one last glance back at her home of nine years, she followed him out into the night.

# Alma

The first thing I noticed when I started to wake up was the nausea of jet-lagged grogginess. That was pretty awful. It took me a few seconds to figure out that I had passed out on the couch of my apartment, apparently with my glasses on, because they were digging into my face and squishing my nose at an awkward angle. I rolled onto my back, adjusting the glasses and rubbing my eyes. Then I realized that I was smelling something delicious—something like beef and maybe vegetables—and that's what made my eyes pop open.

Right across from me, on the kitchen table, was a bag of what looked like takeout food, steaming away and smelling excruciatingly appetizing. I lifted my head and saw that someone was seated next to it, his hands folded in his lap.

"Manuel," I groaned. "Are you trying to kill me?"

"It's for you."

I stared at him. "But I can't—"

"It's kosher. I called the local rabbi and asked if there was someplace to get you food. He directed me to this place." He tapped the business card stapled onto the bag. "I hope you like couscous with meatballs."

I pulled myself up, lurched over to the table, and examined the business card. *Alfassi,* it read. *Restaurante Kosher—bajo la supervisión del Rabino Uri Maimón.*

I swiveled my gaze onto Manuel, who was watching me with a little smile playing at the corners of his mouth.

"Did you ride here on a white horse or what?" I furiously tore at the bag and removed the styrofoam containers. "You're my freaking hero. Oh my God this smells so good." I sat, raced through the appropriate blessing, and started wolfing the food down. Manuel sat there and watched me, his eyes twinkling. "You want some?" I said with my mouth half full, offering him one of the extra plastic forks. He shook his head.

"I'm a vegetarian, remember?"

"Oh, right!" I lowered my eyes back to my food, remembering that really awkward moment at the airport when I said that thing about not marrying him. I gave myself a mental kick in the pants. Sometimes I astonish myself with the tactless stupidity that comes out of my mouth. I cleared my throat. "Well, good—more for me then!"

"How is it?" Manuel asked.

"I'll let you know when I'm not starving anymore," I answered through a mouthful of food. "Right now it tastes like the fruits of Eden." I looked back up at him, raising an eyebrow. "You called the rabbi?"

"Yes. And he said to tell you that you are most welcome to come for the Sabbath, and before that if you need anything. Here's his number." He dug a slip of paper out of his pocket and slid it across the table to me.

"I dunno, Manuel, does your priest know about this?" I grinned. He shifted uncomfortably. I cleared my throat and shoveled another forkful of food into my mouth. "Well," I said, chewing thoughtfully. "It's definitely not my grandmother's couscous. But it's not bad. How much was it? I'll pay you back."

"Don't be ridiculous."

"No, don't *you* be ridiculous. I'm sure it was expensive and I'm sure I have more money than you to spend on such things. How much?"

"Forget it, Alma."

"Oh no you don't." I stabbed my fork in his direction. He dodged back, eyeing the fork nervously. "We are not dating, and I don't have to put up with this from you. Put aside your macho Spanish pride and let me pay for it. Where's the receipt?" I stood up and started digging around for it, but I didn't find it. I threw the bag down and glared at him. "How much?"

He was laughing quietly behind crossed arms. "I'm not telling. Why can't you just accept it as a gift?"

I sighed and sat down, shooting him one last stern look before digging into the food again. Something about this gesture of his felt very, very good, but something about it made me uncomfortable too.

I heard the lock turn in the front door. In walked my roommates, Olivia and Tessa.

"Hey guys," I greeted them.

"I see you're awake! You're lucky he arrived just as we were leaving." Olivia flashed a big smile at Manuel as she set down the grocery bags she was carrying. He gave an uncertain smile back, and coughed.

"Well, I should get back to my apartment and finish unpacking." He turned to me, his eyes softening, and smiled. "Enjoy," he said quietly, then stood up and walked out, nodding at my roommates as he walked past them.

When the door was shut they both burst into giggles. I raised my eyebrows at them.

"Good going, girl." Olivia winked at me as she opened the fridge and started putting away groceries. "Hardly set foot on Spanish soil and you've already snagged a hot Spaniard."

I felt my face get warm. "We're not..."

"Oh, he's totally into you. It's obvious."

I rolled my eyes. "We're just friends."

"Yeah, yeah," Tessa said, dumping a bag on the counter and

opening one of the cabinets. She was a tall African-American with a thin, graceful build and an angular face with high cheekbones. Her thick hair was pulled back into a neat bun.

"Well, does that mean he's single?" Olivia leaned back from the fridge, her eyes shining.

I found myself at a loss for words. It took me a good few moments to recover my tongue.

"Um. Yeah. Yeah, he is."

"Awesome." Olivia dove behind the refrigerator door again.

"But he's a religious Catholic and considering becoming a priest," I blurted. Olivia's head reemerged, her eyebrows arched.

"Ohhh," she said. "*Now* I get it."

"Well, Olivia, there's still hope," Tessa winked at her. "She said 'considering'."

I was not enjoying this conversation at all.

"So which one of you is going to lend me pajamas tonight?" I asked rather loudly.

———⁓———

My suitcase was delivered the following day, and I found the list of kosher products tucked into one of the pots. Olivia and Tessa were politely curious about my dietary needs, and helped me locate the bakery and butcher where I could get kosher bread and meat. I wouldn't be able to use the oven in our apartment, but I figured a frying pan and a pot for milk and one of each for meat would be enough. To use the stove, I would just cover the grating with foil.

I called Rabbi Maimón and accepted his invitation for the upcoming Shabbat. It turned out that he was the Chabad (or in this case, being in Spain—Jabad) *shaliach* here, a representative of the organization that, among other things, provides Shabbat meals and other services to Jewish travelers all over the world. I had known there was a Chabad House in Madrid, and had been counting on going there for *Shabbatot* anyway.

"Excellent," he said, in a vaguely Israeli accent. "You are welcome to spend as many *Shabbatot* with us as you like. I should warn you that there is no *eruv*."

"Oy," I said. That meant I wouldn't be able to carry anything with me outside, not even in my pockets, from Friday evening until Saturday evening.

"Also…don't wear anything particularly Jewish or Israeli looking."

I hesitated. "Why not?" I asked slowly.

"Anti-semitism," he answered simply.

———∽∽———

That Friday afternoon, I put on an ankle-length dress and high-heeled boots, dabbed on a little mascara and lipstick, emptied my handbag of everything except my passport and prayerbook, and headed off to Manuel's place.

Señora Ortega answered the door. I took a deep breath and mustered my best Castilian accent.

"*Buenos tardes. ¿Está Manuel por aquí?*"

"*Sí, en su dormitorio.*" She stepped back to let me in and pointed toward an open door tucked in the hallway on the other side of the small living room. I walked toward it.

"Knock knock," I said as he came into view, curled up on his bed with a book. He looked up.

"Alma!" He sat up and looked me up and down. "You look nice. What's the occasion?"

"Shabbat starts in like an hour."

"Oh, right. Friday evening, when my mother suddenly becomes the most popular woman on the block."

"Huh? Your mother?"

"There is always some neighbor or other who forgot to leave the right lights on or something, coming to ask my mother for help."

"Oh, excellent! Then you know all about being a *Shabbos goy*."

"A what?"

"Get dressed. We're going to the Chabad House for services and dinner."

Manuel blinked at me. "We?"

I walked over to the wardrobe next to his bed and yanked it open. "You've got a suit in here, right?" I scoured the hanging rod and spotted one.

"You want me to come with you to synagogue?!"

"No," I said, snatching the hanger off the rod and tossing the suit at him. "*You* want to come with *me* to synagogue. Don't be so coy. I know you're curious." I paused. "Also, I need you to carry this for me." I lifted my bag.

He eyed it suspiciously. "Why?"

"Because there's no *eruv* and I'm not allowed to carry things outside."

"But you're allowed to make me carry things for you?" One of his thick eyebrows was raised skeptically.

"No...but if you were to *happen* to *feel* like carrying this, for whatever reason, that would be totally fine. Same goes for things like turning on lights and whatever. I'm not allowed to ask you directly."

He narrowed his eyes. "And what if I *don't* feel like it?"

"Hurry up, we need to stop by my place on the way so I can light candles."

I turned and walked out of the room, but before I closed the door, I caught him mumbling something to himself in Spanish about his mother.

"What was that?" I asked.

"Nothing. Admit that the main reason you're dragging me along is that you will get hopelessly lost without me."

I shut the door.

---

Back at my apartment, Manuel stood awkwardly behind me as I set up my tea candles by the kitchen windowsill. I struck a match, lit them, and recited the blessing slowly and carefully: *"Blessed are You, Lord our God, Master of the Universe, Who sanctified us with His commandments and commanded us to light the Sabbath candles."*

My mother had taught me that this was an auspicious time for prayer, and that Jewish women had been offering personal prayers at this moment for many generations. Every Friday evening I used the opportunity to ask God for the things I was hoping for in the coming week, and thank Him for the things He had done for me in the previous week.

I closed my eyes, bowed my head, and prayed silently: "Please send health and happiness to my family, especially my grand-mother, Alma daughter of Mazal," I whispered. "And guide me to the documents and clues that will help us solve the mystery and bring peace to her soul and her grandmother's soul. Thank You for working out the thing with the suitcase," I added, "and for sending Manuel to help me with the food."

That brought my awareness to his presence behind me, shifting his weight from one foot to the other. I decided to leave it at that. I opened my eyes and turned to him.

"Shabbat Shalom, Catholic Boy," I said. He offered an uncertain smile in return.

---

We walked, mostly in silence, through the neighborhoods of Madrid. Manuel kept an eye out for street signs and seemed to know what he was doing, so I gave up trying to figure out where we were going and contemplated my surroundings. I had grown accustomed to the dwarfing urban mass of Manhattan, the feeling of walking through an enormous canyon of brick and stone and glass with just a sliver of sky above me. Madrid was different. Everything felt smaller. The façades of the buildings were painted deep red, pink, yellow, and cream; many of the windows were crowned with neoclassical flourishes, the street lamps decorated with ornate wrought-iron curves. A chilly breeze wove through the streets and made me wish I'd brought a hat and scarf. Unfortunately, my lungs did not seem much happier in the *madrileño* air than they'd been in Manhattan.

*Should have brought my inhaler.* I tried to deepen my breath as I felt my chest constricting.

Manuel noticed me slowing down and holding my hand over my chest. His eyebrows knitted in concern.

"You okay?"

"Yeah, yeah. Just a little asthma." I resumed walking. "I'd hoped the air here would be better than the air in Manhattan."

He shook his head. "I'm sorry to say we city Spaniards do not have a stellar reputation for clean air. It used to be much worse." He eyed me. "Do you have...eh...what's it called? *El inhalador?*"

"An inhaler. Back at the apartment. It's okay, I don't think I'll need it."

He seemed unconvinced, but did not press the issue. We turned into a narrow, badly-lit alley with graffiti on the painted brick walls. Manuel took out the piece of paper with the address he'd scribbled down for me.

"I think it's supposed to be here," he said.

"Really?" I squinted around looking for some indication of an address. I couldn't see any sign of a synagogue. I was about to turn around and tease Manuel that he was just as bad at following directions as I was, when I noticed a gruff-looking man standing outside one of the doorways. He was looking at us with obvious suspicion.

"Looking for Chabad?" he addressed us in what sounded like an Israeli accent. That was when I noticed his earpiece. Security.

"Yes," I said, drawing closer.

"Are you Jewish?"

I blinked. "Um, yeah..."

"No," Manuel said firmly.

The security guy knitted his brow, looking between the two of us. "He is with you?"

"Yeah, he's my *Shabbos goy*. He's got my passport in there." I pointed to the bag Manuel was carrying for me. The security guy extended his hand, and Manuel produced the passport and handed it to him.

"Alma Neshama Ben-Ami. What are you doing in Madrid?"

"Studying. We're students at NYU Madrid."

"You are from New York?"

"Yes, and so is he, but he's originally from Granada."

"*Su pasaporte,*" he addressed Manuel, who drew both of his passports out of his pocket and handed them over.

The security guy flipped through them, then narrowed his eyes at Manuel and asked him something in rapid Spanish that I didn't quite catch. Manuel gave him a sardonic grin and answered simply, "*Mujeres.*" The guy softened into a little smile and nodded, chuckling, handing all the passports back to him.

"Shabbat Shalom," he said, pulling the door open for us.

"What was that about women?" I hissed at him as we started up the stairs.

"He asked me why you were always answering for me."

I rolled my eyes.

"I know security is tight," Manuel said. "But I was not expecting to be cross-examined."

"Well you know what Monty Python says," I turned and grinned at him. He stared at me blankly.

"Monty Python?"

"*No one* expects the Spanish Inquisition!" I wiggled my fingers menacingly.

He just blinked. I flopped my hands down in exasperation.

"Don't tell me you've never seen that! Remind me to look it up for you next time we have Internet access. Seriously, this is required material for people in our line of work..." We arrived at the door to the men's section. I peered inside. There were maybe twenty-five guys, most of them middle aged, squeezed between the crowded wooden benches. I could see the women's section above—a U-shaped balcony across which a few women were scattered. "Well, here's your stop." I stepped aside and gestured for him to go in. His eyes widened.

"What does this mean, *my* stop?" he hissed. "Why should I go in without you?"

"It's the men's section."

"Your prayers are segregated?"

"It's an Orthodox *shul.*"

"Let me understand this—you dragged me here against my will, and now you intend to just throw me in there by myself?"

"*Shabbat Shalom.*" One of the men had drifted toward the door. He looked to be in his fifties, with more than a few gray strands in his bushy black beard and the *payot,* sidecurls, that were tucked neatly behind his ears. He was wearing a black fedora. "Is there a problem?"

"Are you Rabbi Maimón?" I asked.

"Yes, I am," he bowed his head in greeting. "Can I help?"

"This is Manuel. He's shy. This is his first time in *shul*. Would you mind helping him?"

"My absolute pleasure, Manuel." Rabbi Maimón extended a hand to him. Manuel hesitated, but shook his hand. Mid-shake, Rabbi Maimón squinted and pointed at him. *"Are you the one who called me about kosher food for your friend?"* he asked in Spanish.

*"Sí."* Manuel smiled uncomfortably, his shoulder stiff, looking like he really wanted his hand back.

"And you are the friend! Alma, right?" He finally released Manuel's hand and turned his smiling eyes at me.

"Yes. Thanks so much for your help and hospitality."

*"De nada, de nada!* The women's section is just up that way. My wife Ester is there if you need any help." He turned back to Manuel. "So, Manuel. *¿Tú eres un Cohen? ¿Un Leví?"*

"He's a curious Catholic," I tossed over my shoulder as I headed up the stairs. Manuel shot a desperate glare at me.

"Ahh, I see." Rabbi Maimón had an arm around his shoulder now and was steering him in. I chuckled and continued to the third floor.

# Manuel

Rabbi Maimón's openness almost made me feel guilty for having been so hesitant to call him before. He didn't skip a beat when he heard I was Catholic, just steered me right into the synagogue and sat me next to him. Even though the services were clearly already underway and he probably should have been praying, he walked to the bookshelves himself and found me a prayerbook with a Spanish translation next to the Hebrew, opened it to the right page, and showed me where they were in the service. He also handed me a crocheted cap about the size of my hand, yellowed white with a blue design around the rim, and gestured to put it on my head.

Some other guy appeared to be leading the services, standing on a podium at the center of the room and singing the text aloud. It was very different from what I was used to seeing at church.

I looked up at the women's section and spotted Alma by the rail, concentrating on her own prayerbook. She looked up and smiled and waved at me. I shook my head at her. She laughed and went back to her prayers.

I scanned the prayerbook in front of me. The liturgy appeared to be a combination of passages from the Bible—some of which I recognized—along with some other lengthy prayers and poems. I was astonished at how long it was. I flipped back and forth through the book, looking at the prayers for weekdays as well. *Do they really recite this entire thing every single day?*

Services ended with a joyful song. I slipped out of the door as the congregation drifted toward Rabbi Maimón to shake his hand and chat, and waited for Alma at the bottom of the stairs. Finally

I saw her coming around the corner, and her face lit up into a wide, mischievous grin when she saw me.

"Look who Jews up nicely! The *kippa* suits you," she said, gesturing to the cap which I had forgotten was still on my head. The sparkle in her eye as she said this gave me butterflies of pleasure...but something about it also gave me a sort of churning discomfort.

I reached self-consciously for the *kippa*. "Can I take it off now?"

"If you want," she shrugged, "but it's probably more respectful to keep it on for the meal."

"Meal?" I froze. "What meal?"

"I told you we were coming for dinner, didn't I?"

"But...why..."

"Anyone who is here for the *se'udah*—the Sabbath feast," Rabbi Uri's voice boomed over the crowd that had converged on the landing, "please find your seats downstairs in the dining hall."

"Alma, I think I should go," I said, shaking my head. "I can make my own dinner at home."

"Don't be ridiculous." She grabbed my arm and dragged me toward the stairs. I felt the *kippa* sliding off and grabbed at my head to shove it back in place.

"But what if they don't have vegetarian food?" was the only weak protest I could muster.

"They're sure to have something you can eat. This is Chabad, they cater to everybody. Besides, the meal is more important than the services." At this point we had reached the bottom floor, and I noticed an open doorway to our right. Inside, several long tables were set up with plastic tableware, and delicious smells were wafting from somewhere inside. "People are often complaining that women are excluded from the main spheres of religious life, and hey, I'm as upset about that as the next feminist," Alma continued, leading me into the room and toward the table. "The thing about

Judaism, though, is that the main aspects of Jewish life don't revolve around the synagogue. They revolve around the home. When I said it's all about food, I wasn't kidding."

She chose a spot near the head of the table, and finally let go of my arm. Across from her was a blue velvet cloth embroidered in gold Hebrew lettering, covering something lumpy. Next to it was a tarnished silver goblet and a bottle of wine. More people started filtering in: a pair of young women bantering loudly in rapid French; an older British couple; a family of Italians. A woman with an olive complexion, wearing an elegant black dress, came in and greeted every one of them individually with a "Shabbat Shalom," pointing to herself and saying "Ester."

"That's the rabbi's wife," Alma whispered to me.

Eventually, Rabbi Maimón came in and greeted everyone in Spanish, English, French, Italian, and Hebrew, and then began singing a song that everyone but me seemed to know. Ester opened a little paperback prayerbook with a Spanish translation and placed it on the plate in front of me. I nodded in thanks and tried to follow along. It was a song about greeting angels, and something about the haunting melody raised the hairs on the back of my neck. Next came the Biblical song "Woman of Valor", which the Rabbi sang in its entirety while gazing at his wife with such visible and intense affection that I could hardly bear to look.

I found myself watching Alma instead. That serenity that I had seen in her eyes as soon as she had turned from lighting the candles was now positively radiating from her. There was something very unexpected and disarming about it. She always seemed full of nervous energy, with her rapid, tripping-over-itself speech and her emphatic gestures. Now she stood in tranquility, singing along and beaming, and it struck me that this was the first time I was seeing her in her natural environment. At NYU, at her apartment in Madrid, on the airplane, in the streets, she was surrounded by a culture that wasn't really hers—one she accepted and acclimated to, but never entirely fit into. Everywhere else, she was constantly explaining herself. Here, she simply belonged. I had a sudden and vivid image in my mind of her as a little girl in a lacy dress, long black hair tied back with a bow, standing around a table like this with her parents and siblings, all singing this same song. And there was something in me that longed for that myself, especially in contrast to the cold, dark, lonely Christmases with my mother in New York during the past five years.

Alma noticed me staring at her and gave me a bright smile, pulling me out of my reverie. My heart fluttered a little and I smiled back, my cheeks growing warm.

The rabbi then recited the prayer over the wine, and we all drank from the wine distributed on the tables. It was sickeningly sweet, and I tried not to make a face when I took a sip. He explained that we were going to wash our hands before the blessing for bread, and that whoever needed help with this was welcome to ask—but that once he had washed his own hands, he was not allowed to speak until he had eaten. I remained in my seat while Alma went to wash.

Rabbi Maimón pulled the blue velvet cover off to reveal two beautiful braided loaves of bread on a wooden cutting board. He made a blessing over them and began slicing them, eating a piece himself and handing one to his wife. She gathered the remaining pieces in a basket and when it was full, passed it down the table.

"Remind you a little of communion?" the rabbi winked at me. I gave him a relieved smile, feeling my shoulders relax a little. "Where do you think you Catholics got the idea for bread and wine as part of the observance of the Sabbath?" He looked up at everyone else, raising his voice. "Help yourselves," he said, gesturing to a table in the corner where several electric hotplates were loaded with enormous pots and pans of food. "Everything is *pareve* except for the chicken and the brisket."

"That was not completely accurate, Uri." Ester spoke up. "The bread and wine tradition comes from the gospels about the Last Supper. The Passover Seder." She looked at me appraisingly. "I grew up Catholic."

Apparently I did not hide my astonishment very well, because she laughed.

"Or at least I thought I did. I was born in Colombia. It turned out that my family are *Bnei Anusim.*"

Well, that certainly got Alma's attention.

"Descendants of *conversos?*" Alma gasped. Ester nodded. "How did you find out?"

"When I came to America to study, I noticed there were lots of things that we did that other Catholics did not do, and at first I thought it was just a cultural difference; but when I started to look into it, I realized that they were *converso* traditions. I confronted my grandmother and she admitted that we were descended from Spanish Jews."

"What kind of traditions?" I asked.

"Oh, you know, things like lighting candles in the basement on Friday night, separating milk and meat, checking eggs for blood before cooking them, tossing a bit of dough into the oven to burn while baking bread, observing certain fast days... sweeping toward the center of the room..."

"How on earth did your family manage to hold onto their identity in secret for five hundred years?" Alma breathed. "I mean... so... my family is also descended from Spanish Jews, but they apparently left Spain before the Expulsion. I'm actually here to research them and find out what happened to them here."

Ester smiled. *"La sangre te llama,"* she said, and I felt a shiver go down my spine. "The blood calls to you. Some memories are carried in the mind; others are carried in our DNA. The first time my mother heard me recite *Shema Yisrael,* she burst into uncontrollable tears and we couldn't calm her for an hour. She had never heard it before in her life."

Alma was staring at her with her hand over her mouth.

"My ancestors refused to let go of our identity, even under pain of death," Ester continued. "And I guess they were successful enough at hiding it that they were not caught."

"But then why did they keep hiding it?" Alma asked.

Ester sighed. "Unfortunately, another thing they inherited, along with the identity, was the fear. Fear became a completely integral part of keeping those practices and passing them on; it was inextricably linked with Judaism for my family. Even when I finally managed to get my grandmother to admit it, she warned me that being a Jew is dangerous and that I should never tell anyone. She was horrified when I decided to have my Judaism formally recognized."

"How did you do that?"

"I wanted to convert, but it turned out I didn't have to. It's a bit of a long story, but the short version is that I was able to come up with enough documentation to prove beyond a doubt that my maternal line was Jewish. I came to Israel with the help of a few organizations involved in helping *Bnei Anusim*, and I was granted a Certificate of Return."

"What an incredible story!"

I was feeling oddly light-headed. I struggled to stand up from the table.

"Alma," I said, "I am going to get something to eat. Would you like me to bring you something?"

She looked up at me, blinking. "Oh, no, that's okay! I'll go with you." She stood up and followed me to the buffet. She was eyeing me. "Are you okay? You look a little pale."

"I'm fine. I think I'm just hungry." My stomach growled. I approached the table and surveyed the options.

"Can you believe it? A real live descendant of crypto-Jews..." Alma was saying.

"I did not even know that was possible," I said, peering into the pot of soup. "Can you tell if this has meat in it?"

"He said everything is vegetarian except the actual meat."

"Ah, so that's what he said."

"But yeah—to have preserved their Jewishness for five hundred years! I feel like I should interview her for a project or something..."

"You should," I smiled at her. "It fits both your major and your minor."

"Maybe that can be my fallback plan if and when I discover that there is no evidence whatsoever of my ancestors in the national archives." She dumped a generous helping of sliced meat on her plate, and caught me looking at her sideways. She narrowed her eyes at me. "Are you, like, *really* vegetarian, or just vegetarian because your mom is?"

I raised an eyebrow. "This really bothers you, eh?"

"I love meat. Love, love, *love* meat. And I have a cousin who's a vegetarian and she is totally self-righteous and unbearable about it."

"I promise never to be self-righteous and unbearable."

Alma eyed me skeptically and headed back for her seat.

---

Alma ended up interrogating Ester for most of the meal—well, at least when the Maimón kids let their mother sit down. I found myself drifting into conversation with the rabbi, who asked me about my family and my interest in Judaism. He told me about his personal journey toward his Judaism, having been born in Israel and discovered Chabad during a post-army trek in Nepal. Once everyone had finished eating, he led his family in singing Sabbath songs, many of which Alma seemed to know. Then the

Maimóns led the group in the grace after meals—which seemed to take forever—and the guests shuffled out. Before I knew it, Alma and I were the only guests left. Rabbi Uri invited the two of us up to his apartment for drinks, and we climbed the three flights of stairs with him and his family. I turned down his offer of scotch but said I would enjoy a cup of tea. Ester busied herself putting the kids to bed as Rabbi Uri fixed our tea, inviting us to sit on his couch.

"So Manuel," he said, pouring himself a generous glass of whisky, "have you ever thought about conversion?"

I stared at him. "Conversion?"

"To Judaism."

I was too shocked to say anything. Alma sipped her tea quietly next to me.

"I guess that's a no," Rabbi Uri laughed.

"I'm a practicing Catholic," I said. "I have thought seriously about a career in the church."

"This might surprise you," he said, "but practicing Catholics have a lot in common with observant Jews. Or maybe that would not surprise you." He smiled at Alma. "It's okay, I'm just asking. Judaism doesn't actively encourage conversion. We believe that every nation has its place in the world."

My shoulders relaxed a little in relief. "Well... I had never really thought about it before."

"So, what's inspiring you to become a priest?" Rabbi Uri asked. He raised his glass. *"L'chaim."* He closed his eyes in concentration and chanted something else in Hebrew. Alma answered "Amen," and he took a sip.

"Well..." I studied him for a moment. "My priest back in Granada was a very important figure in my life. He was like a father to me after my own father died, and I found a lot of comfort in his teachings. He especially helped me to develop a close and personal relationship with God. I looked up to him and wanted to be like him. He passed away last year."

"I'm sorry to hear that."

There was a pause. Rabbi Uri swirled his drink, watching me intently.

"Well, listen," he said finally, "I teach a class on the basics of Judaism on Sunday evenings. *En castellano.* I've had a few students who did end up converting, but most are just there to satisfy their curiosity. It's free, and you are welcome to come if it interests you."

"I dunno, Rabbi, maybe if it would earn him some college credit..." Alma winked at me. "I've been telling him he should switch to my Judaic Studies minor."

Rabbi Uri laughed. "Well, I'm afraid I can't offer that. But it would certainly enrich the 'Judeo' part of your Judeo-Christian education, if you do decide to go to seminary."

"I appreciate the offer," I said slowly. "I will think about it."

# Míriam

Míriam and León tiptoed through the streets, down past the butcher's house and toward the southern wall of the fortress, trying to stay in shadows. The secret passageway was a tunnel in the fortress wall, accessible through a loose stone next to the Benyemini family's house. León shimmied the stone out of place, then looked back at Míriam.

"I'll go through ahead of you," he whispered. "It's not far. But remember to pull the stone back into place. There's a rope on the other side."

Míriam nodded and he crawled into the tunnel. She waited a few seconds, then glanced back at the *judería* one last time and followed him in.

The rocks were moist and slippery with moss and mud. She fumbled around in the pitch black for the rope León had mentioned, and eventually managed to find it, throwing her weight forward to pull the rock back into place. She slipped around, trying to find something to brace herself against, and finally she managed to get the stone to close behind her. The air was heavy in the tunnel, and the darkness was so thick that it reminded her of the story of the ninth plague in Egypt, when the darkness was so heavy that the Egyptians could not move around in it. She heard León's boots scraping against the stones up ahead and followed the sound, using the narrow walls to guide her forward.

Finally she saw an opening clear in front of her as León's shadow moved out of the way. The half-moon glowed up ahead and the stars were bright; moonlight reflected off the clouds and outlined the silhouettes of the distant mountains. She stepped out of the crevice in the rock, and León shoved the stone back in place. They were at the base of the fortress wall now, with the dark hill stretching treacherously below them. It had been years since Miriam had left the *judería*, and she had never done so at night. She swallowed. The slope looked very, very steep.

"Keep close to the wall," León whispered. "There are guards up on top, but they're less likely to see us if they have to look straight down."

"Which way?" Miriam whispered.

León gestured and she followed. She stepped very carefully, gripping the wall as she walked, terrified she would lose her balance and tumble down the hill.

"How on earth are we going to climb down in the dark?" she hissed.

"We'll walk along the side of the road. It's not as steep there."

They turned downhill when the road came into sight, and used the cover of the bordering trees to start descending the hill. It was less steep, but Miriam still walked very slowly, carefully setting one foot down and making sure it was steady before taking the next step. The night air was cold and crisp, the rocks still damp from a recent rainfall, and several times Miriam almost lost her balance and slipped on them. It was very dark under the trees, and she could only just make out León's silhouette in front of her.

After what felt like hours, they finally reached the base of the hill. Miriam was very relieved to feel level ground beneath her. León hesitated, and turned his head slowly this way and that.

"Don't you know the way?" Miriam whispered.

"Shh." León lifted a finger to his lips and cupped his other hand to his ear. Miriam held her breath, listening. All she heard was crickets chirping and leaves rustling in the breeze. León started walking through the trees, stopping every few seconds to listen. Miriam followed in anxious perplexity. After a few starts and stops, he began to stride more confidently, apparently having heard what he'd been listening for. Eventually, Míriam spotted the gleam of a horse's coat in the moonlight, and heard what León had heard: the stomp of fidgeting hooves. León breathed a sigh of relief.

"Praise God, he's still here," he muttered, and ran toward the horse, checking the rope that tied him to a tree.

He stopped and turned to Míriam.

"My apologies, *señorita*. There is only one horse and we both must ride."

Míriam froze. This was definitely not allowed. Wandering around at night with a man—not to mention a non-Jewish man—was problematic enough. But riding behind him on a horse?

"I can't do that, Don León."

"Your father said you'd say that. And he told me to tell you that it's... I'm trying to remember the Hebrew phrase he used. *Piku... pikua...*"

"*Pikuach nefesh?*" Míriam asked.

"Yes, I think so."

Míriam sighed.

"What does it mean?"

"It refers to a situation where someone is in mortal danger, and we are allowed to transgress most commandments to save a life."

"Well, that would seem to apply here." He had reached the horse now, a large, dark gelding. Míriam looked up at him, her stomach clenching. She had never been this close to a horse, and this one loomed above her. She had no idea how she was meant to get on top of him.

León knelt on the ground. "I would find something for you to stand on," he said, "but we just don't have time. You'll have to use my shoulders."

Míriam took a step back, shocked at the very suggestion. "Climb on your shoulders?!"

"I apologize again. I know this is most unseemly."

"You are out of your mind," she mumbled.

"We are in grave danger, *señorita*." His voice sounded a little agitated. "I did not put my life at risk to argue with you about propriety."

Miriam felt a pang of guilt. In her panic about her situation, she hadn't even given a thought to how much León was risking by bringing her to her father.

"Listen," she said, trying to keep her voice calm, "I'm not really supposed to touch you. At all."

"Because I'm not Jewish?" She could barely make out his face, but his voice sounded a little sharp.

"No," she said, a little more defensive than she had wanted to sound. "Because you're a man."

"Ah." He paused. "Well, I'm afraid it's going to be impossible to follow that rule under the circumstances."

"This entire thing is beyond scandalous—but I don't have a choice, do I?"

"I will keep my head down until you have arranged yourself on top. Tell me when you are ready." He bent forward again.

Miriam swallowed, then put a shaking foot on his shoulder. She stepped up and then scrambled onto the back of the horse, nearly losing her balance and falling back onto León. Finally, she managed to gain her balance, and she arranged her skirts as modestly as she could.

"Ready," she said.

León stood, brushing the dirt from his knees and shoulders, and took hold of the horse's mane. He placed his foot in the stirrup and hoisted himself up, then awkwardly brought his other leg over, trying not to kick Miriam in the process.

"Try and find something to hold on to," he said. "And if it has to be me, I believe *pikuach nefesh* would still apply."

It took her about two of the horse's steps to realize that holding onto León was her only safe option. She gasped and clutched León's waist, and as the horse picked up speed she found herself clinging to him for dear life. She felt very uncomfortable in every imaginable way, but she breathed deeply and thought of her father as they galloped toward the outskirts of Lorca.

# Alma

Classes began the following week, and things started to move into their own rhythm. Manuel and I were studying in different tracks, so we rarely saw each other in class. I was focusing on Spanish for Dummies, as I referred to it, and Manuel was taking classes in Spanish about literature and culture and all sorts of other, far more interesting stuff. Olivia was in most of his classes, and for some reason this made me a little uncomfortable.

On Tuesday we had a meeting scheduled with the Madrid supervisor for the Spanish Heritage Project. I found Manuel already sitting in the classroom, ignoring Zoe and Nicole's giggling and thumbing through a large pile of papers in front of him. I smiled and slapped my own pile of documents on the desk next to his. He looked up, smiled in greeting, and then looked at my papers.

"Are those your family records? Can I see?"

"Only if I can see yours." We swapped piles and examined each other's records.

"What are these?" Manuel asked.

"*Ketubot.* Jewish marriage contracts. It was the craziest thing— I stumbled across them completely by accident in the storage room of my grandmother's store this summer. She had never told me about them! Can you believe it?"

"Even though she knew you were about to do this research? How did she expect you to make any progress?"

"She had the family trees copied down somewhere, so it's not like we didn't have the information. But..." I sighed. "She has this really weird memory issue. She completely forgot that they existed."

"Well... I think memory issues are fairly common in grandmothers..."

"Yes, but you don't know her. She's sharp as a razor. She always seems totally 'with it'. But then there are these completely random things that will just disappear from her memory. Like we'll be hanging out in the living room and she'll start talking to my grandfather, who's been dead for ten years, and she'll get all annoyed that he's not answering her, and I have to remind her that he's gone. And then it'll all come back to her and it'll be like she never forgot. It's like someone just pulled a chip from her brain containing that information and I have to stick it back in there and reboot it. I feel like with other old people, it's like they're in this kind of fog, where details sort of melt in and out of reality, and you can tell over the course of the conversation that something's not right. But with her... it's just weird."

Manuel watched me thoughtfully, and finally said, "I imagine it adds an element of urgency to the research, too. If she forgot that these documents existed, what else might she have forgotten... and what else might she forget?"

I swallowed. "Yeah. There's that."

Something gold glinted in the sun from the window and caught my eye. I looked at Manuel's shirt and realized I was staring right at a gold crucifix. I recoiled a little. He followed my gaze.

"Ah, this." He studied me. "Does it offend you? I could put it under my shirt."

"No... no, it's fine." I wasn't entirely sure about that, though; I had always felt a squirming discomfort around Christian symbols. But it did remind me of something else.

"Oh, and I should show you!" I reached around my own neck and pulled the ring my grandmother had given me out of my shirt. I held it out to him with the chain still on my neck, and he leaned in to examine it.

"Looks like a signet ring. Where did you get it?" He was a little too close and it was making my heart pound, but I waited for him to pull back before taking the ring and tucking it back into my shirt.

"My grandmother gave this to me along with the records," I said. "She said it's been passed down through our family since my ancestors left Spain. Grandma's grandmother told her that it belonged to a Christian family that helped my ancestors escape the Inquisition, and that she wanted her to find the descendants of that family and give the ring back to them."

"That's a fascinating story," said Manuel. "But the chances of finding any records of a thing like this, much less the descendants themselves..."

"Yeah, that's exactly what I said." I glanced at my watch. "Where's the professor? Wasn't the meeting supposed to start at ten?"

"Welcome to Spain," Manuel smiled.

As if on cue, a woman with shoulder-length salt-and-pepper hair strode into the classroom. She had a thin frame, but there was a very solid quality to her presence. *"Buenos días,"* she said, setting her briefcase firmly on the table at the front of the room. "I am Professor Paula García."

She took about fifteen minutes to explain how the program was going to work. She gave us a general idea of how things worked at the National Historical Archive, where we'd be working at first to get a feel for researching historical documents. She then proceeded to give us a brief introduction to the other main historical archives in Spain. She explained that once we really got started, many of us might have to take trips to other archives across the country, depending on the origins of our families.

"I have to tell you," she said, surveying us all sternly. "This is an extremely ambitious project for a group of undergraduates. Professor Rodriguez did not have an easy time convincing me to take this on." She began packing up her briefcase. "I hope you are prepared to work hard."

Manuel and I exchanged an apprehensive look as she left the classroom.

---

The next day we all met at the Archivo Histórico Nacional. I was so excited I could hardly walk straight as we crossed the lawn toward the old brick building with the elegant gray arch above its entrance. Manuel and I paused by the door, looking up at the building's façade as the other students streamed past us. We looked at each other.

"Well, here we go," Manuel said, pulling the door open and looking at me expectantly. But I was busy digging through my backpack. "What are you doing?"

"Aha!" I pulled out my video camera.

"*Dios mío,*" Manuel muttered and quickly walked through the door.

"No no no! Get back here! I want to film you walking in!"

Manuel ignored me and disappeared into the lobby. I rolled my eyes and turned on the camera.

"We are about to enter the Archivo Histórico Nacional building," I told the camera. I pulled the door back open and walked in slowly, filming all the way. "And there..." I zoomed in on Manuel, who was waiting for me with a sour look. "Is Mister I Hate Cameras, who ran in ahead before I could properly record this historical moment." I turned off the camera.

"One of these days I am going to steal that thing from you and throw it out a window," Manuel grumbled at me.

Professor García was waiting for us in an armchair in the lobby. She introduced us to the head archivist, and then led us up the stairs to a heavy metal door. She pulled it open and the first thing I noticed was the scent of old paper, ink, and dust. Good thing I'd brought my inhaler! Shelves stretched in front of us in dimly lit rows, books and files stacked floor to ceiling. I charged forward, but Professor García grabbed my arm firmly and yanked me away from the doorway.

"*Señorita!*" she scolded. "No one but authorized staff is allowed in there."

She released my arm from her iron grip. I rubbed my arm, mouthing "Ow" to Zoe as the professor pulled the door closed.

After her tour of the building, she took us back to the lobby. We huddled around her as she gave us a quick explanation about the rules and policies of the archive. Then she excused us so she could sit with Lucas and Melissa to talk about their individual projects. The rest of us filed outside and set up camp on the steps, chatting. Well, everyone except Manuel. He was sitting off in a corner, staring out at the lawn, apparently deep in thought.

Andrea and Lorenzo were called in next, and then Zoe and Nicole. When it was just me and Manuel left waiting, I wandered over to where he sat, still daydreaming.

"Earth to Manuel."

He looked up at me, startled.

"What are you looking so pensive about?"

He looked flustered. "I... I don't know," he stammered.

I flopped down next to him and started chattering excitedly about our research and the archive and how amazing this was going to be and how I was so excited and nervous. He just watched my emphatic gesturing with amusement. At some point I noticed I'd been monologuing for about five minutes straight and skidded to a stop, studying him suspiciously.

"Are you actually even listening to a word I'm saying?"

He blinked in surprise. "Every one! Do I look uninterested?"

I shrugged. "I guess not. I'm used to people's eyes glazing over pretty quick when I start launching into my rambling monologues."

"I like your monologues."

"Alma? Manuel? Your turn," Nicole called from behind us. I sprang up from the step and offered my hand to help Manuel up. He looked at me uncertainly.

"What, it's not manly to be helped up by a girl?" I teased.

"Your gender has nothing to do with it," he said, ignoring my hand and standing up. "You're maybe half my size."

"Hmph! I'm small, but tough!"

He just laughed.

We sat next to Professor García on the leather armchairs in the lobby and started off with Manuel's family. When Manuel handed her the oldest document he had, her eyebrows shot up. It was a set of church records from the archdiocese of Granada, listing marriages, baptisms, and deaths. The earliest date associated with an Aguilar was a wedding in 1502; there were also several deaths and a few baptisms listed over the following twenty years.

"Your father saved you a lot of work," she said. "The problem is, we don't have any idea where to look for the previous generation."

Manuel's brow furrowed. "Why not?"

"Granada was under Moorish rule until 1492. This wedding was only ten years after that, and the groom must have been at least a teenager. Do the math. He was probably not born in Granada." She handed the pages back to him. "Furthermore, his mother's name is not mentioned. That means she probably died somewhere else. My guess is that the family moved to Granada shortly after the conquest," she said. "There are a few reasons they may have chosen to do that, but if your father was right and they were an important—maybe even noble—family, there's a very good chance that they were running away from something."

"That something being the Inquisition?" I asked.

"Could very well be. There are no noble titles here, so if they were noblemen before they moved to Granada, the Inquisition is a good explanation. We know that it took quite a while before the Inquisition really became active in Granada, and it was a good refuge for people who wanted to start over."

"So what you want to say is that you think they were stripped of their titles and importance by the Inquisition and then came to Granada to start over?" Manuel asked.

"That's my theory, based on what you have told me; but remember that we have no proof at all of your father's claim that your family was important once. And we have no way of knowing why they came to Granada. The only thing I'm confident about is that they moved there sometime between 1492 and 1502."

"So you think we should search the Inquisition records for their names?"

Professor García sighed. "Well…yes, but it's not that simple. We should not rule out other types of documents either. Inquisition records are easier because they are better catalogued, but we have no idea where your ancestors were before they moved to Granada. We could focus in on the tribunals in the surrounding districts, but there are so many of them. Not to mention that our chances of recovering them are greatly reduced the older they are, since many archives were destroyed in the wars over the years. How are you at reading fifteenth-century Castilian script, Manuel?"

He shrugged.

"Oh, don't be so modest." I elbowed him and turned to Professor García. "He's a natural. Professor Rodriguez was having kittens over him. Why do you think I snatched him up as my research partner?"

"I'm pretty good at identifying letters in different hands," Manuel admitted.

"Excellent. Between that and your Spanish you will probably need a lot less of my help than Alma will."

"Speaking of which," I said pointedly.

"Right." She nodded and I slid the *ketubot* toward her. Her eyebrows shot up again. "Hebrew calligraphy. Interesting. *Ketubas?*" she asked, eyeing me over her glasses. I nodded, impressed.

"Do you read Aramaic?" I asked.

"No, do you?"

"Yeah. That is... I can read the script and get a general idea of what it means, at least the relevant parts. Should I translate them for you?"

"Please do."

I pulled out the notebook with the family tree I'd drawn with Grandma, and the list of questions we wanted to answer, and went over them with Professor García. When I was done, she sighed and removed her glasses.

"I'm sorry to say this," she began, and my heart began to sink. "I am even less hopeful about your project." She pulled the oldest *ketuba* before her and put her glasses back on, surveying the document. "The only clue we have about where to search is the last name de Carmona, which implies that they were originally from Carmona or nearby. But that's not necessarily true, because people moved around a lot in those days, especially Jews... and what makes it even more complicated is that the Jews were expelled from that area in 1483, nine years before the Alhambra Decree. Now, this expulsion was not strictly enforced, but it still makes your grandmother's story all the more unlikely, because many of the Jews of Andalusia went straight to the Maghreb at that time. In all likelihood, your family left Spain before the Inquisition really got started."

I stared at the floor, trying to hold back a frown.

"However," she went on, "Carmona is close to Sevilla, where

the first *auto-da-fé* happened in 1481, two years before that expulsion—so it's not entirely impossible that they had a run-in with the Inquisition before they left. But...there's another problem."

I pursed my lips. "What's that?"

"Your grandmother also claims that your ancestors never converted. The Inquisition's authority was really only over Christians. The only reason a Jew might be investigated by the Inquisition is if he was involved in helping a Christian in Judaizing, or something like that. And when that did happen...who knows how carefully they followed protocol? They may not have bothered keeping records of it, or holding a proper trial. Often they passed such cases to the local authorities to deal with. And that's without getting into the same issue we have with Manuel's records: the fact that it is very rare to find records from before the sixteenth century."

I sighed and ran my hand through my hair. "So basically you're saying that we're both on wild goose chases here."

Professor García smiled. "This is often the case with things like this; it's why I was so skeptical about Professor Rodriguez's idea for the project in the first place. Still, difficult is not the same as impossible—I do think it's worth giving it a try. I have a few ideas about places we might want to start." She paused, eyeing the two of us, her eyes lingering on Manuel's crucifix. "And you know... a little prayer can't hurt."

---

"So how's the new job?" I asked Mimi, clenching my phone between my shoulder and my ear as I stuffed clean laundry into my wardrobe. It was a beat-up old thing with scratches criss-crossing the varnish, and one of the doors hung off the hinge at a weird angle, making it hard to close.

"Really demanding," she answered. "But really interesting too. You should see how Abba's chest puffs out whenever he tells someone I just became the youngest attorney at Meyer & Gold. Ima flits around at the *shul kiddush* telling anyone who's willing to listen."

"If I were your mother, I'd do the same thing," I said. "Between the doctor and the hot-shot lawyer, she's living every Jewish mother's dream."

I didn't ask her if Ima was flitting around at *kiddush* boasting about her daughter in Madrid who was researching her family history. I knew the answer.

I swallowed the lump in my throat.

"What about you?" Mimi asked. "Met any cute Jewish guys yet?"

"How about, 'How's your research going? Find anything totally amazing that will blow my mind about my own ancestry?'" I retorted.

"Come on, Alma. You only just started. I know what research is like."

"How's Aryeh?"

"Good," she said, and there was a pause.

I shut the door to the wardrobe as best I could and sat on my bed.

"So..." she continued, "I did want to talk to you about something. You know we've been pretty serious for a while, and we're starting to talk about...the next step."

"Mimi, don't you *dare* get engaged while I'm in Spain!" I jumped off the bed, suddenly filled with giddy excitement.

"Look, Alma...we both just started steady jobs, we've been dating for almost a year...the time is right. I don't want to have to wait until the summer just to get engaged. We won't get married until September at least."

I paced back and forth. "Great. This is sure to seal my fate as the black sheep forever. 'Where's Alma in the engagement photos?' 'Oh, you know, off in Spain...'"

"I love you dearly, sis, and I hate to break it to you, but this isn't about you."

I sighed. "I know, I know. I'm just sad that I won't be there to celebrate with you."

"You'll be here for the henna party and the wedding. You'll be my maid of honor."

"What are you talking about? Jews don't have maids of honor."

"A minor technicality!" Mimi laughed.

"You're such a lawyer."

"I just wanted to tell you…"

"I know. I appreciate it. And I better not be the last one to hear about it when he proposes. I don't care if it's four in the morning here when it happens."

"Noted," Mimi said, and there was a smile in her voice. "I gotta go. My lunch break is over. Love you, sis."

"Love you too. Give everyone kisses for me."

"I will."

# Manuel

For reasons not entirely clear to me, Alma insisted that I accompany her to Plaza Mayor after one of our Tuesday mornings at the National Historical Archive. I tried to convince her that there was nothing to see there except flocks of tourists, but she didn't care. So we took the bus and entered the plaza through one of the brick archways. As I had predicted, the place was swarming with people; and as we pushed our way through, I noticed that it was lined with little stands selling paintings, sculptures, jewelry, and, of course, corny souvenirs. I looked up, taking in the red brick walls, the columns, and the cobblestones, but Alma dragged me right into the center of all the activity, pointing out bizarre trinkets for sale and people speaking languages neither of us recognized. Finally she stopped at one of the souvenir stands. My eyes widened as she scooped up an entire box of refrigerator magnets with pictures of Madrid and proceeded to buy it.

"What are you doing, setting up your own tourist shop?" I asked.

She gave me a sour look over her glasses.

"I told you I come from a huge family. This will probably cover my aunts, uncles, and cousins, maybe some of my friends from Albany." She shoved it into my arms. "Here, put it in your backpack. It won't fit in mine." She turned away from the stand, squinting across the plaza at the area under the porticoes. "Is there a café there? Let's go sit down."

We found a comparatively quiet table and sat down for coffee—or at least I did. Alma ordered orange juice, muttering something about wishing she could have had coffee instead; and when her glass of juice arrived she glared at it accusingly.

"Is it just me, or is this seriously depressing?" she sighed.

"What's depressing?" I asked. "The fact that you can't drink coffee here?"

"Well...that too." She narrowed her eyes at me. "Seriously—why do you Spaniards have to put pig in everything?"

I peered into my cup in mock suspicion. "I don't see any pigs in here."

"Lard. I was told that I can't drink the milk in this godforsaken country because you put lard in there to make it creamier. Why would you do that? What is it with you people and pigs?"

"Why not just drink it black?"

She gave me a withering look. "Why not just drink mud?"

I took a slow sip. "Why are you Jews so hysterical about food?"

"Says the vegetarian," Alma shot back, taking a sip of her juice while I wondered what my vegetarianism had to do with anything. "Anyway. I was talking about our wild-goose-chase research projects, not the coffee."

"Ah, that." I shrugged. "I don't know if it's depressing, but it's definitely frustrating. It takes forever to work through those documents...and it could all be for nothing."

"I don't even want to imagine what it would be like without your paleographical genius. Seriously. I'd never make any headway at all on my own."

"That's not true," I insisted. "You did remarkably well by yourself on that contract you were looking at today."

She just scowled at me.

"What?"

"Don't even try," she said.

There was a pause. I found myself watching the hand she was resting next to her glass, realizing that I wanted to put mine on it. Would that be appropriate?

I figured it was a good time to change the subject. "Why are you Jews so paranoid about food, anyway?" I asked, sipping my coffee. "I may be a vegetarian, but I don't take my pots to a molecular biologist to determine whether they had ever come in contact with a product that may or may not have been derived from an animal."

"Take it up with the Big Guy, not with me," Alma said, pointing at arched ceiling above us.

"Where does it say in the Bible that you can't eat from a pot that once cooked something non-kosher?"

"I told you, the Bible's not the whole Torah. God gave us an oral tradition as well, passed down by the rabbis for more than 2,000 years."

"Or so you claim."

"Hey." Alma raised an eyebrow at me. "Wasn't it your buddy Jesus who said, 'Let he who is without sin cast the first stone'? You Christians also claim lots of things that are a far cry from what God said in the Old Testament."

"Well…" I smiled wryly. "That's why there's a New Testament."

"Or so you claim."

"You just quoted it, no?"

We regarded each other for a moment, our smiles fading a little.

"You know," Alma blurted. "You're gonna miss me when you get to Heaven."

I blinked at her. "What?"

"You're gonna miss me." She was still smiling, but there was a sting in her voice. "At least the way I understand it, according to your stuff, I can be a completely wonderful and righteous and kind human being, but without that little dunk you took as a baby, and without accepting your buddy Jesus as my so-called savior, I'm headed straight for Hell."

I sat in silence for a few moments. I regarded Alma, and I

couldn't help thinking, *Do I really believe that she deserves eternal damnation because she is a believing Jew?*

"And in case you're wondering," she added, "we Jews believe that non-Jews are just as eligible for the afterlife as we are. But whatever."

There was an awkward silence. Alma examined her nails.

"Well," I said, trying to gather my thoughts. "At least maybe that means you won't miss me in your Heaven?"

Alma gave me a wry smile. "Here's hoping we Jews are right, then, huh?"

"Maybe you should consider being baptized, just to make sure we're both covered."

I meant it as a joke, but I should have realized by that point that Alma was not in the mood for it. Her brow furrowed in anger and she shoved her chair back from the table.

"Don't even joke about that, Manuel," she growled. She jabbed her finger toward the plaza. "Don't you even realize where we are? This is Plaza Mayor. Do you have any idea how many Jews were burned alive—*right*—*there*—because someone thought they should *consider being baptized?*"

I felt the blood drain from my face. "Alma, please, I'm sorry, I was joking...it was a stupid joke. I'm sorry. Of course I did not mean it."

Alma took a deep breath and pulled her chair back in, waving away my apology. "No...no...it's okay...I'm sorry...I'm being oversensitive." She cleared her throat and took a gulp of juice. "I'm just frustrated about the research." She looked out through the gray columns, scowling at the tourists who were milling around the stands in the center of the plaza, laughing and eating ice cream. "It's bad enough that they turned this square into some kind of carnival. A statue of King Phillip? Seriously? That's all you people have to say about the history of this horrible place?"

I stared down at what was left of my coffee. I didn't like the feeling that was stirring in my chest, the doubts that were filling my mind, thinking about Heaven and Hell and Alma. I looked up, feeling a surge of anger myself.

"You know, it's curious. It's not okay for me to joke about you converting to Christianity, but it is okay for you to drag me to your synagogue and for your rabbi to talk to *me* about conversion to Judaism?"

Alma looked up from her juice, her eyes wide. "Manuel..."

"No, really, there's a double standard. You expect me to respect your faith, admire it even, immerse myself in it—but you don't respect mine. You recoil from it."

"Manuel..." Alma's eyes were welling with tears. "I respect you and your faith. I took you to Chabad because I thought you were interested..."

"Did you *ask* me if I was interested? Do you care the slightest bit about the struggle I am having to reconcile my interest in Judaism with my devotion to the Church? All you want is for me to think and feel like you do." I stood up, grabbed my backpack and tossed a few Euros on the table to pay for my coffee. "Keep the change," I told her and stalked out of the plaza.

# Míriam

The ride was not long, but to Míriam it felt like an eternity. Her arms were sore from holding onto León, her legs and seat were sore from holding onto the horse and bouncing up and down on his back, and her back ached from the effort of trying not to lean against León as she held on for dear life. She had never experienced movement at this kind of speed. She wanted to ask León how much further there was to go, but she could hardly breathe.

Finally, León eased back on the reins and the horse slowed to a trot. Míriam winced at the pain in her lower body as the bouncing in the saddle became more pronounced, but at least they were no longer moving so terrifyingly fast. She looked up. She couldn't see much in the dark, but there were torches up ahead, casting light on an arched wooden gate set into a high stuccoed wall. When they reached it, León very carefully hoisted himself off the horse, narrowly avoiding kicking Míriam in the process. He pulled a key from his robe and fiddled with the lock, then slowly swung the gate open, trying not to let it creak too loudly. As he led the horse through, Míriam could make out the silhouette of a large building across the courtyard that stretched in front of them.

"Praise God," came a voice from beside them, making Míriam jump. She turned to look. From what she could make out in the gloom, it was an older man dressed much like León, his hair and beard neatly trimmed, who had been waiting next to the gate. He took a few steps toward them. "Come, let's get you down and go inside quickly."

León moved to the horse's side and offered Míriam a hand. She ignored it, struggling to get off the horse without help—and, predictably, she slipped. She gasped and fell straight into León's arms.

"Whoa," he said. "Careful." He steadied her on her feet.

"Thank you," she said, stepping back a little too quickly and almost walking into the horse. She looked up at León, thinking about their tense conversation under the trees, and her moment of realization that he had risked his life for her sake. He walked around the gelding, grabbing the reins and patting him on his neck, which gleamed with sweat in the moonlight. "No, truly, León. Thank you." He turned to look at her, and gave her a nod.

"It was an honor, *señorita*."

As she watched him lead the horse away, she thought about how gracious he was to say that—especially after all the trouble she had given him. She wondered if he was just being gentlemanly, or if he actually meant it.

"Come with me, *señorita*," the other man said. "I will take you to your father and then we will explain everything."

She followed him through the courtyard and into the building. The heavy wooden doors opened up to what seemed like a vast reception hall. There were only a few small lamps lit near the windows, so it was hard to see much, but the echoes of their footsteps gave the impression of a high ceiling. The man led her to a stone staircase in one corner of the room, and they ascended in silence to the second floor. Down a dark hallway was a narrower wooden staircase leading up into what appeared to be one of the house's towers. These steps led to a small landing with a closed door to the right. The man knocked on the door in an odd rhythm, and after a few moments Míriam heard a bolt slide. The door opened, and standing behind it was her father.

"Papa!" Míriam gasped and fell into his arms.

"Míriam," he breathed, holding her as she began to cry in relief.

"Don't cry, it's all right…I'm all right."

She pulled away, wiping her eyes. "What happened? How did you know to come here? I sent Yehuda to warn you but he said he couldn't find you…"

Abraham pulled back in astonishment. "How did you know to send someone to warn me?"

"An Inquisition officer came to our house…was it this afternoon? I've completely lost my sense of time. He took one of our wine barrels."

Abraham exchanged a glance with the man standing behind her. Míriam turned to look at the man, only now realizing who he must be.

"I did not get a chance to introduce myself," he said. "Though you probably guessed that I am Tomás."

"So pleased to meet you, Don Tomás." Míriam gave a curtsy. "We are greatly indebted to you."

"We were together at the market today," Don Tomás said, "and someone told your father that Sánchez had been arrested. I had never seen your father look so white! I insisted that he tell me what was wrong, and he explained about the wine. We decided it would be safest for him to come and stay here while we wait to see if Sánchez implicates him and if the Inquisition decides to pursue the matter…"

"But from what you say, Míriam, it sounds like they are already gathering evidence against me." Abraham stepped back into the room and sank onto the bed.

"A barrel of wine is not exactly evidence," Don Tomás said.

"Of course it is," Abraham responded. "They'll be able to see very plainly that it was the same type of barrel, and they should be able to tell by the taste that it's the same wine."

"Maybe it wasn't evidence against you, but against Sánchez?" Míriam offered. "To prove that it was kosher wine he was drinking. After all…the Inquisition isn't supposed to pursue Jews."

Abraham and Don Tomás exchanged glances.

"The Inquisition has been known to try Jews who are accused of enticing a Christian back to Jewish practice," Don Tomás said quietly. "Your fate now lies in the hands of Sánchez and his ability to hold his tongue during the interrogations." He paused. "And I'm afraid our Inquisitor is particularly talented at loosening tongues."

Abraham sighed. "It is almost dawn," he said, "and we are both exhausted. We should sleep now, and talk more when we are rested."

"Yes." Don Tomás put a hand on his friend's shoulder. "I hope to gather more information about Sánchez's interrogation by the end of the day."

Abraham rose from the bed and embraced Don Tomás. "Please give your son my profoundest thanks for bringing my daughter here safely."

"I will. Have a good rest." Don Tomás closed the door, and Abraham slid the bolt shut behind him. He turned to Míriam.

"Why is he doing this?" she whispered. "He is risking his life and his family's lives for us. Is he a *converso?*"

"No," said Abraham. "Just a good Christian."

"Isn't a good Christian the opposite of someone who defies the Inquisition…?"

"Not according to Don Tomás's beliefs." He held her at arm's length. A grayish glow was filtering through the curtains covering the window, and she could see her father's eyes now, tired, bloodshot, and sad. "Míriam…I wanted to tell you that I'm sorry. I don't think I truly understood how right you were until I sat here waiting for León to bring you…not knowing what might become of you, all alone in the *judería* and then sneaking down the mountainside in the dead of night with a stranger. And now both of us are in danger, and it's all my fault." A tear dripped down his cheek.

Míriam sighed and put her arms around him again. "I know why you did it, Papa. You love God and you love the Jewish people and those loves come before anything else."

"No, my girl. Not before family. I should have realized that."

"Still—you are a good man, Papa. A righteous man. I hope to raise my sons to be like you one day."

"May it be His will."

They stood there together for a few moments, and then Abraham pulled back, wiping his face.

"You must be exhausted. There is a bed for you right there. We should sleep now. When we wake, there will be plenty of time to talk."

When Miriam awoke, the sunlight was already streaming brightly through the window. It took a while for her eyes to adjust to the light; she was not used to waking when it was already full daylight.

She cast a look at her surroundings. The room was small and simple, with a slanted roof, white plaster walls, and a plain, worn rug on the floor. She looked over at her father's bed. He was sitting up, hunched over a small pile of parchment. She smiled. *It's a good thing he carries some of his manuscripts with him everywhere. At least he has some Torah to study.*

He noticed her and looked up from the page. His eyes crinkled as he smiled.

"Good…morning? I suppose it might still be morning," he said.

"Good morning, Papa." She stretched and sat up. "Any news?"

"No. I assume they'll be up to bring us food soon. Well…I certainly hope so. Yom Kippur is tonight."

Miriam's eyes widened. "Oh, yes. I had completely forgotten about Yom Kippur." Her heart sank as she thought about the *judería*…all the men going to bathe in the *mikveh*, the ritual bath for purification…the community wondering what had happened to their cantor and his daughter, who had both vanished overnight. She thought of Hanna Guerson and her children, and how worried and confused they all must be.

"You look troubled, Míriam."

She gave her father a sad smile. "I was just thinking…things are going to be very different this Yom Kippur."

Don Tomás did eventually come upstairs to bring food, which he had cooked himself in a new ceramic pot he had bought for the purpose. Míriam cast an uncertain look at her father as she accepted the bowl. Yes, the new pot solved the problem of non-kosher utensils, but there was a rabbinic restriction prohibiting Jews from eating food cooked by non-Jews.

Abraham accepted his bowl without a word. Míriam watched him lift the bowl to his mouth, and then turned to her own porridge and began to eat. There was, after all, the principle of *pikuach nefesh*. They had to eat to live, and they didn't really have any other options. At least this was preferable, according to the complex hierarchy of Jewish prohibitions, to eating food cooked with non-kosher utensils or ingredients.

Unfortunately, Don Tomás had no news to share. He had, however, brought a pair of beeswax candles for Míriam to light for the holiday. Míriam took them in awe; she usually used simple oil lamps for this purpose, and had never seen candles so smooth and fragrant. Don Tomás warned her to light them in the corner of the room so the light wouldn't show through the window, and then he left. Míriam and her father ate, talked a little, studied a little, and did a lot of staring at the four walls around them.

A little while before sunset, Míriam lit the candles in the corner, her heart heavy. Kindling the Sabbath or holiday lights always made her think of her mother, dressed in her Sabbath finery, the reflection of the flames flickering in pale green eyes so much like her own.

"One light for *shamor,* one for *zachor,*" her mother's voice echoed in her head. "Corresponding to the two different versions of the fourth commandment: '*Keep the Sabbath day holy...*' and '*Remember the Sabbath day in its holiness...*'" She remembered her mother pointing to the lights that shone brightly through the window of their old house in Seville. "Remember: for the past. For our mothers and our mothers' mothers, the generations of Jewish women who lovingly kept the Sabbath, sacrificing everything—sometimes their own lives—to pass it down to us. Keep: for the future. For our daughters, and our daughters' daughters, who will someday kindle the Sabbath lights and think of us, and how much we sacrificed to keep this sign of the eternal love between us and God."

Then her mother would place her hands on Miriam's head and bless her with the traditional blessing that parents gave their daughters every Sabbath: *May God make you like Sarah, Rebecca, Rachel, and Leah...may God bless you and guard you...may God shine His countenance upon you and be gracious to you...may God lift His countenance to you and give you peace.*

Miriam's lip quivered as she stood up, watching the shadows flicker against the wall.

Abraham saw the expression on her face in the candlelight.

"What's wrong?" he asked.

Miriam shook her head. "It's just...I think...Mama would be so sad to see me hiding them like this."

Saying the words out loud made the pain that much more real, and a wave of overwhelming sadness overtook her. She sank onto the bed. Her father sat next to her and put his arm around her, kissing her temple.

"You are right," Abraham said. He was silent for a long moment, and then said, very slowly, "I don't know if I ever told you this...but we were offered the choice to convert rather than leave Seville."

Míriam shrugged. "I knew that they usually offer that option."

Abraham shifted uncomfortably, pulling his arm away and smoothing out his tunic. "Yes, but you didn't know that I seriously considered accepting the offer."

Míriam turned and stared at him, her eyes wide.

"*You* considered converting to Christianity?!"

"Not sincerely, of course. But your mother…I don't know if you remember…she was already quite ill before we left. I was afraid she wouldn't survive the move." He took a deep breath and wiped away the tear that had forced its way out of his eye.

Míriam was too stunned to say anything.

"I thought that we could pretend, and live as many of our neighbors and friends had been forced to, keeping the Torah in secret. But your mother…she would hear none of it. She told me she would rather die on the way out of Andalusia than raise you as a *conversa*."

Míriam stared at the candles, her eyes unfocused.

"I have often asked myself if I should have refused to listen to her…" Abraham's voice cracked. He took another deep breath. "But only God knows what might have been had we stayed in Seville."

Míriam turned back to her father. "I think you made the right choice, Papa," she said gently. "She might very well have died in Seville anyway. And then I would be a false Christian *and* a half-orphan…"

He nodded. Míriam leaned her head on his shoulder.

"I think I understand a little better now why you gave the wine to Sánchez."

Abraham leaned his head against hers and sighed. "I would have hated to see your mother cooped up in here," he said. "She was always so full of energy, always doing things. She would go crazy. Well…before she got sick, at least." He looked toward the window, where the light was fading through the curtains. "Still…I can't help but wish she were with us now."

They sat in silence for a while, and then, Abraham began to chant the words of *Kol Nidrei* in a hushed voice. Miriam closed her eyes and listened, pretending she was in the women's section of their beloved and beautiful synagogue, and dwelt on the memories and emotions that made the presence of her mother almost tangible in the darkness.

# Alma

I sat on the couch in my apartment, starting and deleting a gazillion text messages to Manuel. Finally I dropped my phone into my lap in exasperation and started fingering the ring hanging around my neck.

*Well,* he *started it. That comment about Jews and food.*

*Um, no. That was in response to* my *comment about Spaniards and pigs.*

*...It was funny at the time.*

*His comment about getting baptized would have been funny too, if I hadn't been so cranky.*

My phone buzzed, interrupting my internal argument, and I jumped. It bounced in my lap and I fumbled around trying to catch it, then looked at the screen, hoping to see Manuel's name. It wasn't him. It was from my parents' landline back in Albany, but I had a feeling I knew who was calling.

"Hello?"

"Hi, sweetie!"

"Grandma!" I grinned.

"How are you? What time is it there?"

"Just about noon. What are you doing calling me at six in the morning?"

"Oh, you know me. Been up since five cooking."

"What are you making?"

"Stuffed vegetables."

"Mmmm. Red peppers?"

"And zucchini, and onions."

"This is making me hungry," I grinned. "I have to conserve my ground beef, though. You wouldn't believe how expensive the kosher meat is here."

"Oh, I believe it."

"I'm so jealous. Tell Ima to keep some in the freezer for me."

"I'm not making any promises. How's your research going?"

"Well..." I sighed, hating to give Grandma bad news. "We haven't made much progress yet. Been sifting through documents, trying to get some leads, but... I'm not very optimistic."

Grandma was silent for a moment. I felt my heart sink even further. There was nothing more painful than her disappointment.

"Well..." she said. "That's all right. Remember to enjoy the process. It's okay if you don't find anything."

"It's just really frustrating. I was really hoping. I feel like if I could just get my hands on the right file..."

"You've only been searching for a few weeks, right? What month is it now?"

"February."

"Right. You've got lots of time."

"I know... I know."

I struggled to find the words to explain the frustration I was feeling. My grandmother was being very kind about it, but nonetheless I couldn't help but feel that she had placed this huge weight on my shoulders and was expecting me to carry it alone. Spending Rosh Hashana with our family had reminded me yet again that I was the only one other than Grandma who cared deeply about our Sephardic heritage. Even Eliezer, the cousin who had become ultra-Orthodox, studied at an Ashkenazi yeshiva and spoke in Yiddishisms. Sephardi Jews are a small minority in the United States, and Moroccan Jews an even smaller minority of a minority; I'd never even met anyone else with roots in the Spanish part of Morocco. The once-rich culture of our family was fizzling out.

I couldn't help but feel that it was up to me to carry the torch—and it was a lot of pressure.

Not to mention that my grandmother's memory issues gave my research that much more urgency. What if she started to forget everything before I had any material to check against her memories?

There was a knock on the door.

"Look, Grandma, someone's at the door so I gotta go. But I'm really glad to hear from you, and we'll talk later, okay?"

"Okay, *mami*. Love you."

"Love you, Grandma. Bye." I hung up and jogged to the door, calling *"¡Un momento!"* I unlocked it and pulled it open. It was Manuel, his hands in the pockets of his jeans.

"Manuel!" I had completely forgotten about him.

"You better be careful with that Spanish," he said, peering at me from behind the stray curl that fell over his eye. "I'm going to start refusing to speak to you in English."

"Your mom would kill you." I regarded him for a moment. "Come on in." I stepped back. He came in and sat on the couch. I sat next to him and cleared my throat.

"Well—"

"I wanted—"

We both started at once, then both fell silent at once, then both broke into a smile and a giggle.

"I'm sorry," said Manuel. "I just..."

"It's okay. This interfaith friendship thing is hard. Especially since we both feel so deeply about our religions. We're gonna step on each other's proverbial toes every once in a while."

Manuel took a deep breath, looking like he wanted to say something; but he didn't, so I continued.

"I'm sorry too," I went on. "I hadn't realized at all that you were struggling with your interest in Judaism. I thought you were just shy and needed someone to kind of guide you to it. I didn't mean to be pushy about it."

"Well, there was no way for you to know, because I did not tell you. It's okay. I appreciate what you have done for me. I don't think you were pushy." He paused. "Well... not *too* pushy."

I snorted.

"I think I got defensive..." he said slowly, "because I was struggling with what you said about Heaven and Hell."

I almost interrupted to tell him about something I'd learned since our fight, but he looked like he was weighing his words carefully, so I let him go on.

"One of the things I am coming to understand about Judaism is that it is very much in your head," he said, tapping his head with his finger. "Very logical, very precise, a lot of thinking and calculation. I think Christianity puts more weight on what you believe, what you feel in your heart." He put his hand on his heart and looked at me. "So when your head has doubts, you are supposed to look to your heart, and say 'This is what I believe,' even when it does not make any sense."

"Well, there's plenty of that in Judaism too..." I said.

"I know, I know, it's not completely different that way. But I think our faiths address the subject of doubt differently. I was taught to see doubt as something that keeps us away from God, something to fight and suppress. But you see doubt as the beginning of a question. Jews seem to love nothing more than a good question."

I smiled. "Well, that's really a matter of dispute in Jewish philosophy..."

"That's exactly what I mean! Everything is a debate. Questioning is what you do best."

"Okay, let's say that's true, for the sake of argument. What's your point?"

"My point is that earlier today I experienced doubt about my faith, and instead of silencing it and saying 'If God says so, it must be this way, and it must be for the best...' I thought about it and said, 'It can't be that this is true. I don't want this to be true.'"

I watched him, not really sure what to make of all this. I found my hand absently drifting toward his shoulder, but I jerked it back, awkwardly tugging at my hair instead.

"How can it be that a kind, caring, devout woman like you would be condemned to eternal damnation?" he continued. "That makes no sense."

I felt my face get warm. "Well, gee..."

"I had struggled with that question before in the past—about unbaptized babies and such; and we believe that God has mercy on children, and we come up with other ways to squirm out of the problem; but the fact is that there really is no satisfying answer—at least not that I know of—in the Catholic faith. It's simply one of those things you live with, and I'm sure there are struggles like this in Judaism too. But it had not mattered to me nearly as much before I actually sat in front of someone I care about, who I believe absolutely does not deserve an eternity of suffering, and contemplated the question."

"So actually, about that..." I pulled out my phone, opened my browser app, and handed it to him. He gave me a confused look. "Have you ever heard of Karl Rahner and the concept of the 'Anonymous Christian'?"

"No..."

"That's the Wikipedia article. I did some Googling. Turns out there's a concept that seems to be pretty widely accepted in Catholicism, that people who live their lives according to the principles of God can be saved even if they don't specifically accept Jesus as savior. In general, Rahner talks about people who have never heard of the Gospel, and says that people who *have* heard of Jesus and don't accept him don't qualify; *but* there are theologians—Catholic ones—who argue that Jews are automatically considered 'Anonymous Christians' because we live according to God's word. Bottom line is, maybe you won't miss me in your Heaven after all."

Manuel stared at me incredulously.

"Of course," I went on, "I think it's a bit of a stretch, considering the basic foundations of your theology, but hey—I'm Jewish. What do I know?" I winked.

Manuel glanced from me to the phone and back again.

"I cannot believe that you looked this up," he said when he finally found his tongue.

"Why not? I was curious."

He rubbed his forehead, then handed my phone back to me. "Could you email that link to me?"

"Sure."

"I find it pretty ironic that my Jewish friend is the one trying to help me solve my Catholic religious dilemma."

"Well, I have to keep you on track for the priesthood, don't I?"

Manuel let out a hearty laugh.

"Will you be disappointed if I don't become a priest, Alma?"

"Oh totally! I was really looking forward to boasting to all my friends: 'Some of my best friends are Catholic—in fact I'm really tight with this one priest...'"

"Well...regardless...I decided that I'm going to Rabbi Uri's class this Sunday. Just to see if I like it."

I raised my eyebrows, surprised and feeling a kind of warm glow in my chest. "Boy, you're really dancing with the Devil now, aren't you?"

"You know, to be totally honest with you, when we first met I was a little afraid to be friends with you because I was afraid you would corrupt me."

"Little did you know..."

"Well…" He looked across the living room toward the window, resting his elbows on his knees. "I was right in a sense—knowing you has stirred up some doubt. But it was doubt that was there anyway—and I'm realizing now that ignoring it is not what is going to bring me closer to God." He looked back at me and smiled. "And maybe doubt is not all that bad a thing after all."

"You should give your priest a call," I said. He raised an eyebrow at me. "You might discover that there are different approaches to doubt in Christianity, too." I glanced at the clock on the wall. "Look, I've gotta go. Conversational Spanish for Complete Idiots, I believe the course is called." I stood up and picked up the backpack that had been resting by my feet. I paused and contemplated him. "Manuel…" I struggled to find the words. "I just want to say that I really admire your courage." I felt really dumb, but I kept going. "…In facing your doubt like that."

His eyes lit up. "And I really admire yours, in searching for a Christian answer to your own challenge against Christianity."

We smiled at each other warmly for a moment. Then I cleared my throat.

"You're welcome to stay here if you want," I said, "but I wouldn't advise it, because my roommates will be here soon, and as you may have noticed, they're…um…kind of into you."

He blinked at me, looking alarmed, and jumped off the couch to follow me out the door.

# Manuel

I found it very strange to be going from Sunday Mass at the local church to Rabbi Uri's class that evening. He greeted me warmly and introduced me to the other six students, two of whom were secular Jews who wanted to learn more about their religion, and the rest of whom were a random assortment of non-Jews like me. Then he began teaching about the concept of *kashrut*, taking us from the Biblical sources down through the rabbinical sources and into the practices of religious Jews today regarding the separation of milk and meat and the transference of *"ta'am"* —"taste" in Hebrew. It was interesting to see how Jewish law—*halacha*, which translates roughly as "the way"—worked, and the lecture gave me a much better understanding of Alma's situation at her apartment. Even with her lengthy explanation at the airport, I'd had no idea how involved these rules were. I found myself feeling admiration for her: it was clearly very difficult to keep these laws, but she was doing it and refusing to compromise.

As I left, Rabbi Uri asked if he would see me next week, and I said yes.

I even showed up at Alma's doorstep the following Friday afternoon in my suit. She opened the door and looked me up and down.

"You, um, realize that today isn't Sunday, right?"

"Really?!" I exclaimed in mock astonishment. "I was sure it was! And also that your apartment was my church. But I guess I must be mistaken, because you don't look very much like my priest."

"I should hope not!"

"Well, I suppose I'll just have to go to synagogue instead."

"Tough luck, huh."

"Fortunate for you, though," I said, stepping past her into the apartment. "We can't have you walking over to Chabad without your *Shabbos goy* to carry your passport."

"Um. Well, I did without for the past three weeks..." She winced. "And please, don't ever say '*Shabbos*'. You speaking in Hebrew with a Yiddish accent...my brain can't handle it."

Alma's apartment was always a mess: random clothes draped over the armrests of the couch, papers and books piled high on the dining room table, the sink constantly full of dishes. Olivia and Tessa were at the table hunched over some papers. My heart sank as they looked up and waved at me.

"Hey, look who cleans up nicely!" Olivia sang, and I did not like way she was surveying me. "You guys going on a date, or what?"

Alma rolled her eyes and shot me a commiserating look. "We're going to synagogue, Olivia. It's Friday night."

"Strange date," Tessa piped up.

"Aren't you Catholic?" Olivia asked, squinting at me.

"It's not a date, yes I am Catholic, and did you light candles yet?" I said all this while looking pointedly at Alma.

"No, because it's not really time yet..." she trailed off, casting a look at her roommates. "But maybe I'll light early today, and we can wander around town a little before we get to Chabad."

I followed her into the kitchen, trying to ignore the whispers and giggles of her roommates. She opened a cabinet and stood on her tiptoes to try and reach the bag of tea lights on one of the upper shelves.

"Allow me," I said. "Two candles, yes?"

"Yeah. Thanks."

I plucked them from the bag and handed them to her.

"So," I said, "why are there two?"

"A kind of technical and uninteresting reason," she shrugged.

"Can you explain it to me?"

She gave me a sideways glance. "Oh. Right. You're the one who thought my explanation of how to *kasher* a kitchen was the most fascinating thing you'd ever heard." She placed the candles on the windowsill and straightened the wicks. "So, there are two places where the Ten Commandments appear in the Bible—once in Exodus and once in Deuteronomy. There are some subtle differences between the two versions, and one of them is that in the commandment about Shabbat, in Exodus it says, *'Remember the Sabbath day to keep it holy,'* and in Deuteronomy it says, *'Keep the Sabbath day holy.'* So we light one candle for 'keep' and one for 'remember'."

She struck a match, lit the candles, and recited a prayer; then she bowed her head and continued to pray in silence for a minute. When she was done, she turned to me. It was remarkable how the way she held herself had changed; her face relaxed and her green eyes sparkled behind her glasses. I could almost see the burdens of the hectic weekdays sliding off her shoulders.

"Ahhh, Shabbat," she sighed. "This is my favorite time of the week."

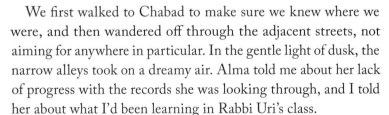

We first walked to Chabad to make sure we knew where we were, and then wandered off through the adjacent streets, not aiming for anywhere in particular. In the gentle light of dusk, the narrow alleys took on a dreamy air. Alma told me about her lack of progress with the records she was looking through, and I told her about what I'd been learning in Rabbi Uri's class.

"I hope you don't mind my asking," I said, "but... how does it not drive you crazy to keep all these laws? So many details that dictate practically every moment of your day. All for no definite reward."

Alma gave me a wry smile. "Weren't you planning to become a priest?"

"That's different. I would be actively choosing to be a clergyman. Taking on extra restrictions because I want to. And even so, it doesn't even come close to *halacha.*"

"In some ways it's worse. What's with the creepy celibacy thing?"

I raised an eyebrow, unsure whether I was more amused, insulted, or flustered. "What do you mean, 'creepy'?" I demanded.

"I—never mind," she stuttered. Did I detect a little pink in her cheeks? She cleared her throat and quickly steered the conversation back to where it had started. "Anyway, your question: I have lots of reasons for keeping *halacha,* some of them rational and some of them emotional or spiritual. So...like...take blessings, for example. You know those little prayers Rabbi Uri says every time he's about to eat something? And that I say when I'm not too distracted?"

"Yes, I was wondering what those were."

"They're short statements thanking God for the food. Which isn't that special—Christians have that too. But the thing is, different kinds of food have different blessings. So you have to really know, and think about, where that food came from, before you take a bite of literally anything. A lot of these laws help us live more consciously that way."

"Okay, that's beautiful," I said. "But saying a little prayer is not much of an inconvenience. Keeping kosher is."

"Keeping kosher takes it a level higher. But there's another layer here, too. In Catholicism, as I understand it, the physical world is perceived as negative because it pulls man toward sin."

"Right..." I said, wondering where this could be going.

"So in Judaism, the physical world is perceived as basically neutral. Whether it's good or bad depends on what we choose to do with it. So when I make a blessing on a cupcake, and make sure the cupcake is kosher, I have turned the ordinary act of eating and enjoying a cupcake into a holy act."

"Interesting," I said slowly. "So you use the commandments to...like...elevate the physical world by...eh..." I made a vague two-handed lifting gesture.

"Channelling the Divine into it," Alma finished for me.

"Yes, exactly!"

"That's the idea," she nodded. "That's why Jewish law gets into all the little minutiae of daily life. Because even the act of saying a blessing over a cupcake increases God's presence in my life and in the world. Even more so doing things that are hard."

I contemplated this as we rounded a corner. The sun was setting now, and the street lamps were starting to glow.

"But you know...beyond all that..." Alma went on. "I don't know, Manuel. My ancestors suffered a lot throughout the centuries. They really should have disappeared as a nation after the first exile, but they didn't. The fact that we still exist today as an identifiable group with a common religion and heritage is nothing short of a miracle. And I have to ask myself—what is this thing they lived and died for? Why was it important enough for them to risk so much and sacrifice so much to preserve it for all this time? If someone went through hell and high water for two and a half millennia just to pass you a letter, wouldn't you want to read it?"

"Reading it is one thing," I said. "Doing what it says is another."

"Sure. And that's where you have to ask yourself if it makes sense to do this. To me, it does. The benefits greatly outweigh the inconveniences, at least in my experience. And I really feel that it's what God wants from me."

I considered this for a moment. "I guess I can identify with that," I said.

The religious dissonance that characterized my weekends was starting to get confusing. Walking Alma to synagogue became part of my Friday evening routine. Sometimes I'd stay for the service, and sometimes I'd go home or walk around for a while and come back afterwards for the meal. We often stayed and chatted with the Maimóns late into the night. Saturdays were lazy and slow and usually spent resting—or studying on my part. Then on Sunday morning I'd get up early and go to the local church for Mass... and in the evening, head back to Chabad House for Rabbi Uri's class. The class focused primarily on the details of Jewish practice, and at least so far did not address the philosophical and theological differences between Christianity and Judaism. For the time being, I was happy with that.

Still, I found myself thinking about church the whole time I was in the synagogue, and about the synagogue the whole time I was in church. The church, obviously, felt more comfortable and familiar. The softly colored light streaming through the stained-glass windows, the scent of the incense wafting through the sanctuary, the gentle harmony of the choir... the architecture and ambiance were definitely more conducive to spiritual contemplation. But something about the passivity of Mass versus the more active engagement of the Jewish services bothered me. It wasn't that the congregation didn't participate at church—we sang and chanted and prayed. But I couldn't help but acknowledge that the main point of the entire service was really Communion, and that was something the priest had to do for me. A Jewish service doesn't even need a rabbi. I learned that the person leading the Jewish services was called a *chazzan*, a cantor, and the only requirements were that he know the liturgy and have a decent voice (and sometimes, unfortunately for the congregation, not even the latter). In fact there was a lot about Judaism that was more "direct". In some ways the idea of facing the Creator of the World with no guide or intermediary was very intimidating—and in some ways, it felt right.

After several weeks of this, I sat in church, so lost in thought about these things that I didn't even notice that a young woman had come to sit down next to me until it was time to line up for Communion. I did a double-take as I stood up and saw her: it was Alma's roommate Olivia. She gave me a little smile and a wave and got in line ahead of me. I stared at her long, sleek curtain of black hair as the line moved forward, my stomach filling with dread.

Just as I feared, when Mass was over, she was waiting for me by the door.

*"Hola,"* she said. She had a wide, dimpled smile with perfect white teeth. "I suspected I might find you here," she continued in Spanish.

I swallowed. "Were you looking for me?"

"No, actually, I was looking for Jesus." She winked. I relaxed a little.

"Did you find him?" I smiled.

"Yes, I think I did." We hung back as the rest of the congregation spilled out onto the street and went their separate ways. "I'm not all that good a Catholic, but my parents are very religious, and when I get homesick I always find a church. Never fails to bring me some comfort." She paused. "Are you hurrying somewhere, or do you want to go grab a cup of coffee?"

I hesitated. I was definitely not interested in dating her. Well... except that I didn't really know why, and I thought about that as I looked at her. True, I found her interest in me intimidating and fairly annoying. She had been insisting on sitting next to me in every single advanced Spanish-language class, and seemed especially talented at asking only tangentially related questions that sidetracked the lecturer for twenty minutes. But... she was pretty, and seemed intelligent and sweet. A Spanish speaker too, and yet fully American culturally. My mother would like that.

And it wasn't like I had taken any vows yet.

"Eh...sure," I said. She flashed her brilliant smile and led me to a nearby café. We sat down outside and ordered lattes.

"So...can I ask you something?" Olivia asked, giving me kind of a mischievous grin. She took my uncomfortable silence as a *yes*. "You and Alma. Is it just because she's Jewish that you're not... you know..."

I gave a frustrated sigh. "Because she's Jewish...because I'm a practicing Catholic...because...it's not relevant."

"But if she were Catholic?"

I shrugged, trying to pull off an air of nonchalance. "I don't know."

"She said you were thinking of going to seminary."

"I was."

"Was?"

"Am. More or less. I'm not sure."

"What's giving you trouble in deciding?"

I studied her, wondering if this was information I felt like sharing with her. She was watching me with earnest curiosity. "Well...many things. I know so little. It's interesting getting to know Jews and how they relate to their faith...you have to know so much to be an observant Jew. I'm taking these classes with the rabbi here on Sunday evenings just to get to know a little more... it's completely overwhelming, the amount of information you need just to get through the day."

"I see it at our apartment. The whole kosher business is totally baffling to me. *Gracias,*" she addressed the waiter who had just placed her latte in front of her. That brought my attention to the fact that he had already given me my latte, so I thanked him also, then turned back to Olivia.

"You don't really need to know very much to be a good Catholic," I went on. "You get baptized, you go to church, you take communion, you confess, you try not to sin, and that's basically it.

A lot of information is there if you want it, but you don't need it
to function spiritually. Our faith is very much about feeling. But
there's something about Judaism's culture of 'knowing and doing'
that I really connect to."

She sipped her coffee. "Well...then maybe you should be Jewish."

I sighed, and gave her a wry smile. "But...Jesus."

She laughed. "Yes. I know. I dated this Jewish guy once...not
religious at all, definitely not like Alma. I really liked him, and
you know, I'm not so religious myself and I have no problem
with interfaith relationships...but at the end of the day, I just
couldn't see myself being with someone who doesn't believe in
Jesus. Someone who doesn't 'get' that part of me. Not to mention,
who could not relate at all to my family culture."

I nodded, taking a sip. "It's the one thing I know I can never
talk to Alma about." I rolled my eyes. "She always refers to him
as *your buddy Jesus*," I quoted in English.

Olivia laughed. "And what's the problem? Isn't he your *'buddy'*?"

I shook my head. "She just doesn't get it."

"No. It's a completely foreign concept to Jews. Even secular ones.
Danny was agnostic, so he looked at all religions critically, but
while he could understand believing in God, he found the idea of
the Trinity totally beyond his grasp."

"Well, I don't really get it either, frankly. Is God one, or is
He three?"

"He is three that are one."

"That doesn't make sense."

"It's not supposed to. No religion makes sense. It's not about
sense, it's about faith. Having a relationship with God. Honestly,
all this 'knowing' you're talking about in Judaism sounds so dry
to me. I see Alma so caught up in her little rules about food
and the Sabbath...I just don't see the connection between that
and spirituality."

I sat back, scratching my chin. "I think I get it, actually. Relationships are not just about feelings, they're also about practical details. My parents had a really good marriage, and I could see this even as a child before my father died. It's the little things, the routine things, that make it work. He never bought her flowers. He never wrote her love poetry. He swept the floor; he cleaned up after dinner; he got up with me in the morning and took me to school. Those weren't romantic gestures in the classical sense, and I'm sure they didn't feel nearly as exciting to either of them in the moment as the flowers or poetry would have. But they meant a lot more in the long run."

Olivia raised an eyebrow. "Sounds like maybe you should be spending more time in that synagogue."

I sighed and ran my hand through my hair. "I don't know. Maybe."

"So is that why you're not sure you want to be a priest? Because you think you might want to be a rabbi instead?"

"No...well, I don't know. In some ways I feel like I connected to the Church because that's what was there. And because I needed a father after my own father's death...and it wasn't just Padre Carlos. He was a priest who became my friend after my father died," I explained at her questioning look. "It's because of him that I considered being a priest in the first place."

"Ah," Olivia nodded.

"I think there is a lot about Christianity that is very 'fatherly'. Judaism..." I smiled. "It's more like my mother." I mimicked her in a sharp falsetto: "Eat this! Don't touch that! Say 'please'! For the love of God, get a haircut!"

Olivia laughed. "So I think the answer to my question was actually 'yes,'" she said.

I blinked. "I don't remember. What was your question?"

"That maybe you want to be a rabbi, not a priest. Hey, at least rabbis aren't celibate. Big advantage there." She winked. I stared down at my coffee, my face growing warm. I cleared my throat.

"Depends who you ask," I mumbled.

"I'm sure," Olivia said, leaning in confidentially, "if you asked Alma, she would agree wholeheartedly that it's an advantage." My face got even warmer and Olivia started to giggle. I looked up at her, smiling hopelessly.

"You think so?"

Olivia laughed triumphantly. "Oh, I *know* so." She cleared her throat. "But look, if you do decide to stay Catholic, I'd love to do this again sometime." She flagged the waiter and gestured for the check. She turned back to me. "It's strange—even though I'm not that religious anymore, I really appreciate having someone to talk to about faith. People are so cynical about this stuff. So if you ever want someone to talk to about Jesus..." She winked again.

I smiled back. "I'll know who to call."

# Alma

It was with a feeling of deep disappointment that I knocked on the Maimóns' door on a Sunday morning. Not that I was unhappy to see Ester; I was actually pretty excited about hearing her story in depth. But starting this new project felt like an admission of failure. Last week, Professor García had finally asked Manuel and me to start thinking about alternative projects for the paper due at the end of the semester. Manuel had suggested that I start by interviewing the rabbi's wife about her genealogical research, and Professor García had been enthusiastic about the idea. I would have been, too, if not for the fact that I was about to abandon the entire reason I'd signed up for the Spanish Heritage Project in the first place.

But really, Professor García had been generous. Midterms were coming up, and we still had nothing at all to show for our efforts at the archive.

Ester pulled open the door and smiled warmly. "Alma! Come in. Watch your step," she waved at the Duplos strewn across the carpet. It was strange to be there during daylight; I wasn't sure if the piles of laundry next to the couch and the toys all over the floor were really absent on Friday nights, or if I just hadn't noticed them before.

The two-year-old and the four-year-old were squabbling over the Duplos; the six-year-old and the seven-year-old were at the dining room table with booklets of some sort and a pile of crayons; and the baby was in a bouncy chair by the couch, batting at a mobile, but squirming and emitting a complaint every few seconds. Ester went over to the baby and stuck a pacifier in her mouth. Then she picked up the two-year-old, who had started screaming and throwing Duplos in the air, and carried him over to his high chair near the table. She handed him a chocolate-chip muffin from a plate on the table, and he quickly forgot all about the Duplos.

"I don't know how you do this," I remarked.

Ester looked at me with a weary smile. "Oh, it's easy. I just never sleep."

She gestured for me to sit at the table across from her kids. I noticed that a thick file of papers was waiting for us there.

Ester began with her interest in Judaism as a child, her discoveries in college, her one fateful conversation with her grandmother about their Jewish heritage, and her eventual decision to trace her maternal genealogy. She said she'd hired someone to do the groundwork at the archives, which disappointed me a little because it would have been nice to interview her about her research methodology. Still, she had copies of all the documents, and I took notes as she went through them.

"This is the family tree from 1562 to 1814," she said, pulling out a page covered in tiny names and lines connecting them. "You see this?" I leaned closer, and squinted at it. Something didn't look quite right about it. "Looks strange, no?"

I nodded.

"A family tree is called a tree because it has branches," she went on. "Opening up, spreading wider and wider each generation. But not this." She traced her finger over the lines connecting the names. "It's more like a helix—cousins marrying cousins."

"To marry within the faith."

"Exactly. There were another few families—you see, here, and here—that were also *conversos*, that must have been within the little circle of trust, because they also married in. But you see how many husbands they had?" She pointed to a few names that had several "marriage ties" marked on the paper. "So many widows. What was happening to all the husbands?"

"The Inquisition?" I guessed.

Ester pulled out another few pages and handed them to me one by one. "Many of those husbands turned up in the Inquisition trials. Burned at the stake. Died in prison. Died during interrogations."

A shiver went down my spine. "That's horrible."

"The women kept changing their names, changing spellings, leaving out former surnames. It made the whole thing quite a mess to research. But that's exactly what they intended—they were trying to cover their tracks." She rested the page she'd been holding on the table, drawing a deep breath, and then glanced toward the hallway. *"Wash your hands, Naomi,"* she said in Spanish.

The four-year-old sheepishly slunk back to the bathroom.

"There's something very powerful about uncovering all this," she went on. "I felt like each time we uncovered a new layer, I got to know each of my ancestors that much more deeply."

I realized at that point that the uncomfortable sensation that had been welling in my chest for the last ten minutes was jealousy. I wanted to get to know my ancestors, too.

"I think of them every Friday night," Ester said, her eyes wandering to the silver candelabras in the glass cabinet behind the table. "When I light the Shabbat candles. I feel their souls standing all around me. Protecting me."

There was a moment of reverent silence.

I asked, my voice hushed: "If you could gather them all in this room right now…what would you say to them?"

Ester's mouth contorted a little, and I noticed that her eyes were welling with tears. She gave a little laugh. "I would probably cry my eyes out," she said, dabbing at the corners of her eyes to avoid smearing her makeup. "I would ask each of them what it was like to be a Jew in her time, how much she was able to keep and remember. I would tell the ones who had forgotten parts of their Judaism that I forgive them, that they did the best they could, and that I cherish every spark they did hold on to and pass down. I would hold their hands and we would cry together." Ester gave up trying to wipe her tears away and just let them stream down her face.

"What do you think they would say to you?" I whispered.

Ester smiled, still gazing at the candelabras.

"I think they would say that they are very proud of me."

---

I walked home so lost in thought that I took three wrong turns and had to ask for directions to get back to my apartment. When I walked in, Olivia and Tessa were sitting on the couch giggling about something on Tessa's phone.

"Oh, hey!" Olivia said when she caught sight of me. "Where were you?"

"Me? At the Maimón's. I was interviewing Ester for my project."

"Oh, cool," she said. "Guess who I ran into at church."

I raised an eyebrow.

"Your Catholic friend," she grinned. "We sat down for coffee afterwards."

A pause.

"Huh." I put my bag down, trying to maintain an air of nonchalance and ignore the sick feeling in my stomach. I headed over to the kitchen and pulled the fridge open, hoping the conversation would end there, but it didn't.

"This Manuel of yours..." Olivia went on. "He's awfully sweet and thoughtful, and gorgeous goes without saying..."

"God, those dreamy eyes," Tessa chimed in. I closed my eyes and clenched my jaw in irritation.

"But geez, is he tightly wound," Olivia continued. "Can he talk about anything other than his deep spiritual struggles or the woes of humankind?"

I slammed the fridge shut. "Well, for God's sake, Olivia, I *told* you he's thinking of becoming a priest. What were you expecting, a party boy?"

Olivia gave me a vague grin. "I wouldn't be so sure about those priestly aspirations, hon."

I stood there with my mouth hanging slightly open, not sure what to say, as she turned back to Tessa's phone.

*What did he tell her that he's not telling me?*

# Míriam

Yom Kippur passed mostly in silence. After Míriam and her father prayed together, there was little else to do but sit, talk, and sleep. By the time it was evening and Don Tomás finally came with some food for them to break their fast, Míriam felt she was starting to go mad from boredom.

"Don Tomás—" she said, taking a breath in between ravenous bites of the porridge he had brought them. He turned to her, his eyebrows raised. "I know it makes sense for my father to stay here in hiding. But perhaps I could pretend to be a new maid and do some housework for you? No one here has ever seen me. They won't know who I am."

Don Tomás looked at her thoughtfully. Then his eyes lit up. "Is it true that you can read, Míriam?"

Míriam nodded. "Yes, I can read. Hebrew and Castilian, and a little Arabic."

"Your father told me you are unusually well-educated for a young woman. I have a collection of records and documents that have been waiting for years to be sorted. None of the other maids or servants can read. I was having León do it, but he has other pursuits, and it's taking him an awfully long time. Would you be interested in putting those documents in order?"

Míriam stood up from the bed. "Oh, yes, *señor!* It would be my pleasure, and the least I could do to return the great kindnesses you have done for me and my father."

"Well, that's settled, then." He regarded her, his eyes resting on the red cloth patch over her heart. "You'll need to remove that."

She glanced down at it. She'd hardly ever given a thought to the badge she always pinned to the front of her clothes. All Jews wore them, and she'd never had any reason to feel resentful about being forced to distinguish herself visually from Christians. In fact, the idea of removing it and wandering about without one made her stomach turn in discomfort. She thought of her hidden Sabbath candles. Removing the badge was another way she was being forced to hide her identity.

"Most of our maids wear wimples. I'll find you one, and I'll send León for you tomorrow morning to show you where the library is. But be very careful around the other servants. You'll need to invent a story about where you come from and who you are. And never let anyone see you coming up here."

"Of course not, *senor*," she said. "Thank you for the opportunity."

Early the next morning, the same strange knock Don Tomás had used when he brought her to her father sounded at the door. Míriam cracked it open and saw León standing in the hall.

"*Señorita.*" He looked down at her. His hair fell softly around his face, his beard was neatly trimmed, and she couldn't help but notice, especially in the soft morning light, that he really was quite a handsome fellow. He was wearing a doublet of embroidered damask, very clean and perfectly pressed. Míriam was used to the flowing robes and modest tunics worn by the men in the *judería*.

"Here is a wimple for you to wear. Come." He gestured for her to follow him and she slipped out, waving to her father before closing the door.

León turned toward the end of the hallway where the stairs led down to the next floor. Míriam followed him down the steps and into the main part of the house, adjusting the wimple as she walked. She hated the restrictive cloth around her neck. She tried to keep her eyes down, but she just couldn't help staring at her surroundings. She had never seen such wealth before: Elaborate tapestries hung from the walls, and high arched doorways were adorned with Moorish-style plasterwork. Servants bustled in and out of every room, cleaning and dusting.

The library was a stuffy little room on the bottom floor, down a narrow, mostly empty corridor from the main reception hall. There was a battered wooden table in the middle, piled high with crates of paper and parchment, and wooden shelves lined the walls from floor to ceiling, most of them empty. A few leather-bound books were tucked onto one of them. Míriam approached these and ran her hand over their covers. They reminded her of the books kept in the *beit midrash* next to the synagogue, and the beautiful Talmud that her father had studied when she was a child. It had been confiscated and burned by the civil authorities in Seville, along with hundreds of other Jewish and Muslim books and manuscripts containing "heresy".

"It's such a mess," León said, gesturing toward the mass of documents on the table. "Makes my head spin just looking at it." He pointed to the far corner of the room, where a few piles of paper were lined up neatly on a shelf. "That's as far as I've gotten. Financial papers from 1487." He pointed at one of the piles of loose papers on the table. "There are probably more of those in there. You'll need to catalogue them according to date."

"Well, this is going to take an eternity," Míriam said, frowning. "I really hope I won't be here long enough to finish the job."

León raised an eyebrow at her. "Where, exactly, do you think you're going to go?"

Míriam just looked at him. It hadn't even occurred to her to think about this, but he was right. If the Inquisition was after her father, the only option would be to flee Castile—and how would they do that? Her father had business contacts in the Maghreb and Italy, and she knew he had two brothers in Fez and several cousins in Cairo, but how would they get there? They had absolutely nothing. Their property had probably already been seized, and the proceeds would be filling the pockets of the Tribunal. They couldn't even afford to sail to Genoa or Tangier, assuming they somehow managed to get to a seaport.

"Well…" She glanced at the door, to make sure no one was nearby, and lowered her voice. "We can't stay here in hiding forever…"

"May I ask you a question?" León blurted. Míriam raised her eyebrows. "I apologize if this is forward. I have never really had an opportunity to speak plainly with a Jew before. Why don't you just convert?"

Míriam gave him a look of utter disgust. "Why on earth would I want to do that?"

León shrugged, pulling up one of the chairs and sitting down. He crossed his arms in front of him. "Aren't you tired of God constantly punishing you?"

Míriam sighed in irritation, picking up the papers on the table and thumbing through them. "What gives you the impression that God is constantly punishing us?"

León laughed. "Isn't it obvious?"

"No," Míriam said loudly, then winced and lowered her voice. "God is protecting us."

"And by God, you mean my father?" León gave a cynical grin.

Míriam narrowed her eyes at him. "You're one to talk about confusing certain men with God."

He just frowned. She thumbed through the papers again, but she was having trouble concentrating with him sitting there. After a few moments, she looked up at him.

"If you're hoping to convert me, I'll have you know that you are wasting your time."

León threw his palms up in a gesture of bewilderment. "I just don't understand why you are so stubborn about this. Even if you have a hard time accepting Jesus as the son of God, wouldn't it make your life easier to be a Christian?"

"My life *would* be easier if I were a Christian. But I'm not a Christian. And I have no desire to be one. Ease is not my greatest concern. Besides, it wouldn't help very much. Haven't you heard what the Inquisition is doing to *conversos?*"

"Only the insincere ones."

"How exactly is it heretical to drink kosher wine?" Her eyes flashed. "Didn't Jesus himself only eat kosher food?"

León fell silent again. She didn't bother going back to the documents. She just scowled at him.

"But all these prohibitions...the food...the holidays...the Sabbath...not touching men."

Míriam raised an eyebrow, feeling her cheeks get a little warm.

"It seems like an awful lot of bother, and for what?" he continued. "Plenty of Jews have converted and God didn't punish them. There are many *conversos* who are successful and prosperous. Why bother holding on to these traditions?"

Míriam glared at him.

"I know what you're doing," she said. "I know that the primary goal of Christians is to get Jews to convert. Stop it. It's not going to work."

"I'm not trying to convert you. For Heaven's sake." León leaned back in his chair, crossing his legs. "I'm just curious."

Míriam squinted at him appraisingly. There were a few moments of silence as they regarded each other.

"Really?" she asked quietly.

"Really."

Míriam fiddled with the papers for a moment, unsure of what to say. "Because…" She sighed. "It's hard to explain, Don León. It's something so deep, so much a part of who I am, I'm not sure I can really put it into words." She paused. "I believe very strongly in God. I believe that He gave us the Torah as a gift of His love. I believe that He shows us His love every day, by giving us everything—food, shelter, the breath that we draw. Keeping His commandments is…" She thought for a moment. "It's my way of telling Him that I love Him, too. So I keep them, even if it's difficult and I don't always understand them."

León's eyes had taken on a soft look.

"I think I can understand that," he said slowly. "There are many things about Christianity that I don't fully comprehend. But trusting in God when He guides you into the unknown, and accepting it with love—that's really the definition of faith, isn't it?"

They looked at each other for a moment, and Míriam felt a sort of warmth pass between them. She knew that faith was a central part of both of their lives; and especially in this environment of hatred and suspicion over religious differences, there was something deeply comforting to her about discovering what they shared.

"How do you know how to read, Míriam?" León asked.

Míriam shrugged. "My father taught me."

"Do all Jewish women know how to read?"

"No. Most women aren't knowledgeable at all. It's just that my father didn't have any sons to teach, and he really wanted to teach someone, so…" Her voice trailed off and she sighed. "And after my mother died, we had a lot of time to spend alone together on the road. There wasn't much better to do than discuss the manuscripts he always carries with him."

He was watching her with that intense gaze of his that made the hairs on the back of her neck prickle. "How old were you when your mother died?"

"Seven." Míriam bit her lip, returning to the papers. There were a few moments of silence.

"I was eight."

Míriam looked up in surprise. León lowered his eyes.

"I... I didn't realize."

He shrugged. "Ten years ago. In childbirth. My sister didn't survive either."

Míriam was speechless for a moment. "I'm sorry," she said quietly. Then she found herself continuing: "My mother fell ill before we left Seville, and she died on the road after we were expelled from Andalusia. We buried her somewhere in La Mancha."

He raised his eyes again to meet hers. "It must have been hard."

She nodded slowly. "We had already lost enough."

He nodded, staring at the floor. "I loved my mother very much."

They sat there awkwardly for a few minutes. Eventually Míriam tried to go back to her work, but she couldn't concentrate.

"What is your Heaven like?" León asked suddenly.

Míriam furrowed her brow, resting her cheek in her hand. "I'm not sure."

León looked confused. "What do you mean?"

"We have the concept of the Garden of Eden, or of sitting in God's presence...but honestly, we're not that focused on what happens after we die. We're more focused on what happens before."

"Don't you sometimes wonder where your mother is?"

Míriam's eyes darkened. "Of course I do."

"Do you think she is looking down on you? Watching you?"

"I...yes, I think so." She looked over at him. He was still staring at the floor. "I was just thinking about her yesterday. I think she would have hated to be hiding here like this."

León stood up from the chair. "Well. I should probably be going. Good luck with the documents."

"Wait, León." Míriam didn't really mean to delay him, but the words were out of her mouth before she could stop them. He turned back and looked at her in surprise. She flushed a bright red. "I... I'm just..." she stuttered. "Never mind. Good day to you."

He paused, giving her a searching look. "Do you want me to stay and help?" he offered gently. "I could, if you want."

"I..." Míriam struggled to understand what she wanted from him. She didn't really need his help, but something in her very much wanted him to stay. She was worried about the other servants coming in and asking her questions. And she had never really talked about her mother's death with anyone but her father. It was comforting to talk about it with someone who had gone through the same thing...and even if their beliefs were very different, Míriam had a sense that they shared a common hope and connection to God.

And...she was curious about León. He was refined and polite, but somehow very candid at the same time. No one had ever asked her so directly about such personal things before. Curiously, it didn't make her feel uncomfortable; it made her feel that he really cared about her—which was not at all what she expected to feel in this situation, especially considering that he was Christian.

She cleared her throat. "If it's no trouble... I suppose," she said slowly.

He pulled a chair over to the table, sat down, and grabbed half of the pile of papers in front of her.

# Alma

Tuesday morning, I stared absently out the window of the bus as the students around me chattered excitedly. We'd been looking forward to this day trip to Toledo since we got to Spain, and I could certainly use the change of scenery. But I was not in much of a celebratory mood.

The nobility section of the historical archives was located in Toledo, and Professor García had arranged for the bus to drop Manuel and me off there while the rest of the students took a really cool tour of a metalworking shop, with medieval swords and armor and stuff. Checking the Toledo archive seemed to be a kind of last-ditch attempt to make some progress on Manuel's project; I couldn't help but feel jealous that he stood even a remote chance of getting somewhere with it.

I drew the ring out from under my shirt, turning it over in my hand, running my finger over the bird carving with a sinking feeling of sadness.

*Why am I supposed to return this, anyway? What's the point? Why was it so important that they had to pass this burden down for twenty-six generations?*

But it *felt* important. It felt more important than anything.

A movement to my right snapped me back to reality and I turned to see Manuel standing there. He pointed at my backpack sitting in the seat next to me.

"Is this saved for me?" he asked.

"Nope. The Messiah," I said, sliding the backpack out of the seat and under the bench in front of ours. "But I think he'll probably be a while."

"Some might claim that he was already here," Manuel winked as he sat down.

"Speaking of which," I said, sliding my glasses off and examining them. "I hear you found a church buddy on Sunday."

He paused. "Yes, your roommate Olivia was there."

"She said you went out for coffee afterwards." I started cleaning my glasses very carefully on my shirt.

"Yes," he said cautiously. "She's nice, you know."

I shrugged. "I thought you found her annoying."

"I did. Less so now."

I nodded ahead. "She's up in the front, I think. You sure she didn't save you a seat?""

Manuel froze now, his eyes squinted in confusion.

"What...why..." He looked at me suspiciously. "It was not a date, if that's what you're implying." He paused. "At least not as far as I know."

I raised my eyebrows, sliding my glasses back on. "It's none of my business."

The engine started and the bus started rolling forward. We rode in awkward silence, watching the buildings along the highway zip past, eventually changing into wide fields and olive groves under a clear blue sky.

The bus dropped us off at the traffic circle outside the Hospital de Tavera, where the archive was housed. We had only two hours, and I was kind of disappointed to miss the metalworking thing. But Manuel and I had thrown in our lot with old libraries, and so we stepped off the bus and approached the building. It was a sprawling, sand-colored, Renaissance-style affair that looked a lot like the main branch in Madrid.

Manuel cleared his throat.

"Alma," he said, "if I did not know any better, I would think you were jealous or something."

I looked at him, a little startled that he was also still thinking about the thing with Olivia. I gave him a pointed look over my glasses. "Well, it's a good thing you do know better," I said. I marched up to the entrance and swung open the door. He followed me inside. "I don't have a problem with you dating Olivia," I said, lowering my tone as I headed for the information desk. "I was just...surprised."

"I am *not* dating Olivia," Manuel insisted, jogging to catch up with me.

We consulted the archivist, a brightly-dressed brunette in her fifties, on our situation. She soon gave us the bad news: every file she had under "Aguilar" was either too early or too late to be of any use to us. But we had two hours to kill before the bus came back for us, so we figured we might as well look through the files anyway, searching for any clues that might help. We sat next to each other in the reading room, and the archivist brought each of us a document to peruse.

I tried to focus on the page in front of me, but the text swam before my eyes.

Finally, I took off my glasses, rubbed my eyes, turned to Manuel, and whispered, "Well, are you *interested* in dating her?"

He looked up from his document with a raised eyebrow and studied me carefully, a little smile playing at the corners of his mouth.

"Did you not say that it's none of your business?" he whispered back.

I wagged my head from side to side. "Well okay then, Mister Cryptic. Sheesh. I'm just asking. You know she's gonna be all over me trying to figure out how to make her next move."

Manuel sighed, rubbing his forehead, and whispered, "I have a feeling that no matter what answer I give, you're not going to like it."

I pushed back from the desk. "Just because you think I might not like to hear something, doesn't mean you shouldn't tell me," I hissed.

A loud "Sshhh!" came from somewhere behind us.

*"Lo siento,"* Manuel said. He stood up. *"Ya terminamos."* He nodded at the archivist, and she came over to take the documents from us, frowning in deep disapproval.

"But I'm not..." I protested weakly.

Manuel grabbed my arm and dragged me up from my chair. I barely had a chance to grab my glasses. He pulled me out of the reading room, past the archivist—who was muttering something about *estudiantes*—and out to the hallway. He pulled me out to a balcony overlooking the interior courtyard.

"What are you doing?" I demanded.

"You clearly have a burning need to talk about this," he said, pulling off the vinyl gloves we were required to wear when handling old documents and stuffing them in his pocket. He folded his arms, leaning against one of the pillars and fixing me with his gaze. I couldn't tell whether he was exasperated, slightly amused, or both. "So talk."

"Well...you..." I said, shoving my glasses back on my face, pulling off my own gloves, and trying to regain my composure. "You've been completely avoiding talking about Christianity with me since we had that argument. It's stupid." His eyebrows went up. "The whole awesome thing about having a friend from another religion," I went on, "is getting to talk about this stuff. I don't know anything about where you are in terms of your religious beliefs right now. I feel like you're just humoring me, asking me all about Judaism, hanging out with my Jewish friends and taking Jewish classes, but I have no idea what you actually think about all of it because you never tell me." I crossed my arms. "You know I don't care whether you end up being a priest, a rabbi, or a Mongolian shaman. I was joking about wanting you to be a priest. I'm getting the sense that you've pretty much decided not to be one, since you're talking about dating—"

"I'm *not* talking about dating!" he protested. *"You're* the one who's talking about me dating."

"Well? So what's going on?" I glared at him.

"Nothing's *going on!* I just...I'm... I'm just not sure, I don't know where I am with religion," he fumbled, staring at the floor and absently digging at the tile with his sneakers. "And I don't think it's a good time to be starting a serious relationship with someone—especially when some of the paths I'm thinking about would rule out that relationship. And I'm not interested in a relationship that is not serious."

"Well, that was easy! Couldn't you have just said that?" I retorted.

"Why are you mad at me, Alma?" He finally met my eyes with that intense look of his. "I really don't understand. I'm not hiding anything from you."

I just looked at him, taking a deep breath and trying to calm my irritation. I didn't really know what I was so worked up about either. "Wait, so what are these 'paths' you are thinking about? One is being a priest, that one I know."

"Another is not being a priest. And another..." He paused, studying me apprehensively.

"What?"

"Well, Judaism."

I couldn't deny the distinct sense of pleasure that washed over me at those words. *"I don't care whether you end up being a priest or a rabbi,"* huh? I scolded myself.

I raised my eyebrows. "See, I had no idea that was an option."

"Well, it's not a very likely one. But I'm enjoying what I'm learning, and..." He narrowed his eyes at me. "Please. Don't tell me this comes as a total surprise to you. Don't you remember how we met?"

I blinked and tried to think back. I was a little disconcerted—it felt like I'd known him forever.

"Your grandmother's store."

"Oh, right! Well...no, it's not a total surprise. It's just that you never talk about it."

He shrugged. "There's a lot I don't talk about."

"Except with Olivia, apparently," I muttered, and started off down the walkway. He remained in place for a moment, let out a slow breath, and then jogged after me.

"Oh, for goodness' sake, Alma. I was unaware that you claim exclusive rights on all expression of my thoughts."

I sighed. "No, you're right. I'm sorry. I'm just..." My voice trailed off, and the end of the sentence hung in the air. *I'm just what? Jealous?*

"I... I understand if it's easier to talk to Olivia about Catholic stuff," I went on. "You know...you love Jesus...she loves Jesus... you both love Jesus together..."

He laughed kind of nervously, falling into step next to me. We walked toward the stairs in awkward silence.

As we started down the staircase, Manuel froze.

"What?" I asked.

"I think she's calling us..." Manuel turned around, looking for the source of a voice I hadn't even registered. But he was right: it was the archivist, moving with astonishing speed down the walkway and looking very excited. She and Manuel exchanged a few words, and then she started leading us back to the reading room. Manuel's eyes lit up.

"What? What's going on?"

"She says she was just filing a document that mentions an Aguilar, one dated in the 1470's," he said, breathless. "It's from a different file, a dowry document from the Angel family."

"Oh, and that's our time frame!" I exclaimed.

"Exactly!"

The archivist ushered him into the reading room, and glared at me when I tried to follow—apparently having quickly recovered from the excitement and returned to her natural disposition.

*"No está permitida la consulta simultánea,"* she said sternly.

"But—"

"We'll get a reproduction!" Manuel said from behind her. "Wait for me outside, don't let the bus leave without me!"

<hr>

I paced the courtyard in front of the building, biting the nail of my index finger. The yard was paved with flat stones, with short hedges rising up in geometrical maze-like patterns, and I followed these, weaving in and out. I impulsively glanced at my phone, simultaneously annoyed with the bus for being late and with Manuel for taking so long, though I should have been grateful for the former because of the latter.

As luck would have it, Manuel came dashing out of the building just as the bus pulled up.

"Excellent timing," I exclaimed as he doubled over, trying to catch his breath. I snatched the papers he was holding and tried riffling through them, but was quickly reminded that I suck at fifteenth-century Spanish paleography.

"So? What did you find?"

"I'll—tell—you—on the bus..." Manuel panted, stumbling over to the door. I followed him onto the bus, and as soon as we were seated, I shoved the papers back into his hands.

*"Nu?"* I prompted.

Manuel grinned, his eyes shining, and he pointed to somewhere near the middle of one of the photocopies in his hand. I squinted at it. It could just as well have been Chinese.

"What does it say?" I asked impatiently.

"Don Tomás Aguilar y Alverez." He closed his eyes and leaned back against the seat, still breathing heavily from his race to the bus. "My ancestor. He married María Pilar Angel y Hernando. She was the daughter of Juan Angel, who was a count in Castilla. The names, the dates, everything matches up."

"Oh my gosh!" I exclaimed. "This is exactly what you were looking for!"

"More than that," he went on, "it says where they got married." He pointed to a different page. I looked at it closely.

"That's...a C, right?"

"Cartagena. It says Cartagena. It's a port city in Murcia."

"So now we have a region to focus our attention on!"

"And," he added, "we have proof that my father was right. And we know for sure that it was this Aguilar who somehow lost his title before moving to Granada. *And,*" he added, flipping to another page, "look at this."

It was a seal of some sort, a coat of arms with an eagle at the center.

There was something about it that looked vaguely familiar. I was sure I'd seen it before, but couldn't remember where.

"My father..." Manuel was saying. "I remember him saying something about an eagle emblem." He sat back again, staring over the seats of the bus ahead of us. "He taught me how to draw an eagle when I was a kid. And he hung my drawing on our refrigerator. It stayed there until we moved to America. My mother thinks she still has it somewhere."

"Manuel!" My exclamation jerked him out of his reverie, and he turned to me. "This is amazing!" I raised my hand for a high-five, and he obliged, grinning from ear to ear. "You'd think there was a God, or something! Looks like all those hours you've been putting in at various houses of worship are paying off..."

"How does Rabbi Uri say? *Baruch haShem*," he said, kissing his hand and looking up at the roof of the bus in a gesture of gratitude to God. "This means we don't have to give up on our project after all!"

My enthusiasm died down pretty quickly. "Well. That *you* won't have to give up on *yours*, anyway."

Manuel studied me. "Maybe there is still hope for you too," he said, but he didn't sound very convinced.

I shook my head. "I don't think so." I looked out the window, swallowing a lump of jealousy in my throat.

<hr />

The rest of the day was a bit of a blur. Even Toledo's famous ancient synagogues and Sephardic history museum didn't hold my attention well. Professor Pérez, who was leading the tour, asked me if I could decipher the Hebrew inscriptions carved into the elaborate plasterwork on the walls of the El Tránsito synagogue, but apparently no one believed in spacing or punctuation in the fourteenth century and it was hard to pick out individual words from the stream of letters. Honestly, it made my stomach turn to see these inscriptions—such clear physical evidence of the presence of my ancestors—on a building that had been converted into a church and was now a museum. Toledo advertised itself as a city of three cultures, but all I could see was how the one culture had swallowed up the other two. All that was left of *my* culture was these silent letters on the walls, calling out to people who couldn't read them. I couldn't meet Manuel's eye in that place.

I left the synagogue before the tour was over and sat down on the curb by the narrow cobblestone alleyway, trying to hide my tears.

# Míriam

"May I ask you something?"

Míriam turned from the shelf, her eyebrows raised. León had been sitting quietly next to her for a long while, sorting through documents, and she had almost forgotten he was there. He had been coming to help her almost every day since she had begun, mostly sitting in silence but sometimes asking a question or two.

"I've come to understand a little more about what makes food kosher—separating milk and meat, and certain animals slaughtered a certain way, and all that. But what about wine? What makes a wine kosher or not kosher? Isn't it just fermented fruit juice?"

Míriam hesitated, watching him warily. "Well…it has to do with the special spiritual status of wine. Not just for us, but for other religions, too. It was often used during pagan rituals. The Sages ruled that wine must only be handled by a Jew, from the moment the grapes are squeezed until it is drunk, to make sure it wasn't contaminated with idolatry."

"So it becomes non-kosher if a non-Jew comes into contact with it?" he asked. Míriam studied his expression closely, trying to determine whether he found this offensive. She couldn't tell.

"Yes."

"Even if he's not an idolater?"

"Well…" she answered slowly, "I think it's one of a series of laws about food that the rabbis prefer to keep in place to prevent close relationships between Jews and non-Jews."

Both of them stiffened, and there was a tense silence.

"Because you're afraid we'll convert you?" León asked finally.

Míriam swallowed, taking a moment to think about how best to answer. "Mostly. Not being able to eat or drink socially is a major obstacle in forming the sort of relationships that lead to conversion and intermarriage. You have to understand...for us, this isn't only about faith. It's about our preservation as a nation. We were banished from our homeland more than a thousand years ago. Maintaining our identity as a unified group is not a simple task when we are scattered all over the world."

León was staring, his eyes unfocused, at the pages before him. Míriam still couldn't read his expression.

"Given the odds," he said finally, "you have been remarkably successful." He looked up at her. "I hope this doesn't offend you, but according to our beliefs, the fact that you still exist as a group is proof that you are being punished by God for rejecting Jesus."

Míriam smiled uncertainly. "According to *our* beliefs, it's proof of the exact opposite—our survival shows that we are still the eternal Chosen People."

They both contemplated this for a few moments.

"Interesting how each of us interprets reality differently, according to our beliefs," León said, resting his chin on his folded hands.

"Yes," Míriam agreed, still watching him carefully. "It is interesting."

The next day, as she was rummaging through a crate of old letters, she found a small bundle that was wrapped in a cloth and bound with twine. She turned it around in her hands, trying to get a better look, and loosened the twine enough to slip one of the documents out. It had been sealed with the usual eagle emblem of the family, but the handwriting did not look like that of Don Tomás. She opened it up and began to read, and put her hand to her mouth in delight as she realized what it was. She quickly fished out the next document and examined it, then the next, and the next; then she carefully replaced the documents in their original order.

She looked up and ran to the doorway, poking her head out to look for León. She didn't see him, so she slipped out the door to the courtyard. It was surrounded on three sides by the house, with a marble fountain burbling in the center, and beyond it stretched a grassy field where the family's horses grazed. She spotted León across the grass, leading his horse to the stable on the far side of the pasture. She had half a mind to run and catch him, but that would be immodest; so she walked as quickly as she could.

"León!" she called once she was within earshot. He waited as she rushed up to him, her face flushed and her breathing heavy, her eyes shining. "You will not believe what I just found."

She handed him the packet of documents. He furrowed his brow, untied the twine, and removed the papers from their cloth wrapping, looking from Míriam to the letters and back again.

"I would have given them straight to your father...but I thought you might want to see them first."

He pulled the first document out and opened it. His eyes widened and he stared up at Míriam. "My mother..."

"The marriage and dowry contracts. From your parents' marriage."

León turned back to the document, then swallowed and tore his eyes away, folding it and stuffing the papers into his doublet. Míriam thought she saw tears welling in his eyes, but he blinked them away very quickly. He smiled at her.

"Thank you. It was very kind of you to give them to me."

She stared at the ground. "I know how much they must mean to you. The only thing I have from my mother...well, *had*..." she sighed, "was a little blue book of Psalms. Her father was a *sofer*—a scribe—and he made this book of Psalms for her, which she bound with an embroidered cover she made herself. It was one of the things I would have brought with me if you had let me."

León shifted uncomfortably. "I'm sorry. My instructions were not to let you pack, to bring you right away. If I had known..."

"I know. I'm not angry at you." She looked up at him. "You are very serious about honoring your father."

He smiled. "It is the Fourth Commandment."

She hesitated. "Isn't it the Fifth?"

"It is possible that we count differently."

"Whichever one, it is admirable."

He studied her, looking unsure what to make of this compliment. "Thank you. I do the best I can."

"I just... I think it is incredible that you are willing to put yourself at risk like this just because your father believes it's right, even if you don't."

He shook his head. "I do believe it's right. I don't think your father deserves to be tried by the Inquisition. I was just not sure it was worth the risk." He gave her a shy smile. "I'm starting to...change my mind."

She stared at the ground again, a rush of warmth flowing up through her chest and to her cheeks.

"Thank you so much for giving these to me, Míriam." He gave his horse a slap on the rump and followed it away to the stable.

# Manuel

"Did you tell your mother yet?" Alma asked by way of greeting, approaching me in the lobby of the Archivo Histórico Nacional. I looked up from the photocopies of the document I'd been staring at. "Tell her what?"

"About your find, you idiot. You made a huge discovery two days ago. In Toledo. Remember?"

"She calls me every Saturday," I shrugged. "I'll tell her then."

Alma rolled her eyes, seating herself in the armchair next to mine. "Ugh! You are such a man. Call your mother!"

"Professor García should be here any minute…"

"You want *me* to call your mother?" She pulled her phone out of her pocket threateningly.

"All right, all right!" I glared at her. "Lord help me. It's like having two mothers." I took out my phone and did as I was told.

"*¿Qué pasa?*" My mother's voice was sharp and tense.

"*Nada, mamá,*" I said quickly. "*That is… nothing bad. I just have some news about the research.*"

"*Ah,*" she said, audibly relieved. "*You scared me for a minute. My son? Calling me? Maybe he was taken hostage by terrorists…*"

Alma made a rolling motion with her hands, urging me to go on.

"*I just wanted to tell you that we found a marriage document with the name of the Aguilar we were looking for, and it confirms that he was a nobleman,*" I said.

"*Ah!*" Mama exclaimed. "*That's very exciting! Congratulations, cariño! Thank you for calling me,*" she said, her voice incredulous. "*That was quite considerate of you.*" A pause. "*Ahhh, I know.*" She chuckled. *"The Jewish girl made you call me."*

I shot an exasperated look at Alma, who was hanging on my every word, clearly struggling to understand the Spanish.

*"I knew I could trust her to keep an eye on you. Thank her for me. Is there anything else? Are you okay?"*

"Yes, Mama, I'm fine. I have to go now. We'll talk on Saturday."

*"Sí, sí. Te quiero, cariño."*

*"Te quiero, mamá. Hasta luego."* I hung up.

"Well?" Alma demanded. "Did you tell her how you found it? Did you tell her about the emblem?"

I blinked. "No. Was I supposed to?"

Alma rolled her eyes again. *"Hombres,"* she said. She studied me. "You are really hard to understand when you speak to your mother."

*"Buenos días,"* came a voice behind us. Professor García slid into the chair opposite mine. "So. How was your trip to Toledo?"

<hr/>

Professor García confirmed that my reading of the marriage document was correct, and congratulated me on the find. "Listen," she said, putting the photocopy on the coffee table in front of us. "Genealogical research is often like this. You toil for months and months and you have no idea if all the time and effort you put in is going to turn up anything. Sometimes it does not, and it's very frustrating. But sometimes it does, and it's the best feeling in the world."

Alma was looking at Professor García with her mouth scrunched to one side. "Remind me never to go into genealogical research as a career. Ever."

Professor García ignored her. "So, what this means is that we should narrow our search to Murcia. And it just so happens that we got a shipment of Inquisition records from Murcia the other day. The head archivist wants them catalogued and digitized, and I had been thinking of handing that project to you anyway. It's an important and exciting educational opportunity, and a great privilege to be able to handle original documents outside the reading room."

Alma and I exchanged excited glances.

"The question is, Alma, if you are willing to abandon your new project to help Manuel with his."

"Sure! At least this would be doing real archival work, which is what the program's supposed to be about." Alma was smiling, but her eyes were sad; and when we got up to leave, I caught her throwing a wistful glance up the stairs in the direction of the main archive, where she had tried and failed to find records of her ancestors. I wanted to console her, but I couldn't think of anything comforting to say.

Unfortunately, at this point we did not have a whole lot of spare time for our labors in the National Historical Archive. Midterm exams were upon us, and both of us were stressed and using every extra minute for studying. I even skipped both church and Rabbi Uri's class one Sunday, frantically racing to finish a paper that was due Monday morning. I turned it in on time, but I couldn't shake free of the guilt—it had been years since I missed Communion.

When the end of midterms was finally in sight, I started to look forward to spring break. It would be my chance to go visit Granada. True, the only people I really wanted to visit there were dead...but I was eager to see my childhood home, to visit Padre Carlos's church, to walk the streets where I grew up and let them flood me with memory.

And the more I thought about Granada, the more I realized that all my mental images were of showing these places to Alma, not just visiting them by myself. I wanted to share my memories with her. I wanted to connect my old life with my new one as her friend.

The Friday after I missed Mass and Rabbi Uri's class, I put on my suit and walked to Alma's apartment to accompany her to the synagogue. I found her dressed in her normal clothes, sitting at the little desk in her room with her books in front of her.

"What are you doing?" I asked, peering over her shoulder. "Twenty minutes before candle-lighting and you're not even dressed for synagogue!"

She turned around slowly, her eyes wild with dark circles underneath them.

"Well geez, Mom, thanks for stopping by!" she said. She turned back to her books. "I wasn't going to go today. I just have so much to do…"

"What is this nonsense?" I demanded. "You're not allowed to write on Shabbat."

"But I'm allowed to read…"

"You Jews and your technicalities." I started shutting all the books on her desk. "Why do you think God gave you the Sabbath? So you could torture yourself studying? It's supposed to be a day of rest. Rest, joy, pleasure! No studying! Get dressed! I'm waiting for you in the living room."

She stared at me as I strode toward the door. "God almighty," she muttered. "I've created a monster."

---

"So what's got you all high on the Sabbath spirit?" Alma wanted to know as we descended the stairs of her building to the street.

"What's got you in such a bad mood?" I countered.

She looked up at me wearily. "What, midterms aren't enough?"

"To skip Shabbat dinner? I doubt it. I have never seen you like this before."

She was shaking her head. "Sometimes I think you know me better than I do." She stopped and leaned against the door to the building. "My sister just got engaged."

I paused. "Eh...congratulations? Why is this a bad thing?"

"It's not...it's not." She pushed the door open and walked out.

"Then why are you upset about it?"

She sighed again and turned to me. "Because I'm a self-absorbed brat, that's why."

I didn't know what to say to that.

"They're having the party next week. I'm just really sad that I won't be able to be there. And kind of mad that they couldn't postpone it a few weeks until spring break, so I could go."

"Are you planning to go to New York during spring break?" I asked, feeling a sinking disappointment.

"Sort of. I haven't bought tickets yet."

"Why aren't they willing to wait?"

Alma's mouth tightened. "Oh, you know...scheduling conflicts, blah blah blah, it's just the engagement, Alma, lots of people won't make it, this isn't about you..." She shrugged. "What can I say? She's right. It isn't about me. Nothing in my family ever is." Her voice was sharp. "I mean...she's completely right that this one shouldn't be about me either. I'm just tired of being ignored by them, that's all."

We continued walking down the street in silence. Then I cleared my throat.

"Well, if you're not sure about going to New York... I have an alternative proposal."

She raised an eyebrow at me.

"I have been planning a trip to Granada during spring break," I said. "And I was thinking that I'd like you to come with me."

Alma's expression brightened. "Huh. Granada. I hadn't thought of that."

"And possibly Cartagena on the way back."

"Why Cartagena?"

"My mother's parents are buried there. And it's the city where my father's many-times-great grandfather got married."

"Oh, right!"

"It's a long train ride, and I don't really have any friends left there to visit. All I really need to see is the cemetery, but I also want to visit some places from my childhood. And I enjoy your company and I would like you to come."

Alma's gloominess from earlier was melting away, and she was looking at me with a warm sort of glow. "How long were you planning to be there?" she asked.

"A few days. I called my mother's friend Marta and she said we are welcome to stay with her. She has a guest room, and a fold-out couch in the living room." Alma's step seemed to get lighter and lighter as I spoke. "I searched for kosher restaurants and there was nothing in Granada, but I figured you could bring food with you and maybe some cookware to use on Marta's stove, since that's the easiest thing to *kasher*. Right?"

"Sounds like you've really thought this through," she said, her eyes shining, and the look she gave me made my heart swell. "Well... now that I know I'm going to miss the engagement party, going to Granada with you definitely sounds like more fun than going to New York."

"And less expensive," I added. "And no jet lag."

"And no family fawning over my sister Mimi's general awesomeness and whining about how useless I am."

I laughed. "I don't know... how would they feel about you traveling around Europe with a Catholic boy?"

She gave me a sour look over her glasses. "Who cares?"

We crossed the street, each of us deep in thought.

"Is this why I never hear about them?" I asked finally.

"Who?"

"Your parents and siblings. For someone so obsessed with her ancestors, you talk surprisingly little about your immediate family."

She sighed. "Look. My dad's an engineer. My mom's a dentist. My sister Shoshana is doing her residency to become a cardiologist and I don't even know how she does it with a toddler and a baby. Mimi—she's the one who just got engaged—had hardly passed her bar exam before she got a job with the most prestigious law firm in Albany. Zack is in high school but he's already an expert programmer. My parents are very practical people, and they pretty much think my interests are nonsense and that I'm never going to get my act together and choose a solid career. They threw a fit when I decided to transfer out of nursing school."

"Good thing you're not an artist," I grinned.

"At least that might have made me interesting. Compared to my sisters and my brother, I'm painfully ordinary, and if my parents ever tried to hide their disappointment they didn't do a very good job." She was smiling, but there was a distinct edge to her voice. I stopped walking and turned to her. She looked at me quizzically.

"Alma," I said firmly, looking into her eyes and resisting the urge to reach out and touch her cheek. "You are not ordinary. Painfully or otherwise."

She shrugged and lowered her gaze. "Mimi and I get along okay, but the rest of them... I don't know. We're not on the same wavelength. I grew up pretty close to some of my cousins, but they've all gone their different ways and we don't have much in common anymore. Like my cousin David... I think I told you about him..."

"The one who is dating a non-Jew?" I said softly.

Alma cast a somewhat startled look in my direction. "Um... yeah." She cleared her throat. "But it's not just that, I mean, that was what made my family stop talking to him, but the point is that even before that, he kind of lost interest in Judaism, which used to mean a lot to him. And even the ones who do still feel a connection to it...they're all about the present and the future, and they think my obsession with the past is a waste of time. My grandmother is the only one who appreciates it."

I smiled. "Not the only one."

"Well, *you* don't count. You have a vested interest in my obsession with history." Alma resumed walking. I fell into step beside her.

"Maybe so, but it's still something I admire about you," I said. "Along with a variety of other valuable traits that accompany it, like determination and persistence."

"'Determination and persistence'? Sounds like a nice way to call me stubborn."

"How about your ability to brighten any room you walk into?"

"It's called 'turning on the light'."

"Then how do you manage to do it even on Shabbat?"

"Very poetic, you Spaniard." Alma gave me a playful shove. "You sound like you're about to whip out a guitar and serenade me under the moonlight. If I didn't know better, I'd think you were hitting on me."

"I—" I stammered, feeling my face grow very warm. *Where did* that *come from?* "Well, it's a good thing you do know better," I recovered, glancing at her and clenching the hand that had yearned to touch her into a fist. Her smile was fading and she was staring straight ahead. "I...did not mean it like that. I was trying to point out that—"

"I know, I know. I'm just bad at accepting compliments. Thank you."

But the silence that followed left me wondering which one of us had said too much.

# Alma

Once midterms were over, we were able to start digging through the boxes in the office we had been assigned in the National Archive building. No doubt it was "an important and exciting educational opportunity, and a great privilege"—but it was also extremely tedious work, to say the least. Many of the documents were arranged in files, but they were kind of haphazard and not labeled very well. There were also lots of loose documents that we had to pore over to figure out what they were. And, predictably, we did not find anything remotely connected to an Aguilar family. Worst of all, the archivist was supervising us carefully—and having her breathing down our necks was pretty unnerving.

So at ten-thirty in the morning on the Thursday before spring break, both of us were exhausted, frustrated, and profoundly bored. The archivist was delivering our latest batch of catalogued documents to the digitization staff; everyone else in the nearby offices seemed to have gone on their coffee break. Manuel was sitting listlessly on the floor, whining that his back was hurting and that he hadn't eaten breakfast.

"Go get something from the vending machine," I told him. "We're almost at the bottom of this box, and I am not giving up until it's empty."

"Why? What's the point?" He pulled off his gloves, dropped them in his lap, and ran his hands through his curls, which were growing pretty wild as he consistently ignored his mother's pleas to get his hair cut. "We have three more boxes to go through. Endless piles of pure historical drivel."

"Because the next file could always be *the one*, Manuel," I scolded him. "Come on, you're supposed to be cheering me on here. This is *your* family we're researching."

He sighed, rubbed his eyes wearily, and buried his face in his hands. I turned back to the box and dove in, pulling out a thick file...and that was when a certain word caught my eye. I froze and looked back at the file underneath the one I had just removed. I stared at the index card that had been stapled to the front of the file, and the words written there in clear blue print.

"No."

My tone of voice must have conveyed my incredulousness because Manuel's head popped right up out of his hands.

"What? Did you find something?" He grabbed his gloves, jumped to his feet, and peered into the box. I backed away from it, blinking, thinking my mind must be playing tricks on me.

"Tell me that doesn't say what I think it says."

He snapped on his gloves, pulled out the file, and squinted at it. His jaw dropped and he stared up at me.

"De Carmona, Abraham? Is that..."

"No no no no. It can't be him. It must be someone else. There's no freaking way."

Manuel opened the file and squinted at the cover page. He looked up at me with a huge grin, then looked back down at the page and began translating out loud.

"'Tribunal of Lorca. Protocol from the trial *in absentia* of Abraham de Carmona, the Jew, who to all appearances escaped the city with his daughter before the warrant for his arrest was issued.' The trial took place on the fifth of September, 1492. It looks very similar to other Inquisition trials we've read."

"Oh my God!" I shrieked. "How...I...how is this even...I can't...it...oh my God! Let me see!" He handed me the file. It contained a relatively thick pile of papers. And yes,

*Abraham de Carmona* was written in very clear lettering on the first page, next to the commonly used abbreviation for *"judío"*.

Manuel and I gaped at each other in total astonishment.

"Oh my God!" I started jumping up and down. "I can't believe this! How did this...how...we found the file! We found the file! I can't even...ahhh!"

Manuel stood there watching me freak out, his arms crossed and a big smile on his face.

"Oh my God. I have to call my Grandma." I whipped out my phone and dialed quickly. The phone rang a few times, and then a very, very groggy voice answered.

"This better be important," my father croaked.

"Oh!" I clapped my hand to my mouth. "Oops! What time is it there?"

"Four-thirty in the morning. Is this Alma?"

"Yes! Oh I'm so sorry! I totally forgot about the time difference. I just...um...I made a really important discovery and I was going to tell Grandma. But it can wait until morning—"

"Important discovery?" my father echoed.

"Um, yes, but it can wait, I'm so sorry, go back to sleep."

"No, no, tell me, what did you find?"

I paused a moment, surprised that he was interested enough to stay on the phone at such an ungodly hour. "Well...I'm here in the National Historical Archive with Manuel. You know how we had given up on our family and started focusing on his? And we were going through these boxes of documents from Murcia?"

"Yes?"

"We found the file! The de Carmona file!"

There was a pause. "The de Carmona file...?"

"Um...Ima's maternal ancestor. The father of the bride in the oldest *ketuba* we have."

"*Ima's* maternal ancestor?" His voice was suddenly sharp. "A record from *our* family?" he exclaimed. I heard my mother's muffled, inquiring voice in the background. "It's Alma," my father told her. "She found something."

"Yes! It was here in these boxes!" I went on. "It's totally crazy, but it's true! It's a protocol from the Tribunal of...what was the name of the city?"

"Lorca," Manuel said.

"Lorca! It says that the trial took place in his absence after he disappeared from his house before the arrest warrant was issued."

"Well, this is wonderful!" my dad said. "I'll tell Grandma to call you first thing in the morning so you can tell her all about it."

"Thanks! I'm so sorry about the time..." I stammered again.

"It's fine, it's fine. Great work, Alma."

"Thanks! Love you!"

I hung up, staring at the phone for a minute. Then I tossed it on a nearby desk and did another little victory dance.

"*¿Qué haces?*" came the archivist's sharp whisper behind me.

Manuel made some excuse for my behavior, explained what we were doing, and convinced her to bump the file to the front of the digitization queue so we could have a couple of printouts of the digital images to take with us on our trip to Granada.

"Good thinking!" I exclaimed when he explained this to me after she had left with the file. "Well...so...what now?"

Manuel pulled off his gloves and tossed them in a nearby garbage pail. "Now we find more information about Lorca."

"Oh, right! Yes! Lorca! Computers!" I got rid of my gloves and charged toward the computer in the corner of the room. I plopped down in the seat and stared at the screen. "Um..." It was a very old machine, with some ancient version of Windows that I wasn't sure what to do with, especially since everything was in Spanish.

"Allow me," Manuel offered. I stood up and let him take my

place. The computer was impossibly slow, and I tapped my foot impatiently as we waited for the browser to load.

"Well, this certainly shifts the focus of our project, eh?" Manuel said, leaning back in the chair.

I looked at him. "Uh…yeah. Sorry to…um…steal your thunder. Are you disappointed that we haven't found anything else about your family?"

He shrugged. "A little. But I'm very happy for you. And once we've worked through the file, we can look through the rest of these boxes. Maybe there is still hope for the Aguilars, too." The browser finally loaded and Manuel started tapping at the keyboard. I leaned over, eagerly looking at the screen in front of him. After a few seconds I noticed that he had stopped what he was doing, his fingers hovering over the keyboard, his shoulders tensed.

"What?" I asked. "Why'd you stop?"

"I…just…" He closed his eyes, wincing a little. "Could you… not lean over my shoulder like that?"

I jerked upright. "Oh." I cleared my throat. "Sorry."

I dragged a chair over to the computer desk.

"Okay, Alma, look at this." He swiveled the computer screen toward me. "Turns out there's this huge medieval fortress in Lorca that housed the *judería*, and there are ongoing excavations there, uncovering all kinds of amazing things. Apparently it has the only synagogue in the region that was never converted into a church or a mosque."

I skimmed the page, looking at the pictures, and then turned to Manuel.

"We are going there!"

"We are definitely going there," he echoed.

"It's close to Cartagena, right?"

"About an hour by car. Longer by bus and train, unfortunately."

"And Cartagena is a major port."

"Yes, that's true."

"I bet my ancestors sailed from there."

Manuel nodded. "Very likely."

"So we should definitely visit Cartagena too."

"I was hoping to get there anyway."

"Well, you know what this means," I said. He blinked in confusion. "Celebratory lunch at Alfassi! Now! On me!" I glared at him, lest he even consider protesting.

# Míriam

"It's absolutely infuriating," Don Tomás said, pacing back and forth between the beds. Abraham and Míriam were sitting next to each other on Míriam's bed, staring grimly at the floor. "There has been no official announcement of any kind. But yesterday I heard that your property had been seized. With no warrant!"

"Even the spices that I was storing for you?"

"Yes! Exactly! So at least I had an excuse to go down to their offices and demand that they release my property to me. They were apologetic and told me where it was all being kept, and gave me a letter for the guards so they would let me take it. I'm sending León to get it today, because I'm due in Cartagena tonight and I'm not going to have time to waste on this scandalous nonsense." He turned toward them, sighing deeply. "I wish there were something I could do to protect all your property for you. I can't believe their audacity—it seems they'll use any pretext to take advantage of a Jew."

Abraham sighed. "This is nothing new, my friend."

Don Tomás crossed his arms, his brow furrowed. "I just can't stand it. I can't stand the corruption, the hatred, the injustice…and it's not being done by some heathen tribe somewhere or by ignorant peasants—these are the most elevated, respected members of the Church! How can they act this way in the name of God? How can they pretend to represent Jesus on Earth?"

"There is corruption everywhere, Tomás, and especially in places of power. This has always been true."

Don Tomás gave him a weary look. "Maybe it's just that you are used to it."

Abraham smiled sadly. "Maybe so."

"Well, I don't want to get used to it." Don Tomás peered out the window and sighed. "I must go." He looked at Abraham and Míriam, his face wrinkled in concern. "I don't want to leave you here like this."

"I'm sure León will take good care of us," Abraham said gently. He stood and embraced his friend. "You have done more than your share for us. God will surely reward you."

"I hope to bring better news when I get back."

"May it be His will."

Don Tomás regarded Abraham carefully. "Have you thought about where you might go if you need to flee?"

Abraham frowned and sank back down to the bed.

"I assume Fez would be the best option for you," Don Tomás continued quietly. "You could join your brothers' business."

"You're probably right." Abraham glanced at Míriam, his brow knitted in worry. "But the situation is not so good there. They have lost several children to plagues and bandits. I would not want to have to bring Míriam to such a place."

Míriam swallowed and stared at her feet.

"Well," Don Tomás said, "let us pray you will not need to consider it."

With León left alone to run the estate, Míriam expected that she wouldn't see much of him over the next few days; so she was surprised when she turned from the bookshelves to see him standing in the doorway. Her heart beat a little faster.

"Good day, *señor*." She curtsied. "I wasn't expecting to see you."

"I can't stay and help today," he said, "but I have something for you." She noticed that he was holding something small wrapped in a white handkerchief. He handed it to her. She looked up at him curiously, then slowly unwrapped it. When she caught a glimpse of sky blue, she gasped.

"How...?!"

It was her mother's book of Psalms. Brilliant threads of gold, green, purple and red were painstakingly stitched in elaborate patterns around the letters that spelled the Hebrew word for Psalms: *Tehillim*. She ran her hand over the embroidered letters, caressing this little piece of her mother she thought had been gone forever. A wave of mixed emotions—sadness, despair, relief, gratitude—washed over her. She tried to brace herself against it, blinking the tears away, but she had been holding back so much pain and fear and grief, for so long, that it was impossible to control herself. Before she knew it she was sitting on the nearest chair, sobbing as she had on the day her mother died, crying as she'd only cried as a child in her father's arms as the shadows grew longer in the drab wastelands of La Mancha...her mother's body freshly buried under a pile of earth, and almost everything they had ever owned, known, or loved left behind them.

She was mortified to lose her composure like this in front of León; she was afraid he would be alarmed or embarrassed by her outburst. But he just stood there quietly, waiting for the storm to pass. After a few minutes he sat next to her, his hands folded in his lap, and stayed there until she finally spoke.

"I'm sorry..." she said. "I'm just...so grateful."

"I was returning your favor." León gave her a little smile.

Míriam found herself longing to embrace León. She hugged the book to her chest instead.

"How did you get this?"

"I may have taken a few liberties at the storehouse where they keep the confiscated property," he said with a twinkle in his eye. "They let me in to collect my father's spices."

"How on earth did you find it among all our things?" She opened the book, breathing in the scent of the parchment, her eyes drinking in the Hebrew letters dancing across the pages.

"By the grace of God and with a little patience," León answered.

"León." Miriam looked up into his eyes. "I can't tell you how much this means to me."

"I think I know." They studied each other for a few moments. Miriam clenched the book in her hands to fight the urge to take León's. "Well, I must be going." León stood from the chair. "Good day, señorita."

# Manuel

Exciting as Alma's find was, we did not have a lot of time to work on it before our trip to the south. We were planning to leave early on Monday, as I was determined not to miss either church or Rabbi Uri's class that week. We'd have some time to work on the file on the train to Granada.

Olivia was in church again that Sunday. When she asked if I'd like to join her for coffee again, I agreed; but as we crossed the bustling street I felt a little pang of guilt. It was followed immediately by a wave of exasperation. *This is ridiculous,* I told myself as we sat down. *There is no reason to feel guilty about spending time with a girl I am not dating, because another girl I am not dating is apparently uncomfortable with it.*

"So," Olivia said. "Really nice service today."

"I think they overdid it a bit with the incense. Good thing Alma doesn't come to church—she'd be coughing for a week."

"They don't have incense in synagogues?"

"No. They can't light fires on the Sabbath, and it's not part of the prayer service anyway."

Olivia watched me as I emptied a sugar packet into my coffee and stirred. Finally she said, "Have you decided which religion you like better yet?"

"It's not a matter of liking it better. It's a matter of which one feels more right."

"And?"

I sighed. "I don't know." I took a sip. "In many ways the synagogue does. But…you know. It's complicated."

"What do Jews think about Jesus?" Olivia asked. "I know Muslims think of him as a prophet."

I stared into my coffee. "I don't know, Olivia. I've been afraid to ask."

Olivia laughed. "Afraid to ask? Don't you think the answer to that question might help you solve your dilemma once and for all?"

I looked at her thoughtfully. "Maybe that's what I'm afraid of."

"What? That it'll change your feelings?"

"That I'll hear an answer that will force me to rethink everything. Or that will create some kind of certainty. I know that seems like what I'm looking for, but there's also something scary about it. Certainty closes doors. It's a point of no return. Nothing will ever be quite the same, no matter what I decide."

"I hate to tell you this," she said, "but you're already there."

I blinked. "Where?"

"The point of no return. You already think differently than you used to about religion. Even if you decide to go ahead and become a priest after all, it'll never be the same for you as it was. You already can't go back."

I swallowed.

"But I think it's a good thing," she went on.

"Maybe in the long run," I said. "It's just... once I'm in, I'm in, and my entire life could turn on its head. I'm not sure I'm ready for that right now."

Olivia laughed. "Manuel, will you ever be sure you're ready for that?"

⌇⌇⌇

That evening, after the last of Rabbi Uri's students had bid him goodbye, I approached him and took a deep breath.

"I want to talk to you about Jesus," I said.

Rabbi Uri looked at me, his bushy eyebrows raised, and laughed. "I hope you don't mean that in the way it's usually meant!"

So he sat me down, took out a few sources from the Bible and the Talmud, and reviewed them with me. I appreciated his style: he wasn't pushy about his viewpoint, he just presented it as "the way we see things". And I had to admit, after about forty-five minutes of this, that I was feeling rather confused.

I let out a long breath. "This Trinity business... it never did make much sense to me," I said slowly. "And the Messiah thing... I think what you believe makes a lot of sense. But..."

He nodded. "I know. I've taught a number of Christians who really struggled with this. Particularly Evangelicals... they really feel that direct connection with Jesus as their personal savior. It's a very intense sort of relationship that's hard to let go of."

I sighed in relief. *He gets it.*

"It's much easier to relate to a God who is—at least in part—embodied in a person, than a God who is unknowable, unreachable, completely beyond human contact or comprehension. It's not the only thing about Christianity that is easier... as I'm sure you've learned by now."

I stared at my hands, discomfort churning in my chest.

"But we Jews simply cannot accept that concept. It's directly contrary to the commandment to believe in one unitary God—the first two of the Ten Commandments. We can't reconcile this."

I chewed on my lip and said nothing.

He studied me. "So... have I answered your questions?"

I gave him a sad smile. "I think you've created more questions than you've answered."

He laughed and clapped me on the back. "Great! That's what I like to hear." He took a book off the pile he had collected from his library for the conversation and slid it across the desk to me: *The Real Messiah? A Jewish Response to Missionaries.* "It's a collection of essays tackling this issue from various angles, most of which we touched on, but if you want to read about it more in depth..." His voice trailed off as he studied the cover. "I'll warn you, it doesn't pull any punches. You might be a little upset by some of the things it says. But it raises some very important questions about Christian theology that you may already be asking yourself. It's up to you whether you want to explore it from the Jewish perspective. Maybe your priest can recommend something from the Christian perspective."

I picked up the book and studied it for a long moment, pursing my lips, torn between curiosity and foreboding.

Finally, I looked up at Rabbi Uri.

"Thank you," I said, and slipped it into my bag. "I'll think about it."

He took a long pause, staring at his folded hands on the table, and then looked up. "Well... if we're already talking about these issues, then I think this might be the right time to have this conversation." He smiled, and after another few moments, took a deep breath and said, "So... you and Alma."

I looked away, dread filling the pit of my stomach. I cleared my throat and looked back at him. "Me and Alma?"

He paused again, and then continued very slowly and carefully. "I can't help but notice the chemistry between you. You seem to get along really well, and... well... I think it's obvious that there's the potential for something there."

I didn't answer. I just stared down at the floor.

"The thing is..."

"I know what the thing is," I interrupted him.

"Okay. But let's put everything on the table so we can be totally honest here. Alma is an observant Jewish girl. She is very devoted to her faith and her heritage. But I can't help but wonder if she and you are being careful enough about boundaries."

Anger started to rise in my chest.

"What kind of boundaries, Rabbi?" I asked, not looking at him.

"This trip to Granada, for example. Or really...all that time working alone together in a little office at the archive..."

"We're not exactly alone there," I protested through gritted teeth. "There are plenty of other people around."

"Still. It sounds very intense, and quite...intimate. I'm not sure it's such a good idea. I don't want either of you to get hurt."

I pursed my lips, trying to swallow my anger. "Let's say, in theory, that we would want to do something about this...'potential', as you call it," I said slowly. "Couldn't I convert?"

"See...that's the thing." He rested a gentle hand on my arm. "If you do decide to convert, having Alma there as an ulterior motive is very problematic for a rabbinical court. We don't want people to convert just to marry; we want them to convert only if they absolutely cannot see themselves living any other kind of life. So either way... I think it would be wise to...maybe...keep your distance."

I turned toward him, pushing my chair back a little. "Keep my distance?"

He nodded, watching me apprehensively.

"What does that even mean?" I demanded.

He sighed, pushing his black velvet skullcap back to scratch the bald spot on the top of his head.

I couldn't hold back my anger any longer. "It's fine for you to be interested in Judaism and to learn, but stay away from our women? Is that what you're telling me?" I spat.

"Manuel...please. I know you're upset."

"She's too good for me?"

"It's not about that at all! No one is better than anyone else..."

"You call yourselves 'the chosen people'..."

"That's not about quality, it's about our mission in the world. A dog is no better than a cat, but they fill different functions—"

"So I'm a dog and Alma is a cat?!"

"It's a metaphor—"

"It's a terrible and racist metaphor!" I raged, getting up from my chair. "We are two human beings!"

"Manuel, please, sit down. I know this is upsetting and I'm sorry, but please let me explain."

I hesitated, and then sat down slowly, trying to breathe deeply to calm the pulsing in my forehead.

"Jews have lived under an existential threat since the destruction of the First Temple. For most of history, that threat expressed itself through hatred, violence, oppression, and genocide. That does still exist today, more in some places than others, but most modern Jews are facing a very different kind of existential threat now. Assimilation rates in the USA are alarming beyond all measure. This isn't about individuals and how they might feel about each other. This is about our destiny as a nation."

I folded my arms. "What if a couple decided to raise their kids Jewish? Isn't Judaism passed down only through the mother?"

"Yes, and that might work for the first generation. But even then, the children might look at their parents and say, 'Well, if this Judaism thing is so important, why is my dad not Jewish?' It certainly wouldn't be important enough to them to go out of their way to marry Jewish themselves. So what about the next generation, and the next? Jews are disappearing this way, Manuel. I'm not talking theoretically. This is very real, and it is happening right now all over the world."

I just sat there scowling at him.

"This isn't only about Alma's commitment to Jewish continuity, either. As a person who values Jews and Judaism and who believes they have something important to contribute to the world, now and in the future...this should be important to you, too."

I stood up again and fixed him with a glare. "I don't need you to tell me what is important to me...Rabbi."

Rabbi Uri looked up at me with sad eyes. "Please, Manuel. I mean no offense. I just don't want either of you to get hurt."

"Well," I said coldly, scooping up my shoulder bag and coat. "I appreciate your concern."

I stalked out.

# Míriam

The next day, Míriam was working in the library and heard some kind of commotion on the other side of the house. She froze, unsure whether to try to find out what was happening or to lie low and wait. She tiptoed to the door and peeked down the hallway, listening carefully.

A minute later León burst out of the kitchen and came sprinting toward her. "María," he called. It took a few moments before she realized he was calling her by her false name.

"What's wrong?" she asked.

"Have you ever attended a birth?" He stopped in front of her. His face was very pale, his hands shaking.

She almost giggled, but then she remembered the circumstances of his mother's death, and her smile melted away.

"Yes," she said. "My neighbor was the *judería*'s midwife and I often assisted her. Is someone having a baby?"

"One of the maids—come quickly—we sent for a midwife but the baby is coming too fast..." They jogged toward the kitchen. "Why do these things *always* happen when my father is away?"

Míriam shoved the door open. A very pregnant woman was leaning against the wall, red-faced and drenched in sweat, letting out a low, loud, grunting sort of moan. Three other maids were scurrying around, shouting at each other in high-pitched voices. They were all very young, probably too young to have had much experience with childbirth themselves. There were grains and vegetables scattered all over the table and the floor.

Míriam stepped forward.

"Everybody calm down!" She commanded. Everyone froze and looked up at her. She pointed at one of the maids. "You! Get a large bowl of clean, warm water." The maid turned right around to do as she was told. "You!" She pointed at the next maid. "Clean cloths and blankets. You! Clean this up." She gestured at the food that was on the floor near the woman in labor. The third maid went right to work.

The pregnant woman let out a howl. Míriam rushed to her side and put a firm hand on the small of her back. "Take a deep breath now, *señora*. Everything will be just fine." The woman breathed deeply and her shoulders relaxed a little. "Now you just tell me when you feel that baby's head. It sounds like you are pushing already." The woman nodded.

Míriam suddenly noticed a movement behind her, and whirled around to see that León was still standing there, staring at her.

"Some privacy, please, *señor!*" she scolded.

He turned and bolted from the room.

Within a few minutes, the woman let out a raucous cry and said she was feeling the baby's head emerge. Míriam delicately lifted her skirts and put her hands on the little head.

"Try not to push now," she said. "Better for him to come slowly. Breathe deeply." A few moans later, a beautiful baby girl slid into Míriam's hands, and immediately began to cry. Míriam laughed in triumphant relief, wrapping the baby gently in one of the cloths the other maid had brought. "Here, sit down," she said, stuffing some extra cloths underneath the new mother to soak up the blood. "Hold your sweet baby girl."

"Thank you, thank you…oh, look at her!" The maid murmured in an awed, breathless voice as she took her child into her arms. She looked up at Míriam with wide eyes. "Are you the midwife?"

Míriam chuckled. "No…but I attended many of my neighbors' births."

As if on cue, the real midwife burst through the door and bustled over to the mother and baby. Míriam stepped back, then looked at her hands covered in blood, and washed them in the bowl the other maid had brought. She backed out of the kitchen, leaving the maids and the midwife to fuss over the mess, and walked out into the hallway where León was pacing nervously back and forth. He looked up.

"Well?"

"It's a girl." She smiled. "They are both fine, thank God."

He let out a long breath. "Thank God for you. They were in such hysterics, I don't know what would have happened…" His eyes locked on hers. "I had no idea you could…do that."

"What, catch a baby?" She laughed. "It's not much harder than catching anything else…they come out quite slowly."

"That's not what I meant." He was looking at her intensely. It sent a pleasant sort of shiver down her spine. "I've never met a woman quite like you."

She blushed and lowered her eyes. She wasn't sure what to say to that; she cleared her throat and mumbled something about getting back to work, and started walking toward the library. But he followed her.

"How is it that you are not married yet?" he asked when they were in the relative privacy of the room. She looked up at him, her heart pounding. *Why would he ask me that? That's hardly an appropriate question.*

"Well…to be honest," she said slowly, "it's probably that I am too well educated. It's uncommon in our circles, and it makes people suspicious. I don't know about Christian men, but Jewish men tend to prefer their wives silent, obedient, and not too bright. My father never got any offers for me, and he didn't really go out of his way to seek them." She studied him. "But I could ask the same of you."

León shrugged.

"I think my father just hasn't been quite ready to bring another lady into the house after my mother's death—so he hasn't tried very hard either." He paused. "And the eligible women I have met match your description of an 'ideal' Jewish wife for the most part…and quite frankly, I find them tiresome."

There was an awkward silence, and Míriam sensed that León felt he had said too much.

"Well, ehhh…thank you for your help. You were wonderful." And he left her standing at the library table, chewing her lip and thinking about their conversation.

León was the only Christian she had ever befriended; she had never had much opportunity to interact with people outside the walled-in *judería*. And she liked him, and found herself thinking about him more than she thought she should. About the way his eyes squinted when he smiled. About his blunt, straightforward manner of asking her questions and sharing his thoughts. About the look on his face when he gave her the book of Psalms. About how much she had longed to take his hand then, and still did now.

She shook her head, trying to clear it of these images of León. He was a Christian. He should not even have mentioned the concept of marriage around her! And marrying him was completely out of the question on every imaginable level. Both Jewish and Castilian law forbade such a union in the most severe terms; for León to marry a Jew meant a choice between being burned at the stake by the Inquisition or permanent exile, while for her the choice would be between the fire and the betrayal of everything she believed and valued. The idea of that happening—on either side—was preposterous, even without the issues of their vastly different social status and what both their fathers might think.

And yet…

*No. Don't even think about it*, she scolded herself. She sank down into the chair, feeling a heavy despair settle over her. She stared unseeing at the piles of papers on the table.

*No. I can't believe I'm even thinking about this. How could I be thinking about this? With everything I've been taught, all my conviction, all my commitment to my faith and my people...all my devotion to God and His law...how could I be thinking this way about a Christian man I met only a few weeks ago? How could this have happened to me?*

She buried her face in her hands. The image of León's face wouldn't budge from her mind. Miriam had daydreamed about meeting a man someday who would make her feel like this; she had imagined butterflies in her stomach, giddiness, the world filling with color and beauty and light—but all she could feel now was the crushing weight of "neverness".

*Never. I could never marry him. Never, ever, ever.*

"God help me," she whispered. "How could I be so foolish?"

*I should never have let him stay and talk with me. I should never have become his friend. I should never have given him those letters or talked to him about my mother or about the book of Psalms. I should never have let the walls come down enough for me to grow to love him.*

*Never.*

*Never.*

*Never.*

# Alma

I stood over my suitcase on Sunday evening, my hands on my hips and my mouth scrunched to one side.

"I may have overdone this a bit," I mumbled. Some clothes were crunched into the bottom of the suitcase, and the rest was piled high with cans of tuna and beans, a carton of shelf-stable milk, packages of pasta, some granola bars, and a loaf of bread, along with all my dairy cookware and utensils.

My phone buzzed in my pocket and I pulled it out.

"Hello?"

"Hi, honey. How are you?"

"Grandma! How was the party yesterday?"

"Loud. Really loud. The food... well, his family was hosting, and it was, you know..."

"Ashkenazi?" I grinned.

"You said it, not me."

"But what about Mimi? Was she happy?"

"Oh, she was glowing. Beautiful. He couldn't take his eyes off her the whole time. I think he can't believe his luck."

"I wouldn't either if I were him. I hope they took lots of pictures."

"You can count on that. We missed you there. You should have heard your parents boasting to the future in-laws about your findings—your father especially."

I was speechless for a moment. "Really? *Abba?*"

"Yes. He's very proud of you, you know."

I sat back, a warm glow washing over me. Tears pricked at my eyes.

"So what's new with you?" Grandma asked.

"Well... I just finishing packing for our trip to Granada tomorrow." I glanced back at the suitcase. "I think I might have been a little over-enthusiastic in the food-packing department."

"Granada, hmm? Another school trip?"

"Um, no. Just me and Manuel."

There was a pause on the other end. "Oh."

The warm glow from earlier now threatened to turn into irritation.

"What happened to you not frolicking on the beach drinking martinis?" my grandmother asked. There was a smile in her voice, but I was not in a joking mood about this.

"First of all," I said sharply, "Granada is nowhere near the beach. Second of all, I couldn't find a kosher martini there even if I searched the whole city door to door. Third of all, I will have you know that we are *also* going to be visiting the old Jewish quarter of Lorca, which is important for our research—you should be really excited about that."

"Why, what's in Lorca?"

"How do you remember my comment about beaches and martinis but not this?" I sighed. "Lorca. Our ancestors. Abraham de Carmona. Remember?"

"Oh, that! Have you had more time to read the file?"

"Not much, but we did go through the first page. What Abraham was accused of was helping *conversos* keep their Jewish practices in secret. They seem to have had concrete evidence of one incident, where he provided kosher wine for some families on one of the holidays."

"Good for him!"

"I know, right? But the rest...it's hard to know what's true and what isn't."

"Any mention of them being aided by a Christian family in their escape?"

"No, nothing that we came across."

Grandma paused and took a deep breath. "Alma...I know this is going to sound crazy...but I just remembered something."

I froze. "What?"

"The rest of the story."

"What rest of the story?" I exclaimed, squeezing the phone between my shoulder and my chin and clawing around my backpack for a pen and paper. "There's more to the story?"

"Yes! I remembered another detail my grandmother told me about the ring."

"Tell me, tell me!" I squealed.

"So, our maternal ancestor? Míriam?"

"Yeah..."

"Abuela told me that Míriam fell in love with the son of the Christian family while they were helping her and her father."

My enthusiasm died down very suddenly and I felt the irritation wash back over me. I chewed my lip. "Uh huh."

"Abuela said that he is the one who gave her that ring."

There were a few moments of silence.

"Are you there?" my grandmother asked.

"Yeah, I'm here," I said, my voice biting. "And that's a pretty good story."

Grandma paused. "Why do you sound angry?"

"Because I don't believe you."

"Don't believe what?"

"That that's the actual story. I know what you're doing. This is supposed to be some kind of morality tale, and you're warning me again about a relationship with Manuel."

There was silence on the other end. Finally, Grandma said, "I can't believe you think I am making this up."

"Because Mimi is marrying a Jew and you're afraid that I won't. When are you going to let this go and just trust me?"

"You don't believe me when I tell you a story I heard with my own ears from my own grandmother, and then you complain that *I* don't trust *you?*" Grandma's voice was sharp.

"Don't Jewish-grandmother me," I shot back. "Very convenient to be remembering a story about a Jewish woman choosing her faith over love right after I told you that I'm going to Granada with Manuel."

"That *is* what reminded me of it, but that doesn't mean it's not—"

"Whatever, Grandma. I'm going to finish packing." And I hung up the phone without another word. I sat and stared at it and waited for her to call back, but she didn't.

---

Manuel and I met at the Metro station the following morning. He was carrying a mid-sized backpack, and his eyebrows shot up when he saw the suitcase I was lugging.

"We're going for three days, Alma," he said. "Did you pack your entire apartment?"

"Only the dairy part. What do you expect me to live on for three days? Apples?" I slipped my pass into the machine and walked through the turnstile.

"Actually, I did a little more research," Manuel said, following me down the stairs to the subway platform. "It turns out that the fastest way to get to Granada is through Málaga. *And* it turns out that there is a kosher café a fifteen-minute walk from the train station in Málaga."

I turned to him, grinning. "I like where this is going."

"That's what I thought you would say. The ride is about three hours. We could stop there for lunch, and then continue on to Granada."

"I told you, you're definitely starting to think like a Jew," I shouted as the Metro train pulled up next to us and the doors slid open. We stepped inside and took seats. Manuel was staring ahead of him, his eyes pensive.

"Well," he said finally, "maybe so, but I think I have decided that I'm not going to be one."

I blinked. "One what?"

"A Jew."

I looked at the floor. This wasn't exactly surprising to me, but still, I couldn't deny a sinking feeling of disappointment.

"Why, what happened in Rabbi Uri's class last night?" I asked.

He shrugged, shifting uncomfortably. "Nothing. Well...maybe something. We just had a little argument. It does not matter." He looked away, and after a few moments he said, "To be honest, it's not so much the idea of *being* Jewish that I have difficulty with. It's the *becoming* Jewish part. There's so much to take on at once... it's overwhelming. I wish there were a way to explore it and my relationship with it more gradually." He paused again. "We talked about the Jewish view of Jesus..."

"Ahh," I said.

"No, actually, that's not what the argument was about. I thought the Jesus stuff made a lot of sense."

"Then what was the argument about?"

"It...I told you, it does not matter." His voice had an edge, though, and he seemed somewhat agitated. I narrowed my eyes in suspicion, but before I could pry any further, he continued: "The point is, a lot of what he said about Jesus and the Trinity rang true for me."

I raised an eyebrow at him. "Wait. Didn't you just say you *didn't* want to be a Jew? But you think the Jews are right about Jesus?"

"I did not say I think the Jews are right about Jesus. I said I understand your viewpoint. And it has forced me to dig around in my own beliefs to work out what I feel is true. I'm still not sure."

I rubbed my forehead in confusion. "At this rate, you'll end up as a Hindu or something. I think we need to get you to seminary pronto."

He laughed.

"Come on, you already worship cows..."

"I do not worship cows! I just don't eat them!"

"Yeah, yeah."

He was digging around in his bag. Finally, he pulled out a book and handed it to me: *The Real Messiah? A Jewish Response to Missionaries.*

"Hmm, Aryeh Kaplan. He's awesome," I said. "Rabbi Uri gave this to you?"

"Yes. I have not started it yet. I was wondering if you would be willing to read it first. Then you can tell me how well you think I'll tolerate it."

I studied him. "What does that even mean? How on earth am I supposed to know?"

He shrugged. "I only... I trust you."

I scanned the back cover of the book. "So does this mean you've decided not to go to seminary?"

"No... it does not mean anything, really. I still want to learn more about both faiths. But I think you're going to have to attend Shabbat meals without me, at least for a while."

Well, *there* was a legitimate excuse to be disappointed.

"Darn!" I whined. "Who's going to be my *Shabbos goy?*"

"You're a Jew," he said with a mischievous grin. "Improvise. You guys are good at that."

I rolled my eyes and cracked the book open. "What if we read it together? Would that make it easier?"

He paused. "I don't know."

"What are you afraid of, Manuel?" I looked him squarely in the eye. "That it'll turn you off of Christianity once and for all? It's just a book. Propaganda, if we're calling a spade a spade. I bet your priest in Brooklyn could offer some decent counter-arguments if you just gave him a call."

"See, this is why I trust you." He smiled at me, his shoulders relaxing somewhat. "You never force your views on me. You have always been neutral and supportive about my exploring things on my own terms."

*Neutral, huh?* said a voice in my head. I ignored it.

"I know it's ridiculous," he went on. "It's just very uncomfortable to encounter beliefs that are so contrary to yours, especially when they're presented in a sophisticated way, and *especially* when you're not sure how to counter them." He sighed. "I'm just afraid it would upset me, and leave me more confused than ever. Maybe it would turn me away from Judaism, too."

"Like I said," I winked, "the Hindus are waiting."

"What is the Hindu heaven like? Would I miss you there?"

I grinned. "Only if you get reincarnated as something really lame."

I pulled my suitcase closer and unzipped one of the outside pockets, dropping the book into it.

"I'll read it and give you my professional opinion."

We sat quietly for a minute. Then I spoke up: "Can I just ask you... this might be a hard question to answer: What is your spiritual experience of God? Like, do you really think He could have been embodied in a person? When you speak to Him, who are you speaking to?"

He nodded, and took at least a minute before answering. "Well... that's the thing," he said finally. "I was told to picture Jesus when I prayed. To speak to him. But I never did. I never could. For me, I pictured Jesus most easily from the stories in the Gospels. I pictured him as a kind teacher, as a leader. Most of all, as a father figure, or a friend. But I could not picture him as being the same as God in any way. And when I prayed, I always felt like I was speaking to something much bigger, much greater than something that could possibly be embodied in a person. That 'person' of the Trinity is basically the Father, so I figured I was speaking to Him. But it never sat very well with me, this whole business of dividing Him up into persons. It was very hard for me to see Jesus as being an equal aspect of God. So I suppose the answer to your question is that my spiritual experience of God is almost exclusively that of the Father. And that seems to me to be pretty similar to the Jewish concept of God."

I nodded slowly. "So...I can see why you are not totally scandalized by what Rabbi Uri said."

"Yes."

"And...well...isn't not believing in the Trinity...heresy or something?"

He sighed, ran a hand through his hair, and said nothing.

"I could burn you at the stake a little if it would make you feel better," I added helpfully after a moment.

He laughed and glanced at me warmly.

"That is very generous of you, Alma."

"Any time."

---

The Atocha train station—the main intercity station in Madrid—was huge and airport-like, with high arched ceilings and a big indoor tropical garden in the atrium. Manuel tried to be patient as I took videos of the turtles in the garden while we waited. We boarded the train to Málaga and spent the ride going through Manuel's copy of the de Carmona file. (Of course, I'd forgotten to pack mine.)

The trial seemed to consist mostly of dubious testimony given by Christian customers of Abraham's spice business—none of which had anything to do with the original accusation. The trial protocol kept referring to the testimony of some guy called Sánchez—apparently the *converso* Abraham supplied with kosher wine—at his own trial; but the de Carmona file did not include a copy of this testimony or any other details of Sánchez's trial. By the time we arrived in Málaga, I was pretty disgruntled at how little useful information we'd found.

Málaga was bright and sunny and smelled of the sea. I was overcome with a sudden desire to see the seashore, but we didn't have time. We had lunch at the kosher café Manuel had found, and then caught a bus onward to Granada.

We arrived in late afternoon and took another bus to Marta's apartment. At this point I was more in the mood to collapse in a heap and sleep than anything else, but Marta had other plans. Apparently she had pre-booked tickets to a night tour of the Alhambra, and she and her husband insisted on taking us out somewhere before that. I tried to suggest that they go without me, but Manuel said, "Oh no you don't!" and dragged me out the door.

Their apartment was in a district that Manuel said used to be the city's Jewish quarter. I didn't see anything indicating as much, but it was an interesting and quaint—if somewhat cramped—little neighborhood, with narrow brick-paved streets weaving through rows of small apartment buildings.

"Where are we going?" I asked.

Manuel pointed past Marta at a storefront set into the stone wall across the street. Through the tall windows, I could see people sitting at a bar. *"Tapas* bar," he said. "Can't be in Granada and not have *tapas.*" He grabbed the handle and swung the door open, gesturing for me to enter. José and Marta filed in after me. I let them go ahead of me to take their seats, and waited for Manuel. The dim lighting, jazzy music, and thick, smoky air did not help me feel more awake.

"So," I said, "I guess we finally get to be the joke now."

Manuel furrowed his brow in confusion.

"An American Jew and a Spanish Catholic walk into a bar..."

Manuel cracked up as I grabbed one of the bar stools and perched on it. "So how does the joke end?" Manuel asked, sliding onto the bar stool next to me.

"You tell me." I stared across the bar at the bottles lining the walls. "I think the Jew says, 'I don't drink. Why am I here?'"

"No, I think that's what the Catholic is supposed to say..."

"But only if he's a priest, and you're not."

"Still. You're making it sound like Jews don't drink. I saw how Rabbi Uri gulps down a huge glass of scotch every Friday night."

"Yes, well, he *is* a Chabadnik," I shrugged. "But you're right, it's not true that I don't drink. I'll have a glass of wine or a beer now and then."

"Wine is problematic, I know, but does beer need kosher supervision?"

"No, as long as it doesn't have added flavor. But I hate the drinking culture. I've always hated how my uncles and cousins act when they get drunk on Purim."

He gave a sardonic smile. "Did you ever go to one of the student parties at NYU?" he asked.

"Ha. I know better!"

"I wish *I* had known better when Rob dragged me to one the first week after we got here."

Marta grabbed the bartender's attention and started ordering for all of us.

*"Disculpe,"* I cut in. *"Nada para mí, gracias."*

Marta gave me a scandalized look and said something in her rapid, sound-swallowing Andalusian Spanish that I could not understand. I opened my mouth to ask her to repeat that, but Manuel lifted his hand and responded to her in equally incomprehensible speech. After a brief discussion with the bartender, he turned back to me.

"I ordered you a beer," he said. "In Granada you get free *tapas* with your drink, and I asked for him to see if there are any fresh fruits or vegetables he can serve you."

I smiled in relief. "Thanks."

The bartender slid two tall glasses of beer in our direction. I took one and examined it.

"What is this?"

"Alhambra Reserva. It's quite strong."

"I thought we were going to visit the Alhambra, not drink it."

Manuel snorted. "Is that how our joke ends?"

"If it does..." I looked up at him over my glasses. "We make a pretty lame joke."

Manuel laughed and clinked his glass against mine. *"L'chaim."*

*"Salud,"* I answered.

---

We took a taxi to the Alhambra, and as soon as we arrived I understood why Marta had ordered us tickets for the night tour of the palace complex. The moonlight dancing on the fountains and streams, casting shadows on the elaborate tiling and plasterwork, gave the whole thing a mystic atmosphere. It was, without a doubt, the most beautiful structure I had ever seen. There was something in its symmetry, the way the arches and domes and rooftops aligned and reflected in the still pools, the constant soothing sound of flowing water... Those Nasrid emirs who built this place—they knew what they were doing.

On the other hand... this was also the place where King Fernando and Queen Isabel signed the Edict of Expulsion in 1492.

I imagined them strolling alongside me, arm in arm, their footsteps and polite laughter echoing through the halls, as the mournful procession of Jews made its way out of the city.

"Thanks for nothing, a-holes," I mumbled.

"Did you say something?" Manuel tore his eyes off the ornate wooden carvings on the ceiling to glance at me.

"Nothing," I said. "Just paying my respects to the Royal Jesus Freaks who humiliated, tortured, exploited, robbed, and expelled my ancestors."

Manuel stiffened.

"Sorry," I said quickly. "I didn't mean—"

"I understand. I have no defense for the behavior of some of my coreligionists. But as for the Catholic Monarchs—they are not the ones who built this place. They're not even buried here anymore."

"Good thing, too, because I'd probably get arrested for spitting on their graves."

"Not that I would stop you," he said, "but you know, it's thanks to them that Columbus discovered America."

"Oh, don't even get me started on Columbus and the colonies in America and what they did to the Native Americans."

"Still, America has been a wonderful place for Jews."

"That's thanks to the Founding Fathers, who were all British stock, and to a bunch of British political philosophers—not to the Spaniards."

"But Isabel—"

Marta interrupted him with her rapid-fire, incomprehensible-to-me Spanish—apparently insisting that we pose for yet another picture under yet another archway. Manuel sighed but faced the camera with me and obliged Marta with a weary smile. "...Isabel was known at the time for being rather sympathetic toward the Jews," he continued after Marta had satisfied herself with what seemed like dozens of shots. "She was very hesitant to expel them—it was

Torquemada who talked her into it. She was primarily concerned with the souls of humanity and the purity of the Catholic faith. She had good intentions."

"Oh I'm sure," I said, running my finger along the tiling on one of the walls. "That's why she signed a document that forbade the Jews to carry gold or silver with them out of the country. Because she was worried about their souls."

"She was probably hoping it would persuade them to stay and convert."

"Okay, *why* are you defending Queen Isabel?" I demanded, turning around to look at him.

"I'm not," he shrugged. "I'm just saying, it's complex."

I sighed, shaking my head. "Spoken like a true historian."

---

When we finally got back to the apartment, I collapsed into the bed in the spare room and fell asleep without even changing into pajamas.

# Míriam

Míriam was tying her apron in preparation to go downstairs to the library when she heard voices from the stairway. She exchanged glances with her father, and they both froze, listening carefully.

*Thump.* Someone tried to open the door.

"Unlock it," came a voice, and it made Míriam's blood run cold. She recognized its smooth, sinister softness.

Míriam cast a desperate look around the room and saw a pile of cloths and blankets lying next to her bed. Trying to keep totally silent, she wildly gestured to her father to come hide with her under the blankets.

"I'm sorry, *señor*," came León's voice. "I think my father has the key. As I told you, we are expecting him home this afternoon... perhaps that would be a better time..."

*Thump.* It was much louder this time, as if someone was throwing his full weight against the door. Míriam tucked herself under the pile next to her father and started whispering every chapter of Psalms she could remember. Abraham grabbed her hand and squeezed it tight.

"*Señor*, please, is this really necessary? This is just a storeroom. I don't want my father coming home to broken furniture..."

*Crash.* The door burst open. From underneath the cloth, Míriam could see a mass of black. Heavy boots clumped along the floor in slow, deliberate steps. Míriam could hear her heart pounding and tried to breathe as slowly and quietly as she could. Her body shook.

"Are you quite satisfied, Señor Giménez?" León's voice was weary and Míriam sensed some relief in it.

Giménez stood still and said nothing.

Then he turned suddenly.

"You realize why I am here, Don León, don't you?"

"No, señor. And I do not appreciate this interruption at all."

"You know your father was friends with the Jew Abraham de Carmona."

Míriam's heart pounded faster. Her father's hand was clammy in her grip.

"De Carmona, señor? Yes. I heard that he disappeared the day the Tribunal decided to investigate him."

Giménez began pacing again. "Do you not think it odd, Don León, that he and his daughter vanished so quickly from the judería on that very same day? I myself went to his house to collect the wine from his daughter on that day, just after Sánchez confessed about it. There was no way she could have warned her father so quickly."

León was silent for a few moments. "Was that supposed to be some kind of explanation?" he asked.

"All I am saying, señor, is that your father had close ties with this Jew, and so had every motive to hide him."

"Ahh, I see. So you stormed in here knowing that my father was away, in the hope that you would find this Jew hiding in some corner of our estate?" León's voice was sharp. "Let me ask you something, señor." Peering between two blankets, Míriam could just make out the blob of brown that was León's boots stepping closer to the blob of black that was his visitor. León lowered his voice to a menacing whisper. "Is it really God you fear, Giménez? Or is it, perhaps, the information that we have regarding you and your colleagues and the allocation of certain funds?"

Giménez was silent.

"I know how the Holy Office operates. My father and I have seen it time and again. Your operations are funded by the property you confiscate, so it is natural for you to target wealthy families in your so-called 'investigations'. And what target could be better than a wealthy family that also possesses information that might be dangerous to you? I know the real reason you are here; this missing Jew is merely a convenient excuse. Well played, my good man."

A pause. Giménez cleared his throat. "Don León, I will forgive you your deeply insulting accusations. God will be my witness that I am here only to protect the purity of the Christian faith." His boots thudded toward the door.

"As far as I know, there hasn't even been a proper denunciation of this Jew," León continued. "This is just a pretext."

"My good sir," Gimenéz said, stopping by the doorway. "Abraham de Carmona is a Jew, and his denunciation was made centuries ago by Lord Jesus Christ himself. He should be grateful we are even offering the opportunity for a trial." He was silent for a few moments, and Míriam wasn't sure whether he had left or not. Then she heard him speak again: "What is this?"

León cleared his throat. "What do you mean? It is a circle of cloth."

Míriam almost gasped. The red badge she had removed from her dress must have been on the floor.

"It looks like a Jew's badge."

"As does every other circle of red cloth in the world," León's voice was sharp and mocking. "Good Heavens, Giménez. Will you accuse us of stealing your horse if you find a horseshoe in our stable?"

After a pause, the boots clumped out of the room. León lingered a moment, then followed, trying to close the broken door behind him.

The door swung back open on its hinge. Míriam held her breath, listening. The footsteps faded down the stairwell. She waited until all she could hear was the pulse pounding through her ears. Finally, she lifted the blanket she was under, tentatively peeking out at the room. She stood, wincing at the cramps in her muscles, and tiptoed to the door to close it. She cast around, trying to find something to brace against it. Abraham found a wooden plank under the bed and propped it against the wooden bedframe. Then Míriam turned to face her father.

Abraham's face was red and dripping with sweat. He wiped his brow with the cloth next to him. Neither of them dared to speak. Míriam pulled the little book of Psalms from the pouch León had given her to carry it and handed it to him. They prayed silently together, side by side on the bed.

# Manuel

I couldn't sleep.

It's not that the sofa was all that uncomfortable; it opened up to a decent-sized bed, and while the mattress was a little lumpy, I'd slept fine in much worse conditions.

Part of it was the memories. Marta and José lived in the heart of the Realejo quarter, just a few blocks away from my childhood home, the church, and the park by the river where I spent so much time as a teenager. I was itching to go see those places but even looking across the living room at the apartment's small balcony, I saw an image of my father standing there, leaning on the banister, a cigarette dangling from his hand as he looked out over the street. I could almost hear his quiet, husky voice, my mother's boisterous laughter in response. I could almost smell the smoke. I buried my face in the blanket, trying to block out the memory of that smell. Those cigarettes were what killed him.

And then there was the argument with Rabbi Uri, which for some reason I could not stop playing over and over in my mind. He had been out of line and offensive and presumptuous—but I couldn't help but wonder if I *was* being careful enough about my friendship with Alma. The feeling that welled in my chest when she turned to me, eyes shining, after lighting the Sabbath candles... the way everything in the room seemed brighter when she walked in... the way she made me laugh, even when I was miserable or frustrated... there was no denying it. If the circumstances had been different, I would definitely have wanted us to be something more than friends; Rabbi Uri was right about that part. But things were what they were, and I had to live with that.

Still, even though nothing would come of it, a part of me wanted to know if Alma felt the same way. Olivia seemed to think so, and she had turned out to be remarkably insightful for someone who seemed to spend the majority of her free time partying. There were those moments, when Alma or I leaned a little too close or made an offhand, slightly suggestive joke... and the tense silences that followed them. And there was also, of course, Alma's strangely hostile behavior whenever I mentioned Olivia.

But it would be totally inappropriate to broach the subject—and what would it accomplish, anyhow? It would be the most awkward conversation of my life, and trust me, there have been a few. It might change everything. It might scare her away, and I didn't want to lose Alma as a friend. It was getting to a point where the thought of spending a few days away from her made me sad; that was part of why I had dragged her down here to Granada in the first place. The thought of possibly destroying our friendship because of a few misplaced romantic feelings was too painful to bear.

But maybe that was exactly the problem.

I sighed and burrowed my face into the pillow. My thoughts wandered to the room just down the hall where I knew Alma was asleep. The image of her sleeping on the couch in her apartment that first evening in Madrid drifted into my mind. The way her hair spilled around her face, her features relaxed, her lips slightly open... her ribs rising and falling with her breath, the way her hips curved, with her body curled to the side and her knees teasingly peeking out from the hem of her skirt. How I had longed, even then, to cross the room and nestle in beside her, to graze my hand over those curves...

*Don't even go there,* I scolded myself. *Don't you dare.*

*"Padre nuestro, que estás en el cielo..."* I began to whisper. Padre Carlos had taught me to recite the Lord's Prayer when I found

my thoughts straying to places they shouldn't go. *"Santificado sea tu nombre..."* I stopped and sighed, feeling a heavy, pining sort of sadness settle over me.

*This is not good,* I thought. *This is not good at all.*

*I think I might be in trouble.*

*And by "trouble", I mean love.*

---

"Wakey wakey!"

Something was poking me in the arm. I groaned.

"Come on, you lazy Spaniard, don't *'mañana'* me. If you want to show me around this place you're gonna have to get up. It's nine-thirty already!"

My eyes fluttered open to see Alma perched on the coffee table in front of me, her black hair wet and smelling like shampoo. She was holding a styrofoam cup of coffee.

"There ya go," she said, uncrossing her legs and standing up. "The Valéz...Gómez...s...zz...es..." She looked confused, then stopped and tried again. "Marta and José are at work. They left me a key." She held it up.

"You," I croaked, "are the most annoyingly cheerful alarm clock ever."

She cackled and headed off into the kitchen. "You want an omelet?" She called. "They have the kosher French brand of butter here."

I hoisted myself up. "Sounds good," I said. I turned to the kitchen and watched her crack two eggs into a glass, examine them, then pour in a little water and beat them vigorously with a fork. I stood up and walked to the kitchen. Alma glanced at me from the stove, which was now totally encased in aluminum foil.

"Your mom is right," she said. "You seriously need a haircut."

"Well, it's a good thing she has you here as her agent to tell me what to do."

"Remember, she wouldn't have let you come otherwise!" Alma lifted the frying pan and expertly flipped the omelet with it.

"Wow," I said. "That's impressive."

"I learned from the best," she said, sliding the omelet onto my plate. "So. What are we doing today?" She turned back to the stove, cracking more eggs into the glass.

"Well, I think we can just...walk around the neighborhood," I said, slicing the omelet and lifting a piece to my mouth. "And then we can take a bus to the cemetery."

"Sounds like a plan," she said.

"Is there anything else in Granada you would like to see?" I asked.

"Well, the Jewish stuff, of course," she said, pouring the eggs into the sizzling pan. "Didn't you say we're in the old Jewish quarter?"

"Well...there is nothing much left from then. It's like most of the places where there used to be significant Jewish communities in Spain. We Spaniards have not been particularly respectful toward your past, I am afraid."

"I noticed that about you," Alma muttered. "Um. That is, not *you*—"

"I know. There's a little museum a few streets over that deals with the *judería*, though. It's in the opposite direction from the places I wanted to see, but maybe if we have time left over we can make a stop there."

---

The sky was a deep blue with occasional white clouds offering intermittent shade from the bright April sun—not that we needed extra shade in the narrow brick streets of the Realejo district. In a surprising show of tact, Alma had left her video camera at home, and stayed mostly silent as we walked. I led her through the alleys, past the stucco façades painted in varying shades of gray, yellow, and red, and stopped in front of a five-story brick building with long, narrow balconies looking out over the street. I stepped back until my back was pressed against the white stucco wall on the opposite side of the street, squinting up at the building's third story. I couldn't see a lot from this vantage point, and I could not recognize much of anything. Even the balcony's banister had been repainted to a darker shade of green.

I pointed. *"Eso..."* I said, and then gave my head a quick shake and switched back to English. "That balcony, on the third floor. The only home I remember from before we moved to Brooklyn."

Alma smiled at me. "You can say it in Spanish—I'll understand. Probably. Most likely. If you say it slowly."

"Don't tempt me to forget my English."

We stood there for a few moments, leaning against the wall and looking up.

"Speaking of reasons for your mom to kill you," Alma said finally, "I'd better get a picture of you here."

I sighed.

"Better yet..." She glanced back and forth down the street and spotted a woman walking past on a perpendicular street. *"¡Disculpe!"* she called out, sprinting toward the woman, *"¿puede tomar una foto de nosotros?"* The woman glanced at her, shook her head, and kept walking. Alma turned back to me, disgruntled. "Sheesh, people here are grouchy. Back up and stand in the middle of the street so I can catch as much of the buildings as possible."

I did as I was told, but before Alma had set up her phone to take the picture she turned, apparently having noticed another woman walking down the street, and called out to her to ask if she would photograph us. This one at least took the phone, even as she pursed her lips in visible irritation. Alma sprinted back to me, threw her arm across my back and smiled brightly. I felt flustered and disoriented for a good few seconds. She had never held me that way before, and I was finding it hard to breathe. I tentatively put my arm around her and tried to relax my face into a smile. The woman snapped a few pictures and then handed the phone back to Alma.

"*Gracias,*" Alma chirped.

"*De nada,*" the woman replied, finally giving a friendly smile, looking both of us in the eye. As she walked away she tossed over her shoulder: "*Que bonita pareja.*"

I was grateful that Alma seemed to miss both that comment and the subsequent reddening of my face as she examined the photos.

"This'll do," she pronounced, and put her phone away. "So. What now?"

I wasn't listening, though. I had caught sight of something that made the hairs on the back of my neck stand on end.

There was a group of young men who had congregated on the other end of the alley. There were maybe five or six of them, heads shaven, dressed in leather jackets and jeans. They were clearly drunk—most of them, anyway—stumbling along with exaggerated gestures and laughing loudly. But the most disturbing aspect of their behavior was the shape they were spray-painting onto the brick wall in front of them.

Alma squinted in the direction of my gaze. "Is that a *swastika?!*"

I surveyed her carefully. She was wearing a mint-green blouse and a full skirt of some black lacy material that hit a few inches above her ankles and fluttered a little in the wind. I tried to steer my brain away from the way the blouse hugged her body and back to the point: she wasn't wearing a Star of David or anything with Hebrew letters.

I turned back toward the gang, feeling dread in the pit of my stomach. "Let's get out of here," I said.

That was when I noticed that Alma was marching straight toward them, and had already covered half the distance.

I ran after her in a panic.

"Alma!" I hissed, grabbing hold of her arm. "What do you think you are doing?!" I whirled around her, shoving myself between her and the gang.

"I'm going to give those cretins a piece of my mind." She tried to step around me, but I gripped her by the upper arms, planting her firmly in place.

"What are you, crazy?!" I exclaimed in a hushed voice. "This isn't America! You can't just march over there and ask them to please stop spraying offensive graffiti!"

"What, and you're just going to let them get away with it?!"

"Those are *neo-Nazis!*" I hissed. "There are only two of us and six of them, and each one of them is twice your size!"

"Would you quit saying that about my size?" she retorted. But at least now she hesitated, casting a wary look over my shoulder.

"*¿Qué pasa aquí?*" came a taunting voice from behind me.

I spun around, trying to look as nonchalant as possible. The thug who had spoken was standing just a few inches from my face—a broad-shouldered, gap-toothed brute whose breath reeked of tobacco and beer. He was flanked by several of his cronies, all of them leering idiotically. I pulled myself up to my full height, which was, thankfully, several centimeters above his. Alma stayed behind me and did not speak. I offered up a silent prayer of thanks that her common sense seemed to have finally switched on.

"*¿Perdona?*" I asked in the breeziest tone I could muster.

"*It's just that she seems very upset,*" he sneered in a hair-raisingly low voice. "*Perhaps she does not appreciate our fine artistry?*" He made a wobbly gesture toward the wall. My eyes flicked toward it briefly, my heart pounding hard.

"*Eh,*" I stuttered. "*Oh, no, that is... that is not...*"

*"Are you Jews?"* he growled, the smile melting from his face.

The crazy thing is that my first thought was, *Oh no. He knows what we are.*

When I heard myself think that, I blinked, staring at him dumbly for a few seconds.

*We?*

I cleared my throat and reached for my collar, pulling my crucifix from beneath my shirt. It dangled from my hand, glinting in the yellow light of the streetlamps. *"Soy católico, amigo,"* I said softly. For a few seconds, it felt like none of us breathed.

*"Want to hear a joke?"* the thug blurted, his gap-toothed grin returning.

I just stared at him, the crucifix still dangling from my hand.

*"How do you fit six million Jews into a VW Beetle?"*

I felt a little sick to my stomach. The goons behind him sniggered.

*"In the ashtray."*

I felt suddenly very thankful for Alma's mediocre grasp of Spanish and prayed silently that she had not understood what he'd said.

I took a deep breath, trying to calm the wave of nausea. *"Well,"* I said, *"we need to be going. If you'll excuse us, gentlemen."*

He stepped back, stumbling a little, his grin unfading. He gave a wild sweeping gesture, and the six of them parted like the Red Sea. Feeling a little dizzy with relief at this sign that we might get out of this unharmed, I turned around and grabbed Alma's hand. *"Gracias,"* I said, and pulled her through.

"Casual," I whispered out of the corner of my mouth, and walked as slowly as I could manage, my muscles screaming to burst into a run. Alma kept in step with me, clinging tightly to my hand.

"Don't look back," she hissed when she noticed me turning my head slightly. "Just until we turn this corner."

After what felt like forever, we reached the intersection and ducked around the corner of a building. Alma let go of my hand, flattened herself against the wall, and peered carefully back down the street.

"So," she whispered. "What do we do about this? Call the police?"

That seemed like a reasonable course of action. I pulled out my phone and dialed 112.

We kept walking, heading out of the Realejo district, as I described the situation to the responder.

"Man," Alma said when I hung up, "I never thought I'd see the day I'd be overjoyed to see a crucifix." She grinned up at me. "Well, look at you," she sang. "My noble Christian hero!" She jabbed her fist in front of her, apparently pretending to ward off an imaginary thug with an imaginary cross. "Back! Back, Nazis!" She bellowed in a ridiculous low voice and a somewhat painful imitation of my accent. "In the name of the Father, the Son, and the Holy Ghost! *Soy católico,* suckers!"

I laughed, feeling a little lighter in the chest.

"I have to admit," I said, "I am pretty shaken after what we just saw. I have never witnessed this kind of overt anti-semitism before. Usually it's more subtle."

Alma cocked her head at me. "What do you mean?"

I shrugged. "Just... the way people talk, certain expressions, certain attitudes... it drives my mother crazy. I would not even have noticed if she was not always complaining about it. Did you know that in northern Spain they still have a festival on Good Friday called *'matar judíos'?"*

Alma's eyes went wide. *"What?* 'Kill Jews'? Are you serious?!"

"Well... it's an expression. It just means drinking spiked lemonade. At least... that's what it means nowadays."

"Spiked lemonade?" she spluttered. She squinted into the distance, trying to make sense of this. "And that's symbolic of... what? When life gives you Jews, make lemonade?"

I gave a sardonic smile. "Actually, there is a theory that the expression came from something King Fernando said when he signed the Edict of Expulsion. *'Limonada que trasiego, judío que pulvarizo.'*"

Alma wrinkled her nose in disgust. "Something about lemonade and pulverizing Jews?"

"More or less, 'For every lemonade I drink, I will crush a Jew.'"

"What an asshole," she growled angrily, and then quickly apologized when she saw me flinch: "Sorry. I mean, um, yeah. What a jerk. I mean..." She paused. "I know killing Jews—I mean, actually killing Jews—was a popular Easter activity back in the day..."

"That's the thing," I cut in. "There *were* no Jews to kill for hundreds of years. The Alhambra Decree was still in effect until the middle of the twentieth century. But somehow the traditions remained. Up until the '70s there were still villages all over Spain where they would go throw stones at where the *judería* used to be."

"What the heck, Spain?!" Alma exclaimed, throwing up her arms as we approached the crosswalk on the two-lane Carrera de la Virgen. "Can you imagine if there was still a festival in, like, Louisiana, called 'Lynch Negroes'? 'It's just an expression! We're just drinking lemonade!'"

I sighed. "Yes. Americans are much more sensitive about these things."

"Sheesh. No wonder your mom wanted to get you out of here."

I opened my mouth to reply, but then closed it again. Honestly, I had never really thought about that in depth before. I knew my mother was upset about the flippant racism and especially the anti-semitism here, but I had always shrugged it off as her making a big deal out of nothing—it's not like there were a lot of Jews around to be offended by it. But she had insisted that wherever there was anti-semitism, there was evil...that it was an expression of the dark side of man's nature. I had thought she was crazy.

"My mother grew up in a small village near Cartagena," I said slowly, as much to myself as to Alma, as we waited for the light to turn green. "She told me she used to go throw stones at the old *judería* with her friends until her mother found out. It was my grandmother who sat her down and explained to her what Jews were... that they were people who had contributed a great deal to the Spanish culture and economy, who wrote philosophy and poetry and managed the kingdom's finances very skillfully... that they were cruelly expelled the same year Columbus sailed. My mother says she was completely shocked to learn all this."

"So that's how she became a Jew-lover?" Alma grinned.

"I think she was teased a lot in school, and I imagine when she started speaking up about anti-semitism it got worse. But you know her. If there's anything that makes her dig her heels in deeper, it's someone else telling her she should stop."

Alma gave me a thoughtful look. "Kind of like you."

I stared at her. I had never before thought of myself as being in any way like my mother.

We walked down the street toward my old church. The trees planted along the sidewalks and in the island dividing the road definitely seemed taller than I remembered. The church had a modest façade: yellow stucco with white plaster flourishes around the windows, and a statue of the crucifixion over the double oak doors. Two spires rose on either side.

"I'll wait out here," Alma said.

I turned to her, my eyebrows raised. "You don't want to come in with me?"

She shifted uncomfortably.

"It's okay," I said quickly. "You don't have to. I'll be out soon."

But when I pulled the door handle, it didn't budge.

"Strange..." I said.

"Is it supposed to be open?" Alma asked.

"Padre Carlos had it left open all day."

"Maybe the policy has changed."

I stepped back, feeling a lump growing in my throat.

"It's all right," Alma said. "We'll visit him at the cemetery later, right?"

I nodded, looking up at the spires. I sighed, then crossed myself discreetly and kissed my hand. I turned back to Alma, who was looking off down the street.

"Let's go to the park by the river and sit down."

# Alma

Manuel led me to an empty bench near a bridge. I pulled a couple of pears out of my bag and handed him one; we snacked on them in silence, watching the tourists drift by, breathing in the damp air and listening to the rush of the water from the river. I asked Manuel about a building nearby, and he started to talk. He told me about walks to the library with his mother and picnics with his papa in this park, about summers without air conditioning, and the time he took an important file from his dad's office and turned it into a fleet of paper boats that he dropped into the river from the bridge. His eyes were sparkling, his gestures animated, and it occurred to me as I watched him that I had never seen him so happy before.

As we headed toward the bus stop to start our way to the cemetery, I finally spoke.

"So...you never really told me. What happened to your father?"

He drew a deep breath, and my heart sank a little to see his demeanor turn somber again, immediately regretting that I had asked.

"Lung cancer," he said. "He was a heavy smoker."

The covered bus stop had just one low, short bench, and a teenage girl was huddled on one side, staring down at her phone. Manuel, ever the gentleman, gestured toward the empty space next to her.

"That's fine, I'd rather stand," I said, leaning against the plexiglass wall behind me. "How old were you when he was diagnosed?"

"Eight." He was staring down at the pavement in front of him, so I couldn't see his eyes. "At first things looked good," he went on. "The cancer responded to the chemotherapy and it appeared that he'd make it. But a year later..." He fumbled for the words. "It got bad. Very fast. It was only about three months from the bad news until he passed away."

"How old were you then?" I asked gently.

"Ten."

"And that's when you met Padre Carlos?"

"Well, no, my father took me to church sometimes and was friendly with him. But I did not know him very well until he started coming to visit my father at the hospital. He would bring board games to play with me while we kept my father company, giving my mother a chance to go take a walk or visit a friend. When my father died, he was there within the hour. He took care of the funeral arrangements. My mother was hardly functioning for the first month or so, and he arranged for people from the community to send us meals, clean the house, do our laundry. Sometimes he would come do it himself. I have a memory of sitting on the sofa in the living room watching him fold my shirts. He was really an extraordinarily kind man."

I studied him. He still wasn't meeting my eyes. "Sounds like a great role model for you," I said, "especially after losing your father."

He nodded, still looking at the ground. "My mother was always very grateful to him, even though she refused to have anything to do with the church and constantly complained about his political and religious views."

I wasn't sure I wanted to know more about that. I fiddled with the zipper of my bag, suddenly picturing Manuel as a little boy with adorable little black curls and huge honey-brown eyes, and feeling overwhelmed with sadness for him.

"How do you even survive after that?" I said finally. "I'm not exactly super-close with my father, but if he had died when I was a kid, I would have grown up a dysfunctional wreck."

Manuel shrugged. "You find strength in yourself that you never knew you had." He looked out at the street. "You would be surprised what you are capable of coping with."

"You, maybe. Not me."

He turned toward me, finally meeting my eyes with an intense gaze. "You seriously underestimate yourself, Alma."

I looked away. We were silent for a while. I found myself staring at his hand, its long fingers tapping an impatient rhythm against the leg of his jeans, just inches away from mine. I felt an urge to reach out and take it.

"So what's the story with your mom's side?" I asked. "Why doesn't she know any of her relatives?"

He shook his head. "The Medranos? I honestly don't know. All I know is that my mother's mother was basically excommunicated from her family when she married my grandfather. No one ever told me why. My mother claims that even she doesn't know. She always got irritable when I asked about it, and my grandmother died before I was old enough to ask her."

"Sheesh. Why would they hate your grandfather so much?"

"That's what makes it even more confusing. He was the least offensive person I have ever known. He was quiet and very kind, and never said a bad word about anyone. I can't imagine what he could possibly have done to make my Abuela's family so angry... I think she did have a few brothers and sisters, but I don't know anything about them."

"My family has some stories of epic dramas like that—family feuds that lasted a few generations—but nothing quite that extreme," I said slowly. "It's such a shame. Everybody mad at everybody else for no rational reason at all."

"Well, at least that anger was not passed down to me," he said. His hand slipped into the pocket of his jeans. "No one ever spoke about the Medranos—negatively or positively. I have thought about trying to find them when I'm done researching my father's line. I probably have cousins I never knew existed."

"That would be cool." I looked at him thoughtfully, trying to decide whether to say what I wanted to say. "It's so...interesting to see you in your natural habitat," I finally ventured. "It's like getting to see a side of you that I could never have known otherwise."

He smiled. "Maybe when we get back to New York, you can take me on a tour of Albany."

I snorted. "As a penance for what, exactly?"

"And your grandmother is really something. I would love to meet her again someday."

My stomach dropped at the mention of her.

I looked at him sideways. "Not sure that would be such a great idea."

The bus pulled up with a screech and a hiss, and I was relieved that he didn't get a chance to inquire further.

The bus took us up through the city and past the Alhambra, which was even more imposing in broad daylight, crowning the lush green hilltop with its stone walls and towers. The entrance to the cemetery was teeming with tourists who had come to look at the historical monuments and gravestones.

"Do you want to see the old section?" Manuel asked as we stepped off the bus.

I raised an eyebrow at him. "A bunch of crucifixes and carved stone angels commemorating a bunch of random famous dead Spaniards? No thanks. We're here to see your dad."

He smiled.

I spotted a flower seller by the entrance and pointed him out to Manuel. He shrugged.

"Papa was not a flower person."

We crossed to the modern section of the cemetery and made our way in. The graves were marked with large marble slabs over the ground; there were lots of trees everywhere, and bushes and flowering potted plants. I followed Manuel as he walked without hesitation through the lots. Finally he stopped at the corner of one of the sections, looking down at the gravestone there and letting out a slow breath.

MIGUEL AGUILAR MORALES
D. E. P.

I knelt down, picked up a pebble, and solemnly placed it on the gravestone.

"What are you doing?" Manuel asked.

"Jewish custom." I stood up. "What's 'D.E.P.' stand for?"

"*Descanse en paz*. Rest in peace."

We stood together for a moment in reverent silence. Then I stepped back.

"I'm going to give you two some time." I turned around and wandered off, examining the other gravestones in the area. I snuck a glance behind me at Manuel, who was now kneeling next to the grave, his eyes closed and his lips moving. I turned away quickly and stopped in front of a tree, staring at the pattern in its bark.

Something about being with Manuel here in Granada was... I don't really know how to describe it. Maybe "intimate" is the right word. I mean, I had known intellectually about some parts of his life, but being here with him really immersed me in his world—and brought up all these warm feelings that I wasn't sure what to do with. Like, right at that moment, I felt this inexplicable urge to walk over there and give him a big, long hug.

But somehow...even though I hadn't given a second thought to hugging male friends in the past...it didn't seem appropriate with Manuel. We were tiptoeing on the edge of this fuzzy sort of boundary that we had never really gotten around to defining. And maybe we should have.

Because the fact was that I felt closer to him than I had felt to pretty much anyone else in my life. There was something so comforting about him. He put up with me even when I was being bossy or cranky or overexcited. He laughed at my stupid jokes and made me laugh at his. And how ironic was it that the person I seemed to connect with most deeply on matters of faith was a Christian? *A Christian.*

I swallowed, feeling a little twinge of doubt, a creeping sense of foreboding. And a voice in my head said, *Maybe Grandma was right. Maybe this trip* is *a little too much.*

My stomach turned over in guilt as I thought about how I had ended my last conversation with her. I slipped my phone out of my pocket, counting back six hours in my head...but even though there was a good chance she'd be awake, pride and laziness got the best of me and I put my phone back.

I turned around to look at Manuel again. He was standing up now, scanning, apparently searching for me. I hesitated, watching him brush back his shock of black curls that had blown in his face in the wind. He spotted me and smiled, and I tried to ignore the butterflies in my chest that fluttered in response.

# Manuel

Our final stop at the cemetery was Padre Carlos's grave. Thanks to the vague instructions I had been given at the front desk, I could not figure out where we were supposed to go, and I was on the verge of giving up when Alma spotted his name on a modest gravestone that we almost walked right past.

I felt a weary sadness settle over me as I stood over his grave. He had been like a second father to me; and now he, too, rested deep beneath this ground.

I thought about him, about his smile, his hug, his words of comfort and encouragement when I felt so alone.

But with Alma standing next to me, I also thought about his harshness, his rigidity, and his stifling of my curiosity. He would not approve of this friendship, for sure—and I realized now, for the first time, with absolute certainty, that I no longer felt ashamed or guilty about being friends with Alma.

As I realized that, I felt a weight lift from my chest. I could still love Padre Carlos. I could still feel grateful for everything he had given and taught me. I could still be devoted to God and to finding the truth. That didn't mean I necessarily had to follow the path Padre Carlos had set for me.

I looked up at the clouds drifting lazily overhead. *Thank you for everything, Padre*, I thought.

I turned to Alma. "Let's go."

I swept past her and walked toward the exit, my steps solid and sure.

We rose early the next morning to catch the bus to Lorca. Marta made quite a scene at the bus stop with her tearful goodbyes, telling me again and again to give her love to my mother and kissing my cheeks every time I stood still long enough. Alma finally managed to pry me away and shove me onto the bus, and we settled in an empty bench toward the back. I had brought the de Carmona file with us; but when I pulled it out, Alma said reading on the moving bus would make her carsick, so I put it away again.

She looked out the window at the city fading into the distance. "Are you sad to leave Granada so soon?"

"A little bit." I paused. "There's nothing really there for me anymore, though. Just ghosts." I was silent for a little while. "You know... I had always thought that after I finished my degree at NYU I would come back here—seminary or not. But now I'm not sure. In many ways, I belong but I don't belong—in both places."

"Kind of the story of your life, isn't it?" Alma looked at me, her face serious. I cocked my head at her curiously. "You and Spain, you and the US, you and Christianity... even you and Judaism. You're always caught in between."

I chewed on that insight for a while.

"In some ways I feel the same about myself," she went on. "I mean, it's not that I don't belong... I have a big family that I belong to, but I never seem to be interested in the same stuff as everyone else. That's why my grandmother and I have always been so close. I identify with her in ways that my siblings and cousins don't. And I've always had this obsessive interest in family stories, in our history."

"Yes, you told me. Your parents think it's a waste of time."

I saw a smile twitch at the corner of her mouth. "I think they might be reconsidering that, though."

We were silent for a while, and eventually I noticed that she had fallen asleep. Her head was drifting toward my shoulder, and at a certain point came to rest on it. I stiffened, not sure whether to nudge her away. Eventually I relaxed and leaned toward her myself, resting my head against hers. I closed my eyes, imagining for just this moment that the barriers between us were not there.

# Míriam

Hours later, the secret knock came at the door, and Míriam and her father got up to remove the plank that was bracing it shut. Don Tomás entered the room, examining the damage to the lock. León was right behind him.

Don Tomás faced Abraham and let out a deep sigh. "Praise the Lord. Where did you hide?"

Abraham pointed to the pile of blankets. "Good thing my daughter kept her wits about her."

León's eyes met Míriam's. A surge of warmth rose in her chest and she quickly lowered her gaze, her heart pounding.

"Well, one thing is clear," Don Tomás said. "You are no longer safe here. You need to leave."

Míriam looked up at Don Tomás in horror.

"Leave?" she breathed.

"I have a ship at the port in Cartagena preparing for a trip to Tangier. It was supposed to leave in a week, but I can invent some reason that it needs to sail a few days sooner. I trust the captain, and he will keep you safe and fed until you arrive. You remember Kadosh, yes?"

"Your contact in Tangier?"

"Yes. He will meet the ship when it arrives, and he should be able to arrange passage to Fez; I'll prepare a letter to him and entrust it to the captain."

Abraham took a deep breath and nodded. "How would we get from here to Cartagena?"

"We will wait until we are sure they aren't watching the roads, and then I'll come for you; you'll hide in the back of my cart. You and Míriam should stay here until then."

"Don Tomás..." Abraham grasped his friend by the elbows. "Don't you realize what this might mean for you? They could take away your title, your land, everything you have!"

Don Tomás waved dismissively. "They won't dare touch us. We have some sensitive information that they wouldn't risk our releasing just because of one Jew who got away from them. You know how they are."

Abraham's eyes welled with tears. "My friend, I cannot thank you enough..."

They embraced. León was standing behind his father in the doorway, his eyes burning into Míriam's; but neither one said a word or moved a muscle. A crushing sadness was settling over Míriam again, and she finally bowed her head and looked away.

Finally, Don Tomás released Abraham and gathered León with him to go down the stairs and begin making preparations for Abraham and Míriam's escape.

Míriam stood by the window, watching the sky light up in shades of rich gold as the sun sank toward the misty mountains in the distance. Thick clouds were blowing in from the north.

"What is it like in the Maghreb?" she asked quietly.

Abraham looked up from his Hebrew manuscripts and thought for a few moments.

"Hot. Dry. Dirty."

Míriam tried to swallow the lump in her throat.

"I won't lie to you, my daughter. The situation is not so good there. The Moors have been more gracious to us than the Christians have, but Fez…your uncles' descriptions…they are not heartening."

A tear streamed down Míriam's cheek. "We don't have a choice though, do we?"

"There are other places we might be able to go…Portugal, perhaps, or Rome. But even if we could find a way to get there, who's to say that it would be a better choice in the long run?"

"I meant staying in Castile."

Abraham sighed. "No." He paused. "To tell you the truth, my feeling is that by this time next year, there will be no more Jews in Castile or Aragon."

"It's just not fair," Míriam whispered, furiously wiping the tears from her face. "I love this land. Our family has lived here for a thousand years. We are Sephardim in our hearts and our souls. How could they force us to leave like this?"

"It's not the first time and it won't be the last. This is the story of our people." Abraham stood up to join her at the window. "But you know, our story is not only about exile and oppression and suffering. It is the story of thriving, of triumph, and of great faith. It is the story of a people that laughs in the face of deepest despair, that stubbornly clings to life and to joy even in the face of horror and death. We take our pain and turn it into poetry. We take our misfortune and transform it into opportunity. God promised our father Abraham that he would curse whoever curses us and bless whoever blesses us. The Spaniards have long prospered from the blessings we brought, and now that they curse us, they will feel the consequences in time. Wait and see."

Just after nightfall two days later, the secret knock came again at their door. Don Tomás led them quickly down the stairs, León keeping an eye out for stray servants ahead of them. They slipped out the back door and strode across the grass to the stable, where a horse and cart were waiting for them. Miriam felt a couple of fat raindrops on her face as she stopped next to the cart.

"Each of you get into one of those barrels. Quickly," Don Tomás said, pointing to several large barrels in the back of the cart.

Miriam turned to León. He was standing there studying her, and in the flickering torchlight she could see the helpless expression on his face. She yearned to reach for him, take his hands in hers, wrap him in her arms, hold him forever...but instead, she clenched her fists behind her back, trembling.

"I...thank you...for...everything," she whispered.

León opened his mouth to answer, but no words would come. Miriam swallowed and turned to climb into the cart. She stood over an open barrel, hesitating a moment to try to catch one last glimpse of León's face, but he had already turned away and was walking toward the house. She bit her lip, blinked back her tears, and stuffed herself into the barrel, hugging her knees. Her mother's book of Psalms pressed against her side through the pouch León had given her. Someone came and closed the barrel, pounding a few times on the lid to lodge it firmly in place; and after a few minutes, she felt the cart rattle and bump as the horse began moving.

Heavy rain began to pound on the lid of Miriam's barrel, seeping through the cracks. Her hair was soon stuck to the back of her neck. She was extremely uncomfortable—her whole body ached from crouching for so long, and her lungs felt so crushed that it was hard to keep her breath steady. Her thoughts kept drifting to León. She tried to push him from her mind; but alone, stuffed in a barrel, there was no escaping her heart, and she could not deny its pain. She leaned her head against the side of the barrel and let the tears flow.

*Never.*

*Never.*

*I will never see him again. And it's just as well, because I never should.*

*Serves me right. Serves me right for letting this happen to me.*

"Mama..." she moaned, grateful for the pounding rain that drowned out her voice. "Mama...how I have let my heart fail you!"

Exhaustion eventually overcame her, and she drifted into fitful sleep. Thoughts of her mother shifted into dreams. She was certain she felt her mother's arms around her, holding her tight and safe, before jerking awake and remembering where she was.

After an eternity, Míriam began to notice a little light seeping in through the cracks of her barrel; the sun was beginning to rise, and they hadn't reached the port yet. Don Tomás stopped the cart and let Míriam and Abraham out to stretch their legs and make a brief visit to the woods before they returned to their barrels for the last part of the trip. As the light grew stronger, Míriam noticed sounds of horses, braying donkeys, and people around her. The wagon finally stopped in a shaded place, and she heard Don Tomás climb back near the barrels and whisper, "I need to go take care of business. You are in my warehouse and you are unlikely to have company, but I recommend staying in the barrels as much as you can—we can't risk anyone seeing you in daylight. Once the ship has left port, perhaps you will be able to come out of hiding a bit more often."

And then he was gone, and Míriam and her father were left to wait, curled up in the barrels. She continued to drift in and out of sleep, caught between mourning what could never have been with León, the guilt she felt for that mourning, and the physical pain of being stuck in a barrel for so long.

# Manuel

We arrived in Lorca. Our plan had been to walk to the castle, since we hadn't found any information about getting there on public transportation. But Alma took one look at the hill with the fortress on top, towering above the city, and said, "We're taking a taxi." I looked down at her suitcase—a little lighter now that some of the food had been eaten, but still not something I would want to drag up that hill—and readily agreed.

I managed to convince the guy at the castle's reception desk to let us leave Alma's suitcase with him, and then we headed straight for the site of the Jewish-quarter excavation. We walked in silence through the ancient stone corridors and archways. There was a constant chilly breeze blowing in from the east. As we walked along the walls of the fortress, I looked out over the modern city of Lorca stretched out below us. The air was somewhat misty, and I could only just make out the vague silhouettes of other mountains in the distance.

I noticed Alma hugging herself as she walked.

"You cold?" I asked.

Alma scowled at me. "Don't you dare offer me your sweater, you macho cliché."

"I'm not a cliché. I'm a gentleman."

Alma snorted.

"Fine. Enjoy your feminist dignity and be cold. I don't care."

I shrugged and kept walking, pointedly adjusting my sweater. We walked for a few more minutes until Alma suddenly stopped.

"Fine yourself. Revel in your pompous chivalry and give me the sweater." She rolled her eyes and held out her hand in resignation. I cackled triumphantly, dug my extra sweater out of my backpack and handed it to her. I watched her put it on, amused at how its knitted maroon folds engulfed her small frame.

"What are you smiling at?" she snapped.

"It's huge on you."

"It's not my fault you're freakishly tall." She tossed her ponytail, her gentle black curls bouncing, and strode ahead of me on the path, trying to roll up the sleeves to free her hands.

"Why, you are most welcome, milady," I called after her.

She stopped and turned around, looking sheepish. "Sorry," she said. "Thank you."

"My pleasure." I watched her as she turned around and kept going. *She likes when I hold doors for her and things like that*, I thought. *What is it about wearing my sweater that's got her all snippy?* Then I remembered her reaction when I told her to forget about paying me back for the kosher food I brought her our first evening in Madrid. *We are not dating, and I don't have to put up with this from you*, she'd said. Maybe it was a similar discomfort with a gesture that was kind of intimate and might be interpreted as romantic. My heart sank a little.

---

We tagged along with a group taking a guided tour of the site. Alma tried to film the entire thing, tripping over herself a few times because she forgot that she was supposed to be watching where she was going. I ended up grabbing the camera from her and telling her I'd do the filming if she would simply focus on not falling into a ditch and killing herself.

There wasn't a whole lot to see outdoors, at least from my perspective: just ruins, which apparently were the foundations for the Jewish homes that had once stood there. But soon enough we reached the covered area marked *"Restos Sinagoga"*, and we found ourselves standing, utterly speechless, in the reconstructed synagogue. The lights reflected yellow on the smooth lacquer of the beautiful wooden arched ceiling, and cast shadows through the wooden lattices in front of the women's section. Something about it sent a shiver up my spine.

"Goosebumps," Alma murmured to me, under the reverent hush of the tour group. "I'm having serious goosebumps. This place... it reminds me of what Ester said about the way members of her family felt whenever they saw something related to Judaism..."

*"La llamada de la sangre,"* I whispered.

"Yeah. 'The call of the blood'. There's this odd... familiarity about this place."

"You know, it's so strange..." I said softly. "I have the same feeling."

We looked at each other. A lock of hair had come loose from Alma's ponytail and fallen over her eye, and resisting the urge to reach out and brush it out of her face was almost painful.

"Well, it's not entirely impossible that the Aguilars spent some time in Lorca too, you know," Alma said. Her eyes lit up. "Hey... how crazy would it be if our ancestors knew each other?"

I shook my head and laughed. "Now you're just getting carried away... and even if they did spend time in Lorca, it definitely would not have been in the Jewish quarter."

"True." Alma nodded, climbing up the step to go back outside.

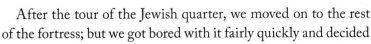

After the tour of the Jewish quarter, we moved on to the rest of the fortress; but we got bored with it fairly quickly and decided to head back down the hill. We took a taxi back into town to visit the Archeological Museum, where some of the items that had been found in the Jewish quarter were on display. Alma struck up a conversation with one of the curators, and when he managed to understand the gist of what we'd read in the de Carmona file from Alma's broken Spanish, he was very enthusiastic and said he would speak to the head archivist at the National Historical Archive about getting a copy for the muscum. Then he gave us a detailed tour of the exhibit.

When we were done at the museum, we headed out to catch the bus to Murcia. Alma had found us a good deal on two rooms in a modest hotel near the port of Cartagena, and she was determined to have some time to work on the de Carmona file before we went to bed. I was starting to get really sick of all the traveling around, and found myself almost looking forward to getting back to our normal routine in Madrid.

We finally arrived at the hotel at about four in the afternoon. Alma deposited most of her stuff in her room, and then informed me that we were going to work on the file down by the port. I've never been a big fan of beaches—the sand drives me crazy—but I figured that the wooden docks would be acceptable. She packed some bread, tuna, and red peppers in a plastic bag.

"It'll be a picnic of sorts," she said.

"What am I going to put on the bread?" I asked.

"What, you don't like tuna?"

I just looked at her.

She didn't get it. "Why are you looking at me like that?" Then it suddenly clicked. "Oh right! *Fish!* I don't even think of fish as meat…" She dove back into her room and emerged with a jar of American peanut butter. "This good?"

I made a face. "Where did you even *get* that stuff?"

"El Corte Inglés. I've found a bunch of American stuff there that's impossible to find anywhere else. Why doesn't anybody eat peanut butter in your annoying country?"

"Why does everyone eat it in yours?!"

She rolled her eyes and disappeared into her room again. She returned holding a jar of jam.

"Will this please His Royal Highness?"

"How much food did you bring?" I asked incredulously.

"A Jew's gotta eat!" She shoved the jar into my hands and swept past me down the hall.

It was a short walk to the port. The boardwalk was lined with palm trees, and we found a bench facing the yachts, with a clear view of the harbor. Two hills rose up on either side of the bay, a pair of shields guarding the ships from the storms of the open sea. A large cruise ship was drifting out through the narrow passage between them.

After we settled in and unpacked our food, it occurred to me that I had forgotten to bring the de Carmona file.

"Well, might as well eat first, then you can go get it later." Alma spread a generous helping of tuna on a slice of bread and bit into it. "Oh my God. So hungry." She sighed and looked out over the water. The yachts rocked gently in the waves, chains clinking softly.

"I wonder if my ancestors really did escape from here," Alma said.

"We'll probably never know." I spread some jam on a slice of bread. "I remember you mentioning that your grandmother said there was a Christian family who helped your ancestors escape..."

"Yeah..." She sighed again. "I think if any evidence of that exists, we should have seen it by now. They would have mentioned it in the file, right?"

"Probably."

We sat and ate in silence, enjoying the steady warm breeze and the strong afternoon sunshine. Alma finished eating and looked out at the horizon. After a few minutes, I heard her voice, soft and low, over the wind and the waves.

*"Hija mía, mi querida, amán, amán, amán..."* she sang, watching the sea as if in a trance. The melody was rhythmic and haunting. *"No te eches a la mar... que la mar está en fortuna, mira que te va llevar..."*

"What is that?" I asked gently. She started and looked at me as though she had forgotten I was there. She flushed a little.

"Um... I don't know," she stuttered. "Just a song... a song in Judeo-Spanish my grandmother always sings. The sea... it reminded me of the lyrics, and her voice just sort of floated into my head."

"It's pretty," I said. "Keep going."

*"Que me lleve y que me traiga, amán amán,"* she continued softly, *"siete puntas de hondor... que m'engluta pexe preto, para salvar del amor."* She stopped, pursing her lips. "I had never understood any of the lyrics before."

"I don't understand all of them either, but it's quite depressing."

"Most Ladino songs are. Either melodramatic or really dumb or both. But yeah. Don't throw yourself into the sea... to save from love...?"

"Seriously, what was your grandmother implying?" I grinned. She responded with something between a cough and a nervous laugh, not meeting my eyes. She turned back to the sea. I watched her, recalling her hesitation when I mentioned that I wanted to meet her grandmother.

*Para salvar del amor...*

I felt a heavy sadness settle over me again, realizing that I identified with these lyrics far more than I wanted to.

*Enough,* I scolded myself. *Get it together and move on.* But all that did was pile shame, anger, and guilt on top of the sadness.

I stood up, brushing my hair out of my eyes.

"I'm going to go get the file," I muttered, turning away to walk back toward the hotel. I found my feet carrying me faster and faster, feeling almost pursued, until I burst into a full-fledged run.

———✦———

When I reached my room, I dug the file out of my backpack. I stood there for a moment, looking at it, and for the first time I noticed that something about it wasn't quite right: it was too thick. We already seemed to have come close to where Abraham de Carmona's sentencing should be, but there was still a good chunk of material left. Curious, I opened it up and flipped through what was left...

And that was when I realized that there was, indeed, something wrong.

For some reason, another Inquisition trial protocol had been filed together with the de Carmona records.

I didn't notice anything special about the additional document at first—and then, on second glance, I could not believe my eyes when they registered the name of the accused... and the single line stating what he was accused of.

For a few moments I could not even move. I just stood there, slack-jawed, staring at the pages in front of me.

Then I turned around and took off in a sprint to find Alma.

# Alma

"Alma."

Manuel's voice snapped me out of my reverie. I had been staring at the horizon, hypnotized by the waves and the fading, orange-y light of late afternoon. He was running toward me, his footsteps thudding on the wooden dock, the de Carmona file in his hand. He looked pale, his eyes wide, and when he reached me I could see that his hands were shaking.

I blinked. "Whoa. Geez. Are you okay? What's up?"

It looked like he was having trouble stringing two words together, much less in English. "*Mira,*" was all he could say as he caught his breath, handing me a page from the file. I took it from him, my heart starting to pound.

"Look at what?" I squinted at the paper, trying to make out what it said. He pointed a quivering finger. I looked closer. I blinked and my heart leapt to my throat.

"Does that say...what...does that say *Aguilar?*"

Manuel could only nod.

"What does it say about Aguilar?"

"They were the ones. A Christian merchant family that lived in the outskirts of Lorca. *They* smuggled Abraham de Carmona out through Cartagena. They were tried in Lorca in 1492."

My jaw dropped.

"Where does it say that?" I asked.

He handed me the next page. "The protocol of their trial was filed together with de Carmona's."

I stared, open-mouthed, from the page to Manuel and back

again. I coughed, trying to gather my thoughts and think critically.

"Well... Aguilar can't have been that rare a name at the time..."

"Don Tomás Aguilar y Alverez?" He jabbed a finger at the page in my hand. *"Don León Aguilar y Angel?"*

I stood from the bench, my hand over my mouth. Manuel and I stared at each other.

"Oh my God." I started giggling in giddiness. "Oh my God, Manuel. This is crazy. This is totally insane."

"I know!" He was pacing back and forth, running his hands through his hair. "Am I dreaming? This must be a crazy dream."

"Holy cow. Yes. I can't wait to tell the real you about it when I wake up."

He stopped and looked at me and we both burst into hysterical laughter.

"Oh my God! Manuel! It's not a dream! It's true! This is crazy!" I pressed a hand to my chest and sunk back onto the bench. My hand landed right on the ring under my shirt. And then I remembered.

*Oh my God. The story.*

A wave of guilt washed over me as I remembered how I had so quickly dismissed my grandmother's words.

*What if she was telling the truth?*

I looked at Manuel, my hand over my mouth. The soft afternoon light lit up his eyes and glowed orange on his tousled black curls. I felt like I was actually seeing him for the first time.

*He really is gorgeous, isn't he?* I heard myself think.

*Wait. What?*

"It is like... it is like destiny," he was saying. "When I walked into your grandmother's store that day..."

"There's something else," I breathed. He froze, his eyes questioning. "I... there's something else..." I put my hands behind my neck, unclasped the chain and drew the ring out. I stared at it.

288

"My grandmother...last time we spoke she told me this story..."

Manuel sat next to me. I could feel his intense gaze and it gave me goosebumps.

I couldn't meet his eyes. But I had to tell him. I had to.

"She said that my ancestor—you know, Míriam de Carmona—she fell in love with the son of the man who rescued her family. That must have been León." I swallowed, my cheeks growing warm. I felt Manuel shift uncomfortably and turn his gaze away. I finally looked up at him. "She said he's the one who gave her this ring." I held it out to him. Manuel looked up and leaned in to examine it.

"Alma!" He said sharply. "You idiot!"

"What?"

"It's an *eagle!*" He took it from me and looked more closely.

"So?"

"*Aguilar,* Alma!" He looked up at me, his eyes wild. "It's the seal! The coat of arms! The Aguilar family emblem! It's been hanging around your neck this entire time!"

I clapped my hand to my forehead.

"Oh my God, Manuel. We are *both* such idiots."

"We are the idiots of the century."

"Of the millennium. Like, *legitimately* the idiots of the millennium."

"*Dios mío,*" he whispered softly, turning the ring over in his hand.

I watched him, my hands shaking, my heart still pounding. I couldn't even describe what I was feeling.

"Well," I said softly, and cleared my throat. "My instructions are to return it to you." I looked down at my lap. "Your family... they lost everything...my family never knew...how much your ancestors sacrificed for them."

Manuel was still staring at the ring as though he were in a trance.

"So on behalf of my entire family, from 1491 until today...thank you. We did not forget."

After a few moments he straightened, looked at me, and extended the ring back to me. "I cannot accept this."

"What?"

"It was a gift. From my ancestor to yours."

"Your ancestor gave us our lives. That was enough of a gift."

He was shaking his head, his hand still extended. "He wanted Miriam to have this."

"*She* wanted us to give it back. At least that's what the family legend says. He probably gave it to her to peddle off anyway. Morocco sucked back then."

He shrugged. "What if he just wanted her to have it?"

"In that case I don't think she should have accepted it." *Why is my voice so sharp?*

"Why not?" Manuel blinked in confusion.

"She said *no*. She was Jewish. He was Christian. It would not have worked out. There was no valid reason to accept a gift from him."

Manuel's brow knitted. "Why—"

"I don't get why she didn't send it back herself," I went on, more to myself than to him. "She clearly wanted to return it to him. Why didn't she do it in her own lifetime? Why drive her descendants crazy with this stupid mission?"

Manuel swallowed, studying the ring again. "Maybe...it was too hard for her to let it go. Maybe she just could not bring herself to do it."

"Well, she should have!" I snapped. There was a tense pause.

"Fine. Well," he said, once again extending the ring to me, his voice now a little sharp too. "Either way, this is a priceless family heirloom and there is no way I could—"

"It has *your* family emblem on it!"

"But it's been in *your* family for five centuries!"

"Your family sacrificed all their wealth, their titles, everything they ever had, for my family." I was practically yelling at this point.

"Can't you at least accept *one* little token of thanks?"

"This is ridiculous, Alma," he said, and finally grabbed my bag and shoved the ring into it. "We're talking about something that happened five hundred years ago!"

I swallowed and looked away. He just sat there for a long moment, and then he took a deep breath.

"Are we...not?" he asked softly, turning to me and looking me square in the eye.

I lowered my eyes. Now I noticed that my whole body was shaking, and I was breaking out in a cold sweat.

I fumbled for an honest answer to that question. "I..." I finally stammered. "I'm not sure."

# Míriam

When Don Tomás finally returned and opened the lids of the barrels, Míriam had to stifle a cry of relief. Abraham bent over and helped her stand up. Her legs were asleep and she could not stand without support. Her father helped her out of the barrel and held her steady until the strength returned to her legs. Míriam looked around her in the flickering light of Don Tomás's torch. The air was dank and smelled of fish and salt. Míriam could hear the pounding of the waves nearby. She froze in fascination—she had never heard the sea before.

Don Tomás handed them each dark cloaks, and they tiptoed out of the warehouse and out onto the docks.

As they walked, Míriam heard the distant sound of hooves pounding. She looked up at Don Tomás, and he quickly motioned for Míriam and Abraham to get behind him. "Keep your heads down!" he whispered. He held up his torch, squinting at the approaching figure on horseback. "Who goes there?" he called.

The horse galloped closer and Don Tomás stood protectively in front of Míriam and Abraham, his hand drifting to the hilt of his sword.

"Stand down," called the figure. "It's me."

Don Tomás jolted in surprise. "León? What are you doing here?" he hissed as the horse pulled to a halt. Míriam gasped and looked up, her heart filling with a hope she didn't even know how to name.

León jumped off his horse and approached the three of them. His eyes glowed in the torchlight.

"I am so sorry, Father," he said. "I just…I can't…I have to…" He looked past his father at Abraham and cleared his throat. "Señor de Carmona, I must speak to you."

Don Tomás stepped aside, looking utterly bewildered but saying nothing. León and Abraham regarded each other for a few moments.

"I know this seems crazy," León said. His eyes were wide and his voice taut with emotion. "Just…hear me out."

"Well, spit it out, boy! You are endangering all of us!" Don Tomás growled.

León stepped a little closer to Abraham. "Please, sir. Let me marry her."

They all stared at him. Míriam couldn't breathe.

"What?" Abraham gasped.

"I know, sir. I know it is unthinkable. But hear me out. I can give your daughter a good life. I can protect her. She will never go hungry. She will want for nothing. Yes, she would have to live as a *conversa*. But I would let her practice your faith in secret in the way she wishes. The Inquisition will never touch her."

Abraham looked incredulously from León to Míriam.

"You know where you are taking her. It is very dangerous and you can't guarantee that she will even survive, let alone lead a decent life. I can promise you that she will be safe with me, and that she will thrive. Please, sir."

Abraham's eyes filled with tears. Don Tomás hung back, saying nothing.

Abraham turned to look at his daughter. She could not meet his eyes.

"How can I make this decision?" he whispered. He shook his head, looking back up at León. "How can I let my daughter marry a non-Jew, be baptized, and lead a life of secrecy, so contrary to the Torah and the traditions of our ancestors? How could I betray God this way?" He turned back to Míriam. "On the other hand…how can I condemn my own daughter to a life of poverty and strife…of danger…of misery…when there is an alternative?" Tears streamed down his face. "I cannot. I cannot make this decision." Míriam finally looked up at him, her own eyes brimming with tears. "I must leave this up to you, Míriam."

Míriam's heart pounded as León shifted his gaze from Abraham to her. He stepped closer and knelt down.

"I promise, I will make you happy," he whispered. "You will want for nothing. You will be safe. I guarantee it. Please. I just… I can't let you leave." Míriam finally lifted her eyes from the ground to meet his. They were welling with tears. She looked past him at Don Tomás, who was standing, his arms crossed, one hand over his mouth, brow furrowed. She looked at her own father, who was watching her expectantly, and then back down at León. His eyes were pleading. "I love you," he finished.

Míriam closed her eyes, hugging herself and bending forward as if in prayer. She felt dizzy with conflicting emotions: sadness, hope, fear, foreboding, guilt. Her mind was flooded with voices, flowing and ebbing to the rhythm of the waves.

"Give me…give me a moment," she stuttered, and she turned away from the three men who waited for her to choose her destiny, and looked out at the sea.

She could just barely make out the horizon that separated the black of the sky from the black of the sea by following the shifting reflections of the moonlight glimmering on the waves. On either side of the harbor, the shadows of two hills rose. Beyond that gateway lay the open sea…from here, it looked like pitch black nothingness. She closed her eyes.

*God…my God…what do you want of me?*

She had spent her entire life trying to do God's will. She had wanted nothing more than to please Him and to carry out the mission He had given her as one of His chosen people.

But she loved León. And she knew that she was unlikely to find someone like him in the Maghreb—someone with his calming voice and his comforting presence, someone who could give her a good life.

*I don't have to give up on the Torah entirely... I can still be a Jew in secret...*

But what about their children? What about the future of her people? Raising children as Jews would be dangerous, even if León agreed to do so; and after a few generations they wouldn't even know they were Jewish anymore—they would be Christians inwardly as well as outwardly, and Míriam's own legacy as a Jew would be lost forever. She didn't want that to happen. She wanted her children and her children's children to be proud Jews. She wanted to bequeath to them the mission God had given her.

But if she didn't survive in the Maghreb, she wouldn't have any children at all...

*Why do You test me like this? Why do You torture me with this most beautiful and powerful of emotions to tempt me away from everything I've ever believed in?*

She drew a deep breath, opening her eyes and looking out at the twinkling stars. Something about their flickering light brought an image to her mind from what seemed a lifetime ago: the Sabbath lights burning by the window of their house in Seville, lending some warmth to her mother's drawn face and reflecting in her sad green eyes.

*Remember...for the past...for our mothers and our mothers' mothers...*

*Keep...for the future...for our daughters and our daughters' daughters...*

And she thought of the candles she had been forced to light in the corner these last few weeks, and imagined herself having to hide those candles forever.

Her mother had known she would probably die on the journey

from their old home in Seville. She had sacrificed everything to pass the burden and gift of the Torah down to Míriam. How could Míriam dream of rejecting it?

Her eyes welled with tears.

She knew what she had to do.

She knew that it was the most painful thing she had ever had to do in her life.

But she knew that she had to do it: for God, for His Torah, for His people.

For her mother.

She looked up. *Please...*she prayed in her heart. *Help me get through this.*

She lingered a moment longer, eyes lifted in prayer.

Then she turned back toward León.

"No," she whispered.

The look on León's face was devastating.

"No," she repeated a little louder, and the tears began to flow. She shook her head. "How could I...how could I marry...in a church? How could I live a life of secrecy and lies, hiding who I really am?" She looked back up at León, her voice trembling. "My mother...she gave up everything so that I would be able to live as a Jew. How could I betray her?"

León bit his lip and took a deep breath, then looked deep into her eyes. The sadness in his gaze was more than she could stand. "You are sure?" His voice was faint.

"Yes," she whispered.

León got slowly to his feet. "Then this is all I ask," he said. He slid a gold signet ring off the little finger of his left hand and held it out to her. "Take this."

Míriam looked at her father, then back at León.

"As a gift," he said softly. "To remember me."

Míriam slowly extended her hand to accept it. León placed the ring in her hand, and then suddenly grasped her hand in both of his. She trembled at his firm, warm touch. This was strictly forbidden—but she could not bring herself to pull her hand away. She knew this would be the last time he would ever touch her.

León brought her hand to his face and pressed it to his lips. They stood there like that a few moments, and then suddenly he let go, as if breaking a spell. Míriam quickly pulled her hand away, her cheeks flushing. The sensation of his lips against her fingers burned into her skin.

"Will I ever see you again?" he whispered.

She blinked back a fresh wave of tears. She shook her head.

"Never," she answered. "I'm sorry."

And then she could not take the pain of being in his presence one moment longer. She turned on her heel and ran—ran straight across the dock and up the gangway of the ship that awaited them. She crouched behind the gunwale and collapsed in grief.

A few minutes later she felt a hand on her back. She started and lifted her head to see who it was, then rose. It was her father. They gazed at each other, then embraced, quietly weeping.

Don Tomás soon joined them and led them down into the belly of the boat, where a large, empty wooden chest waited for them.

"Wait in here," he said. "Captain Ramírez is the only one on board who knows you are here, and he will take care of you until you reach Tangier. You must stay out of sight of the other officers and crew; Ramírez is the only one I fully trust. I hope he will find a way for you to spend some of your time less confined."

"Thank you, my brother. Thank you for everything. May God repay your kindnesses tenfold, and may the house of Aguilar be forever blessed with prosperity and honor." Abraham embraced him one last time, and then stepped into the chest with Míriam. They crouched low, and Don Tomás Aguilar lowered the lid. They were engulfed in darkness.

"I am proud of you," Abraham whispered. "And your mother would be, too."

Emptied of tears, Miriam just sighed, burrowing her head into her father's shoulder. She felt the ring in her right hand, and turned it over and over, fingering its smooth surface.

*One day...one day...I will return this to him, she thought as the boat rocked them gently, rising and falling with the waves. One day, when I have moved on, and prospered, and married a good, devout Jewish man. When I am living a happier, better life than the one I just refused.*

*One day.*

# Alma

A silence fell between us that felt like it lasted a year. I bit my lip and stared out at the sea, willing this conversation to rewind, to go away... praying for Manuel to either disappear or start chattering about the weather or something. He did neither. Out of the corner of my eye I saw him hunched forward, his elbows resting on his knees, his head bowed. I knew we were both thinking the same thing.

*God. What now?*

Finally Manuel lifted his head and slowly sat up. A pause, another deep breath. "Alma, I..."

My phone's ringtone interrupted him, making both of us jump. I sprang to my feet, fishing the phone out of my pocket and offering an unspoken prayer of thanks for the distraction.

"It's my sister," I said, trying to regain composure and forcing a smile. "Just wait 'til she hears..." I walked around the other side of the bench, accepted the call and lifted the phone to my ear.

"Mimi, you will not believe what I just—"

"Alma, I have some terrible news."

Her tone of voice stopped me cold.

"What is it, Mimi?"

"It's Grandma."

My breath caught in my chest.

"The doctors say it was her heart."

I shook my head. My knees felt weak, and I braced myself on the back of the bench for support.

"I'm so sorry to have to tell you like this. I assume you'll want to catch the first plane out of there. The funeral is tomorrow afternoon."

An unearthly moan issued from my lips. I felt Manuel's presence behind me.

"I'm so sorry." Mimi's voice was shaking.

"No, Mimi, you don't understand," I pleaded. "I just found out...I solved the mystery...we had a fight...I...it can't be..."

"I'm so sorry, Alma." She was crying.

"I...I need to...I'll call you back..." I croaked, and hung up the phone with shaking fingers.

The phone fell from my hand and clattered to the ground.

*No. Not this. Anything but this.*

Manuel bent down, picked up the phone, and slipped it into my bag.

"Alma?" His voice was quiet but he sounded alarmed. "What is going on?"

"My grandmother..." The sob broke from me before I could even understand what was happening to me. I felt his hand on my shoulder, and a few moments later his other hand took my wrist.

"What happened, Alma?"

I sobbed again, tears streaming from my eyes. I felt dizzy and nauseated. I hardly managed to squeeze out the words, "She's gone," in a high-pitched, inelegant squeak.

"*Dios mío.* Alma. I am so sorry."

I leaned into his comforting touch, and before I knew it he had gathered me into his arms. I had only a moment of hesitation as my cheek brushed against his gold crucifix, but then I just sank into his embrace, sobbing. He was whispering into my hair. I had no idea what he was saying. My ears were ringing. I couldn't think. Through the fog of sorrow, the pounding of his heart pressed up against my ear was the only steady thing to hold on to. How could I resist his comfort, the woody smell of his sweater, the warmth of his sturdy arms around me?

And when he pulled back...how could I brush his hands away

when they wiped the tears from my cheeks and then gently stroked the hair around my face? And how could I look away when he stared deep into my eyes, his own welling with tears as they took on a strange glint I had never seen before? Or when he drew closer, and his eyes fluttered shut, and his lips met mine?

How could I do anything but kiss him back, sinking into what had just become both the bitterest and sweetest moment of my life so far?

I threw my arms around his neck, pulling him in, drinking him in like the first sip of sweet cool water after five hundred years in a parched desert.

And then, all at once, I came to my senses. I gasped, pulled back, pushed him away—and we both stood there staring at each other in horror and giddiness and shame all at once, our hands clapped to our mouths. Neither of us moved. His eyes brimmed with pain and rejection, and I couldn't believe how much it hurt me to see that. But that same question was still hanging in the air between us...

*What now?*

I tore my eyes away from his, looking out toward the harbor. In the fading light, the silhouettes of the hills rising on either side of the bay were like a pair of hands trying to hold the water as it spilled beyond their grasp. Between them flowed the passage where five hundred years ago a ship carrying my ancestor had probably sailed—an ancestor who had probably also asked herself: *What now?*

And I knew that I had the answer.

"I..." I stammered, snatching up the strap of my bag, "I have to leave."

"Alma—"

"No. Please. Don't say another word." I stared ahead at the horizon, not daring to face him, not trusting myself to look in his eyes again without shattering into a thousand pieces. "I can't..." I whispered. "I just can't."

I turned on my heels and ran.

———∾∾———

I think I cried for the entire train ride back to Madrid. I couldn't stop replaying the last conversation I'd had with Grandma in my mind, how needlessly defensive and cold I'd been.

*Why didn't I tell her I loved her? Why didn't I tell her I loved her?*

And as if the guilt and the grief of losing my beloved grandmother so suddenly did not weigh heavily enough, Manuel's intense golden-brown eyes, brimming with sadness and hurt, would drift into my head, and I was totally overwhelmed with despair and shame and other emotions so raw and painful I didn't even know how to name them.

*I'm so sorry, Grandma,* I thought. *You were right all along. I'm such an idiot that I didn't see this coming.*

I stared at my phone as it rang over and over and Manuel's name flashed on the screen. Finally the text messages started coming in, and I couldn't stop myself from reading them.

*Alma, please pick up the phone.*

*Alma, I am so sorry. I know what she meant to you and I know what it's like to lose someone you love. I couldn't stand to see you in so much pain and I lost my head. Please forgive me. It won't happen again.*

*Please don't make me lose you as a friend over this.*

I just sobbed and sobbed. The other passengers were staring at me, but I didn't care.

*Alma, can you please at least tell me where you are? The hotel clerk says you checked out and I am starting to get really worried.*

I tried to pull myself together. He was right—I should at least let him know I was safe.

*On train to Madrid,* I tapped out. *Flying to NY for funeral.*

Then a few minutes later, I wrote: *I'm so sorry, Manuel. I just can't do this.*

I turned my phone off and slouched against the back of the seat.

I had a sudden sharp memory of that conversation with Grandma shortly before I left for Madrid...

*Love and infatuation are not the same thing... you don't 'fall in love' like you fall in a hole... it's a choice...*

*Yes... but this infatuation business... can be very powerful too...*

*I'm not David,* I'd insisted to my family on Rosh Hashanah.

I buried my face in my hands. *I'm such an idiot. I can't believe this happened to me. How could this have happened to me?*

*I should never have asked him to be my research partner... I should never have become his friend... I should never have talked his mother into letting him come with me to Madrid... I should never have come with him to Granada...*

*But how could I have done otherwise?*

I sighed and stared out the window. He was a great friend—the best I'd ever had. It made perfect sense to fall for him. But that was exactly the problem: there was no way we could have stayed "just friends". And that was why I had to leave him. Once and for all. Cold turkey.

*Never.*

*I will never speak to him again.*

*I will never look into his eyes again.*

*I will never touch him again.*

With that thought came a vivid memory of the sensation of his hand gently stroking my cheek, and a surge of yearning so strong I could hardly breathe.

*Never,* I told myself firmly.

I imagined David holding Cathy's hand, feeling free of the weight of all the generations that chained me to this cushioned seat on a train speeding toward Madrid—and I had a moment of intense jealousy. But then I closed my eyes, and an image of my grandmother floated into my mind. She was lighting the Shabbat candles. I remembered the weight of her hands on my head as she gave me the traditional blessing: *May God make you like Sara, Rebecca, Rachel, and Leah...*

*It's true*, I thought. *I'm not David. I'm making a different choice. The hardest choice I've made in my entire life.*

*I'm in love with Manuel. I can't deny that anymore. And yet... there are other loves in my life. They are the ones that define who I am, even if they don't feel as powerful right now.*

And as I held the image of Grandma and the candles firmly in my mind's eye, I sensed a presence around me: the souls of all my maternal ancestors, whose names I had studied and pored over so many times. Among them, I pictured Míriam—a young woman with flowing black locks and my grandmother's sparkling green eyes. She was smiling, reaching out to stroke my cheek.

*I am proud of you,* she was saying.

"I'm sorry," I whispered.

*You did not forget us, and you did not fail us,* they all said. *We are so proud of you.*

# Manuel

A beam of garishly bright sunlight streamed into my face, waking me far earlier than it had any right to. I was too groggy to get up and close the curtains, so I tried rolling over on the lumpy hotel bed, turning away to escape the light. But it followed me—and by that point, I had regained just enough consciousness to remember why my eyes felt so puffy and sticky, and I knew that there was no chance of getting back to sleep.

I threw off the covers and sat hunched over on the edge of the bed. I cast a withering glare at the open curtains. They were bright blue, floral, and sickeningly cheery. I should have thought to close them last night before getting into bed.

It had not crossed my mind at the time; I'd been more than a little preoccupied.

I stumbled into the bathroom and faced myself in the mirror. I looked about as bad as I felt: eyes red and swollen, hair sticking out in every direction, and fuzz on my chin that could no longer be excused as "designer stubble". I splashed some water on my face and rubbed it vigorously. Time for a shave. And maybe that stupid haircut all the women in my life had been haranguing me about for several months.

A wave of despair washed over me as an image of Alma came to mind, flipping that omelet in Marta's kitchen.

*Dear God. What have I done?*

I reached for my phone, which had been charging on the counter by the sink, and picked it up, hoping but not daring to believe that I would find a message from her there. The emptiness of my

SMS inbox hit me full-force despite my pessimism. I clicked on her name and stared at the picture my phone showed me, probably pulled from her Facebook profile. It was a selfie of us from the restored synagogue in Lorca, her full lips pulled into a radiant smile, strands of hair that had escaped from her ponytail falling wildly around her face, her head touching mine as I obliged her with a tired smile. The collar of my sweater, the one she'd borrowed, lay rumpled over her collarbone.

I closed my eyes to brace myself against another wave of despair.

*"I'm sorry, Manuel. I just can't do this."*

*Can't do what?*

*What did that mean?*

*Would she ever speak to me again?*

This suffocating feeling of pure longing for something that could never be, a door that had slammed shut on me, forever separating me from someone I loved deeply...it was familiar to me. An image of myself as a boy floated into my mind, lying in my bed in the nights after my father had died, calling out for him. I called and called until my mother came into the room, shrieking at me, *"Don't you understand? He's not here! He's not coming! He's never coming back!"*

And then she crumpled to the floor, sobbing. I got out of bed and crawled into her arms, and we lay there and cried together, and awoke the next morning side by side on the floor of my bedroom.

I pulled myself out of this memory and tried to think straight.

*Shave. Clothes. Breakfast.*

*Haircut.*

*Grandparents.*

*Back to Madrid.*

*That is the plan.*

I took a deep breath and reached for my razor.

As I packed up my things, a scrap of paper fell out of my back-pack. I picked it up and glanced at it.

*If I have the gift of prophecy and understand all mysteries and all knowledge, and if I have a faith that can move mountains, but I do not have love, I am nothing.*

I sank onto the bed, buried my face in my hands, and wept bitterly for a long time.

I found a barber shop a few blocks away from the hotel—a brightly lit little place bedecked with posters of models with their hair in strange but oddly beautiful formations. The barber sat me in the chair, and I watched him in the mirror as he snipped and buzzed away. He cut the sides quite short and left the hair on top longer. He then artfully mussed it up with gel, since apparently "bed-head" is a fashion these days. (I wish I were joking about that, but, sadly, I'm not.)

"*¿Te gusta?*" he asked, beaming at me in the mirror.

I studied my own reflection. Yes, I did like it. The haphazard tufts of black hair over my forehead gave me a sort of rakish look. I brushed my hand through it. Fashionable *and* messy-looking enough to continue to drive my mother crazy. Also, a different Manuel than the one who had lost all sense and ruined the best friendship of his life. Win-win-win.

I paid the barber an exorbitant sum and set out into the street to find a taxi.

My mother's parents were buried in a small cemetery near the edge of Cartagena. It was hilly and green, overgrown with vines, and dotted with droopy trees. Fortunately, my grandparents' graves were at the bottom of the hill, easily accessible from the main path. I wandered over to them: a pair of simple stone crosses side by side. But there was an old woman hunched over one of them, leaning over her walker. I stopped short when I realized that she was standing right across from my grandmother's gravestone. She seemed to be arranging a row of pebbles on top of the stone. I hung back awkwardly, not sure what to make of this; could this woman have known Abuela?

I approached her cautiously. *"Disculpe,"* I said. She turned to look at me, and there was something so familiar about her round brown eyes that I forgot my tongue. Her hair was tied in a neat bun at the back of her head, and she bore a striking resemblance to...

"Are you..." I continued in Spanish, "in any way related to Rosa Medrano?"

She looked me up and down. "Yes," she said in a brittle sort of voice. "She was my sister."

My jaw dropped.

*No. It can't be.*

"Who are you?" she asked, eyes narrowed in suspicion.

"I'm her grandson!"

Her eyes bulged. "No," she gasped.

Joyful laughter bubbled up in me and I rushed to her. "My great-aunt! You are my great-aunt!" I kissed her on each cheek, my head spinning giddily, and then took her frail, trembling hands in mine. "My name is Manuel; what is yours?"

"I am Sara," she breathed, cupping my cheek with her hand. "A great-nephew... I don't believe it! I discovered her gravesite here by accident when a friend of mine was buried nearby a couple of years ago. I've visited Rosa every week since then. I felt it was up to me to repair some of the damage our parents did when they cut off contact with her."

"Why did they do it?" I asked, my heart pounding. I had never believed I would learn the answer to this mystery, but here was someone who certainly knew and could tell me!

She glanced around nervously, then leaned forward and whispered: "Do you not know?"

I shook my head. "No one would ever tell me."

Tía Sara looked around again, as though fearful someone would overhear.

"I cannot tell you here," she whispered. "It isn't safe. My apartment is a short walk from here. Come home with me, and I will tell you everything."

My mind reeling, I accompanied Tía Sara out of the graveyard and down the road. I hammered her with questions: did she have any other living relatives? How many siblings did she have? Did she know my grandfather? Where had they lived all these years? Some questions she answered, and to others she simply shook her head and said, "Soon."

The walk seemed to take forever. Clouds had moved in and the breeze was getting chilly; Tía Sara did not move very fast, and I was bursting with impatience. We finally arrived at a small apartment building with a hedge in front and chipped Moorish tiling on its façade. She led me through the wrought-iron gate set into the hedge. The rickety elevator was too small to carry both of us and the walker at once, so I sent her up and took the stairs to the third floor.

I arrived shortly after she did, and found myself facing a huge crucifix hung on her door, with the Savior's head drooping mournfully to one side. The image reminded me of my last conversation with Rabbi Uri, which had started with Jesus and ended with a warning: *"I just don't want either of you to get hurt."*

*He was right.*

*God. He was right.*

"*Ven, cariño,*" came Tía Sara's voice, and I wandered into her apartment. It was immaculately clean, though it smelled a little musty.

"Are you hungry, dear?" Tía Sara slowly wheeled her walker toward the small kitchenette in the corner. "I think I have some stew left over from yesterday."

"No. No thank you, Tía."

"Coffee, then?"

"Please," I insisted, taking her arm, "let me get it." She smiled up at me and touched my face again.

"You are a sweet boy. Everything is on the counter. I will go get the envelope."

She headed toward the hallway, and I approached the counter. I unscrewed the bottom chamber of her coffee maker and filled it with water, my mind racing. *What could be in the envelope? Photos? Records? "It isn't safe," she said. Maybe it has something to do with the Franco regime?*

I set the coffee maker on the stove and wandered into the living room. There were picture frames hung all across the wall behind the leather sofa. My heart pounded in excitement: photos of my grandmother's family! I stepped around the mahogany coffee table to examine them, drinking in their faces. I noticed Tía Sara's form coming out of the hallway next to me, and turned to her.

"Can you tell me who's who in these photos?"

She spent the next minute or so introducing me to my cousins. Then she took my hand and sat heavily on the couch.

"Come, sit," she said.

I did, and looked at the envelope in her lap expectantly. But she just sat there for a while, staring into the Persian carpet.

Finally, she looked up at me and asked: "Are you a Christian?"

That was the last question I had been expecting to hear.

"Eh...yes," I stuttered. I wrinkled my brow, remembering the crucifix on her door. "Aren't you?"

She gazed at me intently, and took a few moments before she answered. "I am," she said, "on the outside."

Now I was really confused.

"On the...outside?" I echoed. What on earth did this have to do with the family's feud with her sister?

She placed the envelope on my lap. Still feeling completely bewildered, I picked it up and opened it. Inside was a pile of documents. I slid them out into my hands. They were yellowed and warped with age and mildew—and that smell, the smell of old parchment and paper that I had gotten so used to at the archives, wafted from them.

I peered at the sheet on top. It looked like a family tree, with names mapped across it and lines connecting them. But there was something odd about it. My father's family tree, as I had sketched it, looked like...well, a tree, with branches stretching out as you moved up. This one looked more like...a corkscrew? Cousins seemed to have married cousins for many generations. Toward the bottom of the page, I spotted Sara's name, and the other sister, Gracia, and...was that Rosa's name, crossed out?

Then I lifted the family tree to look at the page below it.

At first I had no idea what I was looking at. It was a document hastily scrawled in some impossible hand, and upon closer examination I realized that it wasn't even in Spanish.

Then, all at once, I understood.

*"Madre del Amor Hermoso,"* I breathed.

# Alma

The funeral was a huge blur. Dozens of people talking, crying, standing outside huddled under umbrellas in the rain, our shoes sinking in the mud. I'm told I gave a beautiful eulogy; I have no idea what I said. All I remember is the miserably wet, cold, heavy air, the smell of the muddy earth, and the feeling of emptiness and devastation as I stood over the bier where she rested, staring out at the sheet covering the person who I always felt had loved me the most. To whom I hadn't had a chance to say good-bye. Whom I would never, ever see again.

There was so much noise and bustle after the funeral that I didn't really have an opportunity to sit and process what was happening. On the first day of the *shiva,* the seven days of intense mourning, I tried to stay in the room where my aunts and uncles sat on cushions on the floor, passing around pictures, sharing stories about Grandma. But I just couldn't handle it. My mind kept drifting to the other person I'd just lost forever, and I felt guilty enough about the whole thing with Manuel without having thoughts of him intrude on my family's grief for my grandmother and make me feel even guiltier. When people started to ask me about my research, I got up and stammered something about going to find my mom—who I had noticed was missing—and fled.

I eventually found her in the kitchen, scrubbing dishes.

"Ima!" I scolded, grabbing the sponge and plate from her hand. "You're not supposed to be doing housework while you're sitting *shiva!*"

My mother sighed, rinsing the suds off her hands and shaking them into the sink. She dried her hands on a nearby dishtowel and sank into the chair by the breakfast table.

"I just don't know what else to do," she said. "I can't stand all the sitting around. I need to be *doing* something." She ran her hands through her hair, which was showing more streaks of gray than I remembered from before I left Albany. "It drove me crazy during Dad's *shiva*, too. I can't even leave the house. I feel like a caged animal."

I put the dish and sponge in the sink, and sat in a chair next to hers. I put my hand on her shoulder, and her head drooped onto my hand.

"I don't want to have to think," she said in a small voice.

"I know exactly what you mean," I murmured.

She looked up at me, as though suddenly remembering something.

"There was this song," she said, "this song she used to sing. Maybe you remember it? It was in Judeo-Spanish. Something about a daughter and the sea."

I swallowed, remembering the moment that song had come into my mind just two days ago. *"Hija Mia?"* I asked, my throat dry.

"Do you remember how it goes?"

I started to sing it, but choked on the words.

"Yes, I think that's it. She used to sing that to me at night when I was a little girl."

"Me too." I pursed my lips. "It's kind of a dark song to be singing as a lullaby, isn't it?"

She nodded, her eyes narrowing, staring past me at the refrigerator as though trying to draw something up from her memory. "But there was the story she told with it..."

I felt the blood drain from my face.

"What story?"

"One about a Christian nobleman who helped a Jewish woman fleeing from Spain to a dangerous faraway land...before she left, he proposed marriage and promised her a safe and happy life with him if she stayed—but she refused, and chose her devotion to her faith and her people over love, prosperity, and security. He gave her a ring to remember him by, and she waited her whole life to return it to him." She furrowed her brow. "It was a pretty strange story..." She looked up at me, and tilted her head in concern. "Are you okay? You look a little pale."

"I just...um...feel a little sick to my stomach," I stammered. "I'm going to go lie down."

I stumbled out of the kitchen and slipped past all the guests into the hallway, my head spinning.

*Proposed marriage?*

*He proposed marriage?*

I tentatively opened the door to my cousin Elisheva's room, where I had been sleeping on a mattress on the floor; and when I saw that it was empty, I stepped inside and shut the door behind me, collapsing onto her bed.

*The ring was because he proposed marriage?*

I sat bolt upright.

*The ring.*

A wave of panic shot through me. Manuel hadn't accepted it. He'd shoved it back in my bag.

I ran over to the corner of the room where my bag lay, feverishly digging through the pockets.

"Please, oh please be in here..." I begged, cursing Manuel under my breath.

"What are you doing?"

I started and whirled around to see Mimi standing in the doorway.

"I—I'm looking for—yes!" Relief flooded through me as my fingers closed around the smooth band. "Oh thank God. It's here."

"What is?"

I drew the ring out, rubbing it gently with my thumb.

"Wasn't that supposed to be around your neck?" Mimi scolded.

"It was! I just—I was going to give it to…" My voice trailed off as I realized that I hadn't told anyone this story yet—and I wasn't sure I was ready to tell Mimi. But she was watching me with one eyebrow cocked.

"All right, spill the beans," she said. "What the hell happened in Cartagena?"

How could I even begin to answer that question?

I took a deep breath and started with the de Carmona file, and then told her what Manuel had discovered just before she had called me to tell me about Grandma's death.

"Wait, wait, wait," Mimi said, holding up her hand. "Let me get this straight. You discovered, through reading these old Inquisition trials, that our ancestors were rescued by the Christian ancestors of your own research partner?!"

"If I hadn't seen the records with my own eyes," I said, "I wouldn't believe a word of it."

Mimi was shaking her head. "There's no way that can be true. You must have made a mistake. You guys are hallucinating. I don't know… Do you realize the odds—"

"Mimi, I am telling you, *they are the same people.* The names are exactly the same, the dates and locations are right. And the ring has the Aguilar family emblem on it!"

"*What?* Show me!" I handed it to her. "Unbelievable," she breathed, turning it over in her palm. She started pacing around the room, running a hand through her hair and still staring at the ring. "This is insane!"

"I know!"

Mimi stopped short, turning back to me. "So… you were going to give this to Manuel? Why didn't you?"

"I tried…" I faltered, wondering how much to say. "He… didn't want to accept it."

"Why not?"

I shrugged, reaching for it, and she handed it back to me. "I don't know." I polished it on my shirt, and then studied it carefully. "I have to figure out a way to get it to him."

Mimi raised an eyebrow. "Aren't you going to be seeing him next week when you go back to Madrid?"

I didn't answer, still staring at the ring. No, I would not be seeing him next week—or ever. I would not be going back to Madrid.

"Alma."

I looked up at Mimi. She was studying my face with open suspicion.

"You *are* going back to Madrid, aren't you?"

With that, I released a hearty expletive, burst into tears, and buried my face in her shoulder.

"I'm such an idiot, Mimi," I sobbed.

"Yes, you are," she said magnanimously, patting my back. "But I love you anyway."

So we sat on the bed and I told her the rest of the story. She listened, shaking her head most of the time, and then sighed deeply.

"Do I get to say 'I told you so'?"

"No," I snapped. "Listen. I have to figure out how to get this ring back to him." I held it up. "I can't let it stay with me the way our stupid twenty-three-times-great-grandmother did, haunting us for five hundred years with her tragic love story. I need to be the one to put an end to it."

"What's that Talmudic phrase? The one about the deeds of the fathers being a sign for their descendants?"

"*Ma'aseh avot, siman l'vanim.*" The phrase floated up from the depths of my memory from Hebrew school, and I felt a shiver go down my spine.

"Yeah. That." Mimi chewed thoughtfully on the nail of her index finger. "Maybe you could mail it?"

"And trust the United States Postal Service with a priceless, solid-gold historical artifact? No way! Besides, Manuel could always send it back. I need to get around him somehow."

"Well, do you know any other members of his family?"

An image of Raquel Elvira, scrutinizing me at the NYU library, came to mind. She would be sure to keep the ring safe.

"His mother," I said slowly. "She lives in Brooklyn."

"Perfect! You can go on Sunday."

I shook my head, glancing at my watch. "No—she teaches high-school Spanish, and the schools are on spring recess now. How long a drive is it to Brooklyn?"

"Three hours, maybe? You aren't seriously thinking of going today, are you?"

"If I leave now, I can be back in time for Shabbat." I stood up from the bed and stepped over the mattresses to get my bag.

"What are you, nuts?" Mimi exclaimed. "You can't just disappear for the entire day. It's Grandma's *shiva*."

I spun around, giving her a stern look. "Giving this ring back to Manuel's family is the number-one mission *Grandma* gave me," I said. "It can't wait until Sunday. *I* can't wait until Sunday. I have to do this now." I took a deep breath. "Is there an extra car around?"

"Didn't Abba tell you?" Mimi said, rising from the bed herself. "Grandma wanted you to have hers—I guess as thanks for driving her around in it all the time."

———

Mimi helped me come up with a semi-believable cover story. She offered to come with me, but I figured it was more important for her to stay and relay my excuse to the rest of the family.

I crept out of the house as surreptitiously as possible, energized with a renewed sense of mission. But as soon as I sat down on the threadbare driver's seat and shut the door, engulfed in the dusty, cinnamony smell that reminded me so strongly of my grandmother, I was overwhelmed with grief yet again. I broke down in tears as I started the car, and paused to compose myself somewhat before pulling out of the driveway.

"I'm so sorry, Grandma," I found myself sobbing aloud. I stopped at a traffic light and glanced over at the empty passenger seat. It was so easy to feel like she was next to me, as she'd been last time I had driven this car. "You know I love you, right?" I whispered. "Even though I was a total jerk last time we spoke? You know it wasn't really about you… I didn't want to believe you. I was in it too deep to see it." I clutched the wheel and took a deep breath. "But do you think I did the right thing, Grandma?" I asked her silent presence. "Poor guy. I left him all alone there. Didn't even give him a chance to say goodbye. Seems to be a theme with me these days—hurting the people I love most, and then cutting them off forever." My eyes filled with tears again. "Dammit, Grandma," I sobbed. "Why does it have to hurt so much? With both of you…" I wiped my tears away furiously, trying to focus on the road. I sighed. "I miss you so much. At least I know you would forgive me. I don't know if Manuel ever will. I don't know if *I* ever will."

I fingered the ring hanging around my neck.

"But at least I can bring one thing full circle."

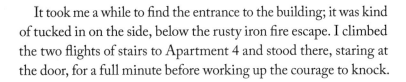

It took me a while to find the entrance to the building; it was kind of tucked in on the side, below the rusty iron fire escape. I climbed the two flights of stairs to Apartment 4 and stood there, staring at the door, for a full minute before working up the courage to knock.

Raquel Elvira pulled the door open. She looked me up and down, and said, "This explains a lot."

I had no idea what to say to that.

"Come in. I'm making lunch." She turned right around and disappeared into the apartment. I was left with no choice but to follow her into the narrow hallway and then into the small, cramped kitchen to the right.

"You keep kosher?" she tossed over her shoulder.

"Um, yes," I said.

"So I'll get you coffee." She pulled out a chair, gesturing for me to sit, and then bustled over to the coffee maker.

I got the sense that there was no use protesting.

"Manuel's plane landed a couple of hours ago," she said. "He should be here any minute."

My heart leapt to my throat. "What?! Manuel's coming home?"

She looked over her shoulder at me, her brow furrowed in confusion. "That's why you're here, no?"

"I...no...I didn't...why is he coming home?"

She turned around, studying me. "He said he made a very important discovery and had to tell me in person. You were with him, no?"

I gaped like a fish, unable to even begin to explain. "We... um...I left..."

She narrowed her eyes at me. "Did you break my little boy's heart?" she accused. "I will kill you." She turned back toward the counter and cracked an egg into a glass. She examined it, and then tossed it into the pan.

In my panic about discovering that Manuel was on his way—and my somewhat milder concern over the possibility of getting bludgeoned to death with a hot frying pan—I almost missed it.

Almost.

I froze, staring at her.

"Um... Señora Elvira..." I stuttered. She looked at me, one eyebrow raised. "Did you..." I cleared my throat, letting out a nervous laugh at how ridiculous this question was going to be. "Um. Did you just... *check* that egg?"

She blinked. "Of course." She squinted at me, as if trying to gauge how stupid I could possibly be to have asked. "To make sure it has no blood in it."

*No. No. Don't even hope.* I tried to stifle the wave of giddiness that washed over me. I cleared my throat again, and was about to ask if she happened to separate her milk and meat, but then my eyes widened. "You're a vegetarian."

"Yes..." she said, still looking at me as though I had asked her to lay an egg herself.

"You never had meat in the house."

"That would be... the definition of a vegetarian, yes."

I took a deep breath, trying to steady my nerves. "Was your mother... a vegetarian too?"

She blinked. "Yes."

I bit my lip and then asked, my voice shaking, "Is it... possible... that you happen to... light candles in the basement on Friday evenings?"

She stared at me.

"What is this, the Holy Inquisition?" she demanded. "No, of course I don't light them in the basement. I don't have a basement. I light them in the closet. My *mother* lit them in the basement." She clicked her tongue and turned back to her frying pan.

I just sat there, reeling, unable to think, unable to speak, and probably with a really stupid expression on my face. And that, of course, is when the door to the apartment burst open.

"Mama!" Manuel called from the entrance. I stood up from my chair, backing into the corner of the kitchen, as he came hurtling into the room. He froze when he saw me, and his eyes widened.

"Alma."

"You…" I stuttered. He looked… different. His wayward curls had finally been trimmed and partially tamed, and it made him look older, more confident, somehow. But there was something else, something I couldn't quite put my finger on.

"So? What is your big secret?" Raquel boomed from behind me. A slow grin spread over his face.

He threw off his backpack, unzipped it, and pulled out a thick manila envelope, very much like the one my grandmother had presented me with before I left for Madrid. He slapped it on the table, and took a step closer to his mother.

"Mama," he breathed. "We are Jewish."

Raquel and I both stared at him, slack-jawed.

"What?!" Raquel demanded.

He yanked the file open and pulled out the pages within it. "It's indisputable. Documented proof going back five hundred years to when our ancestors underwent forced conversion. Your mother came from a family of crypto-Jews who secretly held onto their identity for all these generations. She was ostracized by the rest of the Medranos because she rejected her heritage by marrying a non-Jew. But according to Jewish law," he went on, his eyes flicking toward me, "Judaism is matrilineal. Your mother was Jewish, so you are Jewish. And you are my mother. So I'm Jewish too."

Raquel just stared at him for a long, long moment.

I finally found my voice. "You *idiot!*" I yelled, my voice high-pitched with giddiness. "You *moron!* She checks her eggs for blood!" I jabbed a finger in his mother's direction. "She lights candles in the closet on Fridays!"

Manuel turned to his mother incredulously. "What?! I never knew…" He scrunched up his face. "In the closet? That's a serious fire hazard, no?"

I buried my face in my hands.

Raquel started to laugh and cry at the same time.

"I should have known," she gasped. "I should have known." She shoved past me and hugged Manuel, and they laughed and cried together.

*"I always felt... I always had this feeling... always felt this connection..."* she murmured in Spanish.

*"I know, Mama, me too... me too..."*

I just stood there, leaning against the wall, holding my head as though that might help it stop spinning.

Raquel pulled back sharply, grasping Manuel by his upper arms. *"How the Devil did you find this?"*

*"I met your Tía Sara by chance at the cemetery in Cartagena,"* Manuel answered, picking the papers back up from the table and showing her. *"She invited me to her house and told me, and then she let me copy these documents."* He handed them to her, and tapped the front page. *"This is her phone number. You should call her."*

*"I will!"* She grabbed the papers, and then stood and cast a look from me to Manuel and back again. She cleared her throat. "In fact, I'm going to go do that right now," she said in loud English, and strode quickly out of the kitchen.

Manuel and I both watched his mother disappear into her bedroom and close the door pointedly behind her. Then he turned back toward me.

There were a few moments of awkward silence.

"So," I said. "This is... unexpected."

He gave a mischievous grin. I couldn't get over how handsome he looked with his hair like that. "Well, you know what they say."

I just looked at him blankly.

He raised his eyebrows. "Come on. *No one* expects the Spanish Inquisition?"

I held my hand to my forehead, too stunned to find this funny. "I... you... yeah," I said weakly.

He regarded me for another moment. "You...eh...want to take a walk?"

I paused.

He jerked his head back toward the hall. "She has been known to spy on me."

I bit my lip, peering up at him, my heart starting to pound. The memory of his arms around me, of the sensation of his lips against mine, surged into my skin. A wave of shame immediately followed and I blinked, looking down, trying to erase it from my mind.

"It's only a walk, Alma."

*Yeah,* I thought. *And it was only a research project. Only a trip to Granada. Only a hug.*

*But... technically, he actually appears to be Jewish,* said a voice in my head. I glanced up at him again.

*Well yes, by descent, maybe. But...*

My eyes drifted toward his chest.

"I'm not wearing it," he said quietly.

I swallowed. "Why not?"

"Do you want to take a walk or not?"

---

We walked a full block in total silence, a careful distance between us. The street was relatively quiet; the air was still miserably damp, but a little warmer than the day before. The red brick apartment buildings on either side seemed impossibly tall after the smaller European-style buildings in Madrid. I listened carefully to Manuel's heavy footsteps, the swish of his coat as he walked with his hands in his pockets.

Finally I cleared my throat. "I...I'm really sorry that I—"

He held up his hand. "It's okay. I completely understand."

More awkward silence.

"So…um," I went on. "What happened after I abandoned you?"

He stopped and looked up at the sky, drawing a deep breath. "Well…" he took another few moments, and then resumed walking. "I stayed at the port for a while, trying to call you, as I am sure you are aware." He cast me a sideways glance. I swallowed. "Eventually I went back to the hotel to ask if they knew where you were. That's when the clerk told me you had checked out. Thanks, by the way, for answering that one text message, at least."

"It would have been pretty awkward if you'd sent the police after me."

"Awkward. That's one way to put it." I winced at the bitterness in his voice. I couldn't tell him what I knew he wanted to hear: that I also couldn't bear the idea of him worrying about me on top of everything else. "The next day I went to the cemetery…"

"Before or after you finally cut your hair?"

He shot me an amused look.

"You like it?" he asked, his hand drifting to his temple.

"Yeah," I said, my face getting a little warm. "It suits you. But… anyway. The cemetery."

"So—I met an old woman there at my grandmother's grave, and I asked if she was connected to my grandmother in any way…"

"And she told you she was her sister. Your great-aunt."

"Yes. You understood what I said to my mother?"

I blinked, suddenly realizing that I had. "Yeah. Every word! Maybe my Spanish for Dummies classes are paying off after all!"

"Good for you!"

"Anyway. Your great-aunt."

"Right. So I asked her why her family had been out of touch with my grandmother, and she started looking really nervous, like she was scared someone would overhear. She told me that it was not safe to tell me there, so she took me to her apartment, with this huge, graphic crucifix on the door..."

"And she gave you that pile of family documents?"

"At first I had no idea what they were. Then I realized that the second one was a document written in Hebrew script. I thought I must be hallucinating—why would she have a paper with Hebrew on it? I looked up at her and asked her what it was. She said it was her *ketuba*."

"A *ketuba*?!"

"I know! I was shocked. I could not even speak for a minute. Then I asked her why she had a *ketuba*. That's when she told me she was Jewish."

"But...but..." I stuttered. "Why would she have a *ketuba* but a cross on her door?"

"That's exactly what *I* asked—why she was hiding the fact that she was Jewish. She said that it is dangerous to be a Jew and that our family has been hiding it for centuries. That our ancestors were forced to convert in the fourteenth century, and had managed to keep the secret and pass it down for all these years."

"But..."

"I told her that it's not dangerous anymore. I told her about you, that you are openly Jewish, that your ancestors had always been, and it was perfectly safe."

"Well...mostly."

"Yes, well, bringing up neo-Nazis did not seem very prudent. But she still refused to believe me."

"The inherited fear..."

"Exactly. But what happened then was even stranger." He took another deep breath, turning a corner, brushing past a woman walking a dog. "She looked at me and said, 'You understand what this means, no?' I wasn't sure what to say. 'You are Jewish too,' she said." He stopped and turned to me. My heart started pounding again in response to his intense gaze. "It's not that

I did not understand that intellectually before she said it," he said. "I understood that it meant that I was Jewish by descent, at least according to *halacha*. But to hear her say, *'Eres judío también...'*" His voice trailed off. He was staring out past the small trees lining the sidewalk. "At first I was stunned and did not know what to say. Then I started to argue with her. I told her I was a Catholic, I was baptized, that was how I was born and raised and educated, that was how I had always identified, and that was who I am. She just looked deep into my eyes and said, very simply, 'You know that's not true. You have always known that's not true.'"

A shiver ran down my spine. I waited, but he didn't go on.

I coughed. "Well. Um... Was she... was she right?"

He stayed silent for a while. Finally he said, "I think she was, Alma." He kept staring, unseeing, into the street. "I think she was."

I bit my lip, unsure how to take this. "So... like... you and Jesus." I tried to smile. "What's... what's going on there?"

He laughed, snapping out of his reverie. "That reminds me of every single time someone would catch me away from you. 'You and Alma... you and Alma... what's going on there...?'"

"What? Like who?"

"Olivia, Rabbi Uri..."

I buried my face in my hands. *Everyone knew but me. I'm such an idiot.*

"So Jesus and I... we're just friends."

I peeked out from between my fingers, my brow furrowed in confusion. I had no idea what he meant by that. "You're... not going to marry Jesus," I said slowly. "Well, um, that's good, because he's dead. According to some prominent opinions, anyway." I looked at Manuel sideways. "Also, he was a dude, and I have some fairly persuasive evidence that you are not, in fact, gay."

He completely ignored my irrelevant rambling. "I want to be

Jewish, Alma." Now he was looking at me, those soulful eyes boring into mine. "I will always love and respect Christianity and feel that it is a part of who I am. But the call to Judaism has been there since before I can remember—even when I knew nothing about it. And now I know why." He sighed. "You are right, there are some things about Christianity I might have trouble letting go of. I know that Judaism totally rejects Jesus as a prophet and a teacher and I'll have some trouble accepting that, even if I can let him go as Messiah and the son of God. But I don't think it really takes that much to reconcile any of this. I think Tía Sara was right. I thought I was a Catholic because that's what everyone told me I was—the Church was all I'd ever known. But spiritually... I have always been Jewish. I was always curious about Judaism because my soul knew that was where its home was, and it wanted to return. And now... that's what I want to do. I want to do what Ester Maimón did."

I swallowed. "You mean... the Certificate of Return thing?"

"Yes. This documentation makes me eligible, no?"

"Yes. Yes, it should."

I paused, my heart welling with hope and warmth.

He watched me thoughtfully.

"Well, you know what this means," I said.

His eyes searched mine.

"You can't be my *Shabbos goy* anymore."

He burst out laughing, and laughed so hard and so long that he had to grab a nearby bench and sit down.

I cleared my throat. "And also, you know, that it's actually okay that I am totally in love with you."

He looked up swiftly, glowing in joy and surprise, his eyes welling with tears. He watched me intently as I sank onto the bench next to him, taking my glasses off.

"These, um, kind of got in the way last time," I mumbled. He froze for a moment, registering what I meant, and then leaned close to me, reaching a trembling hand toward my cheek. I threw my arms around him and kissed him eagerly, my whole body charged with giddy joy. He responded in kind.

When I pulled back, I noticed that my cheeks were wet. His face was streaming with tears.

"Why are you crying?" I murmured, reaching up to brush them away.

"I never thought this could happen," he said, his voice choked with emotion. He closed his eyes and leaned into my touch, resting his hand over mine. "Never in a thousand years."

"See? And it only took five hundred! We're ahead of the game!"

He opened his eyes and chuckled. "That's one way to look at it…"

"I gotta say, this entire thing has been outrageously, stupidly, ridiculously unlikely."

He took my hand off his cheek and held it in both of his. "You would think there was a God or something."

I snuggled up next to him on the bench. He put his arm around me and held me close, resting his head against mine. A peaceful bliss settled over me, melting away the shame and guilt and despair that had been tormenting me since I left Cartagena. We sat that way quietly for a few minutes.

"I don't know about this, Alma," he said finally, pulling away and grinning mischievously. "I'm still a vegetarian."

I burst into laughter. I laughed until I cried. And then I cried… and cried.

Manuel dug into his pocket, pulled out a tissue, and handed it to me. I blew my nose, trying to calm down.

"I wish…" I gasped. "I wish I could tell Grandma…she knew about you and me all along too. Tried to warn me about it ages ago, but I was an idiot. If only she could have known that you are Jewish after all… *and* a descendant of the family that rescued our ancestors... she would have gotten such a kick out of it! She would be telling this entire crazy story over and over for the rest of her life... she would be so happy..."

Manuel held me, stroking my hair, as I slowly composed myself. I sighed as the clouds of grief cleared somewhat, and burrowed further into his embrace, knowing that he understood better than anyone how I felt.

"I'm sure she knows," Manuel murmured. "Wherever she is. I'm sure she's very happy."

I sat up, blinking away the last of my tears. "I'm sure she's laughing her head off at us right now." I smiled. "Along with your dad."

"And our ancestors from Lorca."

"And Fez. And Granada. And Tétouan. And Cartagena."

"And even Padre Carlos." He grinned. "Well, you know, on the assumption that the Jews are right about Heaven after all." He blinked and corrected himself: "That *we* are right about Heaven after all."

"*We...*" I echoed, savoring the word.

"Yes... we."

After a few moments of contented silence, the image of the ring popped into my head. "Oh!" I exclaimed, and reached behind my neck to unclasp the chain. "So listen," I said, sliding it off the chain, "the entire reason I drove down here today was to convince your mother to take this."

"Oh, so *that's* why you're here! I thought I was hallucinating when I saw you standing there in the kitchen. You're the last person on earth I had expected to see."

"Any chance I'm going to get you to accept it now?" I held it out to him.

He raised an eyebrow. "Alma, that thing is a priceless historical artifact passed down in your family for twenty-six generations. How could I possibly—"

"It *should* have been passed down in *your* family for twenty-six generations. And I already—"

"Alma," Manuel laughed. "We are not getting into this argument again."

"Listen," I said sharply, "My grandmother's most important mission for me revolved around my giving this back to you."

I paused, feeling the lump in my throat again. "She and I had a fight about the trip to Granada right before you and I left Madrid. That was the last time I ever spoke to her. I literally hung up on her."

"Let me guess," Manuel said gently, with a knowing smile. "She warned you that we were not being careful enough about 'boundaries'?"

"Yes..." I gave him a questioning look.

"Interesting. Rabbi Uri told me the exact same thing that night when we argued."

I stared at him. "What?"

Manuel chuckled. "He gave me the Intermarriage Talk."

"Ohhh...so *that's* why you were mad at him!" I wrinkled my nose in distaste. "Well, that's obnoxious."

"Obnoxious perhaps, but right on the mark, as it turned out."

"He's going to have a heart attack when we get back and show him your papers."

"I think he'll actually be quite relieved. He seems to like both of us very much." He smiled. "He said we have good chemistry."

I snorted. "Well, thanks for the *shidduch*, rabbi."

"The what?"

"Never mind. Just take the ring. Please. To give rest to the soul of my grandmother and the two dozen generations before her." I held it out again.

"All right, all right," he sighed. "How can I refuse?" He opened his hand. I dropped the ring into it. He brought his other hand over and rested it on top of mine, clasping the ring and my hand in both of his. "As long as I get to keep this too."

I smiled up at him. "I don't know, Manuel. You *are* still a vegetarian." He grinned, his eyes twinkling. "But you know, all things considered, it's a compromise I'm willing to make."

 THE END

# Acknowledgements

First and foremost, I must thank the First and Foremost, the Master of the Universe, Who guides my heart and my fingers, Who led me to the people, circumstances, and stories that inspired this book, gave me the skills and the courage to write it, and led—and sometimes dragged me, kicking and screaming—through the exhausting process of bringing it to print. Thank You, thank You.

In the human department, there is no question who I must thank first: my beloved friend Abigail Levitt. Her friendship was the fertile soil from which this book was able to grow and blossom. Without her enthusiasm, cattle-prodding, and constant support, it would still be a three-page draft hiding in the depths of my hard drive. I honestly have no idea how other writers do it without an Abi.

However, it is only by virtue of her particular dedication to my writing that she comes before my husband, Eitan. His love is the fertile soil from which I, as a person and as a writer, have been able to grow and blossom. His support is the solid ground where the foundations for my dreams can be laid. His contributions to this book were less direct, but more fundamental, and I can't imagine doing any of this (or anything, really) without him by my side.

Next up: my dear friend Jordi Martí de Conejeros (a. k. a. "Josep" of my first book, *Letters to Josep)*, without whom this book would certainly not exist. Aspects of our friendship and its context inspired some of the central concepts of the story. He also provided advice, translations, and insight, and responded with patience to my bizarre interrogations on topics ranging from Spanish parent-child relations to coffee percolators. *Moltes gràcies*, Jordi.

I want to thank my parents, Jeff and Jill Shames, for raising me with a deep sense of the importance of my roots, and Mark and Nisa Levy, for their endless love and support. An honorable mention goes to my Bubbie, Betty Shames, the sassy Ashkenazi inspiration for Grandma Alma; and my Grandma of blessed memory, Seena Kronenberg Baker, who got to read the manuscript and express how proud she was of me before she passed away. Much gratitude as well to my grandfathers, Alvin Shames and William Baker, whose nurturing love for me is woven into the bedrock of my being.

My publishers Yael Shahar and Don Radlauer swooped in like a pair of fairy godparents to grant me the wish of a lifetime. Thank you for your vision, your dedication, your humor, and your faith in this book and in me.

Emma Riqué-Hussein helped polish the Spanish dialogue, and Ari Moshkovski, Haim Machluf, and Erika Rain helped me develop and research the historical story. A number of my friends read early drafts and provided insightful comments and advice, and I am very grateful to all of them—especially Jo Levitt, Tammy Paul, and my sister Yonit Arthur.

Dr. Gloria Mound, of blessed memory, was the director of the Casa Shalom Institute of Marrano-Anusim Studies, and the first to welcome me to the world of crypto-Jewish scholarship and activism. There is so much more I could have learned from her, and I regret that I did not spend more time basking in her knowledge.

My "virtual teacher" Dr. Roger L. Martínez-Dávila contributed immeasurably, both to my understanding of Jewish-Christian relations in medieval Spain and to my knowledge of paleography and working with medieval Spanish manuscripts. His successor as president of the Society for Crypto-Judaic Studies, Genie Milgrom, shared her incredible story and inspiring insights with me, and these also made a very visible mark on this book. I am privileged to call both of them friends. *Muchas gracias.*

Likewise, I am very grateful to Professor Yaakov Bentolila for sharing details of his childhood in Tétouan and his knowledge regarding the Jewish community that lived there; and to Dr. Nina Pinto for directing me to him—but not before answering a few questions and offering encouragement herself.

I would also like to express my gratitude to all those who let me pick their brains on Christianity, interfaith encounters, and conversion from one religion to the other—most notably Jonathan Rafa'El Alphonso Alfaro, my "cousin-in-law" Egon Levy, Stephanie McCourt, and of course, once again, Jordi.

And...

Rachel and Carmi...wherever you are...whatever you are doing...you know how much I owe you for this book. My profoundest thanks, and blessings on wherever your journey has taken you.

# About the Author

Daniella Levy is a mother of three, rabbi's wife, writer, translator, self-defense instructor, bridal counselor, black belt in karate, and certified medical clown—and she still can't decide what to be when she grows up. She is the author of *Letters to Josep: An Introduction to Judaism;* and her articles, short fiction, and poetry have appeared in both English and Hebrew in publications such as *The Forward, Writer's Digest, Pnima Magazine, Reckoning, Newfound, Rathalla Review,* and the *Jewish Literary Journal,* as well as online platforms such as *Kveller, Aish.com, JWire, Ynet News,* and *Hevria,* and in the international poetry collection *Veils, Halos & Shackles.*

Born in New York, Daniella immigrated to Israel with her family as a child. She wrote her first book at age ten and completed her first full-length novel at fourteen. Her Talmud Studies notes from high school consisted of a series of silly dramatizations of Jewish sages yelling at each other; she's pretty sure her teacher would have been horrified.

Daniella enjoys blogging about Judaism and life in Israel at LetterstoJosep.com, and about resilience for writers and artists confronting rejection at RejectionSurvivalGuide.wordpress.com. You can visit Daniella online at daniella-levy.com, follow her on Twitter at @DaniellaNLevy, or "like" her on Facebook at facebook.com/daniellalevyauthor.

# About Kasva Press

*"Make its bowls, ladles, jars and pitchers*
*with which to offer libations;*
*make them of pure gold."*
(Exodus 25:29)

וְעָשִׂיתָ קְּעָרֹתָיו וְכַפֹּתָיו וּקְשׂוֹתָיו
וּמְנַקִּיֹּתָיו אֲשֶׁר יֻסַּךְ בָּהֵן
זָהָב טָהוֹר תַּעֲשֶׂה אֹתָם
(שמות פרשת תרומה)

*Kasva* means "a jar or pitcher". The word appears in the Torah exactly once, where it describes the solid-gold vessels made to hold sacrificial wine and oil in the Tabernacle the Israelites carried with them in their desert wanderings.

We believe that a good book is a vessel for the fluid thoughts of its author—its words, the outpouring of the writer's soul, as precious as the sanctified wine and oil of the Tabernacle.

It is our aim to provide worthy vessels for our authors' creations.

# Glossary

*Abba (Aramaic/Hebrew):* Father.

*Abuela/Abuelo (Spanish):* Grandmother/Grandfather.

*Aleha hashalom (Hebrew):* "May peace be upon her"; said of the deceased.

*Amigo/amiga (Spanish):* Friend.

*Ashkenazi (Hebrew):* Jews of central or eastern European descent. Around 75-80% of Jews today are Ashkenazi.

*Baruch HaShem (Hebrew):* Literally "Blessed is the Name". Used as an equivalent of "Thank God".

*¡Basta! (Spanish):* Enough!

*Beit midrash (Hebrew):* House of learning (Torah).

*Belén (Spanish, derived from "Bethlehem"):* Nativity scene, commonly on display during Christmas-time in Andalusia.

*Besamim (Hebrew):* Spices.

*Bimbriyo (Judeo-Spanish):* Quinces, or a sweetmeat made with quinces.

*Chazzan (Hebrew):* Cantor.

*Converso/conversa (Spanish):* A convert. Usually refers to Jews and Moors who converted to Christianity, often due to coercion, in Christian Spain.

*Eruv (Hebrew):* An artificial boundary that symbolically makes a public domain into a private one, thus making it possible for Jews observing the strictures of the Sabbath to carry items around.

*Goy/goya (Hebrew):* Gentile.

*Halacha (Hebrew):* Jewish law; literally "the way."

*HaShem (Hebrew):* Literally "the Name"; the term religious Jews often use to refer to God.

*Havdala (Hebrew):* Literally "differentiation"; the ritual marking the end of the Jewish Sabbath.

*Ima (Aramaic/Hebrew):* Mother.

*Judería (Spanish):* Jewish quarter.

*Judío/judía (Spanish):* Jew.

*Kapara (Hebrew):* Literally "atonement"; used as a term of endearment.

*Ketuba (Hebrew):* Jewish marriage contract.

*Kol Nidre (Aramaic):* Literally "All Vows". The traditional prayer recited at the onset of Yom Kippur, which annuls all religious vows one took upon oneself in the past year. The prayer is said to have been particularly significant to crypto-Jews, who drew hope and comfort from the idea of being forgiven despite outwardly professing a foreign faith.

*Kosher (Hebrew/Yiddish):* Prepared in adherence to the dietary laws of Judaism *(kashrut)*. These laws include restrictions on which animals are permissible to eat, how they must be slaughtered, and strict separation of dairy products from meat products.

*L'chaim (Hebrew):* "To life." Traditional Jewish toast.

*L'shana tova u'metuka (Hebrew):* "To a good and sweet new year." Traditional greeting and blessing for the Jewish New Year.

*Madre del Amor Hermoso (Spanish):* Literally "Mother of Beautiful Love"; an expression used like "Sweet Mother of God!"

*Mami (Spanish):* Literally "mommy", but used as a term of endearment, like "sweetie".

*Membrillos (Spanish):* Quinces.

*Mensch (Yiddish):* Literally "man"; a good, well-mannered, upstanding person.

*Mikveh (Hebrew):* Ritual bath used for purification.

*Pareve (Yiddish):* Food that is considered neither dairy nor meat, and can be eaten with both, according to the laws of *kashrut* (see: "Kosher").

*Pikuach nefesh (Hebrew):* Preserving life. A concept in Jewish law that saving a human life overrides virtually all other Jewish laws.

*Rosh Hashana (Hebrew):* The Jewish New Year. Usually falls in September.

*Salud (Spanish):* Literally "health". Used as a toast: "To your health."

*Señor/señora/señorita (Spanish):* Sir/madam/miss.

*Sephardi/Sephardic (Hebrew):* Jews of Iberian origin. The definition is often expanded to include North African, Middle Eastern, and Asian Jewish communities, since the character of those communities was strongly influenced by Spanish Jews who arrived after the expulsion of 1492; their customs tend to be more like those of Sephardi Jews than those of Ashkenazi Jews. (See: Ashkenazi)

*Sfenj (Moroccan Arabic):* A deep-fried dessert, like a donut, traditionally made around Chanukah-time in Moroccan-Jewish cuisine.

*Shabbat/Shabbos (Hebrew):* The Jewish Sabbath. (Sephardi/Ashkenazi pronunciation, respectively.)

*Shabbat shalom (Hebrew):* "A peaceful Shabbat." Traditional Sabbath greeting.

*Shabbos goy (Hebrew/Yiddish):* "Sabbath Gentile." Since non-Jews are not obligated by the laws of the Torah according to Jewish law, it is sometimes permissible to have a non-Jew perform a necessary task that a Jew would not be allowed to do on the Sabbath.

*Shidduch (Hebrew):* Match (as in a couple).

*Shiva (Hebrew):* Literally "seven". The traditional seven days of mourning following a death. During this period first-degree family members of the deceased are required to sit low to the ground (on stools, benches or mattresses laid on the floor), and they usually stay in their homes as other members of the community visit, comfort them, and cook for them. For this reason the tradition is also known as "sitting *shiva*".

*Sofer (Hebrew):* Scribe.

*Ta'am (Hebrew):* Taste.

*Tehillim (Hebrew):* Psalms.

*Tía abuela (Spanish):* Great-aunt.

*Treif (Yiddish, derived from Hebrew treifa):* Non-kosher (see: kosher). "*Treifing*" as a verb, meaning "making non-kosher", is Jewish-American slang.

*Ya mahabool (Arabic):* "You idiot!"

*Ya terminamos (Spanish):* "We're just finishing up here."

*Yikhrib beitak (Arabic):* An Arabic curse: "May your house be destroyed!"